The Prisoner's Wife

MAGGIE BROOKES

CENTURY

1 3 5 7 9 10 8 6 4 2

Century
20 Vauxhall Bridge Road
London SW1V 2SA

Century is part of the Penguin Random House group of companies
whose addresses can be found at global.penguinrandomhouse.com.

Penguin
Random House
UK

First published in Great Britain by Century in 2020

www.penguin.co.uk

A CIP catalogue record for this book is available from the British Library.

ISBN 9781529124286 (Hardback)
ISBN 9781529124293 (Trade Paperback)

Typeset in 13.25/15.75 pt Fournier MT by Jouve (UK), Milton Keynes
Printed and bound in Great Britain by Clays Ltd, Elcograf S.p.A.

Penguin Random House is committed to a sustainable future
for our business, our readers and our planet. This book is made
from Forest Stewardship Council® certified paper.

In memory of Alfred Arthur Brookes and all the other prisoners of war, who endured so much in the hope it would never happen again.

And for Katie, Amy and Tim. All love.

It happened, therefore it can happen again:
this is the core of what we have to say.

Primo Levi

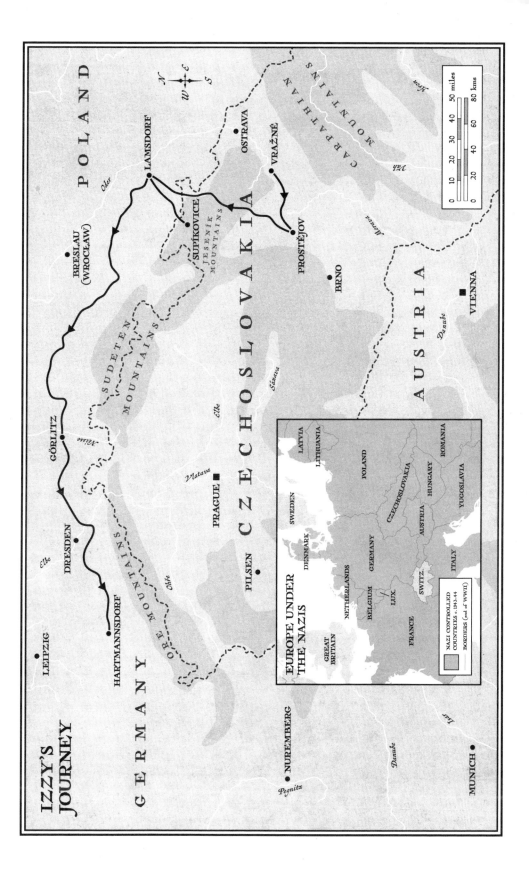

IZZY'S JOURNEY

POLAND

LAMSDORF

BRESLAU
(WROCŁAW)

OSTRAVA

VRAŽNÉ

CARPATHIAN MOUNTAINS

SUPÍKOVICE

JESENÍK MOUNTAINS

PROSTĚJOV

BRNO

CZECHOSLOVAKIA

AUSTRIA

VIENNA

GÖRLITZ

SUDETEN MOUNTAINS

Elbe

Vltava

PRAGUE

Sázava

Morava

Danube

DRESDEN

Elbe

Ohře

PILSEN

GERMANY

ORE MOUNTAINS

HARTMANNSDORF

LEIPZIG

NUREMBERG

Pegnitz

Danube

MUNICH

Isar

Oder

Nisse

Neisse

Iser

| 0 | 10 | 20 | 30 | 40 | 50 miles |
| 0 | 20 | 40 | 60 | 80 kms |

EUROPE UNDER THE NAZIS

GREAT BRITAIN

SWEDEN

DENMARK

NETHERLANDS

BELGIUM

LUX.

FRANCE

GERMANY

SWITZ.

ITALY

LATVIA

LITHUANIA

POLAND

CZECHOSLOVAKIA

AUSTRIA

HUNGARY

ROMANIA

YUGOSLAVIA

NAZI CONTROLLED
COUNTRIES c. 1943–44

BORDERS (end of WWII)

Historical Note

This incredible story was related by Lance Corporal Sidney Reed, who was a prisoner of the Nazis during the Second World War at Lamsdorf, Stalag VIIIB / 344, in Poland, and at the labour camp E166 at Saubsdorf quarry, Czechoslovakia. During the war Poland and Czechoslovakia were under the control of Hitler's Third Reich.

By 1944, when this story begins, the Nazis had established huge prisoner-of-war camps at the eastern reaches of Czechoslovakia and Poland, in order to keep the captured Allies as far as possible from home. It is estimated that they had taken almost 200,000 British prisoners. The officers were held in PoW camps, but the 1929 Geneva Convention allowed the lower ranks to be deployed into labour camps, known as *Arbeitskommandos*. Lamsdorf PoW camp alone could hold 13,000 British prisoners, but also sent 12,000 men to labour camps to build roads and work in the mines, in factories and on the land.

This story starts in the Czech region of Silesia, which had been part of the Austro-Hungarian Empire until 1918. Many of the people who lived there were German-speaking and welcomed the Nazi annexation of their lands. However, in March 1939 Hitler rode into Prague, declaring the rest of Czechoslovakia a 'protectorate' of the Third Reich, and the entire country began life under the Nazis. By 1944 Czech resistance was becoming strong.

The names of many places have changed since 1944. This novel uses a mix of modern and wartime names. For more information about this, see the Author's Note on page 397.

Prologue

Everything was quiet and still, apart from the light crunch of our boots as we crept down the deserted street. The sliver of moon disappeared behind a cloud and we slowed our pace, barely able to make out the way ahead.

That was when we heard the dogs. Only one bark at first, carrying in the quiet of the night. We clutched each other's hands and stood still for a moment.

Then another bark. And another. Not muffled by the walls of a building, but out in the night, like us, out in the streets.

Instinctively we moved away from the sound, and the buildings glowered at us, closing in. My heart was drumming and my breath came fast. We walked more quickly. The dogs were barking, closer, echoing off the buildings – perhaps two of them, perhaps three. We turned to see if they were in sight, but the darkness was too absolute. We were acutely aware of the noise of our boots on the cobbled road.

And then there were shouts behind us: men's voices, excited to have something to do in the boredom of the night-watch, egging on the dogs, eager for the hunt. Whichever way we turned, the dogs and the men grew closer and our boots clanged louder.

It became a town of sounds: our breath, the pounding of our own blood in our ears, the clatter of our boots on the road, the dogs barking, men running and calling, closer, closer. Perhaps we could have stopped, knocked on a door and begged for help, but we didn't. We just kept going, faster and faster, running, Bill dragging me with him. I was breathless to keep up, my kit-bag banging awkwardly against my legs.

At last there was an opening in the terrace, an archway leading into a narrow arcade lined with dark shops. Towards the end of the alley was an even darker place that looked like another turning, but it was only a wide doorway, up two steps, set back and hidden until we drew level with it.

Now the dogs were almost upon us, and Bill pulled me up into the doorway, threw his arms around me, squeezed me very hard and whispered, 'I'm so sorry' into my hair. Then he pushed me away from him, so we wouldn't be found touching. I shut my eyes and waited for the dogs' teeth, hoped it would be over quickly.

Everything seemed to happen at once: the dogs, the men, a searchlight in my face. I raised my arm to cover my eyes and heard the panting breath of the men, the loudness of their voices. My teeth were chattering and I had to clamp them shut. The voices behind the light became one disembodied shout in German from the senior officer. 'Hands up! Against the wall!'

We stumbled down the two steps. Bill went to one side of the doorway, and I to the other. I raised my hands and leaned my face against the wall to stop myself from falling, feeling the roughness of the brick against my cheek.

Behind the wall I sensed the people who lived there scurrying like mice, listening with excitement and maybe – who knows? – with pity. I bit my lips, determined not to sob, not to let it end this way.

PART ONE

VRAŽNÉ, OCCUPIED CZECHOSLOVAKIA
June to October 1944

1

War had ripped across Europe for five years – a great tornado, scattering families, tearing millions of people from their loved ones for ever. But sometimes, just sometimes, it threw them together. Like me and Bill. A Czech farm girl and a London boy who would never have met, were hurled into each other's paths. And we reached out, caught hold and gripped each other tight.

We had the Oily Captain to thank for bringing us together. I always thought of him as the Oily Captain because there was something too eager to please in his manner that made me despise him. Although he was a Nazi officer, he was nothing like the bands of SS who descended without warning to search the farm and interrogate us about my father and older brother, Jan.

We knew at once that the Oily Captain was different, because the first day he turned up at the farm he even knocked at the back door before he pushed it open. He stood silhouetted in the door frame, stocky and well fed on 'requisitioned' farm produce.

My mother was by the sink, cutting potatoes. She dropped a potato in the water and turned, keeping the knife in her right hand.

In one glance he took in the kitchen – the knife, my mother

in her apron, me with my books spread out on the table, and Marek playing on the floor.

'Do you speak German?' he asked her politely, although most people in our region spoke nothing else.

'Of course,' my mother replied in her impeccable High German accent, brushing a wisp of hair from her eyes with the back of her left hand. I nodded too, imperceptibly.

His face brightened. 'May I come in?'

My mother made a small flick of her fingers, which meant 'Can I stop you?' and he took a step forward.

She rested her knife-hand on the edge of the sink and frowned at the mud he'd walked onto her clean floor. My little brother Marek stood up. He was only eight, but took his position as man of the house very seriously.

The captain removed his hat. Beneath it his hair was short and peppered with grey. He had the open face of a countryman used to looking at the sky. His lips were thin and maybe mean, but the wrinkles around his eyes spoke of someone who liked to laugh. He seemed older with his hat off.

'I've been looking over your farm . . .' My mother's face darkened, and he waved his innocence. 'I want to offer you some help to bring in the crops.'

Only so that you can confiscate them, I thought, and knew my mother was thinking the same. They requisitioned every turnip, every bushel of oats, every ham we produced.

'I've got a working party of prisoners of war from the sawmill at Mankendorf. They're improving the road for the timber lorries, but I could spare a man or two to help you at the busiest times. My orders are to improve forestry and agriculture in the region. It's a big farm for the two of you.'

6

'Three,' said my brother, and my mother put a warning hand on his shoulder.

The captain nodded seriously. 'Three.'

He was right, of course. Even if we worked from sun-up till sun-down there was no way my mother and I could do the work of my father, my brother Jan and the two hired men we'd lost.

'What's your name?' the captain asked my brother in a friendly way.

He hesitated and then said, 'Marek', the name he had from his Czech grandfather. Outside the house and at school he normally used his other name of Heinrich, from our mother's father. My mother and I glanced at each other, but didn't speak.

'It's a very nice farm,' the captain continued. 'I grew up on a farm, and I know how much work it can be.'

I was thinking that I preferred the real Nazis, who didn't bother to make conversation, but searched in every room and turned over the contents of every cupboard without asking, as if it was their right. You could hate them with white-hot venom. We kept our eyes fixed on the floor when they were in the house, knowing that our faces would betray our loathing.

But with the Oily Captain, even the first time, when I stared at him, he was the first to look away.

'What's most urgent?' he asked.

'First, the hay must be cut before we have a thunderstorm,' my mother said, and he nodded. It was odd to hear her speaking German in the house. We'd only spoken Czech here for five years, ever since the Nazis marched into Prague.

'Tomorrow morning then,' he said, and replaced his hat and raised his arm in a salute, which looked more as if he was trying to keep the sun out of his eyes. 'Heil Hitler.'

We muttered unintelligibly, and he turned and left. Marek sat down again.

The captain's footsteps clicked away from the house. He held one leg stiffly, and you could hear it in the irregular clack of his boots. I supposed that was why he wasn't away slaughtering Russians or hunting down partisans like my father and Jan. Perhaps he had a false leg.

When he was out of earshot, my mother exhaled and reverted to Czech. 'Well,' she said, 'I can't say it won't help. As long as he isn't around poking his nose in all the time.'

At five-thirty the next morning my mother and I were still having breakfast when there came a loud thumping on the waggon doors that open from the road into the courtyard of our farm.

My mother drank the last of her coffee and pulled a light shawl around her shoulders.

She held herself very erect and her jaw was set firm, as if she expected to have to prove to them that she was the farmer, not just the farmer's wife. She'd pulled her curly hair back under a black headscarf, which made her look severe and almost frightening. We slipped on our clogs as the Oily Captain knocked at the back door and politely asked if we were ready for them. He looked so pleased with himself that I could have smacked him.

'I'm afraid I have to leave a guard as well, because of your husband and your older son.' He shrugged apologetically.

My mother didn't speak, but closed the door in his face, crossed the kitchen and swished out into the courtyard to lift the great beam behind the waggon doors. Outside was a small truck with about twenty men on it. Five prisoners and an elderly guard were climbing down. My mother held one of the huge doors open sufficiently for them to pass through in single file, and scrutinised each man as he passed. Behind them came the Oily Captain, who fussily and quite unnecessarily helped her to lower the beam back into place.

The five prisoners of war marched into our courtyard, and the guard gave a loud, stamping order to halt. I yawned as I leaned against the kitchen doorway, looking on. Marek peeped out past me.

The men lined up, and that was the first time I saw Bill. He stood out from the others because of his blond hair, slate-blue eyes and baby face, almost too pretty for a man. I thought he might be Polish; I didn't know that Englishmen could have that kind of colouring. All the prisoners, including him, were gawping at my mother, who stood in front of them beside the Oily Captain. For a moment I saw her as they did: her womanly shape, her dark eyes and head held high. Despite her worn work-skirts, she looked somehow regal, a queen disguised as a peasant.

'They'll do,' she said, and clacked across the yard in her clogs to fetch tools from the stable. The prisoners were looking around them, taking everything in: the house, stables, barn and hay barn, which formed a tight, enclosed square around our courtyard. Perhaps they were looking for ways they might escape. Their gaze locked on me as I approached. When I stared back at them, their eyes dropped to the ground or skittered onto something neutral in the yard: the water pump, the old tin bath, our bright-red roof tiles. They knew the guard was watching them closely. But Bill continued to regard me in a clear, appraising way, and I raised my chin and looked back. It wasn't love at first sight, or even lust, but there was a something: a metallic frisson in the air, a kind of challenge thrown out and returned. Maybe a kind of recognition.

The Oily Captain made small talk with my mother as she handed out the scythes, rakes and pitchforks, but the guard kept his rifle trained on the young men who had just been issued with tools they could use as weapons. He cleared his throat and spoke to the prisoners in English. 'Don't any of you boys try anything stupid. Don't forget I was in the trenches, and I have many scores to settle.'

They nodded, and I filed away the information that the old guard spoke excellent English.

My mother opened the hay-barn door and led the way through it and out into the fields. I brought up the rear. For a few steps the Oily Captain was lolloping beside her in his stiff-legged way, trying to finish the conversation as she strode off. I couldn't help smiling, and again I caught Bill's eye and saw both amusement and approval of my mother. His face seemed to light up when he smiled.

The Oily Captain must have realised he was being made a fool of, because he suddenly stopped, clicked his heels and wished her a very good day. My mother turned and politely thanked him for providing her with help on the farm. He looked very pleased with himself as he marched away to his car.

At the edge of the first field, my mother demonstrated the correct use of a scythe to the four men who'd been issued with them. Two men hardly watched her at all, but Bill paid keen interest, mirroring the movements she made. I guessed he was a city boy, and this was new to him. She made them practise until she was satisfied that they would do a good job. The two who hadn't been watching had obviously harvested plenty of fields before, but Bill and his friend made several blundering strokes before either managed to cut anything. I felt hot with embarrassment for them, but my mother was patient and stood behind Bill, lowering his right elbow to the correct position until he swished cleanly through the stalks and looked up at me in delight and triumph. I couldn't help smiling back.

The guards had done well to rouse the prisoners early, because the heat was soon hammering down from a cloud-free sky. We were cutting hay and it was tiring, thirsty work, trying to get it all into the barn before any rain might come. There was always a danger of thunderstorms on these hot days. One by one the men asked permission to remove their battledress jackets and the shirts beneath. I was shocked at how thin they looked, with ribs standing out like those of a neglected horse. Some, including Bill, wore tattered vests. Ignoring the guard who was shouting at him to hurry and get back to work, he carefully tied his shirt into a makeshift hat and cover for his neck and scrawny shoulders. Looking at the blue-whiteness of his skin, I thought: I bet he burns really easily. I would only turn brown in the sun, not burn.

My mother and I worked with them to make sure they did everything in the way she liked. Who knew in what strange ways such things were done in England?

Four of the men, including Bill, were working down the rows with scythes, cutting the sweet-smelling hay, while Mother and I and the fifth man came along behind, bending to swish the hay into sheaves, tying them roughly with one stalk and standing them together to dry in the air. We worked slowly and steadily, not talking, and every now and then Mother and I would straighten our backs and look around.

She was checking on the men with the scythes – whether they seemed to know what they were doing, whether they were missing anything, whether they needed the whetstone to resharpen

11

their tools. I was looking at the gold of the field, the china-blue of the sky and – out of the corner of my eye – at the easy swinging movements that Bill was now making with the scythe. I could see how all the muscles in his back and shoulders worked together in the swing. There was something quick and fluid about his movements. Bright and mercurial.

As Bill worked, he whistled tune after tune, swinging the scythe in time with the music. I didn't recognise any of the songs, but sometimes the other men would join in and sing a chorus.

When it became apparent that the guard expected them to work all morning in the heat without anything to drink, Mother sent me back to the farm for water, which I took round to each of them, pouring some into a tin cup and letting them drink. Bill gave a wide, joyful smile. One of his top front teeth was chipped.

'I wish . . . beer,' I said in my halting English, and he beamed even wider.

'I'll pretend it is.' He grinned, smacking his lips appreciatively. I could see him trying to think of something to say to extend the conversation. 'Do you make beer here?' he asked.

I nodded. 'We grow . . .' I didn't know the word for 'barley'.

'You grow beer?' He play-acted amazement. 'I've died and gone to 'eaven.'

A laugh escaped me and the guard strode over to poke Bill hard in the ribs with the barrel of the rifle in a way that I knew would bruise, shouting at him in English, 'Get back to work. Lazy swine.'

I learned quickly that I mustn't laugh out loud or draw the guard's attention to the prisoners.

The guard stood at the edge of the field in the thin shade of a straggly tree and watched us all work, fiddling with his rifle and his tight collar. Sweat poured down his face. He kept batting away a persistent horse-fly or mosquito and I willed it to bite him. He was a postern, rather than regular army – perhaps happy to have work guarding PoWs rather than being on the front lines again. I'm sure he knew how easily this bunch of young men could overcome him, if they chose. All that lay between them was his rifle and his sense of self-importance. And the fact that if they ever tried to escape, they were deep in the heart of Nazi Europe, with more than a thousand kilometres between them and the neutral countries of Switzerland and Sweden. I felt Bill watching me watching the guard, but I didn't look at him.

The prisoners were allowed to stop at noon for lunch, and pulled tiny squares of bread from their packs. Mother took one look at their rations and signalled to me to go back to the farmhouse for the loaf she'd baked yesterday, for farm butter and cheese. I brought beer too, for the guard, to keep him sweet and make sure he would continue to bring the men back to us. I was careful to take him his lunch first, and swallowed my dismay at how much of the cheese he took. I wished I'd hidden the total amount and just brought his separately.

I carried what remained to the prisoners, who were lying in the shade of a big oak tree. Some were asleep. Only Bill was sitting, with his back against the tree trunk, watching me as I went round to the others. They each looked as if I was giving them the best meal they'd ever tasted. I saved Bill's till last.

He grinned at me as I leaned down to him with the tiny portion of food, and I smiled back. As he squinted up at me, his eyes were bluer than they'd seemed in the yard. His mouth was wide, as if it liked to smile. The other men were only interested in the food I gave them, but he held my gaze.

'Do you make the bread and cheese here too?' he said slowly and clearly.

I struggled to retrieve my poor English and wished I'd worked harder at it in school.

'Yes, we make.'

'Best I've 'ad for years.'

He smiled at me until I dropped my eyes. I wasn't often lost for words, but I couldn't think of the English vocabulary.

'I . . . hope . . . like,' I said slowly.

His eyes twinkled mischievously. 'Oh, I like very much.'

My stomach tightened, knowing he didn't mean the cheese, but I retorted in Czech, 'You haven't got many girls to compare me with', kicking myself for not being able to say it in English.

I felt his gaze on me as I walked back to my mother.

By the end of the afternoon the biggest field was cut, and the sheaves were being forked onto our horse-drawn waggon. It was my job to look after the mare, holding her head and leading her forward, though she was so used to the work that she didn't really need me. I petted her nose and brought her the sweetest grass.

I knew where Bill was working without even looking, because of his habit of whistling or humming as he worked. He vibrated with music.

It was hot, sweaty work, and I returned twice to the house to get cold water for the prisoners to drink. Each time I carried water to them, I saved Bill till last and tried to snatch a word or two with him, under the watchful eye of the guard.

'I'm Bill,' he said. 'What's your name?'

'Izabela,' I told him.

He repeated it seriously, twice – 'Isabella, Isabella' – as if it mattered to him to say it right. 'Does it mean something?' he asked, but I didn't know how to say it in English.

I shrugged and shook my head.

'I think there was a Queen Isabella. Of Spain,' he said and I shook my head in wonder.

'Bill,' I said. 'What mean?'

'I dunno. It's a king's name. William the Conqueror.' Ruefully he indicated his shabby clothes. 'Queer sort of conqueror.'

I had no idea what he was talking about or why he started to laugh, silently, so that the guard wouldn't hear, but his delight was infectious and I started to giggle quietly too. I had a sudden overwhelming sense that in all this hardship and mess, it might be possible to feel joy. The same feeling was written all over Bill's face.

By the end of the day we were all covered in the dust of the hay, which stuck in our hair and on our sweaty skin.

The guard stood over the men as they took turns to pump the handle for one another to wash in the yard. One by one they stripped to the waist and leaned their heads and bodies under the freezing water, gasping and laughing at the shock of it, pushing and flicking each other with water, like children. I stood in the entrance to the barn, trying to appear unconcerned, busy with something just out of sight, as if I wasn't watching, wasn't waiting for Bill's turn.

But out of the corner of my eye I watched as he stripped the vest from his china-white torso. I took in his terrible thinness and the tight muscles on his sinewy arms, and something flipped over inside me, like a newly landed fish. He rubbed his hair with his fingers under the running water and then stood back and threw his head up, laughing, as if he was not a half-starved prisoner in a land far from home, but just a boy, knowing that

15

a girl was slyly watching him and liking what she saw. He pulled his clothes back on. His hair was darker when it was wet and gradually lightened as it dried.

I took off my clogs and crept up to the window on the landing, over the waggon doors, so that my mother couldn't see me watching the truck drive them away. But Bill somehow knew where I was and threw me a tiny salute as they turned the corner in the road.

When I entered the kitchen, my mother was pounding a double-sized portion of bread dough on the table. Marek was on the floor playing with his toy cars. Mother was smiling in a way I hadn't seen since my father and Jan went away, but as she saw me, her smile turned to a frown.

'Be more careful,' she said.

I blushed again and wondered if I would ever be able to hide anything from her.

'The guard can see everything I see,' she continued.

I doubted it.

'I know it's hard when all the boys are gone, but this isn't possible.'

'What boys?' asked Marek. We both ignored him.

I always hated to be told something was impossible, deciding immediately that I must prove it wasn't. I inherited that from my mother; she was just the same. If someone had told her she couldn't join the partisans, she would have tried, just like me.

Her idea of parenting was to bend my will to hers, but I'd always been a match for her. When I was small, I decided I wouldn't eat rabbit. I clamped my lips tight and refused the meal she'd cooked. So she brought out the same plate of stew for meal after meal and refused me any other food, saying, 'You can't be hungry if you won't eat that.' I ate nothing for days, until I was light-headed with hunger. When she clattered the rabbit-stew plate in front of me for breakfast on the third day, it had started to grow a fine furring of mould. Then my father stepped in, as I knew he would, giving the stew to the pig and telling my mother, 'She's just like you.' Later she always gave me a plate of boiled turnips when the family had rabbit stew, even after I'd told her I liked it now.

But she was right about the lack of boys. There wasn't one over the age of fourteen for kilometres around. The tiny handful of Czech-speakers had run away to join the resistance, like my dad and Jan, but the German-speaking majority had volunteered for the Nazi army or gone to work in factories across the Reich. Many of the girls I'd known at school had gone too, and of those who stayed, Matylda and Dagmar were rumoured to give themselves freely to the soldiers who were billeted nearby. At least their lives were moving on, while mine was caught like a fly in amber, an unchanged daily routine since I was fifteen. Five long years when I should have been discovering so many new things, but instead my world had narrowed down to just this farm and this house, punctuated only by occasional trips to market or to church. A life that chafed like outgrown shoes.

'You worked hard too,' she said, trying to make it up to me now.

I smiled grudgingly. 'And you.'

When had a day ever passed that she didn't work hard? What else was there in her life, apart from work?

After our meal, I slipped to my room and took down the dusty English reader I'd had at school, opened it at page one and applied myself with absolute concentration. My mother's life wasn't going to be mine. I would make sure of that.

17

2

When his working party was unloaded at the farm in Vražné that first morning, Bill felt a tingle in the back of his head, as though something important was going to happen. For the past five years he'd had the repeated sensation that his world was alternately expanding and shrinking, expanding and shrinking, as if he lived within the ribcage of some live, breathing creature. And this morning it was about to expand.

He glanced at his mate Harry, but he was yawning and scratching, oblivious to anything special about the day. It had been an early start and there was another day's hard labour ahead of them. The only thing Bill could see that was different today was that they had the old guard with them, as well as a smartly dressed captain. Usually they were just dumped at the day's workplace – a forest clearing, the roadworks, a farm – and left under the eye of some zealous, gun-waving, Nazi-supporting local man. Bill wondered what was so special about this farm that it required two soldiers.

The kitchen door opened and he smiled. A shapely woman in her mid-forties stepped out, with clogs and dingy skirts and her hair in a scarf, but an air of imperious elegance, as though she was attending a ball. Bill thought: Ah, that's why they're here. They ain't watchin' *us* at all.

A moment later a girl half her age emerged and leaned casually against the doorpost, as if completely unaware of the effect she was having on these women-starved young men. If the mother was attractive, the girl was an oasis in a desert. Bill felt Harry straighten up beside him, and he pulled his own shoulders back. The girl's eyes ranged over them, assessing, sizing them up. She had black curls, eyes like a cat and a body as lithe and slim as her mother's was rounded and womanly. Bill held her stare, and the walls of the farmyard seemed to move back.

He'd felt this world-expansion before. First of all, back in 1939, when he was eighteen and his Sunday-league football team had downed too many pints after a game and dared one another to go and join up for the army. He'd hardly been aware then that he was signing away any control over his own life for an indeterminate period; hardly realised that, from now on, somebody else would tell him where to be, what to wear, what to eat, when to go to sleep and when to wake up, who to kill. But marching to the training camp, he realised that his life was no longer going to be confined to the Stoke Newington pub where he'd grown up, the familiar London commute to his job at Paddington station, and home to practise his saxophone or play the piano in the bar in the evening.

After their basic training, his world expanded again as he mounted the gangplank of the ship at Portsmouth to an unknown wartime destination, stepping out into a life full of possibilities and dangers, including the new sensations of seasickness and homesickness. He longed to see his mother, his cousin Flora, even his boss in the ticket office. He missed the piano keys that had been like extensions of his own fingers, part of his body, for as long as he could remember. He suffered the boredom of the high seas, where there was no entertainment but endless card games on the long voyage around South Africa and up the Suez Canal. On some days he played his harmonica for sing-songs. He saw Table Mountain as they rounded the Cape, and eventually he felt the gritty sand of a desert under his boots.

His battalion pitched their tents in the freezing-cold dark, and in the morning, when Bill flicked back the tent flap, there was a bloody great pyramid.

'I think we're in Egypt,' he said over his shoulder.

'They'd better have tea in the NAAFI,' replied Harry.

But Bill wasn't interested in tea; he couldn't wait to climb the pyramid, and stood at the top with his arms thrown wide, looking out over a world grown so much bigger than he could have imagined.

That night Harry set off with some of the lads for the local brothels, but Bill refused to join them. 'Don't come crying to me when you've got the clap,' he warned. Instead he made do with memories of the girls back home and wandered the bazaars and streets, soaking up the strangeness, tingling with the excitement of it.

Bill's world continued to expand and then to contract, from the glittering wonders of Cairo, to the sweaty, suffocating confined space inside a tank lumbering across the sands for days on end. The gunners took turns to stand in the turret for some fresh air. They became irritable with each other, squeezed together in a metal box under the roasting sun – a metal box that might be their coffin. On Harry's twenty-first birthday they opened a tin of corned beef, and it was so hot in the tank that the meat ran out as liquid. They suffered mind-numbing boredom, roasted all day and shivered all night, until suddenly they were in the terror and ear-splitting din of battle, with shells exploding all around them, as exposed as a row of ducks at a fairground shooting gallery.

He and Harry had been through it all together, like a couple of book-ends: blond Bill at one end of the shelf and Harry, with his wavy brown hair, at the other. Girls couldn't resist Harry's half-closed, sleepy eyes, while men of a certain kind were drawn to Bill's prettiness, and more than once Harry had to set them straight. It was more than any peacetime friendship. Bill had seen the horrors Harry saw; Harry had felt Bill's terror. They trusted each other implicitly, watched each other's backs, shared each other's food. They had their disagreements of course, and often drove each other mad, but each knew the other would sling him over his back and carry him off a battlefield until he couldn't walk a step further. Brothers-in-arms.

They'd been captured together during the battle of Tobruk in 1941. Their tank took a hit and they all scrambled out of the smoke-filled interior, straight into the barrels of waiting Nazi guns. There was nothing to do but raise their hands above their heads and walk towards their captors.

'My legs feel like jelly,' Bill told Harry.

Harry smiled grimly. 'At least we won't have to get inside a tank ever again.'

They'd all laughed when one of the Nazi soldiers announced, 'The war is over for you Tommies.'

'Blimey,' said Bill, 'I didn't think they actually said that. I thought that was just in the pictures.'

*　*　*

After three months in a viciously guarded prison camp in Libya, where they all got the runs and shivered without blankets in the sub-zero nights, where the tribesmen who guarded them would hang a man by his wrists in the baking sun all day, just for amusement, they were taken by boat to Sicily. The hold was so full of captured prisoners that many couldn't fit below and they had to lie like sardines on the deck. But Bill and Harry were delighted to be up on deck, surrounded by the blueness of the sea, as dolphins played beside the boat. Bill felt he could breathe for the first time in months as the sky stretched away above him. But no sooner had he acknowledged the world expanding than it contracted down again, into the cramped quarters of a dark cattle truck that jostled and shook them all the way up through southern Italy to the closed quarters, watchtowers and barbed wire of a prisoner-of-war camp.

Mussolini's guards were kinder than the Libyans, and the food was better, but there was nothing to occupy themselves with from morning to night every long, long day, and nothing to protect them from being eaten alive by mosquitoes as soon as the sun went down. Some men passed the time by laying bets on the speed that a lizard would climb a wall. Others tried to teach a group to speak a language or learn algebra. Harry went gymnastics-mad. Bill shut his eyes and played an imaginary piano, or sometimes made real music on the harmonica he'd had in his pocket when their tank was hit. Once, he and Harry tried to escape, climbing into the dirty laundry as it was being driven out of the gates. The threat of a firing squad, commuted to solitary confinement, made them decide never to try again.

'Let's just concentrate on getting through this thing alive,' said Bill, and Harry agreed.

As the news of Allied advances up the leg of Italy reached their camp there was an undercurrent of buzzing excitement, and then the news that Mussolini had capitulated. For a few days they talked about nothing but freedom and release.

'D'you reckon they'll let us go home for a bit, or just put us back on the front line?' asked Harry. Bill was pretty sure they wouldn't be sent home.

One morning the guards were gone, and just as Bill and Harry were certain they'd be liberated, trucks covered with swastikas pulled up, and new guards took over, speaking German now, not Italian. Hope of freedom vanished again, as they were rounded up and taken by cattle-truck trains, on the move for day after day, night after night, up through the Alps and right across Austria and Czechoslovakia into Poland, to the giant camp at Lamsdorf.

Within the camp the regime was similar to the one in Italy, with twice-daily roll calls, cramped conditions, insufficient food and guards patrolling the fences with rifles. But Bill soon discovered that Lamsdorf was really an enormous processing centre to provide labour for the factories, mines, quarries and forests of the Third Reich. It wasn't just the Romans who needed slaves to run their empire. The Geneva Convention said that captured officers weren't allowed to be put to work, so they remained imprisoned for the duration of the war, but the NCOs and enlisted men like Bill and Harry could be sent out to *Arbeitskommandos* labour camps, across vast tracts of Poland, Czechoslovakia, Austria and even into Germany itself.

'Let's get out of here,' said Bill, scanning the watchtowers and barbed-wire fences. 'I can't stand this no longer.'

He and Harry agreed that they didn't want to actively assist the Nazi war machine, so they wouldn't make armaments or build tanks, or mine the coal that drove the operation, but they thought they could live with themselves helping out with forestry and agriculture, so they signed up for a work detail at the Mankendorf sawmill deep in the Nazi-run countryside of Czechoslovakia. They were both city boys, and neither of them had ever cut down a tree or even seen a cow close up.

It was freedom compared to the string of prison camps Bill had been in for three long years, ever since he was twenty. Here they were hardly under guard at all, just a rota of old soldiers and wire netting that was no more frightening than a tennis court, but nobody tried to escape because there was nowhere they could run away to. As Harry reminded Bill, they were more than 600 miles from Switzerland, and all the way they would be surrounded by ardent and trigger-happy supporters of the Third Reich.

No wonder Bill was intrigued when their old guard and the captain both accompanied them to the farm for the first time. He couldn't understand why they needed guarding here, and nowhere else. Until he saw the girl and her mother. Bill glanced at Harry and thought the girl would be bound to fall for his charms, like they always did. But Harry was yawning, and the girl hardly gave him a second look.

Instead she met Bill's eyes and held his gaze. He felt the horizon draw back all around him, and the sky lifted into blue.

3

My job the next day was to lead the mare and hold her head while the hay waggon was loaded and unloaded. Bill and Harry were in the fields with the rakes and pitchforks, heaping the sheaves onto the back of the waggon to be taken to the farmyard, where other prisoners were obeying my mother's instructions for stacking the hay inside the barn.

The weather grew more and more humid until we were all slick with sweat. Even Bill's whistling stopped, so I knew he must be tiring. I wanted to tell my mother that we were working the prisoners too hard, but her mouth was fixed in a line, and I knew there wouldn't be any point. A dark cloud was building on the horizon. The time for lunch came, but she wouldn't let us stop.

'We have to get the hay in before the rain,' she said in German to the guard.

I went round the men as they worked, giving them water and bread, but they only stood still for a few moments. Bill was out of breath, and his eyes were dark blue like wet slate. I thought it was strange that they changed colour all the time, but perhaps I'd never paid so much attention to anyone's eyes before.

Through the afternoon we continued, clearing up and down the rows, until more hay was in the barn than in the field.

Bill and I criss-crossed in the field, smiling secretly at each other whenever we passed. We all worked faster and faster, driven in an old battle of man against weather. The dark cloud covered the sun, dimming the light like evening, and the wind turned over the leaves on the oak.

Bill and Harry were pitchforking the last of the cut hay onto the waggon when the first flash of lightning lit the whole sky. The horse shied, and we all jerked our heads up. I comforted the mare and counted aloud – '*jedna, dvě, tři*' – as thunder shook the hills.

'Three miles,' shouted Bill.

Kilometres, I thought.

'Just like *Far from the Madding Crowd*,' he yelled.

I smiled my incomprehension, holding tight to the bridle.

'It's a book. There's a terrible storm' – he hurled the last forkful of hay into the waggon – 'and a beautiful girl.'

That part I understood. I promised myself I would learn to read English well enough to find a copy and know the whole story. Harry looked at Bill and at me and said, 'I'm off', running back towards the house and barn. I clicked to the horse and she began to walk quickly towards the house. Bill fell in step beside me.

'I'll read it to you one day,' he said as the first fat raindrop fell on my nose.

Before I could stop him, he leapt up onto the moving waggon and pulled a tarpaulin over the hay that he'd worked so hard to cut. Lightning flashed again, and he was illuminated against the sky. I struggled to hold the mare's head, with no time to count before deafening thunder shook our whole village. I glanced round quickly to check if lightning had struck a tree, but no flames shot into the sky. Bill jumped down beside me again and the rain came on, sudden and heavy, as if we'd stepped under a fireman's hose.

The rain was soaking us, streaming down our faces and into the neck of my dress. Half-walking and half-running beside the horse, I held my hand out to him. He grasped it very firmly and lolloped alongside me, gazing at me through the rain. In that look was a question, a recognition, a hunger. I pulled him towards me and we were kissing, stumbling, out of step, teeth bruising our lips. I wanted to let go of the horse and kiss him properly, but Bill pulled away. 'You have to go. It's too dangerous,' he said.

He dropped back and ran round the waggon and into the main barn. My mother rushed out into the rain to make sure the hay on the waggon was covered.

'Bill did it,' I told her. We unbuckled the mare from the shafts and I led her into the stable adjoining the barn.

Out of the corner of my eye, I could see Bill bent with his hands on his knees, puffing at the exertion of the day and the run, laughing and saying something to Harry. I hoped he wasn't telling him that he'd kissed me. The rain thundered down on the roof of the barn.

The guard caught me looking at Bill and I turned to Mother. 'We did it!'

She took the horse's bridle from me. 'You're soaking! Go into the house and get dry, and then get some food for everyone.'

I forced myself not to glance at Bill and pelted from the barn to the house, splashing water up my legs from the muddy puddles forming among the cobbles.

I tore up the stairs and yanked off my wet clothes, dropping them where they fell on my bedroom floor. In my mirror I could see that I appeared flushed and pretty, despite my straggly wet hair. My pupils were so enormous that my eyes no longer looked green, but as dark as Mother's. I couldn't take the grin off my face as I rubbed my hair, quickly pulled on dry clothes, loaded a basket with food and swung my mother's waxed cloak over my head and the basket, to run back to the barn.

The Oily Captain arrived as I was handing out the food, and my mother greeted him as if he was an old friend, holding her hand out to shake his. 'We did it! Thank you so much.'

He clicked his heels and saluted, with his fingers to his cap, rather than a full-armed Nazi salute. 'I'm very glad.' He looked like Marek when he's licking the cake mix from the bowl. 'Is it all covered?' he asked.

She was flushed with eagerness. 'Yes, the waggon has a tarpaulin, and the hay barn's full. I couldn't have done it without the working party. Would you like to see the barn?'

He looked even more pleased and pulled his coat round his shoulders. My mother took the oilskin I'd hung on a nail to dry and they half-ran across the muddy yard. She could have run faster, but I thought she was hanging back in deference to his bad leg.

I didn't like to see her being nice to him and wished my father were hiding somewhere to take a shot at him. From where I stood I could have got the Oily Captain clean between the shoulders. The guard was watching me again when I turned round, and I reminded myself that I had to be much, much more careful. I took him a piece of cake and tried to arrange my face into a semblance of kindness.

'They did good work,' I said in German. He seemed pleased I'd spoken to him. He was old, with grey skin blending into grey hair, and lips so thin below his grey moustache that they added no colour to his face. When he spoke, his teeth were stained yellow.

'Yes, good enough workers when they want to be. Though not as good as German workers.'

'No, of course not,' I said, slipping away to take bread to the prisoners, who were flopped around the barn. They were much more tired than my father and brother would have been, and far more tired than I felt. I was zinging with adrenaline and could have gone out and done the whole day's labour again. For a moment I was scornful of their weakness, and then I realised how hard it must be to exert yourself after months, or even years, of relative inactivity and poor food. It made me feel like a stupid little girl.

I went to Bill last. I could feel the guard's gaze on my back and I signalled to Bill with my eyes. He understood immediately and gave a big fake yawn as I came close to him. He didn't look me in the face or speak, but our hands brushed as he took the food from me, and it felt as if lightning sparked between us in the dark of the barn.

I turned as carelessly as I could and sauntered back to the barn entrance, swinging my hips slightly, feeling Bill's eyes on my back, to find the rain easing and my mother and the Oily Captain returning, deep in conversation about the repairs our outbuildings needed.

Yes, I thought. Yes, yes, yes, find him work and keep them coming here for ever.

The Oily Captain was as good as his word, letting us know every few days when the prisoners would next be coming and what the jobs would be. We would hear his knock at the kitchen door, and he would politely enquire what needed to be done. My mother would invite him in and offer him mint tea or coffee. Sometimes she would leave her hair uncovered, loose to her shoulders, as curly as mine, though shot through with silvery streaks since my father and Jan left. She talked to the Oily Captain about the farm and the weather and the town where he came from, and he showed her photographs of his children. I hated to see them chatting easily together, and made sure never to leave them alone in case he tried something with her. I never trusted him, but I needed him to keep bringing the work party.

Some days he said the prisoners couldn't be spared from some other task on another farm, or on the road they were improving, and I was initially furious and then plunged into a pit of gloom. I was sharp with my mother on those days and refused to play with Marek. I turned to my English primer with furious determination, learning ten or twenty words a day, repeating the difficult irregular verbs over and over again to myself as I walked or sewed or washed up. 'I am, you are, he is; I am, you are, he is . . .'

4

Two long, slow weeks inched past after the day of the thunderstorm before there was any chance for Bill and me to steal a moment on our own, though we'd exchanged frequent smiles and glances across the potato field. I listened for his whistling tunes to know exactly where he was working. Only when he was tired towards evening did he stop whistling, and then I worried about him and kept looking to check if he was all right.

We were always under the watchful eyes of the guard, the other prisoners and, most vigilant of all, my mother. Our hands touched as I passed Bill water or bread, and the same sparks flew between us. The desire to be alone with him, to kiss him properly, became an ache in my stomach.

I worked at ingratiating myself with the guard, bringing him titbits from our larder, discovering that he had a sweet tooth and taking him cake whenever I could.

'Do you mind if I speak to you from time to time?' I asked him.

'Why's that?' he asked. 'So you can take secrets to your traitor brother and father, I suppose.'

I looked shocked and hurt. 'No. Not at all. Quite the opposite.'

He glanced up at me, his moustache coated with strawberry jam.

I continued, hesitantly, 'I think I could be more useful to the Reich as an interpreter than as a farm girl. I speak German and Czech, of course, and I would like to interpret in English too, but I only have my school books and no chance to practise. I heard you speaking perfect English.'

He licked his lips, though some jam remained on his moustache. He studied me carefully and I tried to look as hopeful and guileless as possible.

'I used to be a schoolteacher,' he said.

I prayed my father would forgive my disloyalty. 'If my father and brother hadn't gone off with the . . . traitors, I might have been able to go to university instead of being stuck on this farm with my mother, hoeing turnips for the rest of my life.'

I put on my sulkiest expression and hoped he would be taken in. It was partly true, of course. I had hoped to go to university, and my father had been preparing me for the entrance exams when he left. I'd been taught at home by him, ever since the school had asked me to leave when I was fifteen, for refusing to obey the head teacher.

I'd repeated a silly joke about President Hácha's bushy eyebrows trying to mate with Hitler's moustache. It wasn't even very funny, but I was wiggling my eyebrows and my top lip, and my friends were giggling so hard they were almost crying. Then they started to wave at me, still helpless with laughter. I thought they wanted more, but they were trying to signal a warning that the school principal had come up behind me.

He dragged me to his office, with a huge portrait of Hitler behind his desk, and ordered me to apologise to him. I pressed my lips together, and although words were buzzing in my mouth like wasps, I wouldn't let them out. They certainly weren't the words he wanted to hear. He wasn't used to being disobeyed and told me to go home and not come back to school until I was ready to say I was sorry. My mother was furious and said I had to return at once.

Dad said, 'At least the child has principles.'

My mother retorted, 'Principles won't milk the cow. And won't get her to university.'

'You can teach her German literature,' said Dad. 'I can teach her everything else.'

After I went to bed that night they had a terrible row, but Dad won the argument and I never went back to school. Until he went away a year ago, I had lessons from him and my mother. I missed my friends and even missed my lessons, but I wasn't going to say sorry. It was my act of resistance – the only way I could go into battle.

Then my father had left, taking Jan, but refusing to give me the chance to go with them to fight the Third Reich properly. I was angry with my dad and furiously jealous of Jan. I missed them, feared for them and deeply resented them leaving me stuck on the farm. Five years of nothing but work, work, work, under the constant scrutiny of my mother. A sulky look wasn't hard to manage for the guard.

He shifted the rifle from one hand to the other and relaxed, obviously making a decision.

'I will help you with your English. I was a very good school-teacher, and I hope you will be a very good pupil. I will set you a lot of homework.'

'I will. I promise I will.' I was trying not to grin too widely.

33

'Shall I bring my books to you at the dinner break tomorrow? Would that be all right?'

He agreed, looking at his watch. 'Tomorrow then. Bring me your books and we'll see what can be done. And now those lazy dogs need to go back to work. Look at them all taking their ease as if this was a holiday.'

I looked at the five skinny men lying under the trees, trying to recover their strength for the afternoon's work, and fury whipped up in me. But I kept my head turned away, clenched my fists and counted to ten.

'Lazy dogs,' I agreed. 'This won't get the turnips hoed.'

The guard called, '*Raus, raus*' and the prisoners struggled to their feet, picking up their hoes.

'Thank you so much,' I said. 'I will be your best student. But what should I call you?'

He hesitated for a second and then said, 'My name is Weber. You should call me Herr Weber.'

A bee buzzed around him and I wondered whether to tell him about the jam on his moustache, but thought it would be just retribution if the bee stung him – perhaps on the end of his grey nose.

'Thank you, Herr Weber. Until tomorrow.'

The next day I sat down during the dinner break with Herr Weber and he set me dull grammatical exercises. The prisoners watched me with surprise, but I felt that somehow Bill would know this was a way of getting closer to him. I was more careful with my homework than I'd ever been before, and after just three lessons Herr Weber told me I was a good student and would be of excellent service to the Reich.

'You are a quick learner,' he said. 'You could become an interpreter one day.'

I paused, as if a new worry had crossed my mind. 'Would I need to improve my spoken English as well as my grammar?'

He glanced at me with a flicker of suspicion, but my innocent smile reassured him. 'You certainly would.'

'But how can I do that?' I said in a puzzled tone.

He laughed. 'That's easy!'

'Is it?'

'Of course. We have all these teachers in the work detail. So many prisoners. Do you know we have taken millions of prisoners of war? They just hold up their hands and allow themselves to be captured.'

'That's marvellous,' I said, and very quietly, 'Heil Hitler.'

Herr Weber continued. 'Instead of lazing about at dinnertime, they can teach you English!'

I clapped my hands in astonishment. 'That's a wonderful idea. I would never have thought of that. How can it be arranged?'

The next day at dinnertime Herr Weber led me to where the men were sprawled beneath the trees.

He kicked one of the other men with his toecap, to wake him up, but I sat down firmly next to Bill, and Herr Weber just shrugged and left me to it.

'I have English class,' I announced.

'You're a bleedin' miracle-worker,' whispered Bill.

I opened my primer and pointed at the third chapter: Meeting and Greeting.

Bill jumped to his feet. 'How do you do?' he said and held

out his hand. I stood and gave him mine, and he shook it firmly but not too hard.

'How do you do?' I replied.

The men lying about around us turned to watch the show, but I didn't care.

'Do you come here often?' he asked, separating each of the words and saying them a little loudly.

'I live.'

'I live here,' he corrected me, and I was pleased. Bill was really going to help me learn, not just muck about.

'I live here, on farm,' I said.

'I live here, on *this* farm.'

We sat down again and worked our way through the chapter. I scribbled notes all the time.

After this, I was able to join Bill every day, quite openly. We sat where we could be seen, but there were always ways to brush each other's hands. My English improved fast, but the desire to be alone with him became desperate. When you are starving, a little food only makes you hungrier.

Sometimes our conversation was guided by a chapter in the book, but more often we just talked.

'Today I'd like to take you out,' he announced one day.

'Where we go?' I asked.

'Where *would* we go?' he corrected me, and I wrote it down.

'First, I'd come and pick you up. I think that's better than meeting under a clock or something. I'd bring you a little bunch of violets for your buttonhole.'

I didn't know what this word meant. In his London accent it sounded like 'bu'n'ole'. I repeated it: 'Bu-u-nole?'

He laughed. 'Blimey, I'm going to have to talk proper. Buttonhole,' he said, sounding the t's and the h. He pointed at his tunic. 'Button. Buttonhole.'

I nodded and wrote it down.

'Then we'd catch a bus up west and go for tea at Lyons Corner House, and the Nippy'd bring us great plates of sandwiches and scones.'

'Scones?'

'A kind of bready cake with butter and jam and cream.'

'It sound very good.'

'*Sounds* very good, with an s,' he said kindly, and I scribbled the correction as he continued. 'Then we'd go to the pictures. Just stroll up to Leicester Square, looking at all the people. Would you like that?'

'Pichers?'

'Movies, film, cinema.'

'Ah, yes, I like pichers.' I didn't tell him what a rare treat it was for me to see a film. We had a cinema in Neutitschein, but it wasn't easy to get away from the farm. Sometimes us local girls would go together on our bikes.

'What kind of film would you like?' he asked.

'Film of love,' I suggested, with a shy sideways glance, and he laughed. 'With music,' I add decidedly.

'OK. We'll go to a romantic musical. *Top Hat.* Music and dancing.' Bill began to sing softly, ' "Heaven, I'm in heaven, and my heart beats so that I can barely speak . . ." '

It was the first time I'd heard him sing, and his voice was a pleasant tenor. I wanted to know the song, and be able to sing along with him.

' ". . . when we're out together dancing, cheek to cheek." '

I sighed, a deep sigh of longing for a world where this could be true.

'So then, after the pictures, I'll take you dancing. Do you like dancing?'

'I love dance. But not get much . . .' I didn't know the word, so waved my hand around me at the farm.

'Not much chance. No, I can see that. A bit short of dance halls!'

The guard cut in, calling the men back to work. '*Raus, raus.*'

Bill ran his hand up through his hair. He stood up and reached down to pull me to my feet.

'Well, that was nice, Izzy. Now I'll walk you home and,' he lowered his voice, so the others couldn't hear, 'we might kiss at your door.'

'I like that.'

'Me too.'

He let go of my hand, and I bent to gather my books.

Later that week Mother decided it was time for the cherries to be picked. I never knew how she hit on the exact day when they'd be ripe. She said one day I would know it too, but I had no intention of staying on the farm that long.

We used long poles to carefully lift the nets from the three cherry trees and then it was a race – us against the birds. My mother set two men to each tree and moved between them, watching that the fruit didn't get bruised. Bill and Harry were picking one tree – 'larking about', as Bill would say – dangling pairs of cherries from their ears, laughing and singing a song called 'Cherry Ripe' in high falsetto voices.

When the baskets were full, my mother came and inspected the tree, to make sure no cherries had been missed. Wasps were already busy at the fruit. Mother brushed a wisp of hair from her eyes.

'You'd better take these baskets and the nets up to the house,' she said, then stopped and looked at Bill. 'Oh, it's you.'

She hesitated and looked around, but the other prisoners were high in the trees, and she didn't dare leave them unsupervised.

'Oh, I suppose it'll be all right.' She scowled at me, 'No dilly-dallying and no funny business, or you'll be locked up for a fortnight. Do you understand me?'

'I promise, Mother,' I said in my most saintly voice. 'We won't be long.'

She looked very deliberately at her watch. 'You'd better not be.'

I lifted one brimming basket and Bill the other. He said, 'Blimey, you're as strong as I am.'

I strode away as fast as my heavy load would allow, and Bill hurried to keep pace. When I glanced back, Mother was helping Harry to sling the nets across his shoulders, keeping them clear of the ground.

Bill said, 'I see there's a lot more to you than a pretty face.'

He thought I had a pretty face! 'We go gentle must,' I said, hunting for the words.

He guessed, 'We must be cautious? Is that it? Not let them see too much?'

'Yes, yes. Cautious. My mother sees.'

'Mothers see everything,' he agreed.

Inside the house we laid the baskets on the kitchen table. Bill quickly took my hand, and it was as if an electric jolt passed up my arm. He raised my fingers to his lips and we heard Harry whistling the 'Cherry Ripe' tune as he approached. My insides flickered with fire.

Harry coughed a warning as he pushed through the door, festooned with nets. Bill dropped my hand, and we laughed like children as we disentangled Harry and carefully laid the nets on the flagstones for mending.

Bill was saying, 'I had no idea there was so much to do on a farm. City boy, see. London', and looking all round him like a bird, this way and that, taking in everything: the sink, the table, the larder, the pans. 'Oh, Lord, it's so good to be in a house again.' He stroked the table. 'So normal. I'll be able to picture you here.'

Harry winked at Bill. 'I'm just going outside to keep cavey.'

'Keep watch,' Bill explained as I closed the door on Harry's retreating back.

I glanced quickly through the window into the farmyard and drew Bill to the dark wall between the door and window. He took my face between his hands and gazed at me, as if committing each element of my face to memory.

'Your eyes are so green,' he said, 'like a cat's.'

He bent and kissed me, and it was different from any of the boys I'd kissed before, like currents up and down my spine. I pressed myself tightly against him, kissing so deeply it made my knees tremble. The farm and my mother were completely forgotten until a whistle came from outside, and Bill pulled away.

'I mustn't get sent back to Lamsdorf,' he said. 'Not now.'

I laid a finger on his lips and led him to the door. 'You not go Lamsdorf,' I said firmly. 'I stay you here.'

'By God, I think you will.' He shook his head in admiration.

As I opened the door and light flooded into the kitchen, he looked beyond the stairs into our dining room. 'A piano!' he said. 'You've got a piano!'

'Can play?'

'It's my best thing – after kissing you! Can you play?'

I almost had to push him out of the door, he was so reluctant to leave the piano.

'I learn long time, but play bad.'

'And I ain't never had a lesson,' he said. 'But I play good. Funny old world.'

We turned towards the fields and Harry followed at a considerate distance. Bill looked back at the house, as if knowing the location of the precious object would somehow enable him to play it.

'We could play duets.' He ran his hands up and down imaginary scales in the air.

I asked, 'What music you like?'

'Jazz tunes, ragtime, dance music – anything that goes down well in a pub.' He paused. 'I play by ear.'

'What "by ear"?'

'Without music. I don't know how to read music. I can play the tunes if I hear them. Almost any tune off the radio.'

I had never met anyone who could do this.

'This gift from God,' I said in wonder, and a beaming smile lit up his face.

5

In the wired-off compound outside the Mankendorf sawmill, Bill and Harry were playing shuttlecock over a rope. Bill was using a table-tennis bat and Harry had an old tennis racket, but that wasn't why Bill was losing so badly. Every few seconds he glanced up at the road from Vražné – the road Izzy would cycle along, if her mother allowed her to come. The jittery anticipation in his stomach overrode his ever-present hunger. The shuttlecock landed at his feet.

'Thirty-six to seven,' called Harry. 'You ain't even trying.'

Outside the wire, the tarty girls from the village were holding court with a group of prisoners inside the fence. At dinnertime today Bill had told Izzy that other girls came down to the camp and asked if she could come too. She doubted her mother would allow it, but he couldn't help hoping.

Bill flipped a shot over the washing line, just as a bright movement caught his eye on the road from Vražné. The dress of a girl on a bicycle. It was. It was her. His stomach tightened, and he missed Harry's return shot.

Harry shaded his eyes and looked in the direction of Bill's gaze. 'Oh, now I get it,' he said. 'Off you hop then, chummy.'

Bill thrust the tennis-table bat at him and moved to an empty section of the wire fence, watching as Izzy dismounted and scanned the faces inside the compound. The tarty girls spoke to her, but she barely replied. Herr Weber sat smoking with the owner of the sawmill, watching the men half-heartedly, and he started up when he saw Izzy approach, but she waved her school books at him to show her serious intent.

Then she spotted Bill at the wire and smiled with obvious relief. Something jumped inside him as he grinned back.

Feeling nervous, as if this was his first date, Bill smoothed his hair down with one hand, then ran his fingers back up through it with the other. He watched as Izzy laid her bike down on the ground and walked towards him, clutching her books. He drank in the supple movement of her slim body, her skirt swinging, until she stood, perhaps a metre away, on the other side of the wire.

'Hello,' he said awkwardly. 'I'm so glad you came.'

'My mother say is good,' she replied, hardly meeting his eyes.

'Did she really?'

Izzy pulled a wry face. 'Not good, for sure, but OK.'

They both laughed, and the tension broke.

'I see you've brought your books,' he said, grasping for something to say. 'That's a pretty dress.'

But she was looking at the sawmill and the wire.

'Is bad here?' she asked anxiously.

'No, it's not bad. Not compared with Lamsdorf and the other Stalags. We get extra rations here, because we're doing what's

43

classified as heavy work.' He followed the direction of her gaze towards the factory, and pointed to the first floor.

'We sleep upstairs there, above the factory floor. Two big rooms with thirty men in each. On bunk beds. Harry sleeps below me. We're locked in at night, of course. But we get a bath every Saturday and' – he swept his arm around at the surroundings, at the countryside, which was so new to him and which he'd fallen in love with – 'all this. Beautiful trees. Fantastic sunrises over the hills, and look over there. They let us grow tomatoes, lettuce and spring onions – and sometimes we're allowed to swim in the river.' He paused. 'And now you're here.'

'Now I am here.' She smiled.

Bill put his hand up to the wire, and she checked to see if Herr Weber was watching before stepping forward and touching her hand to his. Her hand was warm, and heat seemed to pass into Bill's from it. After a moment she stepped back again. He wanted so much to have something to give her, some flowers or chocolate. But he had nothing.

'I want to know everything about you,' he said.

She smiled. 'Not much say. I am Czech farm girl.'

He shook his head. 'You are beautiful and clever. You are learning English so fast.'

'I have good teacher.'

He grinned again. 'I have *a* good teacher.'

'*A* good teacher,' she echoed, shaking her head. 'A very good teacher.'

'So let's sit down and tell me – tell me about you. Tell me everything.'

'You tell when I say thing wrong. I have bring dictionary.' She corrected herself. 'I have bring *a* dictionary.'

Bill sat cross-legged in the dust on his side of the wire, and she sat down on the grass on the other side. He had so much he wanted to ask. He wanted to know everything about Izzy and her family, and this mysterious country he'd washed up in. 'Tell me why most people speak German, if this is Czechoslovakia,' he said at last.

She shrugged. 'Is history. War.' She drew a line on the grass with her finger and said, 'One nine one four.' Then she rubbed it out and drew another line further away. 'One nine one eight.'

Bill repeated the numbers, running his hand up through his hair, then, 'I get it, 1914 and 1918. The borders got moved after the Great War?'

Izzy nodded and rubbed out the line again. 'And now' – she opened her arms wide – '*Lebensraum.*'

This was one of the few German words that Bill knew well.

'Hitler has taken it all,' he said.

And she agreed. 'All.'

They both sat in silence for a moment until he said, 'You. Tell me about you. What do you want, when all this is over?'

'I want go university, but too late now. Too old,' Izzy said, pulling a wry face.

'*It's* too late. *I'm* too old.' Bill corrected her. 'No, you aren't. Anyway, how old are you?'

'Twenty. You?'

'Twenty-three. Eighteen when I joined up.'

She made an irritated sound with her teeth. 'My father say I not go join partisans when I nineteen.'

Bill wondered if he'd misunderstood. Her accent was very thick. 'You tried to join the resistance?'

'For sure. My big brother Jan, he go. I want too. Kill Hitler soldiers. Fight for country. Leave farm. Big adventure. But my father say not girls.'

Bill agreed absolutely with her father, but she looked so angry that he thought he'd better not say so. 'I wanted adventure too,' he said ruefully. 'And look where it's got me.'

She was still frowning. 'But you have see world.'

'That's true. We sailed all round the Cape of Africa. Camped under the pyramids. Then captured at Tobruk, worst luck.'

The images and noise of that last battle threatened to crowd in on him, and he forced himself to concentrate on Izzy.

'Where Tobruk?' she asked.

'Libya.' As he said the word, the stink of the camp flooded back to him and he clenched his fists.

'So how you here?' she demanded.

He shook his head to rid himself of the sounds and sights. 'The Jerries want us as far as possible from home. Stops us running away. Now you. Tell me about you.'

Haltingly she told him about her mother, a German-speaking farm girl from Vražné, and her father, a music teacher from Prague, the Czech socialist who'd won her mother's heart. As she spoke, Bill gently corrected her or supplied a word, and she scribbled the new vocabulary in her notebook. He thought perhaps his meeting her was somehow meant to be: another musician meeting a farm girl, as if history was repeating on a loop. Izzy told him how her parents had gone to live in the capital and the excitement of their life there. The sun was beginning to set as she described her mother's father becoming ill, and them coming to Vražné together to take over the family farm. Her father had given up his career as a musician to be close to her mother. Bill wondered if he could have done that.

'She teach Dad everything for farm,' Izzy said.

'Like me,' said Bill. 'You've taught me about scything and hoeing.'

'And taking *hnuj* – from horse and cow, to field.'

He looked puzzled for a moment, then laughed and wrinkled his nose. 'Muck-spreading the dung. Yes. I know all about that.'

He watched as she wrote down *muck-spreading* and *dung*.

Before coming to Vražné, he'd never thought about where his food came from, or the work that went into producing it. His aunt had a small garden where she grew raspberries and rhubarb, but in his mind, those things simply grew, without any human effort. They didn't have a garden at the pub, just a yard full of barrels. Now he was wondering if he could ever go back to that closed-in brick-and-concrete life.

'Could you live in a town, do you think?' he asked.

'For sure. I want leave here. See world. Like you. See Table Mountain and pyramid. I want adventure, see life.'

He rubbed his face. 'And I've had enough adventure for a lifetime.'

They looked through the wire at each other for a long time, and Bill realised it was beginning to get dark. He looked up at the sky, at the evening star, and she followed his gaze and jumped to her feet.

'If not home by night . . .' she began.

He stood too. 'Your mother won't let you come again. Go – go quickly. But take care.'

He reached a hand forward to the wire again, and she touched his fingertips.

'See you soon,' he said.

He stood watching her cycle away until she disappeared around the bend in the road.

The next day Bill was working in the yard at Izzy's farm when she ran in shouting that the pigs had escaped and she needed help. As if at random, she grabbed Bill's sleeve and pulled him with her towards the empty sty. He ran behind her, bemused and not sure what was coming next. He was beginning to understand that life with Izzy would never be dull. They stopped near the pigsty, where two sows were loose. He'd never been so close to a pig before, and they were bigger than he'd expected. Izzy began shooing them back to the sty, instructing him to block their escape. He stood well back and waved his arms, not knowing if pigs might bite or charge and trample him. The smell made his eyes water, but Izzy didn't seem to notice. He suspected she had let them out on purpose.

Once the pigs were back in the sty, she looked around, checking that nobody was about. Her eyes were bright with merriment and she held out a hand to him, in the shadow of the sty. He drew close and then they were kissing, and he never wanted it to stop. One of the pigs sneezed and Bill jumped. Izzy could afford to be reckless, but he was a soldier, alert to danger. If they were caught, she would remain here on the farm, free to come and go, with good food and fresh air, and she'd probably find another prisoner to kiss. But he'd be sent back to the closed-in, stifling hell of Lamsdorf.

Regretfully, he kissed her on the nose and turned back to the yard.

During the light July evenings, Bill waited by the wire for Izzy. Sometimes she didn't come, and he climbed into his bunk full of the despair of long imprisonment. He was always tired after his long day's work with too little food, but the sight of her bicycle whizzing down the road made adrenaline surge through his body, filling him with energy. On her second visit he brought out his harmonica and shyly asked if she'd like him to play something. He tried to put everything he couldn't find the words for into his music: how strange and wonderful it was that fate had brought them together.

Every time she came after that, she would ask him to play something on the harmonica, and sometimes the other prisoners would begin to sing along with him, like a male-voice choir. Bill chose romantic tunes, allowing his fellow prisoners to speak for him: 'There were angels dining at the Ritz, and a nightingale sang in Berkeley Square'. He hoped she could understand the words.

Most often, though, they talked about themselves: the things they liked and loathed, their families, their friends. Bill told Izzy how much he hated being an only child and that his cousins who lived on the same street were his closest friends, especially his cousin Flora. He told her about the journey he and Harry had taken through various prison camps. He didn't say how they'd been beaten by sadistic guards but did tell her that Harry had become like a brother to him.

'Different than brother, I think,' she said cheerfully. 'I want kill my brothers sometimes.'

They talked about the things they liked to eat. He was astonished that her favourite food was goose. He thought all girls liked chocolate.

'Mine's jam roly-poly. Or spotted dick. Or Christmas pud . . .' His mouth watered, and for a moment he could taste each of the long-lost delicacies on his tongue.

49

They talked about things they were good at, and things they were terrible at. Izzy made him laugh by telling him how her father despaired at her inability to learn to play the piano, how he called her 'sausage fingers'. Bill looked at the elegant hands holding her pen and book and wanted to kiss each 'sausage' finger.

'Perhaps I could teach you to play? I'd like to teach people, one day, when I've learned to read music.'

'I can teach read,' she said, 'but nobody teach me play!'

He asked her what she was afraid of, and she said she didn't like spiders.

'What you afraid?' she asked.

'Getting sent back to Lamsdorf,' he said.

'I afraid that too.'

They looked at each other for a long moment. For Bill, Izzy was some kind of miracle, a bright flower growing out of concrete, unexpected and unimagined. He couldn't believe that he meant the same to her – she who must have had so many men to choose from. To her, he couldn't be any more than a passing diversion, a novelty to be played with. It was too soon to tell her the truth: that the thing he most feared was never seeing her again. So instead he said, 'And being put in front of a firing squad again.'

She was horrified. 'When that?'

The terror of it swept through him once more, but he tried to make light of it. 'Down in Italy, on our way here. Me and Harry thought we'd try to escape, and we got caught within a day. The Eyeties handed us to the Jerries, who put us up against a wall.' She clapped her hand over her mouth, but he continued, 'I'd always wondered what people thought about when they were in front of a firing squad, and now I know.'

'What think?'

'I thought: I wish they'd bloody well hurry up. I don't think I can stand here much longer.' He shivered at the memory and she reached out to touch his fingers on the wire.

'I am glad they not shoot,' she said.

'I'm glad too. Very glad.'

On the days when Bill and the other prisoners were taken to work on a different farm, or on the road, his body seemed to become heavy and old beyond his years, and the work was hard, hard, hard. But on the days their truck turned in the morning towards Vražné, he began to whistle, wondering when he would see Izzy and how she would contrive to find them time to be alone for a few minutes.

By late July he was sometimes left to work by himself, fixing the tractor or one of the other farm machines, and that helped them to grasp a few minutes out of sight of her mother or Herr Weber. Izzy had been surprised that Bill knew how to mend engines, but he explained that gunners like him were trained in how to take things apart and put them back together.

'I've always been good with my hands,' he said. 'Piano-playing, mending cars, you name it.'

He was too delicate to name the kind of soft touching he'd almost forgotten – as erotic to the toucher as to the one being touched – reminding him what desire felt like, licking through him, strong as a flame.

As the weeks of summer passed and July became August, she'd let him slide a hand inside her dress as they kissed, cupping her breast; and later she didn't stop him from lifting her skirt, running his fingers up the inside of her thigh and up the wide leg of her knickers into the silky wetness. Then he bent down and tongued her hard nipple through the fabric of her cotton dress until he felt her shudder of release.

Each time it became more and more difficult to pull himself back to the task in hand, to remember that at any minute they might be discovered and it would all be over.

At the sawmill one evening, Izzy looked along the fencing to where Matylda and Dagmar were posing provocatively in their tight clothes, with a gang of admirers, including Harry, inside the wire. As Bill watched her, Izzy blushed deep red.

'You aren't like them,' he reassured her. 'What we do isn't like them. This is something different.'

Sometimes they talked about the progress of the war. Izzy brought snippets of information about the rapid advance of the Soviet front, which he was able to pass on to his friends. By late August he learned that the Russians were in the Carpathian Mountains in Czechoslovakia, and close to Warsaw in Poland. He had only the haziest idea of the geography, but realised that as the Red Army drew nearer, he and the rest of the prisoners would be moved back to Lamsdorf. His time with Izzy was coming to an end just as surely as the summer had passed.

A few days later Bill was at the farm, working on an old string-binding reaping machine that he'd pulled out of the barn to fix, when he recognised Izzy's footsteps behind him. She had brought his dinnertime bread and cheese, and he turned to her with a rush of anticipation. They looked all around to make sure her mother wasn't coming, and ducked into the cool darkness of the barn, kissing and clinging to each other.

Bill pulled back, gasping for air. 'You are too beautiful.' He breathed in the smell of her hair and lifted her curls in one hand, feeling their weight. 'I love your hair.'

Izzy laughed. 'My mother say must cut hair. She want make me into boy. She is put boy clothes – my brother clothes – for me to wear when Russian soldiers come.'

The thought was like a cold slap in the face. Bill's whole body froze and he tried to see her expression in the dim light, as he thought through the implications of her mother's plan and the need for it.

'They're getting closer then,' he said at last. 'The Jerries ain't holding them.' He began to pace away from her and then back. 'If they come, you must do what your mother says. You're too beautiful. They would . . .'

She nodded, miserably. The village gossip was alive with what happened to the women in every village and town the Soviets took. Slowly she told Bill one of the stories she'd heard. 'A mother with two daughters – my age. Mother know soldiers come, hide girls in' – she searched for the word – 'room at top of house.'

'Loft. Attic,' supplied Bill, motioning for her to continue.

'Hide them in loftattic room, pull cupboard to hide door. Two soldiers come and ask for *molodaya zhenshchina* – any *Fräulein*. The mother she say no, but then one girl . . . atishoo!'

Bill said, 'Sneezed.' He already knew where this was going, but Izzy couldn't be stopped. The words were tumbling out of her.

'Soldiers hear sneeze. One punch the mother and she fall to floor. Other man kick her. Then they pull the girls downstairs. Girls scream and cry help. Pull girls into mother and father bedroom and lock door. Mother bang on door with hands . . .'

Izzy wouldn't meet Bill's eyes as she told him the story. Her

53

terror filled the barn and he paced up and down, swishing help-lessly at the straw with a stick. He could hardly bear to listen, seeing Izzy's face on one of the girls, her body about to be violated, and not knowing how he could put himself between her and the might of the Red Army.

Taking a deep breath, Izzy went on, telling him how the girls resisted, scratched and spat and twisted away, until one of the soldiers pulled out his revolver and shot them both.

'One girl shot in leg and one in stomach. Then men do . . . that thing . . . to both girls, bleeding and crying and maybe die. After, soldiers hold down mother and do it to her too. They go off, laughing.'

Bill punched the door of the barn, enraged by his own pow-erlessness. 'If you stay here and they find you . . . I can't save you. My God, I can't bear to think of it. Promise me you'll do what she says, dress like a boy. Promise.'

And Izzy promised, though he didn't believe it would be enough to protect her. If only she could escape to the partisans, he thought. If only he could help her escape.

They moved back outside and he began to work again in furi-ous silence, while Izzy trudged back to the field. Despite the glorious sunshine, he was overtaken with despair. Soon everything would change. He and the others would be taken back behind the wires and watchtowers of Lamsdorf, and Izzy – darling Izzy – would be left here at the mercy of the bestial Russian army.

6

We harvested the potatoes and sugar beets in September, my mother working without rest. To my joy, the Oily Captain brought the working party almost every day. Bill and I met for snatched moments in the buildings where the crops were being laid up for the winter. I told Bill that some farmers buried their potatoes surrounded by straw, to ensure they didn't get damp. My mother and I would probably find a place to do the same, to keep some the local inspector wouldn't know about.

Harry was careful to go outside for a smoke from time to time, and then in the earthy-smelling dark of the barn, Bill and I whispered and kissed, kissed and whispered.

One day Harry said, 'I'm just off to stretch my legs for a bit' and sauntered back towards the potato field, his head wreathed in smoke.

I took hold of Bill's head and pulled it to me, hungrily. I let him touch me wherever he liked, knowing now that it was where I liked too, pushing against his fingers.

'You know I'll come back for you, when it's all over,' he said. 'You know that, don't you?'

I studied his face, the three thin lines etched across his brow when he was deeply in earnest.

I picked my words carefully. 'But everything is different then.'

He was almost angry. 'I won't be different. I won't feel any different. I love you. I love you.'

The words were small and clear, but also like a great wind rushing in my ears. I couldn't stop myself grinning as I said the words I had been practising in front of my mirror for weeks. 'I love you also.'

'Then you must know I'll come back?' He was urgent.

'I will be wait for you. Even if long, long time.'

He pulled me tight into him again and kissed my eyelids.

Now that we'd said we loved each other, it felt as if everything had shifted so that we were the still eye of a storm, with all the madness of the world whirling around us. The hours we didn't see each other were almost unendurable, and the snatched moments when we were alone were more tantalising than satisfying. In the evenings I cycled down to the sawmill as fast as if all the hounds of hell were on my tail. And as the swallows returned to their nests and I reluctantly rode away, the pedals seemed almost too heavy to turn. Bill always watched me until I was out of sight. I lifted myself round in the saddle on the last bend, and he raised his hand.

Every evening Bill and I sat on the ground, or stood if it had rained and the ground was damp, on either side of the wire, and talked and talked. He told me about his job as a railway clerk. 'Paddington ain't the prettiest station,' he said. 'That's St Pancras.' Nostalgia swept over his face and he went silent for a moment, then continued, 'It's the smell of it – the trains, the coal dust, the smoke, a kind of metallic . . . I don't know how to describe it, but it smells like home.' He struggled to find the words. 'It's like when Mole is following Ratty and gets a scent of his old home, and it floods over him . . .'

I shook my head in bewilderment. 'Mole?'

Bill laughed. 'Of course, you ain't got *Wind in the Willows* here. Mole and Ratty and Badger and Toad.'

I had no idea what he was talking about.

'And I bet you don't know Winnie-the-Pooh or Piglet, either? Never mind. They're kids' books. You can read them to our children.'

A great rush of love came over me. 'Our children,' I repeated. 'Yes, our children!'

We looked at each other without speaking for a long time; then he promised that after the war we would marry and have children together. And the world would be peaceful and so beautiful. It would be all wind through willows and a house at Pooh Corner.

Once I knew that Bill loved me and we would be married one day, I became desperate in my desire to be with him. I waited until the next time he said, 'I wish you didn't have to go', as he did every night, and then, flushing deeply, I said, 'I come back when my mother is asleep? Are you locked?'

'Would you do that?' he asked, sounding a little breathless at the prospect. 'If I left the laundry-room window ajar, perhaps I could squeeze through. They hardly ever check it. I'll try it tonight and tell you tomorrow.' He laughed aloud at the prospect.

By now it was mid-September and darkness was falling earlier and earlier. Before the war, we'd have seen lamps in windows, families going about their business, making their dinner, darning their socks. But now the shutters were firmly shut before the lamps were lit, as if everyone was closed in their small worlds, unable to contemplate the enormity of what went on beyond their walls.

For two nights running, Bill had left the laundry-room window slightly ajar when the guard came round to lock them into the factory, and it had gone unnoticed. Tonight he would use it to sneak out. He'd told me that every night the prisoners had to leave their trousers and boots in the washroom, as it was assumed that nobody would try to escape in their socks and underwear. But most of the men had spare trousers and boots. I was glad Bill had spare trousers. I didn't think it would be romantic to see him in his underwear and socks.

I pretended to go to bed as usual and lay down in the dark, but didn't undress. When my mother came upstairs, I pulled the bedclothes up to my chin and pretended to be asleep. I could hear her breathing as she stood and looked at me for a long time. Eventually she sighed softly and went out of the room, closing the door behind her. I lay completely still and focused all my attention on listening. I heard her moving about her room. One floorboard creaked and creaked and creaked again. And then, finally, it was quiet. She was quiet. The thin sliver of light under my door vanished as she blew out her lamp. I'd decided I must now wait for an hour, unless I heard her snoring. I practised irregular past participles to keep my mind occupied, although excitement and anticipation effervesced in my tummy. 'To be: I am, I was; I bring, I brought; I come, I came; I do, I did . . .' What would I do tonight? And would it change who I was?

When I was sure my mother must be asleep, I sat up and gathered my shoes in one hand. I turned the doorknob slowly and silently and pulled open my bedroom door. It scraped slightly and I stood in the doorway, waiting and listening. Nothing but the sounds of the night outside: a dog barking far off, which set off the honking of some geese kilometres away. I took one step at a time across the landing and onto the stairs, hugging close to the wall to reduce the creaking to a minimum. At the foot of the stairs I stood and listened again. Nothing. I crept through the dark kitchen, slid the bolts and opened the back door. It was impossible to do in complete silence. I waited again, but there were no noises from upstairs. The door clicked shut behind me, and I knew my mother and Marek were in an unlocked house, but I dismissed the thought. I wouldn't be gone long, and she'd never know I'd been away.

I'd left my bicycle outside the house, leaning against the wall, so I was able to wheel it quietly onto the road. There was half a moon and it was brighter than I had expected, so I was glad I'd worn dark clothes. I'd been afraid I might not be able to see the road, but it was picked out in the moonlight like a ribbon of water. I thought of all the people sleeping behind the shuttered windows of their houses, not knowing I was on my way to meet my love! I pushed the bike until I was out of sight of the house and then I mounted it, letting the thrill of the night rush through me as I flew away through the darkness.

Five minutes from the sawmill, I hid my bike in the hedge and crept nearer on foot, making my way around the perimeter wire to the back of the mill, away from the road where we normally met. I cupped my hands around my mouth and made the owl hoot that was to be our signal. I waited, my stomach churning in anticipation, but nothing happened. What if the guard had noticed the unlocked window? What if Bill hadn't managed to sneak away? What if his spare boots had been discovered?

I hooted again, and this time there was an answering movement inside the wire. At first I thought it wasn't Bill at all; perhaps
a guard come to denounce me, to tell me Bill was under arrest
for attempted escape. But then I realised it was Bill with a dark
woolly hat over his blond hair. He crept forward to me over the
thin strip of ground between the building and the wire, waved
his boots to me and threw them over. I caught them easily and
laid them on the ground. One bare foot at a time, he began to
climb the fence, up in four steps and over the top, dropping down
on my side with a soft thud. We both stood and waited, listening,
looking at each other. I was so nervous I began to giggle, clapping a hand over my mouth to stifle the sound.

'Shh,' he whispered. 'Where are my boots?'

I handed them to him, and he yanked them on roughly over
his bare feet.

'You must tie laces,' I said, imagining him tripping up before
we could make it into the trees. He bent and stuffed the laces
down into his boots,

'There,' he said. 'Satisfied? Come on now.' And taking my
hand, he pulled me beside him across the strip of grass into the
woods.

Under the canopy of trees it was darker and hard to see our
way forward. We felt our way with our feet and hands, touching
the tree trunks as we passed them, kicking through the bracken
underfoot.

Eventually we reached a small clearing and he stopped, looking back towards the black shape of the sawmill, just visible
through the trees.

'That should do,' he said. 'Come here.'

I almost ran into his arms, turning up my face to be kissed.

After a moment he pulled back. 'Are you cold? You're trembling like a rabbit.'

'Not cold,' I said. 'Just . . .'

I didn't have words for the shivers that passed through me. This was the adventure I'd longed for. It felt as if my life was starting at last.

'Are you afraid?' he asked, gazing at me in the moonlight. 'I'll never do anything to hurt you. Nothing you don't want to do. I love you.'

'Not afraid,' I said. And I wasn't. 'I love you. I want . . .'

The novelty of hearing myself say the words was still an arrow of joy in me. Bill drew me into the clearing, where we could see a little better.

'Here, let's sit down. It's just so wonderful to have you to myself for a little while without any guards . . .'

'Or mothers.'

He sat with his back to a broad oak tree and patted the earth beside him. I took off my coat and laid it beside him on the ground, which I knew would be damp, then sat close, cuddling into him. He wrapped his arms around me and we sat watching the small movements of leaves against the sky, listening to tiny rustlings in the undergrowth. We must have looked peaceful, but my heart was banging against my ribs, and I wanted him to start making love to me. I wanted to be a woman.

I turned in his arms and kissed his throat, his carefully shaved chin, his lips, which opened for me. I ran my tongue over the chipped edge of his front tooth, claiming every imperfection as my own. As we kissed, he gently laid me down on my coat. He had one arm under my neck, but the other hand was free, and it went to the small buttons on my blouse. He fumbled unsuccessfully with one button and then moved his hand to my breast, then back again to the infuriatingly tiny buttons. I wished I'd worn something else and broke away from the kiss, pushed myself up onto my elbows, twisting towards him as I sat up. His eyes were steadily on me as I undid the buttons one by one and removed my blouse. It was chilly in the September air, and the hair stood up on my arms, but I didn't care. I lifted my camisole over my head and reached behind me for the fastening of my bra. As I took it off, I automatically covered my breasts with my arms, but as he watched me and made no move, I slowly dropped my arms to my sides, so he could see me properly in the moonlight.

He let out a very long, low sigh, then reached forward to trace the curve of my right breast to the tight nipple. I shivered with cold and delight as he took my left breast in his warm hand and bent with his mouth to the right until I thought I might die with joy.

Kissing me again, he guided my hand to the hard lump in his trousers and pressed it there. The thing inside jumped of its own accord and my hand jerked away in surprise. He drew back to consider me. 'Have you ever? No, you ain't, 'ave you?'

'I am a good Catholic girl,' I said indignantly.

'Of course you are.'

His head was bowed, and I couldn't tell from the way he said it whether he thought this was bad or good. In peacetime most girls were married long before they reached twenty. Many had children. But in war, nothing is the same. Now was the right time for me, married or not. A cold breeze ran over my bare torso, making me shiver and wrap my arms around myself.

He raised his head at the movement, and I could see the struggle on his face. He gazed at me for a long moment, as if making up his mind. 'Then we won't do it till we're married,' he said. 'There's no way of knowing what'll happen, and I don't want to leave you with a kid.'

This proved more than anything that he loved me, and now I wanted him to do it even more.

Bill said, 'You know I'll come back after the war and marry you? You do believe that, don't you?'

I ran the tip of my nails along the bare patch between his sweater and trousers, hoping this would encourage him to resume.

'Why not marry now?' I asked, meaning the consummation, as much as the sacrament.

He shook his head. 'You're crazy! There's a war. I'm a prisoner.'

'But we love each other. Perhaps there is way.'

'Even you couldn't make that happen!'

'Do you want I try?'

'Yes, yes, I'd marry you tonight, right here, if this tree was a priest.'

He struggled up onto his knees and turned towards the tree. 'Yes, I do!' he said, and I knelt beside him and exclaimed, 'I do too!' and he pulled me into his arms again, running his hands over the goose-pimpled skin of my bare back. I thought now we might do it, and I wanted him to so much, but soon he told me to put my clothes back on, because it was too cold.

I was filled with a cocktail of frustration and disappointment, love and pride in him, but he was right: it was becoming really cold. So I began to dress myself.

'When we're married, I'm going to make love to you all night,' he said.

We sat huddled up to each other for a long time, not speaking.

I wondered if a time would ever come when it would be so normal to be together like this that we would take it completely for granted.

As I approached the house I knew that something was wrong. I leaned my bike against the wall and turned the handle of the back door. Nothing. It wouldn't open. I pushed harder. Nothing. Then I heard movement inside. For a terrible moment I thought it might be the Russians, but then the bolts were thrown back and instead I faced the fury of my mother.

She hauled me into the kitchen and slammed the door. The candle on the table wavered in the draught.

'I know where you've been,' she hissed, smacking my arms with her open palm and then with the back of her hand, blows buffeting me with each thought. 'You little slut, you'll bring shame on all of us.'

I dodged a blow to my head and pulled myself out of the reach of her slaps, around the table.

'Don't you know that Bill could be shot?' she raged. 'That *you* could be shot?'

'He's going to come back and marry me. We're engaged,' I protested.

She faced me across the flame of the candle, and it threw witch-like shadows up over her face.

'You little idiot, don't you think they all say that? Don't you think that's what men have always said? How will he come back, when we're the slaves of Russia? He'll be back in London with his old girlfriend and will never think of you – the stupid little farm girl who let him have his way.'

'That's not true. I didn't. It's not true.'

'He'll promise you anything, to do dirty things to you. I didn't think you were such a fool. You'll be pregnant with his bastard child, and nobody will ever marry you. They'll all know you'll do it for free. We'll be a laughing stock.'

'It's not . . . I haven't . . . He wouldn't . . .'

'You're the same as Matylda and Dagmar. I thought you were better than them. Does he give you money?'

'Mother!' I was shocked.

'They say Matylda and Dagmar do it for cigarettes and choco-late. Is that it? Did you sell yourself for a square of English chocolate?'

Now I was outraged too, hot with the temper I'd inherited from her. 'I don't know how you can think that. You brought me up. You know me. Or perhaps you do it for chocolate your-self? Is that what the Oily Captain gives you?'

We stared furiously at each other across the table, and she flopped into a chair. The light of the candle cast angry shadows on the kitchen walls. I sat down opposite her, barely able to keep still or quiet.

Her voice was softer, and I knew she was struggling to bring herself under control, just as I was. 'As soon as the road and the harvest are finished, they'll go back to Lamsdorf and will be sent somewhere else, to another place. Captain Meier has told me. Your Bill will be sent to a munitions factory or a mine, and you'll never see him again.'

'That's not true.'

'Look. The Russians are coming, and the Nazis are getting ready to withdraw into Germany. They won't let their prisoners run free to join the Red Army and fight against them. They aren't such fools.'

I looked across the table at her and, in the flickering light, her face seemed older than I'd ever seen it before. The heat of my anger slowly drained and I tried to speak calmly, to sound like a grown woman, not a petulant child.

'And I'm not such a fool, either. I haven't done the thing you think. Not without being married. He's going to come back. I know he will, and I'll wait for him.'

My mother bit her lip and nodded. 'Then you're going to be terribly hurt. He'll never come back. Once he gets home, you'll be like a dream – the only good thing that happened to him in all these years of hell. But his old life will close around him, and it'll be easier for him to slide back into that, than come looking for you.'

'Then I'll go to find him.' I saw myself setting out, with a new hat and suitcase, climbing on a train that would take me to Bill.

'Izabela, listen to me. I know more about the world than you.'

'We *will* be married. You'll see. I'll prove you wrong.'

She pulled the candle towards her. 'It's late. We have the turnips to harvest in just a few hours. We both need to sleep.'

I stood up. She was right. We were both exhausted.

She crossed the kitchen with the candle and stopped at the foot of the stairs. 'One thing.'

'What?'

'Promise me you won't go down to the sawmill again at night. It's too dangerous. If they catch Bill outside the wire, they'll shoot him or take him straight back to Lamsdorf for punishment.'

I hesitated a long time, and the candle flame stuttered.

'All right,' I said sulkily, 'I promise. Not at night.'

I was already forming other plans for us.

7

The next morning I left the house early and went to confession. As I'd hoped, there was nobody else in the church, not even the busybody village ladies who almost seemed to live there, polishing brass and fussing with flowers. I confessed my anger with my mother and blushed to mention my impure thoughts and deeds. The priest gave me absolution, but before we left the cocoon of the confessional box I said, 'Just a minute, please.'

Beyond the carved screen, I heard him sit down again.

Before I could have second thoughts, I stammered, 'I need to . . . Can I ask you something, Father?'

'Anything, my child.'

He was a young priest, new to the village, and not much older than me.

'Will it be a secret if it's not a confession?' I checked. 'Nobody else must know. Not even my mother.'

There was a moment's silence behind the screen, and then he said, 'You can tell me anything, and I won't repeat it.' I thought I could sense the interest, the curiosity he was trying to keep out of his voice. I wished I could see his face. I took a deep breath.

'I want to know if it would be possible to be married in secret, without banns being read.'

He was cautious. 'Banns are always read. How else would we know if the couple are free to marry?'

I persisted. 'But in wartime, if the lives of the people depended on it being a secret, would it be possible? Might it be possible?'

'Who's the man?' he said sharply. This time he didn't call me 'my child'.

'A prisoner. A British prisoner of war.'

He let out a long, slow exhalation. 'I'd have to ask the bishop for special permission.'

The bishop had once been outspoken in his opposition to the Third Reich, and I was hopeful.

'Then will you ask him very soon, please? The Russians are coming, and the prisoners could be taken away any day. We want to be married before they go. We might never have another chance.' I played my last card. 'Or we could ask the British camp chaplain perhaps. He comes round to the work details sometimes, but he's a Protestant, and I wouldn't feel properly married in the eyes of God.'

'No,' said the young priest, 'that would be a sin. As it happens, I'm cycling over tomorrow to see the bishop about another matter.'

'Thank you. Oh, thank you so much.'

'Just one more thing.' I could almost feel the heat of his blushes. 'In wartime, people do things they . . . wouldn't normally do. What I mean is – don't allow yourself to be drawn into the sin of fornication.'

'No, Father, we both want to be married,' I said sanctimoniously.

'Yes, good. Very good. I'll see what can be done.'

I thanked him and we both left the confessional box. The church was empty and we walked down the aisle to the door together.

The priest opened the heavy door and golden late-summer sunshine lit his boyish face. He tried to pull a sober expression, but his wide, honest eyes were dancing with excitement. 'Even if the bishop says yes – which I doubt – how could it be managed?'

'Oh, if he says yes, I'll find a way to manage it.'

He laughed out loud and suddenly he seemed more like a friend than a priest.

'Izabela,' he said, and I was surprised he even knew my name, 'I believe you will.'

He shook my hand.

'I'll come the day after tomorrow,' I said.

If my mother was surprised at my new desire to attend mass, she didn't say anything. She could hardly criticise me for being a whore one day and a saint the next, and so I sat through the early-morning mass two days later in a welter of anticipation.

Afterwards I positioned myself on the grassy bank below the church and waited for the last of the pious ladies to leave. Finally the priest came to the door, beckoning me inside.

We sat in one of the back pews, under the balcony. It felt private and safe.

'I saw the bishop,' he said cautiously.

'Thank you.' I twisted my hands together in impatience.

His eyes were raised to the paintings of the Stations of the Cross. In profile, his nose had a hooked shape, like a Roman emperor's.

'The bishop said it is most irregular and has little precedence in canon law.'

'But can it be done?'

He glanced quickly at me, full of concern for a moment, and then smiled. 'I have permission. Under the circumstances of the war.'

I moved to hug him and then held back, remembering he was a priest. 'Oh, thank you, thank you!'

'We'll have to have two witnesses. Does the prisoner – your fiancé – speak Czech or German?'

'No.'

'And I can't speak English. So we'll have to have a witness who can translate everything.'

My heart fell like lead. To have to tell another person could risk everything.

But the priest had already been thinking. 'The organist, Mr Novak, speaks good English. He might be willing to help.'

Mr Novak was no good. I'd known him since I was a child. He was a dear friend of my father's, another Czech musician.

'He'd tell my mother,' I blurted out. 'He was my father's closest friend. He's eaten meals with us so many times. He wouldn't keep it from her—'

'He's a good man,' cut in the priest. 'I think he's a man who knows many secrets and keeps good counsel.'

Was he trying to tell me that Mr Novak was in touch with the resistance and that he might even be able to get a message to my father to hurry us to safety?

I nodded uncertainly. 'OK. Please, will you ask him? And please tell him it must be a secret from everyone. Especially my mother.'

70

'We'll need a second witness.'

'I'll ask Bill to ask his friend. I'll pretend to be taking them both to the dentist in Mankendorf.'

'Very well. I can see you've thought of many things.' He paused. 'When will it be?'

'My aunt lives in Český Těšín. She's expecting a baby to arrive in a couple of weeks, at the end of September, and my mother's planning to go to her and take my little brother. The crops should all be gathered in by then.'

'I see.'

'I'll come with a message when she leaves.'

'Very well. I'll speak to the organist. And I'll pray for us all that you aren't making a terrible mistake.'

Bill was working in the turnip field when I got home, but my mother and Herr Weber were both in the field, so I schooled myself in patience, inching along behind Bill, watching him bending and lifting, bending and lifting, loving the fluid grace of his movements, until finally he was within whispering distance.

'Keep working,' I said softly. 'Don't look at me.'

He gave a wonderful impression of a man for whom turnips were the most fascinating thing in the world, and a pretty young woman of no interest at all.

'Hello, Izzy,' he said, not looking back. 'Darling Izzy.' And a warm glow spread through me.

'I have to ask you something,' I said shyly, banging mud from a turnip root and placing it on my cart.

'Yes?'

Suddenly I was worried that I had run away with my own

71

ideas and ambitions, that my mother was right and only the heat of infatuation had made Bill mention marriage.

'I . . . I have talk to priest.'

His head jolted as if he had to stop his instinct to swing round to me, but he continued working, pulling and shaking the turnips.

I thought I could detect a tremble in his voice as he replied quietly, 'And what did he say?'

I took a deep breath. 'He has yes said. He will marry us, if you still want.'

Bill risked a backward glance at me, and the force of his smile was like a light switched on in a gloomy room. He was happy. It was all right!

'Of course I want. You are the most astonishing girl I've ever met.'

Now I was smiling too. How could I ever have doubted his love?

'We must be many time careful,' I said, turning my attention back to the turnips.

He continued his harvesting as I walked slowly behind him.

'Yes, yes, I understand. But how will it be managed? When will it be? I can't believe it.'

'Is true, and I have plan.'

He laughed quietly. 'Of course you have. Tell me everything I have to do.'

I told him about the different elements that would have to come together. First, about my mother going to Český Těšín as soon as my aunt went into labour.

'She is have bad time with last baby. My mother will leave me to look after farm. This bad part.'

'Why? Oh, I see. You feel sad about being married without your mother there?'

I realised I hadn't yet told Bill that my plan was to abandon the farm, abandon the animals I'd fed and cared for, abandon my whole life and family for this one chance to be with him. I hadn't told him that I hoped we would be picked up by the partisans and would be able to fight with Dad and Jan for the resistance. I truly believed I could escape the oncoming Russians, fight the Third Reich and be with Bill, all in one.

'No. Yes. But is only way.'

I reminded him that I'd been allowed previously to take prisoners to the dentist in Mankendorf and he nodded, remembering. 'Jim came back with half his teeth missing!'

'Yes. So you and Harry must start to have bad tooth. Each have pain. Different time.'

'I get it!' The delight was evident in his voice. 'So on the day your mother goes away, me and Harry both have terrible toothache, and you take us to the dentist. But actually, well . . . actually to our wedding. And he'll be my best man.'

'Our wedding,' I repeated, because I couldn't help myself saying it aloud. 'Our wedding.'

8

At the end of September a telegram finally arrived with the news that my aunt was in labour, and my mother buzzed around the house like an annoying fly. She reminded me I wasn't to climb ladders when I was alone on the farm. I must take care not to fall down the well, must dress as a boy if the Russians came. She'd already darned and mended my brother's out-grown clothes. She'd made me try on a pair of his boots, which were in better condition than my own, because he'd grown out of them so quickly that they had hardly been worn. They were too big, and I watched her boiling wool into felt and sewing them into slippers to make a thick lining for them. She'd even climbed up into the attic and eventually came down with a strange-looking pink corset, a stiff band of fabric with shoulder straps and lacing down the side. She said it had been my great-aunt's in the 1920s when it was fashionable to bind your breasts flat. Everything was ready for my transformation into a boy.

'You're only going for a couple of days,' I pointed out. 'The Russians aren't likely to advance that fast.'

She ignored me, refolding a blouse. 'And you're not to see that boy, Bill.'

'I won't be able to help it, if the Oily Captain brings them here to work,' I retorted.

'Don't call him that. He's Captain Meier. You're not to go out to meet Bill at night, like some . . . bad girl. D'you hear me?'

'I hear you,' I snapped with the degree of petulance I knew she'd expect. Inside, I could hardly contain the glee that fizzed through me like bubbles in lemonade. It was coming. My wedding day was finally coming!

My mother continued to pelt me with instructions and warnings as she carried her suitcase downstairs. I followed with my brother's case. Marek was already waiting by the door, eager to be off, to see his cousins, to be the important child who was taken to the birth of a new baby.

Our neighbour was waiting outside with his cart to drive them to the station. It was only then, with one foot out of the door, that my mother stopped and really looked at me, as one woman to another. 'Will you be all right?'

I laughed. 'Of course I will. I'm twenty. I'm a grown woman. You were married and had Jan on the way by the time you were my age.'

She nodded, but still hesitated. 'Don't do anything stupid,' she said eventually and reached out to give me a fierce, quick hug, which took me by surprise. Her arms were as strong as ropes around me, and I held the feel of them in my memory, because I didn't know how long it might be till I saw her again.

'I'll be fine,' I said, and my voice cracked slightly, though I intended it to be reassuring. I cleared my throat. 'Everything'll be fine.'

She stared at me with her quick, penetrating eyes, trying to see through me to where the truth was hiding, then walked quickly towards the cart.

'Give my love to Auntie,' I called. 'I hope it all goes well.'

I watched until the cart lurched around the bend. Then I returned to the kitchen, where I began to dance and sing, 'It's today, today. It's going to be today!'

I ran out to the barn and pulled the oilskin kit-bags from their hiding place in the rafters. They were dusty already, and the dust made me cough. I peeked out of the barn to make sure the coast was clear, before I carried them back across the courtyard and up to my bedroom. I rushed to Jan's room to gather up the clothes I'd chosen to turn me into the boy of Mother's dreams, the boy who would have been allowed to join the partisans. And from my father's drawer I took the clothing to transform Bill from a British soldier into an itinerant farm worker.

At first, Bill had objected to my plan that we run away together, with me dressed as a boy. He'd said it would be too dangerous, that as soon as he went missing, the Nazis would be looking for him and would find us both. His face had closed down with worry at the thought of a dog patrol snapping at our heels. We might both get shot, he'd argued.

But I worked on him, first of all reminding him what would surely happen to me if I stayed on the farm and the Russians came, repeating to him the hair-raising stories of Russian atrocities circulating among the village women, until he knew that he had to help me get away. I also assured him that my father would find us. Of course I wouldn't tell Mr Novak about our plans to run away, but once we had both gone, I was sure he'd find a way to let my father know, so he could come and take us to join the resistance. I painted a picture of us with my father and Jan, hiding out in the mountains with the partisans. Bill told me about Robin Hood and Maid Marian, and I said yes, that was how we'd be, living in the forest and fighting the bad guys side-by-side until the end of the war. Together. And doing all the private things that a married couple could do, whenever we liked.

And, slowly, he'd come round to my idea – perhaps seeing no alternative in the face of the Soviet advance, or perhaps seduced by my certainty of our rescue by the partisans and the picture I painted of us fighting together for the resistance. And maybe, like me, thinking mostly about sex.

So as I made our preparations I couldn't help singing, and every now and then darting to the window to be sure the cart wasn't bringing my mother back home. I lifted up my great-aunt's bust-flattening corset, giggling at the stupid, ugly thing. I pulled open a drawer and took out my sanitary belt and rags. At the bottom of our kit-bags I'd sewn a false bottom, which formed a secret compartment, and I folded the belt and rags into it, with a small vest of Marek's.

The rattle of hooves on the road made me clutch the bag to my chest, but when I looked out of the window, it was just our neighbour, returning alone. My mother had really gone. It was my wedding day! I was dizzy with joy and excitement.

I packed hastily, mentally ticking off the items I'd identified for each of us. I'd found an old brown coat of Jan's for myself, and Bill would wear the short oilskin cape and hood over his greatcoat to make it look less military.

When all my preparations were done and our kit-bags were packed as tight as sausages, I put on my newest underwear and my blue dress. It was a little faded, but I admired myself in the mirror in Mother's bedroom and thought: This is me. I am a bride. My curls were shining, and my eyes were full of excitement. I took my grandmother's wedding ring from its hiding place, slipping it into my bra for safe-keeping. I pulled my coat over the dress and buttoned it to the neck. In the larder, I opened my mother's last bottle of plum brandy and poured out a mugful, topping the bottle back up with water and replacing the stopper. Wrapping the bottle in cotton, I laid it in my bicycle basket. Then I wheeled my bike out onto the lane, eagerness leaping through my veins.

First, I cycled to the train station, taking the route my mother would have followed if something had gone wrong with her trip and she was walking back. I leaned my bike against the station wall and looked cautiously along the platform. Empty. They'd definitely left.

Next, I pedalled to the church, glad that it wasn't on the main road, like Mankendorf, where anyone might see me, but up the hill, behind the trees, only its red roof and onion domes visible from the road. I had to dismount and push the bike up the last steep section, afraid of the smell of sweat on my wedding dress. I laid my hand for a second on the reassuring white walls of the church and hid my bike behind it, before pushing open the big door. My stomach was tight as a knot.

The priest saw me coming and crossed himself.

'It's today,' I blurted out. 'That is, could it be today? Could it be now?'

He asked, 'Are you sure?'

'I've never been so sure of anything in my life!'

'Very well. If you fetch the groom and his witness, I'll bring Mr Novak.'

I was in the saddle in one swift movement, then freewheeling crazily down the slope from the church out onto the road. A car coming from Mankendorf swerved to miss me, almost flying off the road, and I wobbled furiously, most afraid that the bottle would be smashed.

The driver yelled, 'You idiot, you could have been killed!' before he squealed away.

This shocked me into carefulness, and I looked all around me as I pedalled hard. Everything was so beautiful – the greens of the trees and the fields, the singing of the birds, the hills in the distance.

I reached the field where the working party was harvesting sugar beets. At the sight of me approaching, Bill let out a groan and clutched his cheek. 'Ow! It's that bleedin' tooth again. I was awake all night with it. It's going to have to come out.'

As I laid down my bicycle and approached, I heard Harry chime in, 'I've got one playing merry hell too.'

Herr Weber scoffed, 'Crying like a couple of babies at a little toothache. What fuss would they make, having them pulled out?'

I studied Bill and Harry. 'That might be the best thing.'

'The quickest way to have them back to work,' said Herr Weber.

'My mother can't take them. She's gone to her sister's, and I haven't really got time today,' I said crossly, 'but I suppose I could fit it in, if I leave the pigs till later.' I bent and pulled the bottle of plum brandy from my bicycle basket, saying, 'Oh, Mother said I was to bring you this, Herr Weber.'

I held it to my chest as I looked at an imaginary watch. 'I'd have to take them now or leave it till another day. The dentist closes at twelve.'

Bill groaned, a bit too dramatically, and Herr Weber looked carefully at me for a second or two. I tried to appear nonchalant and slightly irritated at the same time, which was tricky.

Finally he held out his hand for the bottle and waved us away. 'Go on, then. Soonest there, soonest back.'

'That's just what I always say.' I beamed at him.

I turned to Bill and Harry. 'Come!' I ordered strictly, in English. 'I have not the whole of day.'

They exchanged a smirk, out of sight of Herr Weber, who was busy hiding his bottle.

I pushed my bike, and they walked beside me towards the village and the church. As soon as we were out of sight of the guard, we began to grin.

'Did you see his face?' asked Bill.

I laughed aloud. 'You such bad actors.'

'You'll never be able to believe a word she says,' Harry remarked. 'I couldn't credit the bare-faced way she lied to him.'

'And she's so bossy,' agreed Bill. 'Are you going to be like that when you're my wife?'

At the words 'my wife', my heart jumped in my chest.

Harry asked, 'Do they have to promise to obey here?'

'Oh, yes,' I said. 'I promise obey!'

'That'll be the day,' said Bill, raising his eyebrows.

We all laughed again and turned onto the hill towards the church, which towered above us from this approach. Bill looked up at it and his pace slowed.

'Did you bring the ring?' Harry asked me.

I touch my chest. 'Yes. I have.'

Bill stopped, and I thought: Oh, no, he's changed his mind, but he shifted from foot to foot and said, 'Look, Izzy – give us a mo, Harry – are you sure about this? Are you sure you know what you're getting into?'

Harry turned aside to examine a section of tree bark.

I was nodding furiously, trying to read Bill's eyes, to understand if he still loved me. 'Yes, yes. I know. I want.'

He smiled, that mercurial smile which lifted his whole face, and I relaxed, but only a fraction.

'And you?' I asked. 'You want?'

But now his face was smiling all over. 'Oh yes, I want very much.'

Harry turned. 'Well, I'm glad that's settled. I thought I was out of a job.'

We leaned my bike behind the church and entered its cool darkness. The priest hurried forward to meet us and to lock the door behind us. The organ was playing softly, which meant Mr Novak was already here.

I unbuttoned my coat and laid it on the back pew.

Harry whistled appreciatively and Bill said, 'You look so beautiful.'

I couldn't stop grinning. 'Excuse,' I said, turning from them to extract the ring from my bra.

We approached the altar steps. The organ stopped, and Mr Novak appeared. He looked anxiously at me and asked in Czech, 'Are you really sure you are doing the right thing? It may be many years before you can be together.'

'Yes!' I insisted. 'Yes, please help us. The prisoners might be taken away at any time.'

'And if you are married, he'll come back for you one day.' He smiled. 'Very well. It's what your father would have done, so I'll give you away in his name.'

Mr Novak stayed close to us on the altar steps, translating every sentence for Bill, who nodded constantly to show he understood. Some of the words were difficult and specialist, but Mr Novak translated so unhesitatingly that I could tell he'd been practising. How can I thank him? I thought.

Before I knew it, we were at the point of saying each other's names and making promises. Bill looked steadily into my eyes as he said, 'I do.' And when it was my turn, I made my promises in Czech for myself, and in English for Bill.

'*Dělám* – I do.'

My grandmother's ring, now cool from lying on the Bible, was pushed onto my finger by Bill. It was a little loose. I held it on tightly with the neighbouring fingers and felt the strangeness of it.

'You are man and wife,' said the priest, and it was done. I was married to Bill! I was Mrs King!

Bill kissed me and I had to push him away, laughing. He threw his arms around Harry, who pumped his hand up and down.

The priest congratulated me stiffly and moved away.

'I'm so grateful to you,' I said to Mr Novak. 'We're so grateful to you. You could never know how much.'

He softened a little. 'You've always been an adventurer, Izabela, just like your father. I hope your parents will forgive me when they see you together, after the war. I'm sorry your father isn't here to see how beautiful you look.' He shook Bill's hand. 'Be good to her,' he said. 'If I ever hear you've been unkind to her, I will regret my part in this day.'

'Never, sir,' said Bill. 'Never in my life, I swear.' And his face shone with such joy that nobody could have failed to believe him.

I turned to Mr Novak. 'Could you get a message—'

But he cut across me, holding up his hand for silence, as if this was something he'd anticipated, and his voice was clear and oddly loud. 'Nobody in the village has any contact with them. You must know that.'

'But . . .' I stopped. Did he think someone in the church was listening? If so, they'd have heard the whole wedding service and would surely be on their way to pick up Bill.

Mr Novak waved his hand. 'Go on, then. Get him back to work, before someone comes looking for you.'

We thanked him hastily and headed towards the door. I looked for the priest to thank him too, but he was nowhere to be seen.

I pulled my coat back over my dress as Bill said goodbye to Harry. I watched as they shook hands, then Bill pulled Harry to him in a fierce hug. I hadn't thought how it would be for Harry, without the friend who'd been with him through the worst possible experiences, even facing a firing squad together. They hadn't been separated for five long years.

'Good luck, mate,' said Harry in a strangled voice.

Bill released him, and I could see the tears in his eyes. 'I'll find you when we get home.'

Harry gave him a play-punch on his arm. 'You bloody better.' And turned away.

The plan was for Harry to go back to the field and say he'd had his tooth removed, but the dentist needed to keep Bill in overnight as he had a nasty abscess and had fainted after his tooth was pulled. Later, when they discovered Bill was missing, Harry would say he had no idea where Bill might have gone.

I shook his hand and thanked him and we parted company, Harry heading to the field and Bill and I back to my house. Bill turned as we rounded the corner, but Harry was already out of sight.

Bill chattered all the way back, recounting moments from the service as if I hadn't been there, and I slowly realised that he was as nervous as I was about what would happen next.

'And you've got it just right,' he said. 'You're supposed to have something borrowed, something blue, something old and something new!'

'My dress blue,' I agreed. 'My grandmother ring old, and borrowed.'

'Two for one!' he laughed.

I tried to think what I had that was new. My newest thing was my underclothes, but I was too shy to say that word to him. 'New?' I repeated as if it was a puzzle that must be solved or our whole marriage would be doomed to failure.

'It's me!' he exclaimed with delight. 'I'm new! I'm your new husband!'

We looked at each other as if neither of us could believe our luck.

Back at the house, I pulled the kitchen door shut behind us and locked the bolts top and bottom, and then Bill was kissing me, pressed hard up against me, until I could hardly breathe.

'Wait,' I said, pushing him away. He perched on the edge of the table to catch his breath and watched me opening the larder for the mug of plum brandy.

'You're so beautiful,' he groaned. 'I can't wait a moment longer.'

But I poured the brandy into two big glasses, and we clicked them together.

'Here's to us,' said Bill, 'the bride and groom.'

'To us,' I said. '*Na zdraví!*'

'*Na zdraví!*' he repeated badly, and dashed off his glass in one swig, which made him cough.

'Fire-water!' he choked, and I laughed at him, sipping from my glass more slowly and leading him by the hand from the kitchen and up the stairs to my bedroom.

I pulled the curtains, wishing it was darker, and he began to kiss me again. The plum brandy had gone to my head, and I felt dizzy and wet between my legs. Bill was trembling so much I had to help him unbutton my dress. I dropped it down onto the floor and stepped out of it in my underclothes. He held me at arm's length and looked at me in my underwear, then placed something from his pocket on the bedside table. I knew this must be a johnny, because he'd told me we must use one so I wouldn't get pregnant. I hoped it wasn't such a sin in wartime.

And then we were kissing and touching everywhere, like we did in the barn or the woods, but nothing like it, because now we took off each other's remaining clothes one by one until we were both quite naked and I caught sight of his thing, standing up to attention. He seemed to be quite proud of it. I hoped he liked my body more than I liked that. He stood me away from him and looked greedily at me, at my breasts and my triangle of hair, until I wanted to cover myself. I thought how long it had been since he'd seen a naked woman – even a picture of one – and tried not to wonder who the last one was.

'Perfect,' he breathed and lowered me onto my narrow child-hood bed, lying half beside me and half on me, skin against skin for the whole length of our bodies. The wickedness of this, in my parents' house, in my girlhood bed, was utterly thrilling. He turned away to do something secret with the johnny and then lifted me on top of him. There was a pushing sensation and then a sliding, and we were joined completely, but then he stopped moving, and it all seemed to be over. I wasn't sure what had happened, and if that was how it was meant to be, but he looked humiliated, and I guessed there should be something more.

'I'm so sorry. It'll be better next time, I promise. You were just too much for me.'

'Everything beautiful,' I said. 'You beautiful. I love you.'

He slid a finger between my legs but I stopped him. It was enough that we were properly married.

So he wrapped me in his arms and legs, kissing my forehead, and I lay there, wanting more and more of this closeness, and wanting never to move again, until my skin began to cool and I felt goosebumps down my flank.

When I went to the bathroom, there was blood down my inner thighs and I exalted in it, because it meant I was truly married; I was Bill's wife, till death do us part. I wondered if I should take my sanitary belt from its hiding place in my kit-bag, but as I cleaned myself, the blood was stopping already.

I came out of the bathroom wrapped in a towel, and Bill kissed me. His thing now bounced limply against his thigh, and I liked it better like that. But now there was time for me to take in his desperate thinness. His arms and legs were muscled, but bony as sticks. I could see all his ribs and, when he turned, he had no bottom. It twisted my insides with fear. What was I doing if his captivity had brought him to this? This was not a game; it was serious. I must have a chance to fight in the war which had done this to him. And we must never get caught. He grinned at me, and I banished the thought. There was a little blood and wetness on my quilt. I thought I must wash it before we left the house.

I dressed in my brother's long underwear and was putting my arm into my great-aunt's bust-flattening corset when Bill came back into the bedroom with a small towel around his waist. My stomach contracted with lust at his smooth, white body. He was looking at me the same way, and I automatically crossed my arms over myself. Bill took them down gently and kissed one breast and then the other, and I could feel his thing hardening again. So soon? I thought. There was so much I didn't know. But he didn't try to do it again, just helped me wrap the corset around me and lifted my arm to tighten the lacing down the side.

'I'm sorry you have to squash them like this,' he said, placing a hand on my chest.

I had to concentrate, or I would be begging him to make me a wife again.

'Tighter,' I said. He tugged at the laces and the bandeau squashed me flat.

'Whatever is this thing?' He stared at me with his head held on one side like a bird, studying me from the front and then from the side.

'Was old-fashion. To look like boy.'

'Yes,' he said slowly, 'it works. If someone didn't know to look. What an odd sort of fashion. Who'd want that?'

'Nineteen-twenties,' I told him. 'Girls want to look like boy. Want to do things they did in war. Drive truck. Work.'

He laughed. 'Who'd want to drive a truck?' he asked, and I could see that I had so much to teach him about women.

'You dress,' I ordered, and he laughed.

'See – still bossy.'

As I pulled my brother's clothing on over the corset, I watched Bill. It was odd to see him dressing in clothes that had belonged to my father and brother. Bill would have to be husband, father and brother to me now. I pushed away the thought before it made me cry, and went to return my grandmother's wedding ring to its hiding place and wash the blood from my quilt. When the bed was properly made again, we picked up our kit-bags and I gazed around my room carefully and seriously.

Bill knew I was saying goodbye and gave me a moment, but not long enough to get emotional.

'I'm starving,' he said, and I realised I was too. In the kitchen we tucked into bread, cheese and sausage, packing more into greased paper, filling our kit-bags to the top, only leaving room for metal water bottles.

'Hair,' I said.

'Hair,' he agreed.

I draped a towel round my shoulders and handed him a comb and scissors.

'I love your curls,' he said. 'I hate to do it.'

'Cut,' I ordered, on the verge of weeping myself.

As each lock fell, the shorter hair curled tighter to my head and I found I liked the light feel of it. He stood back.

'I think that'll do,' he said doubtfully. 'I'm not much of a barber.'

'I go look.'

There was a mirror over the fireplace in the parlour, so I crossed the hallway and opened the door. In the half-light coming from the kitchen behind me, I saw a boy walking towards the mantelpiece. My hair was short, but not too short. It curled around my face. I looked very different, but not ugly, as I'd feared.

Bill came in and stood behind me, looking at our reflection.

'Boy?' I ask.

'A very gorgeous sort of boy,' he said and twirled me towards him, seeking my lips again. I kissed him back and then we broke away, knowing that unless we stopped now we'd be having to undress again. 'You're still the most beautiful girl I've ever seen,' he said.

'Boy!' I said firmly. 'Now boy.'

He fingered a few notes on the piano – the wedding march – then swung himself into the seat and played it, full and glorious, moving as if his body was part of the instrument.

'You play,' I said. 'I listen while work.' He didn't need persuading.

Back in the kitchen, I swept up every strand of my cut hair and burned it on the range, then washed our plates and cutlery. Bill's music swirled around me, lifting me up. This would be our life together, filled with harmony.

When my chores were finished, Bill wrenched himself away from the piano to accompany me out into the twilit yard, where he watched as I milked the cow, fed the horse and pig and chickens, giving them all double rations. I touched the horse and pig and cow on their noses and whispered, 'Goodbye. I'm sorry.' The Oily Captain would look after them.

In my mother's bedroom I hid the note I'd written her under the bedcovers, on her pillow:

Dearest Mama,

Bill and I have been married, properly married in church, and have gone north to try to make contact with Father and Jan. Please try to be happy for me. I'm sorry for the extra work I'm leaving you. Please give Marek a big hug from me. I love you,
Izabela King

It had given me such a rush of joy the previous night to write my name as Izabela King, even though I wondered if I was tempting fate to write it before the wedding. But now the marriage had taken place, and that was really who I was. I hoped she would be fooled by the lie that we were travelling north.

I'd also written another note, in German, for the Oily Captain, which I was going to push under the door of our nearest neighbour to the north, before we turned back and headed west. This one read:

> *Dear Captain Meier,*
> *I have had a telegram to go to my aunt's in Český Těšín. I hope you can take care of the farm until my mother and I return.*
> *Izabela*

I hoped that would buy us a few days.

Then we pulled on our coats and hats, shouldered our bags and blankets and headed out into the darkness.

9

Bill and Izzy had agreed to move by night and sleep in the day, but Bill wasn't used to night-time without street lamps and found he had to walk quite slowly. Night in the countryside was darker than he'd ever imagined.

Izzy knew the area well enough to have planned where they'd hide for the first two days, and she led Bill from the road across an uneven field and onto the railway tracks that would lead through Hranice and Lipník to Přerov. She was bubbling over with the thrill of it, but Bill thought they wouldn't get far before the guards started looking for him, even with the false trail Izzy had left in the notes. The best he could hope for was to get her out of the path of the oncoming Russian soldiers and deliver her safely to her dad and her brother.

The stars were often obscured by cloud, and Izzy sometimes lost the rhythm of stepping over the railway sleepers and tripped. Bill's stride was longer and he seemed to find it easier to set up a slow, steady rhythm to whatever song was playing over and over in his head.

Each time the dark shape of a building reared up beside the

track, he would fall silent and his heart would thump louder in his chest, as he listened for patrolling soldiers. This was worse than escaping with Harry. Now he was responsible for Izzy, and she was just like an excited child who wouldn't stop talking. How hard she made it to keep her safe, he thought.

It was already becoming light when they left the railway tracks to find the farm Izzy was seeking. She'd told Bill there was only one woman on this farm now, and he thought it was true, judging by the disrepair of many of the outbuildings. Izzy pulled him into the disused stables and led the way up the rickety staircase to the old ostler's quarters.

They pushed open the door, and a dust cloud rose to meet them. Bill was pleased. Nobody had set foot in here for years. The dust made them sneeze, but the room was private and out of the wind, and there was even a bed. Bill wedged a chair-back under the door handle, and Izzy was impressed, because she'd never seen that before. He didn't tell her how ineffective it would be against guards trying to break down the door. He had other things on his mind.

Slowly he stripped all the clothes from her, dropping them one by one to the floor. He unlaced her corset then stood back to look at her in the light falling from a tiny, cobwebbed window. This time he was determined to make it last.

'Lie on the bed,' he said, pulling off his boots and socks, never taking his eyes from her. He turned to remove his shorts and fit the johnny, then sat on the bed beside her. 'Now I'm going to show you what it's all about,' he said.

During the course of the day they made love five times, falling entangled in a deep, sticky sleep afterwards and waking to drink a sip of water or creep down to the stable to pee in a corner. When Bill woke for the third time, he was aware of every rustle in the old stable, but mostly he was listening to Izzy's quiet breathing. He lay on his back with her head resting in the dip below his shoulder and thought: This is heaven . . . not dancing cheek to cheek.

When they woke again and discovered it was beginning to get dark, they started to gather their clothes from around the room, where they'd been thrown down in the dust. Bill decided tomorrow he'd fold Izzy's clothes properly.

'I want wash,' she said pettishly, and Bill did too, but he tried to be cheerful. 'I know. Me too. I stink like a goat.'

Outside in the twilit yard he found a water barrel and dipped a rag into it, so they could wash as best they could.

Bill refilled their water bottles and, as soon as it was completely dark, they set out again along the railway tracks. Usually Izzy talked, but sometimes they simply held hands and listened to the sounds of the night. Then Bill's mind wandered back and forth from the past to the present to the future, looping and curling on itself. Only when they reached a station did he remember to be afraid, to look for movement or light, which might mean an end to everything; only then did he remember that all this happiness was as fragile as an eggshell.

As day broke after their third night of walking they found an abandoned cottage, barely even stopping to lock the door before peeling off each other's clothes. Bill had used up his supply of johnnies and forced himself to withdraw quickly.

'That not so good,' Izzy complained.

Bill laughed. 'Don't I know it! But I'm not going to make you pregnant.'

'I don't care,' she said, running a hand down his chest and stomach. 'I like have your baby.'

Bill gripped her hand. 'But not here, and not now. Though, God knows, I can't leave you alone.' He bent his head to lick her from throat to navel. And later he slept like a baby himself, although he'd promised himself he'd stay awake to protect her.

And so they continued for five days, walking through the nights and spending the days wrapped together in haylofts, barns and outbuildings. When their food ran out, they began to steal. Izzy suggested she should go to a farm and ask to buy food, but Bill didn't want her to be seen, in case the guards were out questioning farmers. They tried to guess if her mother had now returned from Český Těšín and whether the guards knew they'd run away together.

On their sixth day they found an abandoned hunting shelter. It was one room with a single bed in an alcove, plus a table, two chairs and a fur rug in front of a fireplace.

'Could have fire?' Izzy asked pleadingly. 'To lie, no clothes.'

'You were such a good girl, and I've turned you into a harlot,' said Bill, thoroughly pleased with himself.

'What is har lot?' she pouted, and in answer he pushed her up against the wall.

Later Bill lit the fire, despite his fear of the smoke being seen from miles away in broad daylight. 'Look at your green eyes, like some kind of witch,' he said, stroking Izzy's face. 'I've always thought of myself as a sensible sort of bloke. How did you make me run away with you, if it wasn't by casting a spell? Why have I lit a fire, which might bring Nazis from miles around? You've put an enchantment on me.'

'Spell is love,' she said, running a finger down his hairless chest. 'I make you do anything.' She touched the tip of his penis. 'I make you do this.'

He groaned. 'Again?'

'Again,' she breathed in his ear.

Afterwards it was as if a new thought had struck her. 'How you know all this? What to do?'

Bill was sleepy and didn't want to talk, but she jabbed him in the ribs.

'How you know?'

'Know what? I need to sleep, Izzy. You wear me out.'

'Yes, sleep, but first tell. How know what girl like?'

Suddenly he was awake. 'Ha! Just a natural, I suppose,' he joked.

'No. Not laugh. Tell. What other girl you do this with?'

'Oh, come on – not now, surely?'

'Husband tell wife everything,' she ordered.

'You knew I'd done it before,' he said.

'I know. But now must tell name of girl. Was Flora, yes?'

Bill was appalled. Whatever had made her think such a thing? 'Good God, no. That'd be like doing it with my sister.'

'Name, then.'

Bill hesitated. His better judgement told him to laugh it off, to cajole Izzy into a safer topic. But part of him thought they should have no secrets from each other. Everything should be clear as crystal between them.

'London's not like Vražné,' he started. 'And not all girls are good girls, like you.' He sat up and could see the lovely curve of her body in the light from the coals penetrating the thin curtains.

'I must know,' she insisted.

'OK. If you "must know", in the pub – my parents' pub – there's a couple of working girls. Not so young any more.' He saw she didn't understand, and he was beginning to think this was a really terrible idea, but couldn't see how to backtrack now. 'On the game. Not bad girls, but they ain't got husbands and have to make a living.'

'Do sex for money?'

'Yes. That's it.'

'You pay money?' She was outraged, and he was equally indignant.

'No. I've never paid. Not even in Egypt. One of the girls – her name was Kath – when I was eighteen said she'd give me a birthday present I'd never forget.'

'*Děvka!*' Izzy spat, but Bill protested.

'It wasn't just that. We went to her place.'

Izzy was listening now in silence.

'She said she was going to give me a lesson more useful than anything I'd been taught in school. She was going to show me how to make my wife happy.' He chuckled smugly. 'And she bloody did!'

Izzy smacked his back, hard, and Bill jumped, taken completely by surprise at the stinging blow.

She hissed, 'You think it funny to put that thing in filthy *děvka* and then put in me?'

She's jealous, Bill thought, a little pleased.

'You are disgusting,' she spat. 'I not same as filthy *děvka*.' And she tried to hit him again.

He grabbed her wrists to keep off the blows. She was almost as strong as he was, and they struggled together, hampered by the blankets around their legs. He fell back and took her with him. Her mouth made contact with his shoulder and she bit down, hard.

He shouted out in pain and surprise, and pushed her away from him. Izzy fell back and he jumped to his feet, one hand holding the place she'd bitten. He backed away from her, behind the table.

'Get yourself under control,' he ordered.

They circled the table, both naked, and he was aware of blood coming from below his fingers. Izzy covered herself with one arm across her chest and a hand over her groin.

'Not look!' she ordered.

Bill lifted his wet hand towards his face. 'You drew blood.' He looked down at the circle of teeth marks. 'I didn't know you had such a temper.' He thought: She's a bloody wildcat. I don't know her at all. 'Aren't you going to say sorry?' he asked, pressing a dirty rag against the wound.

'I not speak,' she said.

'Well, that's not very nice,' he said. 'I only told you the truth, like you wanted. He paused. 'And anyway Kath was right, and you did like it. You loved it.'

Izzy wrapped a blanket around herself and went to lie on the cold single bed in the alcove, turning her back to him while he returned to the makeshift bed by the fire. He lifted the rag from the wound, and when it had stopped bleeding he dressed slowly.

'It's warmer to sleep here,' he suggested, but Izzy didn't move.

He lay, missing her warmth, wondering what other things they would discover about each other; wondering how much time they had left.

When darkness had fallen and it was time to get on the move again, he had trouble waking her. Izzy still seemed determined not to speak, so he kept up a barrage of light chatter. He talked about different kinds of fireplaces, and how they burned coal in London, not wood, and didn't remark on her failure to reply. They packed up their things and set out, both feeling like something was broken between them that could never be mended.

She stumbled on the railway tracks and he caught hold of her elbow. She shrugged him off.

'Look, Izzy,' he said, almost in a whisper. 'We might be captured any minute. We might never see each other again. I'm sorry you weren't my first. But I can't change what happened before I met you. You are the love of my life.'

As soon as he started to speak, tears began to roll from her eyes and she tripped. This time when he steadied her, she let him. Then she stopped walking, as sobs came in great gulps. Bill took her in his arms and she howled into his shoulder, tears and snot running down the oilskin cape. He held her, stroking her short curls, until she was cried out; then he pulled a rag from his pocket for her to blow her nose. It was crisp with dried blood from where she'd bitten him.

'Sorry,' she sobbed. 'Sorry for bite, for smack, for shout. You can hit me.'

He shook his head. 'I'd never hit a woman. Seen too much of that. Never. Never.'

She kissed him on the lips. 'You right. We alive. We never fight. And I never do not speak. Too hard.'

But although they were lovers again, something subtle had changed, and the reality of their situation at last began to dawn on them. Bill knew they were moving too slowly and finally acknowledged the truth: the partisans weren't out looking for Izzy; they'd got more important things to do, like blowing up bridges and fighting battles. He and Izzy were tiny and alone in the centre of a huge continent teeming with Nazi soldiers who would crush them like beetles under their boots.

They walked for two more nights, more sober, more realistic, more hungry now. They burrowed themselves down in cold barns and outbuildings during the day and held onto each other with a new desperation.

As they walked, they began to talk about what would happen if they were caught. Bill knew what they'd do to him: send him back to Lamsdorf for thirty days of solitary confinement in the cooler; but he didn't know what the punishment might be for Izzy, for helping a prisoner escape. He feared they might shoot her. Impossible though it sounded, it might be safer for her to pretend she was another escaped prisoner of war.

'You wouldn't be able to speak,' he warned, and Izzy nodded dismally.

'We'd have to come up with a name for you, and you'd have to learn a serial number and how to write them, like an English person would.'

He told her that her British 'next of kin' would be informed, and said that would have to be Flora, if only they could think of a way of letting Flora know that this fictitious prisoner was connected with him.

'I know! His name will be Cousins, because me and Flora are cousins.'

Bill tried out various possible first names as they walked through the dark, and eventually decided that Cousins' first name should be Algernon, because he and Flora used to play at being Biggles and Algernon.

'Characters from books,' Bill explained. 'She'd know right

away. We used to play it all the time when we was kids. So you'd be Algernon Cousins. He'd be young, to explain the fact that you don't shave. Maybe he lied about his age and joined up when he was only fifteen or sixteen.'

Izzy nodded. 'I am small for a boy.'

'He'd have been bullied at school, for being so small, for having a stupid name like Algernon, but that would have made him tough.'

'And what work he do? Farm boy?'

'No, because he'll have a London address – Flora's address. He could be a stable lad who looks after the horses that pull the coal waggon, but who dreams of being a jockey. That's it – an ostler, who looks after the gee-gees. Like Al-gee. That'd be his nick-name for sure: Gee-gee Cousins.' He explained to Izzy that young English children called horses 'gee-gees', but he couldn't tell her why.

When they rested that day, he showed her how to write her new name and address, and she memorised an invented serial number: Harry's with two numbers changed.

'Will this work?' asked Izzy doubtfully.

And although Bill couldn't see how it would, he tried to sound confident. 'Of course. It *has* to work.'

As afternoon slipped into evening on the eighth day, they were sleeping in the hayloft of a barn when they were woken by voices from the yard outside. They gripped hold of each other, and Bill raised himself to a sitting position. It sounded like two people.

'Fuck!' whispered Bill as he recognised Captain Meier and Herr Weber. 'Quick, hide.'

They scrambled to their feet. Bill grabbed their boots and Izzy rolled up the blankets. Above their heads the thick beams of rafters criss-crossed, supporting the roof.

'Up there,' Bill ordered, quietly.

Izzy passed Bill the kit-bags and blankets, and he stretched on tiptoe to lay them on top of the beam nearest to him.

The great door of the barn swung open below them and a shaft of evening light streamed in. Bill kicked the straw about, where they'd been lying.

The captain and Herr Weber entered the barn beneath them, speaking in German. Bill wished he knew what they were saying. He led Izzy on tiptoe to the darkest corner of the hayloft, then wrapped his arms around her knees and lifted her, so that she could reach the beam. With a massive pull, she heaved her body up onto the rafter and lay along it.

'Bombardier King,' Herr Weber called, in English, 'are you in here? If so, I arrest you. Give yourself up now, and it will not go so badly for you.'

Izzy reached her hand down to help Bill, but he moved silently across the hayloft, as far from her as possible. If they found him first, he'd say they'd quarrelled and split up days ago. Anything not to turn Izzy in.

There was another discussion in German below, presumably Captain Meier telling Herr Weber what to say, and he called out in English again.

'Are you here? Is Izabela with you? The SS will shoot her, for helping a prisoner escape. Her mother is back on the farm and she is beside herself with anxiety. You must hand yourself over to us now. This is your last chance.'

Although Bill had been able to reach the beam to hide their

belongings, it was harder for him to get enough of a grip now to pull himself up. Halfway up, his hand slipped, and he fell back onto his feet.

Herr Weber said something excitedly and moved towards the ladder to the hayloft. Captain Meier remained below.

Bill leapt into the air, grabbed the rafter and yanked his body up. Slowly Herr Weber ascended the ladder, and Bill lay flat just as the other man's helmet appeared in the hayloft. Bill pressed his face to the timber beam, saw the streams of light from Herr Weber's torch playing around the space. His heart was banging so loudly he thought Herr Weber would be able to hear it.

Herr Weber stuck his bayonet a few times into the pile of straw where they'd been lying. Bill looked over and could see the skirt of Izzy's greatcoat hanging below the rafter she was lying on. He felt sure Herr Weber would spot it, so he prepared to let himself down to distract attention from her. But the beam of the torch swept around the hayloft one more time and Herr Weber called down, '*Nein, nicht hier*' to Captain Meier. Finally he swung his bayonet back over his shoulder and felt for the first rung of the ladder with his foot.

There was another conversation in the barn below, before Herr Weber called in English once more, 'If you are here, Bombardier King, please know this was your last chance. Now we must report you as missing, and soon the SS will find you with their dog patrols. Then we can't help you. And, Izabela, if you are here, think of all you are throwing away. You are such a good student. I could still help you to be a translator or go to university.'

The two soldiers waited, listening, for several minutes before they agreed, '*Nein, nicht hier*' and left the barn. A few more moments passed before Bill heard the distinctive limping gait of Captain Meier as he came back alone and said something in German. Something, apparently, to Izzy. Her name was all that Bill understood. He held his breath and waited, thinking perhaps she ought to go with them now, but she didn't move. Then Captain Meier left, the doors clanged shut and a heavy wooden beam was slid down from outside, shutting Bill and Izzy into the barn. Bill thought they'd die of thirst in here in just a few days, if the SS didn't find them first.

They heard Captain Meier and Herr Weber banging on the farmhouse door, and an old-sounding woman speaking to them.

Bill raised his head and looked at Izzy across the gloomy barn. He signalled to her to tuck her coat under her legs. They might still come back. He pressed his face to the rafter. 'Be calm, be calm,' he told himself. 'Listen now.' It seemed the soldiers had gone into the house. 'Wait,' Bill told himself, 'wait and be calm.'

Eventually they came back into the yard and there was a further discussion, before the doors of their armoured car banged shut. Bill listened as it drove away into the night. He and Izzy waited in silence.

After about twenty minutes footsteps quietly crossed the yard. Someone was struggling to lift the locking beam. Bill heard it swish down and bang slightly as it came to rest. In the barn beneath them, two elderly voices were whispering in Czech. The people scuffled about like rats and then pulled the door closed behind them, but didn't lock it.

The dim light in the barn faded as the day ended. Bill and Izzy waited a long time. A long, long time. They didn't speak. Bill's leg developed pins and needles from being too long in one position. They waited until it was completely dark outside.

Finally Bill whispered, 'I think it must be safe now' and swung himself down from the rafter. But even as he said it, he was thinking: Izzy will never be safe again, and it's all my fault.

He moved under the beam where Izzy was hiding. 'Izzy, are you all right? Let yourself down. I'll catch you.'

She lowered herself into his arms.

'What did the captain say?' he asked. 'How did they find us?'

'He promise my mother he try to find us first and bring me back. He knows all farms in district, and they are try all the barns and outbuildings. He will have to say that you missing, but he not say I might be with you. He will tell story that I go to help my aunt.'

They both fell silent, and Bill wondered why Captain Meier would want to help them. Surely it was a risk for him, and for Herr Weber. Perhaps they had both developed a soft spot for Izzy; he could understand that. Or maybe Captain Meier loved her mother. Or perhaps . . . perhaps they were simply good men, a teacher and a farmer caught up in horrors beyond their imagining and trying to do what little they could to make it right, by rescuing one foolish girl.

'You should have gone with them,' Bill said.

She wrapped her arms around him. 'I'll never leave you.'

He kissed her forehead, and they held onto each other like two frightened children. This felt like their only place of safety now, flimsy as a tent in an avalanche.

10

On our tenth night of walking, everything was quiet and still, apart from the light crunch of our boots on the stony country road. The sliver of moon disappeared behind a cloud and we slowed our pace, barely able to make out the way ahead. The road and the hedges were dark as soot, and I couldn't see where one ended and the other began. The ground was uneven, with tufty hummocks of grass running down the middle of the road, and I put out each foot tentatively, in case I twisted my ankle in a pothole or tumbled into a ditch. I gripped Bill's hand to keep myself from falling, and reminded myself that if we could hardly see the road, then nobody could see us, either. That was a small comfort.

Out of the darkness, the side walls of houses reared up on each side of the road.

'Here we go,' said Bill, 'a nice hayloft maybe to snuggle down in', and I knew that desire leapt in both of us at the thought. A blush warmed my throat and face, and I was glad he couldn't see me and make fun of it.

But as we got close, we realised this was the start of a village street. We hesitated, then crept forward. The front doors opened directly onto the road and, as we passed each one, I tensed myself in case it flew open and we were discovered. My pulse beat as loudly as rain on a barn roof.

Bill adjusted his stride in time with mine, so that we only made one set of footsteps, which echoed slightly off the buildings. He squeezed my hand tightly, and I wondered if he was afraid too. We walked on up the street, ready to turn and run at any moment back into the enveloping dark.

At first I tried to tell myself that the houses were just a hamlet – somewhere whose name I'd forgotten – which might offer the possibility of food and shelter, a disused hen-house or garage where we could hide. I imagined a pie left to cool on a windowsill and forgotten at bedtime, apples stored in a shed. But as we walked on, it became obvious that this place was larger than a village.

A cat's tail flicked and my stomach lurched. Figures seemed to lurk in the deep shadows of every doorway, and I strained my eyes in the hope that it would be my father or my brother, or one of their band of partisans sent to gather me up, to hide us. I pleaded with him silently, 'Find me, Daddy – tatinku – please find me now.' But as we passed each house, the imaginary figures dissolved into a deeper blackness, and hope faded that they'd ever find us. I told myself I was a fool. How had I expected my father to know where we were and carry us to safety? Had I just been trying to prove to him that he ought to have taken me with him? Did I think I could show him that I was as brave as Jan?

We held hands and crept on – an odd-looking couple, if anyone had seen us. Bill in ill-fitting farmworker's clothes, me decked out like a boy, both of us fat with layers of woollens, as the nights were chilly already and it seemed the easiest way to carry them;

both with my home-made oilcloth kit-bags and a blanket strung across our backs. No more than a couple of tramps.

The town gathered around us, cutting off our lines of escape. I feared I must have led us into Prostějov, though I didn't know how, because I was sure it was further to the north. The houses became grander and the roads widened. We passed a small park. I thought for a moment that we might hide in the bushes there, and then realised how quickly dogs and children would sniff us out in the morning. Beyond the park, tall public buildings began, banks and offices where cleaners and clerks would soon arrive to work. We came across a stretch of the old city wall and a stone guard-tower with a pointed roof like a witch's hat, and I knew we were going the wrong way.

'This old town. Centre town,' I whispered, pulling at Bill's sleeve.

I sensed rather than saw Bill shake his head and run his hand up through his hair, making it stand in blond spikes. He lowered his voice so that I could barely catch his reply. 'No, I'm sure we're circling the town to the south. Soon we'll be out in open country again. This way.'

I felt a lick of exasperation. 'No. Wrong way.'

'Look, so far we've done everything your way. It's my turn.'

'But wrong turn,' I insisted.

'I thought you promised to obey,' he joked, but irritation twisted within me.

'Not obey stupid idea,' I snapped.

'And whose stupid idea was all of this?' he replied, with a wave of his arm, which took in our wedding and our escape. 'Running away, with you dressed as a boy? Being rescued by your dad? Stupidest thing I've ever done.'

I was stung, but I swallowed my anger and forced myself into silence. I didn't want to argue with him ever again, after the last time. I had to learn to keep my temper. I struggled with myself until I managed to say, 'OK. Your way. Crazy man.'

He set off again and I followed him, treading softly in case the guard-tower housed Nazi soldiers. Ducking left, we found ourselves on a long road of terraced houses facing the old wall. We crept round the tower and along in the shadow of the wall, listening for any movement – boots on a floor, voices in the dark. When we were clear of the tower, I tried to lighten his mood, whispering, 'What stupidest thing ever done, after this?'

It was a game we played as we walked through the nights: What's your earliest memory? What's the most embarrassing thing you've ever done?

He whispered, 'Going onto the shed roof to get a ball, because Flora told me to. Fell off and chipped me front tooth and broke my wrist. It still hurts in the cold. Should've learned not to do what girls tell me.'

I gave him a play-punch. Flora again. Well, I'd shown Flora, because now he was all mine and she couldn't ever have him back. He didn't ask me about my stupidest thing, but held his finger to his lips and paused, looking down the deserted street, then we crept forward slowly.

That was when we heard the dogs. Only one bark at first, carrying in the quiet of the night. We clutched each other's hands and stood still for a moment.

'Just a pet,' murmured Bill. 'Barking at shadders.'

Then another bark. And another. Not muffled by the walls of a building, but out in the night, like us, out in the streets.

Instinctively we moved away from the sound of the dogs, and

the buildings glowered at us, closing in. My heart was drumming and my breath came fast. Without deciding to, we walked more quickly, no longer towards something, but away. The dogs were barking, closer, echoing off the buildings – perhaps two of them, perhaps three. We turned to see if they were in sight, but the darkness was too absolute. We were acutely aware of the sound of our boots on the cobbled road, being unable to muffle our footsteps at this faster pace.

And then there were shouts behind us: men's voices, excited to have something to do in the boredom of the night-watch, egging on the dogs, eager for the hunt. And whichever way we turned, the dogs and men grew closer and our boots clanged louder.

'At home I had a dog,' panted Bill. 'Rusty.'

Of course we had dogs too, but they were farm dogs, working dogs – their teeth bared as they cornered a rat in the barn. I glanced up at the sky, the strip of it between the buildings, trying to shut out the image of the dogs tearing apart a rat. Their saliva. The blood. One star disappeared behind a cloud, and its dim light went out.

Prostějov had become a town of sounds: our breath, the pounding of our own blood in our ears, the clatter of our boots on the road, the dogs barking, men running and calling, closer, closer. Perhaps we could have stopped, knocked on a door and begged for help, but we didn't. We just kept going, faster and faster, running, Bill dragging me with him. I was breathless to keep up, my kit-bag banging awkwardly against my legs.

At last there was an opening in the terrace, an archway leading into a narrow arcade lined with dark shops. Towards the end of the alley was an even darker place that looked like another turning, but it was only a wide doorway, up two steps, set back and hidden until we drew level with it.

Now the dogs were almost upon us, and Bill pulled me up into the doorway, threw his arms around me, squeezed me very hard and whispered, 'I'm so sorry' into my hair. Then he pushed me away from him, so we wouldn't be found touching.

A doorway was a hopeless hiding place, and the sound of the tracker dogs was deafening in the alleyway. They found us easily, barking, growling and snapping at our feet in triumph. Three big Alsatian dogs longing to tear us apart like wolves, but trained to wait for the men who came behind, shouting in excitement. I shut my eyes and waited for the dogs' teeth, hoped it would be over quickly.

Everything seemed to happen at once: the dogs, the men, a searchlight in my face. I raised my arm to cover my eyes, could see nothing beyond the lights, but heard the men close, their panting breath, the loudness of their voices. My teeth were chattering and I had to clamp them shut. The voices behind the light became one disembodied shout in German from the senior officer. 'Hands up! Against the wall!'

We stumbled down the two steps. Bill went to one side of the doorway, and I to the other. I raised my hands above my head and leaned my face against the wall to stop myself from falling, feeling the roughness of the brick against my cheek.

Behind the wall I sensed the people who lived there scurrying like mice, listening with excitement and maybe – who knows? – with pity. I bit my lips, determined not to sob, not to let it end this way.

Then there were hands on me, banging on the thick wadding of my clothes, searching for a weapon and finding none. In Bill's pocket they found my dad's wire-cutters and trowel and sent them clattering onto the cobbles. They picked up our kit-bags and slung them over their shoulders. I was stupidly glad to be wearing the jumper my mother had knitted. At least that stayed with me, for now. They spun me round and the searchlight was blinding.

The light swept down from my face as they discussed what to do with us. Still blinded, I was pulled and pushed onto the street, a gun barrel urging me to walk, stumbling forward as if into an abyss.

Gradually my eyes adjusted to the dark again, although a round purple glow persisted where the searchlight had etched onto my retina. The dark cobbled street swam back into view, the blacked-out buildings, just as they were before, as if the whole world hadn't changed for ever. The barrel of a rifle poked into my back through the layers of clothes.

Bill was walking beside me, another soldier close behind him with a rifle. Ahead were the one in charge and two dog handlers. Each of them had a torch lighting their shiny boots. Behind, I could hear the snuffling of the third dog. My faltering footsteps became steadier as my eyesight returned, and I focused on the torchlight ahead. I could make out clouds of steam from the breathing men and panting dogs in front of me. My stomach twisted in terror, but I marched, because there was nothing else to do, concentrating on my feet – left, right, left, right – saying it to myself in English: 'Left, right, be strong. Left, right, be strong . . .'

We took a winding route down arcades and alleys, until one of them opened through a stone archway onto a large square surrounded by grand buildings – hotels or mansions perhaps.

On the far side was the town hall, draped with Nazi flags and banners. Its domed and colonnaded clock tower was silhouetted against the sky. As we got closer, the clock told us it was 6 a.m., almost day. Armoured cars and trucks marked with swastikas were parked outside in the square. Two sentries stood on guard beside imposing glazed and gilded doors. The sentries greeted our party with a salute and a 'Heil Hitler'.

One door opened briefly and we were pushed inside, hurriedly, so as not to let the light and warmth escape. It was bright in the hall compared with the darkness outside, and I raised my hand to shade my eyes. A gun barrel knocked it down and I almost cried out. I fixed my hands to my sides, formed fists of my fingers, concentrated on the pulsing pain where the steel had hit my hand. Curious eyes looked at us from more sentries and a sergeant at a desk, but nobody pointed a finger and asked if I was a woman.

We were in a long hallway with a high ceiling. Once, not so long ago but in a different world, the town-hall receptionist would have sat here, an older woman with iron-grey hair and sensible lace-up shoes. The hallway was lit by huge bulbs, which hung from four massive mahogany columns, casting a cavernous glow. To the left were steps leading to the doors of Prostějov's magistrate court. At the other end of the hall were more high glass doors with windows above, showing the first lightening of the sky, too late for us.

The soldier who had cornered us explained the details in German, exaggerating a little about the length of the chase and the difficulty of the capture, and how we resisted arrest. I thought how strange it was that Bill understood so little of this. Now it seemed we were really two parts of one whole. I could hear and understand everything, but only he could speak.

The soldiers had assumed we were both escaping prisoners, but if I was to say one word, make one noise, they'd know at once that I was a girl. Was I a girl still? A woman or, should I say, a wife? I thought of the proverb *Mluviti stříbro, mlčeti zlato* – Speaking is silver, silence is gold. From now on, I must be a woman of gold.

The man at the desk cocked his thumb, and we climbed two flights of ornately decorated stairs. On the second floor the landing opened out to a waiting area with a red-and-yellow chequered tiled floor, like a chessboard. I thought what very small pawns we were in this game. A tired-looking sergeant with orange hair sat at a desk and indicated for us to stand in front of him. A boyish private with a rifle slouched to one side.

'Name, rank, serial number,' said the sergeant, in English.

This had been no more real than a game of make-believe when Bill and I practised it. Now it was actually happening, and it made my head spin.

Bill gave his details and they were written down. The sergeant looked at me. I made a mime of my left hand as a notebook and my right hand as a pen.

'He don't say nothing,' Bill told them. '*Stumm.* Mute.' He covered his mouth with one hand, turned to me and nodded. His blue eyes were dark with anxiety.

I started to move my left hand, as slowly as I could, and the young private trained his rifle on me. My heart was thumping as I reached inside the lining of my pocket to pull out the rolled-up cigarette paper Bill had given me and unfolded it unsteadily.

The sergeant sighed exaggeratedly and beckoned me to give him the paper, as the guard stood at ease. I handed him the paper, on which Bill had written *Private Algernon Cousins* and my

113

fictitious rank and serial number, in his English writing. I'd also practised writing this, careful to form my letters in the English way and not to cross the number seven. The cross of a seven could be the end of everything. Panic swooped and dived in me.

He smoothed out the paper and read the details aloud. Then he beckoned again for me to bend towards him. I thought for certain he'd see I was a girl and not Private Cousins, that I'd be dragged away from Bill and never see him again. The sergeant stared so hard at me, it made me dizzy with terror. He checked again what Bill had written on the paper, then sighed and waved me back against the wall.

Our names and serial numbers were meticulously copied into a book and the sergeant motioned for us to sit on two chairs against the wall. I almost fell into the chair, so grateful to sit, aware again of the uncontrollable shaking in my legs and the dull throbbing in the back of my hand.

With a sigh, the sergeant stood, walked around the desk and tipped our kit-bags onto the floor to sift through the contents. Bill's harmonica, in the felt pouch I had made for him, went spinning across the tiles and the sergeant approached it carefully, as if it might be a hand-grenade. When he realised what it was, he laughed in relief and passed it to the young soldier, who sucked and blew inexpertly, making them both roar with laughter. The noise of the harmonica and their laughter echoed in the high-ceilinged space and they both suddenly looked like ordinary young men having what Bill would have called 'a lark', until another soldier appeared and barked at them for silence. They had woken the captain. The sergeant blamed the private, who furiously shoved the harmonica back in its bag.

The sergeant returned to the other contents of our kit-bags, scrutinising Bill's photographs, seeking cigarettes, weapons, food – who knows what? He handled the muddy 'spuds' that we'd pulled up from a field with the tips of his fingers. He didn't find the hidden compartment at the bottom of my bag, with the sanitary belt and rags that I'd be unable to explain. Of course Bill didn't know they were there, either. How could I tell such a thing to a man? Blood thumped in my throat.

Finding nothing of interest, the sergeant ordered the private to stuff everything back in the bags and place them at our feet. Some of Bill's things ended up in my bag and vice versa.

Sitting there under the gaze of the soldiers, unable to move, to touch Bill, to escape, I was overwhelmed by the selfishness of my decision to run away with him. My desire to fight for my country, to be with Bill, and to see my dad and Jan again had led us both to this. What a fool I'd been to hold on so long to the childish illusion that my father would find us and carry us to safety. I looked at the date on the wall calendar above the desk – October 1944, fifteen months since Dad and Jan left to join the resistance and refused to take me with them. Perhaps it was even true that they were dead. I tried to count the red-and-yellow tiles on the floor in an effort to calm the panic sweeping over and over me.

Time inched slowly forward – minutes that might be our last together – and, as it passed, the shaking in my legs and the throbbing of my bruised hand subsided. Nazi soldiers marched in and out, but none of them took any notice of us. They weren't even curious, let alone concerned. We were less than pieces of furniture, in their eyes. I looked up at the fake-medieval coffered ceiling and the fancy staircase. I became aware that I was terribly thirsty.

Bill leaned forward, with his fair head in his long delicate fingers. I wanted to reach out, to wash the sweat and mud from his face and neck with a cool flannel, but I dared not touch him. His bowed head looked so fragile, so easily broken or lost. What had I done? What had I done?

A cramp began to grip my guts repeatedly. I pressed my hands on my stomach and then, as the spasm passed, I stood. The sergeant at the desk glimpsed the movement and his head jerked up. I wrapped my stomach with both arms and bent over in a pantomime of diarrhoea.

'Take him to the crapper before he shits himself,' he barked at the private. I shrugged off the blanket I'd had strung across my body, and felt Bill's worried eyes on my back as I followed the private back down the stairs and out through more palatial doors to a walled yard. We entered a normal-sized door to the toilets.

The guard left one foot in the door as I fumbled under my coat with the unfamiliar trousers and underwear, but he turned away from the noise and stink I made. I was pleased Bill wasn't there to hear me. When my stomach was truly empty and the griping pain had ceased, I smiled wryly to find carefully cut-up squares of German newspaper at hand to wipe myself with. It felt good to smear excrement on the propaganda words, and as I flushed the toilet and came out of the cubicle, there was even water and soap to wash my hands. How soon those things had come to seem like luxuries.

Back upstairs, Bill was still half-watching the door through which I'd left, and there was a tension and exhaustion in his face that I'd never seen before, which made him look so much older than twenty-three. His eyes asked me, 'Are you all right?' and I nodded and gave a ghost of a smile. He'd begged a glass of water, and we shared it, sipping carefully, not knowing when food or drink would come our way again. My stomach was empty now, and I was hungrier than I'd ever been in my life.

It became warm in our seats, and I unbuttoned my coat, but didn't take it off. Sweat trickled down my spine into the crack of my bottom. The heat made me drowsy and I dozed for perhaps an hour, before we were roughly shaken and hurried to the stairs leading down into the yard. A truck drew up, our details were given to the driver and we were shoved into the back. I wanted to tell them that pushing us till we stumbled actually made us slower rather than faster, but dropped my eyes and held my tongue. In the back of the truck were piles of crates and, on wooden benches, a guard and four other recaptured prisoners wearing a strange assortment of coats and hats.

We all nodded at one another, and one man said in an American accent, 'Here we are again.'

'Happy as can be,' replied Bill, like a secret mantra.

Another American replied, in a phoney German accent, as if it was a very old joke, 'The war is over for you, Tommy.'

Bill laughed so loudly, it made me jump. The two Americans introduced themselves and Bill told them I was British, but mute from shell-shock. They looked at me with interest and pity. One of the other recaptured prisoners was French, and Bill said, '*Bonjour*', pronouncing it very badly.

'He's Russian,' said one of the Americans, indicating the fourth prisoner. Nobody spoke any Russian.

The truck started up and we jolted out of the cobbled yard. The clock in the tower now showed 8 a.m., and it was light enough to see that the town hall's ornate domes were green. Bill and I sat side-by-side, as the truck rattled and swerved back through the town. Our thighs pressed hard into each other, both knowing it might be our last touch. I could hear bells from a number of different churches, reminding me that it was Sunday. I thought of my mother and Marek, hurrying, late as usual, into the familiar comfort of our parish church. I pictured them there, my mother's eyes red-rimmed and her mouth held in a tight line, as they were for so long after my father and brother left.

'Never marry a foolish idealist or a daredevil,' she'd told me bitterly. Now I thought that I must be both – my father's traits running through me like a fault-line through marble.

I focused on what I could see from the back of the truck – Prostějov drawing away from us, more churches, a fancy theatre, the grander buildings of the centre giving way slowly to three-storey, two-storey houses and then the low terraces of the outskirts, before we were back out in the open country.

The Russian man sat and stared straight ahead, as if none of us were there. I watched him curiously out of the corner of my eye. He was the first of this terrifying breed I'd ever laid eyes on. He looked just like a man.

'Do we know where we're going?' Bill asked the Americans.

'Lamsdorf,' said one, and the Russian prisoner made a choked sound that might have been a groan. Bill shook his head in sympathy.

'Dropping off groceries en route,' said the other American, indicating the piles of crates. 'Might take some time.' He smiled at me encouragingly. 'Enjoy the trip!' He must have seen how terrified I was and thought I was very young. I wanted to tell him I wasn't a cowardly boy, but a reckless twenty-year-old girl who had leapt from the comfort and security of home into the arms of an almost stranger, putting both our lives in appalling danger. Instead I stretched my face into a smile.

As the truck followed the twists and turns of the road, we were thrown about and it made me feel nauseous. I held my body away from the American on my left, and let myself lean into Bill on my right.

The shape of the houses began to change. The roofs got steeper, and one of the Americans pointed out a woodpile up one wall of a house, right to the roof.

'It must get pretty cold hereabouts?' he said.

Bill nodded. 'A bit chilly. Like Canada.'

'I'm from Florida,' said the soldier.

'Blimey, you're gonna feel it. Brass monkeys,' said Bill.

I didn't know what it had to do with monkeys, but I thought the American would soon feel very, very cold as the Polish winter drew on. I wondered if I would live to see the first snow.

From time to time I allowed myself to glance at Bill, rationing the frequency so it wouldn't be obvious. I took in his slightly ski-jump nose, the patchy blond-red stubble beginning to push through his chin, the tightness of his earlobe to his face, his pale eyelashes, and I loved all these things, wanted to hold them in my mind for ever. More often I let myself look down at his hands resting on his thighs, the dirt under the nails, the long white fingers, a turquoise vein running down the back of the left hand. I wanted to cover them in kisses, knowing that each kiss might be the last. Sometimes I felt his eyes on me, and looked up to exchange the briefest of glances. This close, his eyes were the grey-blue of a lake on a thundery day.

About mid-morning the truck stopped at Mährisch Schönberg,

and we were allowed out of the truck so they could unload some of the crates. The prisoners were permitted to pee up against a tree. I did my diarrhoea mime again and was given a sheet of newspaper and allowed to go a little further from the road. The guard kept his rifle trained on me, in case I was trying to escape. He didn't know that wherever Bill was, that's where I must be, now and for ever.

On the road again, the countryside stretched out below us as we climbed higher. Out of the back of the truck, we could see only where we'd been, not where we were going, but as the road bent we glimpsed the mountains that lay ahead, hills behind hills, bluer and bluer as they faded into the distance.

'*C'est comme les Alpes*,' said the Frenchman.

'It's a long way from Piccadilly,' replied Bill.

The farmhouses we passed now were tall and square, with storage in an undercroft and living space above. None of them were the familiar shape of the farms I knew, with four buildings around a courtyard. There were stony fields where it wouldn't be possible to grow anything, and fast-flowing shallow rivers. We'd covered such a short distance, but it was all so foreign already.

We had one more stop, at Frývaldov, and we stood to the side of the truck while the rest of the crates were unloaded. By now it was lunchtime, and the Nazi driver and guard sat on a wall and chewed on sausage and bread. We watched them like starving dogs, and I thought I might faint from hunger.

There was a short discussion and then the guard gave a small nugget of bread each to me, Bill, the Americans and the Frenchman, but not to the Russian. I nibbled at my bread like a mouse, trying to make it last, and balled up a small amount, which I meant to give to the Russian, once nobody was looking.

But then hunger overcame me, and I ate it. I reminded myself of the stories of what Russian soldiers had done to women, but I didn't feel good about my behaviour. It wasn't Christian. The guards passed around a canteen of water and we all took a swig, wiping the top of it with our sleeves. I handed it to the Russian, but the guard snatched it away.

We passed through a checkpoint, and I realised I'd left my homeland for the first time in my life. It was a shock to know that here, if I spoke, I wouldn't be understood; in fact, people would laugh at me, because Poles found Czech speech funny. I thought: I wouldn't want to be laughed at; then immediately I wondered that, in such danger, I could be concerned about being ridiculed. I was still such a child.

And then we were descending the other side of the Jeseník Mountains, into flat farmland again. Fog was closing in and the trees were charcoal smudges on the horizon. Tall avenues of trees spread out behind our truck on the long, straight roads. The road stretched out behind, taking me further and further from my mother, my brother, everything I knew, leaving them in fog.

It was mid-afternoon before the truck trundled through the gates of an enormous PoW camp, with watchtowers and barbed-wire fences. Dread clutched my stomach, sending waves of sickness through me. I pressed my leg into Bill's, from hip to knee, like one last lingering kiss. My imagination galloped ahead, to me being discovered as a girl and dragged, screaming, from Bill, never to see him again. I saw Nazi soldiers lining up to rape me, forcing Bill to watch, until one did me the favour of a bullet through the brain. I hoped he wasn't thinking the same.

We were unloaded just inside the gates, and prisoners watched us from beyond more barbed-wire fences. Perhaps they were interested because we were the only things that lifted the monotony of the hours, although every day must have brought new prisoners through the gates. Perhaps they were hoping to see old friends. They checked out our clothes and faces, and I wondered what movement or expression would betray me as a girl.

'British?' someone shouted.

Bill looked in the direction of the voice and nodded.

'Welcome to the holiday camp,' called the voice.

Bill smiled grimly and shouted, 'What time's the knobbly-knees contest?'

Laughter erupted around us and the guard looked over. I'd never understood the British need to make jokes out of everything, but now I began to recognise that it was an aspect of courage.

Bill was scanning the faces to see if there was anyone he recognised. He'd told me it wasn't likely, because men moved through here so quickly into the *Arbeitskommandos* work camps. Perhaps he was thinking about Harry and wishing he hadn't left him behind. Or just looking for a familiar face in this ocean of strangers.

We were prodded forward through another set of gates into the compound. The two rows of wire fencing looked flimsy until I raised my eyes to the tower and saw the guns, and pictured the guards, wounded or too old for the Russian front, itching to pull a trigger to prove themselves still men.

During our long nights of walking Bill had warned me about what might lie in wait if we were captured. First, we'd be entered in their endless books. Name, rank and serial number again. Then they might de-louse us, and here lay the greatest danger. In some camps prisoners would be taken to the de-lousing station, stripped naked, showered or hosed down and then painted on the underarm and genital areas with louse-killer. If I was taken there, I'd be finished. We'd be finished. Everything would be finished.

He'd also told me that escaped prisoners were normally put in the 'cooler' for thirty days. I could barely imagine half an hour in a damp, cold cell on my own, let alone a whole month away from Bill, away from any other people, so far from my mother.

I bit my tongue, hoped a 'Hail Mary' would contain the fear, prevent it bubbling, like a hot spring, from my lips. 'Hail Mary,' I said, over and over again in my head.

Ahead I could see block upon block of long single-storey buildings that must have been the 'huts'. The ground below our feet was mud, which had been stamped as hard as a road by so many feet. We were prodded into the third building, where an overweight Nazi sergeant asked Bill for his name and serial number. Bill replied smartly, looking straight forward. I practised in my head the details we'd agreed for me.

'Which working party did you escape from?' the sergeant asked.

'I can't remember,' said Bill. 'Went for a stroll and got a bit lost.'

I feared they would strike him for his insolence, but the guards seemed to be used to this British humour.

The sergeant motioned me forward and asked my name. I placed two fingers on my lips and mimed writing on a paper.

'Permission to speak,' said Bill.

The sergeant raised his eyebrows and turned to a young soldier with a lazy eye. 'Call Sergeant Maddox,' he ordered in German, and as the soldier left, the telephone rang. Perhaps this would be someone reporting a Czech girl on the run.

'Wait,' he said to us, picking up the receiver. 'No, the turnips have not arrived,' he said. A conversation about supplies of vegetables! The normality of it slowed the crazy beating of my heart. I focused on translating it into English.

We waited. He regarded us, unseeingly, as he talked into the phone, and I avoided his eyes, taking in his office with its filing cabinets, table lamp, typewriter, coats and hats on pegs – so many ordinary things in this unnatural world – until the door opened again and the lazy-eyed guard returned with a young British soldier, presumably Sergeant Maddox.

Maddox's worried expression had carved one prematurely deep furrow into his forehead, and his metal-rimmed spectacles were held together with tape. He was probably only our age, but the glasses and the worry-line made him look older.

The fat sergeant ended the vegetable conversation with a 'Heil Hitler' and waved to Bill to indicate that he should speak to the British sergeant.

Bill pointed at me. 'It's a rum do. He can hear, but doesn't speak. I think it's some sort of shell-shock. I found him on the road. He'll have to write his details.'

Maddox flicked back a flop of brown hair and translated, in correct schoolboy German, pushing his glasses up onto his nose. The sergeant stood up slowly from behind his desk and walked towards me. I kept my eyes fixed on the wall behind his shoulder, trying to read the smallest words on a notice. He bent in very close, so I could smell his breath and almost feel his stomach pressing against me. I stared straight ahead, past his ear, at the clock on the wall. I thought he must be able to hear the tick-tock of my heart.

Finally he pulled back and called over his shoulder to the

young soldier, 'Beardless boy. Mad, silent, beardless boy. This is our fearsome enemy. The British are as desperate as the Russians. They know we will win.'

He indicated the form on the desk and gave me a well-sharpened pencil.

'Write,' he said in English.

I wrote my invented details. Where the form asked for my mother's name, I wrote Flora's name and her address in London. Bill had told me that when the Red Cross sent her a card to report me as her captured 'son', she would recognise my name as one invented by Bill and would know not to give us away. On the line for 'occupation' I wrote *ostler*, as we'd decided. I tried to make my letters in the English way, but my hand was shaking badly.

The lazy-eyed soldier took the form and overtyped all my details, then unlocked a drawer and reverentially removed a camera to photograph Bill and me. For the first time in my life I tried to look ugly for the camera, allowed my face to go slack and sullen, as if I was fifteen and furious with my mother.

He wound the form out of the typewriter and pulled a small inkpad from a drawer. Holding my hand too tightly and pressing on the bruise that was forming, he forced my thumb down onto the pad, before rolling it into a pre-marked section of the form. I wanted to tell him I could do it perfectly well on my own – in fact better – but I bit my lips together. Once he'd finished with me, he did the same for Bill. A machine pressed out dog-tags with our newly issued details, and the young guard handed them to us. We both passed the chains over our heads. We were labelled. I was Private Cousins.

The phone began to ring again and the sergeant picked it up

and put his hand over the receiver. Maddox met my glance and smiled encouragingly. He had a small, neat mouth and soft hazel eyes behind his glasses. We could hear shouting from the other end of the phone, and the sergeant looked flustered. He obviously wanted us out of the way.

'I can get them de-loused,' offered Maddox, in German.

The sergeant waved at me and covered the mouthpiece. 'Confiscate those clothes, and get the boy a haircut. He looks like a queer.'

Maddox repeated, 'Haircut', and I wondered how much uglier I'd look when they'd finished with me.

The sergeant nodded, indicating for us to go with Maddox, and spoke respectfully into the phone. We were dismissed.

'Hail Mary,' I said inside my head, 'Hail Mary, I'm alive; hail Mary, hail Mary.'

PART TWO

LAMSDORF PRISONER OF WAR CAMP, POLAND
October 1944

11

Bill's stomach churns with dread and misery; Lamsdorf is the last place in the world he wants to be with Izzy. His eyes dart about, aware of men watching them from every side as they follow Sergeant Maddox between the long rows of huge wooden huts.

It's so much worse than the first time he was brought here, with Harry. Then, after their days of travel, crammed into stinking, dark cattle-truck trains, it was almost a relief to be back behind wire and under watchtowers. But this time his precious girl is right in the hands of the Nazis. He doesn't let himself think about what they'll do when they find her, as he's certain they will. It's only a matter of time. Izzy being discovered in Lamsdorf could be even more dangerous than leaving her at home for the Russians, and he's filled with anguish.

He glances at her as they walk. Her head is down, eyes on the compacted dirt beneath their feet. Her hands are clenched into fists, her slim body held tight to run or fight, and he knows without any doubt that he would die to save her.

His eyes flick around again, taking in the familiar blocks of huts with their window shutters. He remembers how astonished he and Harry were at the size of this camp, how many thousands of young men must be processed through this place and out into the labour camps.

As they walk, they pass khaki-clad prisoners lounging or walking in twos and threes who stare at them, knowing by their farm clothes that they've recently been captured.

'Hard luck, mate,' one calls, and Bill nods. Izzy doesn't raise her head.

Two rats shoot across the path in front of them and under one of the huts. Maddox kicks dust ineffectually in their direction. There have been rats in every camp where Bill has been imprisoned. He can never understand how they look so sleek, when all the human inmates are starving. What he hates most about them is that they are free to come and go, tunnelling back and forth under the barbed-wire fences.

'Filthy things,' Maddox says. 'The shipment of rat poison is overdue. We'll put it under the huts when it arrives.'

Bill notices he says 'huts' like a Northerner, and Maddox continues his official introduction. 'The camp can take up to thirteen thousand British prisoners, but this is a transit camp really. There's another twelve thousand of us out at the work camps. And God knows how many other nationalities; the Americans, the Aussies, the French . . .'

Bill nods towards Izzy. 'I've been here before, but he hasn't.'

'As you know then, escapees are normally sent to the cooler,' Maddox continues, 'but they brought in a gang of RAF boys two days ago, so there's a bit of a waiting list. They'll put you on extra-dirty work instead, so be prepared.'

This is a small relief to Bill. At least Izzy won't have to face solitary confinement, and they won't be separated – yet. He closes his mind to the voice that says, 'But for how long?'

'You missed the Red Cross parcels,' Maddox goes on. 'We had them yesterday, I'm afraid, but I'll see what I can find. Need to get those clothes confiscated first.'

He leads them inside a hut with a counter. Behind it, a British soldier stands up to meet them, saying, 'Hard luck' to Bill and Izzy as he looks them up and down. Bill sees that Izzy is staring straight ahead, not making eye contact, and his heart thumps as he waits for the soldier to notice that she's a girl, but he just calls back to someone out of sight, 'One about five-foot-ten and skinny. The other better be the smallest you've got: five-five maybe. Short-arse. No offence, mate.'

The soldier leans over the counter to look at their feet and asks Maddox, 'Do you think they'll do? Boots are in awfully short supply.'

'I think so,' says Maddox. 'They aren't army-issue, but they aren't shoes.'

'Underwear? We haven't got any socks.'

Bill tries to keep his breathing steady. The conversation about clothes seems unreal, given the danger Izzy is in. He forces himself to speak, to get them away from here as quickly as possible, away from these appraising eyes. 'I think we're both all right for underwear,' he says.

'I haven't got any greatcoats, either,' says the soldier. 'You'll have to persuade the goons to let them keep those. We might have some Belgian ones in, next week.'

Bill struggles to remove his waxed cape and hood. 'My coat's army-issue,' he says. 'I just added these extras.'

Maddox and the soldier scrutinise Izzy's old brown coat,

and she pulls it around her defensively. They decide it will do, for now.

A private appears with a neat pile of supplies: British-army trousers, battledress top and shirt, a mess tin, spoon and fork for each of them.

Walking away, they thread their way between groups of men, who stand around with nothing else to do but stare at them. Stationed at intervals in the compound and in the towers, the armed guards are watching, watching, watching. Bill is a jangle of nerves. A very tall guard looks them up and down carefully, and Bill's stomach freezes.

As they move away, he mutters to Izzy, 'He was here before. Sharp-eyed bastard.'

They follow Maddox to another building. Bill can feel the eyes of the tall guard on their backs, and thinks how much the guard would like to use that rifle. Maddox opens the door with an ironic flourish. 'Welcome to the Ritz. Latrines and wash-house for our compound. Forty-holer. You can change your clothes here and I'll take the others for confiscation.'

Even though they have to walk through a washroom to the latrines, the smell hits them as soon as the door is opened. In the latrine, long planks with holes in them run down each wall, where men sit opposite each other in open rows to do their business. Bill doesn't dare to look at Izzy, all too aware of the disgust she must be feeling. Two men are enthroned and raise their heads uninterestedly.

Maddox says, 'There's an apple tub in the hut for night-time. Rota for cleaning that out.' He pauses and indicates the plank. 'Do you need . . . ?'

Izzy glances helplessly at Bill and starts to move towards the bench. Maddox digs in a pocket and hands her one square of shiny toilet paper.

'Be prepared,' he says kindly, and she looks blank. 'Not a Boy Scout then?'

Bill forces himself to laugh, 'Dyb, dyb; dob, dob', and Izzy stretches her face to a smile as if she understood.

Bill marches towards a hole in the bench and begins to unbutton his trouser fly. Izzy lifts her brother's heavy coat, but keeps it draped to the front of her as she wiggles down her trousers and underwear to pee into the stinking hole.

Maddox is waiting for them in the washroom, beside a row of low metal sinks. Taps jut out of a copper pipe above them. The taps are splashy and the water's freezing. Bill washes his hands next to Izzy, and fresh alarm surges through him. How can Izzy ever wash herself without everyone seeing what she is? How can he possibly protect her on his own? He tries to concentrate on what Maddox is saying.

'Have you got lice? There's a de-lousing station.'

Bill shakes his head. 'Been on a farm, very clean.'

'Lucky you,' says Maddox. 'Can you change now?'

Bill undresses quickly, watching out of the corner of his eye as Izzy removes her boots to pull down her brother's trousers under the cover of her long coat. She steps into the army trousers, rolls up the bottoms and takes the old belt from her brother's trousers. She shoots Bill an anguished glance as she begins to unbutton her coat. His insides lurch with fear and pity.

Maddox offers to hold their coats, as there's nowhere clean and dry to lay them down. He smiles encouragingly, and Bill thinks there's something trustworthy in his bespectacled eyes. Bill yanks his jumper over his head, and in the second of blackness as he shoves his arms into the holes, he realises the total impossibility of watching out for Izzy every moment.

'You can have your jumpers back,' says Maddox. 'It's just the trousers I have to confiscate. Civilian shirts are allowed, as long as they haven't got collars.'

When she's dressed, Bill meets Izzy's eyes again and nods slightly to tell her that she looks like a British soldier now and won't attract so much attention. Her fingers run around the itchy neck of the battledress jacket, and her face is white and pinched. She's biting the inside of her lip.

He looks over to Maddox, waiting patiently for them, cleaning his glasses on his sleeve, and makes a decision. He has to tell Maddox. He can't protect Izzy on his own.

Outside the washroom, as soon as they are out of earshot of anyone, Bill looks up and down the rows of huts and touches Maddox's sleeve. 'Excuse me,' he says.

'Oh, sorry, I'm Sergeant Maddox, Ralph Maddox – call me Ralph.' He holds out a hand to Bill and then to Izzy.

They shake hands as Bill says, 'I'm Bill. He's Cousins. But before we go any further, I need to tell you something.'

Izzy shakes her head violently, but it's no good. Bill needs help, and it's now or never. Ralph Maddox realises that the 'something' is serious. He also glances up and down the rows, before nodding for Bill to continue. They walk more slowly, with Bill between Ralph and Izzy. Bill indicates Izzy, and she stares at the ground.

'This bloke here – Private Cousins. I'm sorry if this causes trouble for you, but he ain't a soldier. The truth of the matter is, well . . . he's a she, and she's my wife.'

Ralph's eyebrows shoot up into his flopping hair as he squints at Izzy, but he doesn't lose a stride. 'Bloody, chuffing hell. Well, I'm . . . jiggered.' Bill knows he's trying not to swear in front of a lady. 'If that doesn't take the biscuit! What to do, what to do?'

They take another few paces, and Izzy raises her head. Bill can see misery and terror written all over her face and prays that Ralph can read it too.

They stroll a few steps further towards the hut they must be heading for, with three men outside, smoking.

Bill and Izzy wait for Ralph to say something, and he stops to look her full in the face, pushing up his glasses onto his nose and narrowing his eyes. The furrow between his brows deepens as the seconds pass. Trouble ferments in his face. And then he slowly relaxes.

'You could be one of my sisters,' he says simply, and Izzy's eyes fill with tears. Bill is flooded with relief. With another man to share the burden, he might just be able to protect her.

They reach the entrance to Hut 17, with its number over the door. It's right under a watchtower. A guard on the tower platform surveys them idly, but his gun is trained on the wire fence.

'Let's just take another turn,' says Ralph and they set off around the exterior of the hut, close to the fence. 'I need to think.'

They walk on in silence beside the long block of three huts joined together, each with a door and two windows. Bill glances in the windows and thinks that each hut is full of strangers who might be more observant than Ralph Maddox.

'I'm going to have to tell them,' says Ralph decisively.

Horror rushes through Bill, and he can see the consternation in Izzy's expression. 'Really?' he says. 'Couldn't it just be our secret?'

He might be able to trust this gentle-looking man who has sisters, but how could they trust the strangers in a whole hut? There might be a hundred of them, and any one of them might betray Izzy.

'It's the only way,' says Ralph. 'You and me can't be on guard all the time. We'll need help.' He consults his watch. 'We've just got time now. The main working parties won't be back for another half-hour. Now there'll just be twenty or so in the hut. Trusted men.'

They turn back down the long side of the adjacent block, and Bill feels he has no choice. It's as though all ability to control his life has been taken away from him.

'Whatever you think,' he says unhappily.

Izzy's eyes are blazing with fury, and Bill has to look away.

Ralph Maddox opens the door to Hut 17 and ushers them inside, ahead of him. Bill sees Izzy quickly taking in her surroundings – a huge square room, with a walkway between the rows of bunk beds. Two windows and a door behind them, and the same at the other end of the gangway. There's a buzz of chatter that stills momentarily when they enter. The air is smoky and smells of bodies, as if a window hasn't been opened for a long time. The bunks are three high, end-on along both sides of the walkway. To their left is one row of about ten bunks, with just enough space between them for a man to climb into bed. It looks the same to their right, until their eyes adjust to the semi-dark and they see there are two sets of bunks there, backing onto each other. Between the rows nearest them, men are sitting facing one another on the lower bunks, playing cards.

'Like sardines,' Bill apologises to Izzy, as if it's somehow his fault that beds for ninety men are crammed into this small space.

In the centre of the walkway is an iron stove, but it's chilly in the room and Bill knows it won't be lit till the weather is much colder. On either side of the stove are tables with benches, and a couple of khaki-clad men sit there. A few others are lying on their bunks, sleeping or reading or just staring ahead into the darkness.

Ralph Maddox asks a man on his right, 'Is B Company here?'

The man nods. 'All present and correct.'

'And nobody else?'

'Not yet.'

'Post a lookout. I've got something to tell everyone.'

At the suggestion of news, people look up. Nobody wants to be the lookout who'll miss the news, but Ralph points to two men and promises to tell them later.

He gives them each a cigarette, and they pull on coats to step outside. One exits the door behind them, and the other the door at the far end of the room, while the rest of the men obey Ralph's call to 'Gather round'.

Once the watchmen have given the 'all clear', Ralph raises his hand for silence. The twenty or so men are quiet immediately. Bill can see that they obviously respect Ralph, but he has no idea if he'll be able to control them once they've heard about Izzy. He is racked with misery and guilt.

Ralph's voice is low, but everyone can hear. 'This is Bill, joining us from the Eighth Army and a work camp in Czechoslovakia.'

A murmur begins and Ralph raises his hand again.

'And this . . . Steady now, men—' He pulls Izzy forward to stand beside him, keeping one hand on her shoulder.

She looks hard at her boots and chews the inside of her cheek. Bill forms fists and parts his feet for balance, in case he needs to defend her.

'This is his wife.'

A riot of noise erupts around them. One man bangs his tin cup on the table. Others cheer. Close by, someone says, 'A woman in the camp!'

Men call out, 'Will she do us all?'

'I'm first.'

'Put her in a different bed each night!'

Bill steps in front of Izzy, raises his fists and wishes Harry was here beside him.

Ralph keeps his hand on Izzy's shoulder and yells, 'Quiet!', but this time it takes several seconds for the excited murmuring to die away. All around them men are pressing closer, where they can get a good view of Izzy.

Slowly she raises her head, and one by one she looks them in the eyes. Bill watches their faces, on the alert for any rush towards her. He sees exhilaration and thrill in their eyes, but nobody moves to grab her.

Ralph barks, 'That's the last time I hear anything like that, or God help you! She's the wife of a British soldier, and we'll all have to work together night and day to keep her safe. I don't know if we can do it.' He pauses and looks around him. 'But I know we can't do it unless we all pull together.'

An electric charge of excitement runs through the hut.

Ralph pauses and calls, 'Max?' and the other prisoners turn to a man who is still lying on his bunk, curled away from them. Slowly Max turns over and gazes blankly at them. And then, as if they slowly come into focus, he sighs and climbs down from his bunk, his dark hair standing up on end. Everyone's watching him. He's a stick of a man, with a long, mournful face and deep black circles under his eyes, as if he hasn't slept for weeks. His cheeks are hollow, and Bill can see his skull beneath the flesh. The crowd parts to let him stand beside Ralph.

'I'm in,' he says. He speaks with the faintest trace of an American accent. He clears his throat, and everyone listens carefully. 'We have to remember she isn't military. Not covered by the Geneva Convention. If they find her now, they'll say she's a spy.' He nods to Izzy and Bill, and his eyes are deep-brown pools of sadness. 'Sorry to say this guys, but they shoot spies.'

Bill and Izzy glance at each other, aghast. How could she be a spy? Bill thinks. What would she tell? Who would she tell? This is a new horror, something he's never considered. He looks around at the other prisoners' faces and wonders what the Nazis do to men who harbour spies.

Over to Izzy's right, a short, square man with sandy hair and piercing blue eyes pushes through the crowd. His Scots accent rips and jars the words, so that Bill can hardly understand him. 'I'm with ye.' He looks around the hut. 'And by the by, I'll kill the man who messes with the lassie.' Bill suspects, from the silent way they receive this casual threat, that the men know he means it.

Another steps forward, a man with a thin moustache. 'I'm with you,' he says. But there's something in the way his calculating scrutiny rests on Izzy too long that Bill doesn't like. His eyes are fringed with long black eyelashes, like a cow's, but he has none of the softness of a bovine gaze.

'OK. I'm in,' says one man, and then another and another.

'Don't worry, love,' says someone. 'They'll have to take us down first.'

There's murmured assent and a buzz of excitement from all the prisoners. Bill slowly lowers his fists.

Ralph nods. 'OK, lads. This must be our secret. Our deadly

secret. He'll be known by everyone as Cousins. He's listed here as Private Algernon Cousins.' He chuckles. 'You may remember that Algernon was Biggles's cousin.'

A laugh explodes around the hut and seems to release the pressure in the room.

'The story is that he's got shell-shock and doesn't speak.'

Bill looks round with a hopeful grimace. 'If we can do this . . .'

Someone says, 'You'll have a lot of godfathers for your first', and the tension breaks again into laughter.

'Tell us the story,' says someone else. There's a mix of amusement and admiration on every face, and Bill can't help himself rising to it.

'I was on a work detail based at a sawmill in Mankendorf. Five of us was sent to her mother's farm to help bring in the crops. I suppose you'd say it was love at first sight.'

There's a mix of groans and cheers from the men.

'We was married about ten days ago' — Bill pauses for effect, lifting his eyebrows suggestively, and there are more cheers and groans — 'and we've been movin' at night. Her dad and brother are in the resistance, so we thought we might get lucky and make a home run . . .'

Five clear raps come at the far door of the hut, and instantly everyone moves back to their previous places. A buzz of innocent chatter begins. The door opens and the lookout comes in, with a gust of fresh air. 'Goon on the block,' he says. 'And the working parties returning.'

The day's turning darker outside the windows. Ralph nods, and the men return to their bunks, to their card games, dissolving in the gloom.

Ralph taps his lip with his forefinger and addresses Izzy. 'I think we'll hide you in plain sight, Cousins,' he says, indicating the first bunk by the door. 'I'll shift over, and you'll come here by the window, in the middle bunk, with Bill below you. It's warmest on top, but insects drop out of the ceiling. I'll move to the next bunk.'

Bill feels Izzy shiver and remembers her fear of spiders. How trifling that seems now.

Ralph continues. 'We'll keep the bunk above you free as long as we can.'

'Thank you,' says Bill. 'Sorry to be so much trouble.'

As the removal of Ralph's belongings is being managed, the door closest to them opens again and a line of filthy and exhausted-looking men files in. They don't speak much, but seek out their own beds, pull off their work boots and lie down. Izzy shrinks back into the shadows of the bunk, but Bill can see they are too tired to pay any attention to the newcomers.

The lookout calls, 'Goon up!' and three Nazi guards enter by the door at the other end of the gangway.

'Hut inspection,' says the fat sergeant who signed in Bill and Izzy.

Ralph motions to them to stay where they are and hurries down to meet the guards, calling, 'Look lively, men. Stand by your beds.'

From the shadows to the right someone shouts, 'Oh no, I was just dreaming of giving a fat English sausage to the commandant's lovely missus.'

There's laughter, but the guard ignores it. Bill thinks perhaps he doesn't speak English.

The prisoners stand at the ends of their bunks as the two guards march forward, turning over a game of chess in progress

141

on the table, deliberately knocking over tin mugs from which the men have been drinking tea, poking into the precious parcels open on some of the beds.

Bloody bullies, Bill thinks, staring at the opposite bunks as they approach.

The young lazy-eyed guard slings their kit-bags, blankets and a straw mattress each onto their bunks. The sergeant glances at them and addresses Ralph in English. 'They should be in the cooler. Will be, when we finish with those RAF *Terrorflieger* bastards. For now, latrine duty.'

Ralph protests, 'But the Russians do that.'

'Well, now they do it too. It's their punishment. The ostler can hold the horse.'

Ralph begins to speak and thinks better of it. 'OK, I'll give them the gen.' He hands the Nazi their trousers. 'Confiscated civilian clothes.'

The sergeant looks them up and down, then passes on to the next bunk. He doesn't pay any particular attention to Izzy, and the relief is so great, it makes Bill feel unsteady. He looks up, and the man with the thin moustache is studying Izzy with an expression Bill can't read.

12

Twilight is falling on the camp. We line up to be searched as we leave the hut. Ahead of me the prison guard is patting down prisoners, and wild terror pulses through me as the line moves and I get nearer and nearer to my turn. Now he's searching Bill, his hunger-skinny arms and chest, and then the horrible Nazi hands go up my legs, my hips.

From the dusk ahead of us someone calls, 'Fat-arsed square-head. Going to lose the war. Like you did before.'

The guard searching me freezes momentarily. I can smell the cigarettes on his breath and can't tell if he's looking at me or past me. A joyful, derisive chorus starts up outside in the twilight.

'Going to lose the war, like you did before!'

The guard motions me forward and starts to search the man behind me, and I stumble out into the air, shaking all over, taking deep breaths. I force myself to march like a man, left, right, repeating it over and over to myself in English.

On the parade ground, thousands of men line up. Guards move up and down the rows, count each man and return to the commandant with their tally. Our guard has great bushy white eyebrows and white hair sprouting from his ears. His eyes scan my face, and I expect him to notice at once that I'm a girl. I look out beyond the wire, at the top of a fir tree, as he passes. I force myself to concentrate as the cold wind riffles the tree's uppermost branches. I try to imagine I'm a bird sitting up there observing us, my feathers lifted by the breeze, ready to take off at any moment and fly to freedom. Fly home. The guard passes on, and my heartbeat slows. One group has to be counted twice, and the early-autumn chill starts to penetrate my clothes.

At last 'the count' is completed, and the prisoners all move towards the latrines and wash-houses. I choose a dark corner hole in the stinking latrine, while Bill, the sandy-haired man, the thin-moustached man and the mournful man stand with their backs to me, introducing themselves to one another. I hear the sad-faced man say his name is Max, and the sandy-haired man calls himself Scotty. The man with the thin moustache is Tucker. He's the only one who flicks a glance over his shoulder at me sitting on the latrine. They're blocking me from the view of the tall guard who passes the washroom door from time to time and looks in. I guess the guards don't want to be in this stinking place any more than we do.

The twenty men from 'B Company' contrive not to use the holes near me, but allow me a respectful distance. A man who doesn't know my secret plonks himself beside me, farting loudly.

As we come into the washroom someone hands me a sliver of soap, someone else a well-used toothbrush and another a small, grubby towel. I have to blink back tears at their kindness, and pin my tongue to the roof of my mouth not to thank them. I hope they can see my gratitude.

The soap is poor-quality, but it feels good to wash my hands. I use a small corner of the towel as a cloth to wash my face. I wonder when I'll be able to wash my body again. The cold water on my face tingles and I've never felt more terrified, but oddly too I've never felt more alive. Everything is brighter and louder and more acute than I've ever seen it. The men's banter ricochets around me. The guard pauses at the door, watching two men who are fooling about. He isn't interested in me. They start up a rollicking song, and others join in: 'Roll me over, in the clover, roll me over, lay me down and do it again.'

I wonder if those who know my secret are thinking of Bill and me as they sing. Tucker is singing heartily, with his cow-eyes on me and his thin moustache hopping up and down on his lip, and I'm the first to look away. My scalp prickles with uneasiness.

By the time we leave the washroom, it is almost dark and the searchlight from each tower around the compound plays back and forth along the double lines of perimeter fencing, over the thousands of prisoners.

Back in our hut, the window shutters have been closed from the outside. It's terrifying to be locked in, but at least I'm shut away from the Nazi guards. Some men sit on their bunks to unlace their boots and tie them together in pairs. I notice how few of them have socks. Most seem to have their feet wrapped in strips of linen.

'*Fuss-lag*. Foot-rags,' says one of them wryly, noticing my stare. 'Not as good as woolly socks.'

The men begin preparing their meagre evening meal. Terror has prevented me from feeling hungry, but now I realise it must be many hours since Bill and I sat on the railway embankment and ate our morsels of bread.

I think of the dumplings my mother will be serving now, and the memory of the smell of cooking in our kitchen is almost overwhelming. I must be careful what I allow myself to think about.

Ralph Maddox tells Bill that we two will be a 'combine', to share food and Red Cross parcels when they come. Tonight we get one-third of a black loaf to share between us.

The sad man called Max says, 'The Geneva Convention says they're supposed to give us the same rations as they give their military. I pity the poor schmucks, if this is all they get.' I wonder if he's a lawyer. He has that kind of serious look about him.

A few men can fit around the tables at the centre of the hut, but most retreat to their own bunks to eat or sit on a mate's bottom bunk. We sit on Bill's bed, with Ralph and Max facing us. Scotty has disappeared back to a group of his own friends, but sometimes I catch his eye and he winks at me. His eyes aren't the grey-blue of Bill's, but bright and clear as a lake under ice. It comforts me a little to know that he's watching, alert for trouble. Tucker is also playing cards, sitting where he has a clear view of me. I try to nudge myself as much as possible into the shadow of the bunk above, draw myself back, like a snail into a shell. If I could, I'd make myself disappear.

Most of the men around us are using the edge of their metal PoW ID tags as rulers and knives to get an exact division of the bread, but Bill just tears ours roughly in half and gives me the bigger share. I don't protest, but when he isn't looking I swap them over. The men bring out yesterday's parcels, and in their 'combines' of two or three they earnestly debate whether they will have margarine on the bread, or jam to make it a 'pudding'. Some have pink tinned meat, which they call Spam, and that too is divided into carefully ruled portions. I can see already that the parcels mean the difference between slow starvation and survival.

Ralph and Max each give us a sliver of their pink meat and I understand, without being told, that this is quite a sacrifice.

'I'll try to get you a parcel tomorrow,' says Ralph. 'It's usually Tuesday or Friday, but you never know.'

Up to now I've been too frightened to be hungry, but as the bread and meat go down, they remind my stomach how much it wants to eat. I'm hungrier when it's finished than when I began.

Many of the men bring out strange devices made from old tins. One vertical tin and one lying horizontally are joined together by a belt made from a shoelace, all fixed to a board.

Bill explains, 'Blowers. They're called blowers. See here. You can light your wood, or whatever, in the bottom of this tin and then turn the handle, and that winds the pulley and cranks a fan to get the fire really hot with a tiny amount of fuel. You can make a brew whenever you like. Bloody genius invented the blower. I'll make us one as soon as we've got empty cans.'

I watch as Ralph conjures a small flame — enough to heat water for a cup of tea. They take the tea-making very seriously, and I nod my thanks when a hot tin mug is pressed into my hands, even though I don't like the taste of the powdered milk.

Scotty approaches the end of my bunk. He doesn't speak, but reaches up to the end of my bunk and balances something on the wooden frame. He winks reassuringly as he turns away, and even in this half-light his eyes are astonishingly blue. Other men who are 'in the know' watch him and, before they pack away their parcels, a few of them select something and walk to our end of the hut, to leave an offering on the end of my bunk.

Some bend down and smile shyly at me as they do so, and I'm filled with a childish desire to jump up and see what they have left. But I'm trying to make myself invisible as well as silent, so I hunch back in the shadows. I'm glad Tucker doesn't come any closer. Tentatively I poke the bruise on my hand. The fact that it hurts proves this is all horribly real.

Bill's deep in conversation with Ralph Maddox and sad-eyed Max. Their English is too fast for me to be able to follow everything, and they all have slightly different ways of speaking. I gather that there's been an influx of American prisoners and RAF fliers from a battle to the west of here. They keep looking at me, seriously, anxiously and, with a sudden lurch, I fully understand that it's not only me in danger, but that I've put every man in the hut at risk too.

Bill smiles encouragingly at me from time to time, but doesn't draw me into the conversation. I sit and watch the three of them, who now control my fate. Mournful Max is always moving; one leg or other jigs rapidly up and down and he motions with his hands as he speaks. He keeps his voice down, but his face is dramatic. I see emotion scudding across it, but there's a darkness in him and he has deep shadows under his eyes, like a man who doesn't sleep well. I think he might be good to have as a friend, but not as an enemy.

Ralph Maddox is slower and more considered in his movements, like a man double his age, though none of them can be much older than me and Bill. Only Scotty might be as old as thirty. I focus on listening to the way they speak, to give my mind something to hang onto, to stop myself from howling in fear.

Ralph's always pushing his spectacles back up his nose, as if they are too big for him since they were mended with tape. His brown hair flops onto his forehead and he flicks it back. When he speaks there's some quiet authority about him that makes the others listen attentively.

And dear Bill, graceful and languid, lounging on the bed, so easy in his body, quietly telling our story to the others, smiling sometimes like a switch has been flicked, which makes other people smile too, even if they don't intend to. I look at him and know I would go anywhere with him, even if it was my last day on Earth.

After a while I look out further into the bunkhouse, through the gathering thickness of cigarette smoke, watching the patterns of the men – how they form into small groups, mostly two, but sometimes three, talking or reading, or writing in notebooks or on letter cards, or most often playing cards. Scotty is sitting in a foursome around an upturned carton, playing cards with a screwed-up face and an air of absolute determination. Many cigarettes lie on the carton, obviously as bets. Tucker is playing cards too, and is still watching me.

'Shall we turn in?' asks Bill.

I don't know what this means.

'Go to bed,' he explains. 'Up the wooden hill to Bedfordshire. See if we can sleep.'

I nod gratefully. Perhaps I'll wake up and find this has all been a nightmare, and Bill and I are still out on the road, walking west, waiting for my father to find us.

As we stand, Ralph breaks off his conversation and comes close to us, indicating the apple tub near the door.

'Do you need to use this?' he asks me. 'We can stand around you.'

I think about my bladder. I've not had much to drink since

the last visit to the latrine, and I decide I can hold it until morning, but I'm so grateful for his thoughtfulness and kindness. I try to put all that into a slight shake of the head and a smile.

'Sleep well, then,' he says. 'Sweet dreams.'

Nobody's paying any attention to me as I climb up to the middle bunk. Bill pops his head up and touches my shoulder fleetingly, before he drops down to the bed below. From the safety of my bunk, I look out at all the men, engaged again in their games or books, or deep in their private thoughts. The smoke seems to hang in the air up here and it makes me cough. When I turn to my right, the shuttered window is within reach; to my left is another bunk, where at arm's length a strange man will lie watching me, close as husband and wife. I take the newly issued blanket – as rough as those we use for horses at home – and tuck it under the slats above, making a curtain to hide behind.

On the foot of my bed are the little offerings the men have made: there are seven single squares of chocolate. I want to call out my thanks, but I know I mustn't. I wonder if I should eat them all now, in case this is my last night alive. I wonder if I'll have the will-power to limit the chocolate to one square a day, to make it last a week – if I manage to live so long. It seems odd to wonder if I have a night or a week left to live. All my hopes and dreams have closed down to this place, these few hours, Bill's body on the bunk beneath me. I carefully line up the chocolate squares, above my kit-bag pillow. I must be hoping to last for a week.

It's too chilly to take off any clothes, so I lie down as I am in my British-army uniform and wrap my home blanket over me. I look at the bruise forming on my hand, and think I'm lucky to have escaped so far with so little injury. I lay Jan's coat

150

over my feet, to pull up if it gets colder in the night. The straw mattress is hard and lumpy, but it smells of farms, under the powerful reek of cigarette smoke and unwashed bodies that fills the hut. I could almost be in our stable, wrapped in a blanket still carrying the faint scent of my mother's laundry soap. I close my eyes, and somehow I'm comforted to know I'm resting my head on my kit-bag filled with clothes from home, my brother's long underwear and cast-off sweater. As I wriggle to get comfortable, the whole bed rocks a little. The underside of the top bunk is close above me, and I hope there aren't any spiders. How stupid to be scared of spiders, with the whole Nazi army just outside the walls, ready to drag me from Bill and shoot me for a spy, or do much worse.

I drop my hand down the side of the bed out of sight of the hut, beside the shuttered window, and Bill reaches up and gives it a squeeze, as I knew he would. My new wife's body longs for his, to wrap my arms around him and sleep in his arms just one more time.

Then he releases his grip, and I withdraw my hand. I feel for one square of chocolate and put it on my tongue to melt as slowly as possible. It tastes of all the happiness we've known in the last ten days.

Listening to the hum of voices from around the hut, I think I should work harder at being Algernon Cousins, the boy who grooms and feeds the horses and wants to ride at the races; a boy who left home young to fend for himself in the world; self-reliant and tough. A boy who's almost invisible. He's not a thoughtless chatterbox like me, but is silent because he prefers the company of horses to people. You know where you are with horses, he'd think. He watches and listens, alert as a mare to a little click of the tongue, but speaks only when it's absolutely necessary. He's considered in all his actions, not impulsive like me; he wouldn't frighten the horses by sudden movements or loud sounds. He's schooled himself in self-control, which makes him slow to anger. Cousins has spent so much time with horses that he seems to have taken on some of their qualities, their alert wariness, but also their patience, strength and endurance. That's who I'll be tomorrow. The new me. Gee-gee Cousins.

I curl into myself and count up – I've not slept for twenty-seven hours, apart from a few minutes in the truck and the town hall. They have been the most exhausting hours of my life. I say my prayers. I pray most ardently for a miracle to keep me undiscovered, to keep me alive with Bill, for us both to survive unscathed. I pray for my family and, when I think of my mother, tears prickle the back of my throat. I force myself to think of something else: how the square of chocolate has almost melted in my mouth; how all this is worth it for even one more day with Bill.

13

When I wake the next morning I know immediately where I am, with a sick lurch in my stomach. The wooden bunk bed is hard through the thin straw mattress, and my kit-bag makes a lumpy pillow. I lie for a moment, listening to the sound of so many men breathing, snoring, snuffling like pigs. I've woken up because I badly need to pee. Terror grips me. How am I to do this?

I hear the voice of Gee-gee Cousins, the new me, in my head. 'Easy now,' he says, as if I was a skittish pony. 'Easy now.' The shutters are still closed outside the window, and a thin streak of grey light appears around the edges of them. It must still be very early.

I pull the blanket around me and swing my legs over the edge of the bunk on the window side. I feel for Bill's bed below mine with my feet, then ease myself out and down. I stand beside him, bending to try and make out his face in the dark; then I edge cautiously out into the gangway. Nobody else is moving. I smell rather than see my way to the apple tub, and feel around the rim.

Praying that this will not be the moment when the shutters are thrown back, or the door flies open, or a strange man wakes to urinate, I unbutton my army trousers, push down my brother's shorts, cautiously lift the blanket behind me so I don't wet it, and struggle uncomfortably into a position where I can wee into the tub and not onto the floor. Letting go of my full bladder is a relief, but I have to shake like a boy, and have nothing to dry myself with but my hand. I hope it won't be long before I can wash.

I pull up my clothes and creep back to bed, pausing only to kiss the fingers of my other hand to touch Bill's hair lightly. He stirs, but doesn't wake. I throw the blanket up ahead of me and climb back to my bunk.

In bed, I sit back against the wall and reach up under my clothes to readjust the bust-flattening corset. It's the first time I've slept in it, and it feels tight and uncomfortable. I feel sorry for my poor little breasts, squashed under it. When it's in a better position, I wriggle back down, to lie curled towards the shuttered window. Sleep won't return, so I lie and look at the grey sliver of light becoming whiter and wonder if these are the last hours that Bill and I will be together. If this will be my final day in this world.

When the shutters are thrown back, with a simultaneous loud rapping on the door and a shout of 'Raus', I jerk up and hit my head on the bunk above. My heart is beating wildly and misery sweeps over me. I know the time has come for discovery and all that means.

I fold my blanket and smooth the top of it with my hand, as if it's a friend I must say goodbye to. Everything in life suddenly seems so precious. I touch the kit-bag that has come from home with me, and pull Jan's coat with me as I climb down. Bill winks at me anxiously and quickly pats my arm.

The door's hurled open, and a cold blast of air swirls round my legs, even through the army trousers. I thrust my arms into the coat sleeves, wrapping it around me, and sit on Bill's bunk to pull on my boots, ever grateful for the felt lining my mother made – blessing the thought of her, in case it's the last time I have the power to do so. We form up into a line. Ralph is at the head with Max behind him, then me, then Bill, then Scotty, then Tucker, and all the nameless others stretching out behind.

Ralph leads us out of the hut into the cold air. I guess it's about 7 a.m., and the sun is just rising over the compound. We follow Ralph between the huts onto the parade ground and form up into rows to be counted again. The guard who's counting approaches me along the row. It's a man I haven't seen before. As he walks, he scratches himself obsessively, first one arm, then the other. The closer he comes, the faster my heart beats. As he comes level, I hold my breath and look straight ahead, but he's not really looking at me, just muttering numbers under his breath. I see an angry patch of eczema rising from his uniform collar. He probably wants to finish as soon as possible to get inside for a hearty breakfast and a good scratch. As he moves away, my fear ebbs a little.

The count is not satisfactory in some way and has to be done again, to the loud groans and jeers of the prisoners. This time the guard looks closer at me and I fold my arms over my chest, but he goes on past without comment. It begins to drizzle lightly and I turn up my coat collar. My wrists are covered with goose pimples. I'm glad my brother's coat sleeves are long enough to almost cover my hands.

Eventually the count is complete. Ralph turns to me. 'You must be hungry.'

I nod, watching the ground, trying not to make eye contact with anyone, not to be visible. I want eggs and cheese and a big hunk of my mother's rye bread.

'It must be the devil of a job not to say anything. I wouldn't have a hope,' he says.

I lift my head and smile at him. If only he knew what a chatterbox I am.

'That's better.' He grins. 'Now then, I've got a little present for you.'

From his pocket he draws half a roll of toilet paper. I hesitate.

'Can I spare it?' he continues. 'Yes, look, I've got another. Been stockpiling them, just in case we get a chance to scarper.'

I reach out and take it, nodding my thanks, wondering how long I have to make it last.

Most men, including Ralph, Max and Tucker, set off for the latrine and washroom, but first Bill and I have to double-back to the hut to pick up the apple tub containing the night-soil. Scotty has volunteered to help us. He says the tub will be too heavy for me and Bill. I want to protest that I'm stronger than I look.

Scotty crouches down beside it and indicates to me and Bill to come round, so we can take the weight between the three of us.

I hope that having Scotty to help won't draw undue attention to us, but the tub is surprisingly heavy and the contents slosh about alarmingly as we make our way to the latrine to empty it. It's difficult for three people to walk in rhythm. A powerful stench of ammonia comes off the urine, and we all walk with our heads turned aside and our eyes watering. Somehow we manoeuvre it into the latrine and tip it down one of the holes, splashing everywhere.

Bill carries the empty tub over to the taps, and Scotty shows us where a stiff brush and carbolic soap are kept on a window ledge. I take it from him, kneeling on the washroom floor, scrubbing out the tub. The water is freezing and my hands turn bright red, but the tub is clean, and I'm glad to have done something useful.

To wash myself, I choose the tap nearest the wall, where the water runs down into the drain. The tall guard regularly passes the doorway to the washroom, but Bill or Ralph or Max or Scotty or Tucker, or one of the other twenty prisoners we've trusted with my secret, seems to be able to casually position himself between me and the door. Now I begin to see why more men had to be told. Some of the prisoners around me strip to the waist, while others just splash their faces. I wash my face with my cupped hands, like a man, and use a rag to wipe beneath my clothes. I sense the other men casting curious glances at me – the ones who know. Some of them are unshaven, but Ralph makes a show of carefully scraping his face. 'It's a way of proving to them that they haven't beaten us,' he says.

Bill moves to the sink next to me and hums as he shaves in a scrap of mirror. When he's finished, he hands me the razor and soap. For a moment I don't understand, then I go through an act of soaping my face and gently pulling the razor through the thin scum on my cheeks. Max and Ralph saunter off, so the guard can see me 'shaving' if he looks my way. I must think more like a boy, if I'm not going to give myself away. Bill holds my hand for a second as I give him back the razor.

'All right, chum,' he says reassuringly.

With our ablutions done, Max leads the way to the cookhouse. My eyes skitter around me at everything, aware all the time of the guards and the guns, trying to watch the other prisoners and do whatever they do, sick to my stomach with anxiety. I lengthen my stride to match Max's.

'Walk like Gee-gee Cousins,' I tell myself in English. 'Tough boy.'

'Don't bother with the acorn coffee,' Max says. 'The mint tea isn't so bad, once you get used to it. And you can have a brew of your own once you get a parcel.'

Back in the hut, I sip my mint tea, and Bill and I share another thin slice of the loaf we were given last night. I'm already so hungry that my stomach seems to be glued to my spine. Ralph has disappeared and comes back triumphantly with a Red Cross parcel for me and Bill. Apparently this one is Canadian, which means it doesn't have cigarettes like the British and American parcels. I think: That doesn't matter, we don't smoke. But Bill explains, 'We need the cigs to trade. Fags are like cash here.'

I cut the string with my ID tag and open the brown paper like a child, impatient to see what's inside. A woman far across the sea has carefully packed neat rows of tins. I lift each one out and study the label carefully, trying to translate the English: milk powder, butter, cheese, corned beef, pork luncheon meat. Luncheon. What could that mean?

'That's the pink meat we had last night,' says Bill. 'We'll give some back to Max and Ralph.'

I'm pleased to see soap and puzzled by things called kippers, prunes and marmalade.

Tucker saunters over to our bunk and scans the contents of

our parcel, nodding to Ralph. 'Good going to get one so quick.' He winks at me as he walks back into the hut, and I'd like to run after him and knock him to the ground.

'Bloody coffee, not tea,' says Bill ruefully, though I am delighted.

'I'll swap you my tea,' offers Ralph, and I want to shout 'No', but Bill looks overjoyed, so I turn my face to hide my disappointment. I prefer coffee, but if I'm meant to be an English boy, I realise tea is what I'm supposed to drink.

'I'm for a brew,' says Bill, and Max lends him the ingenious little blower and retreats to his own bunk with a book. The dark circles under his eyes seem even deeper today and I wonder why he can't sleep. Straining my eyes in the gloom, I see he has a small library above his bunk. I'd like to know what he's reading and where he's found books.

'What'll we have for breakfast?' Bill asks me. 'This lot has to last a week – maybe more, if the parcels don't get through. A little slice of cheese?'

I nod, with one eye on the biscuits. They are called Pilot biscuits. I begin to see that while I can't speak, Bill will make all the decisions for both of us. How astonished my mother and father would be to see me so docile, when I fought them for my own way over every small thing.

'You are a selfish, wilful girl,' my mother used to say. I pick up the biscuits, pleadingly.

'Just one then,' says Bill.

But as I'm about to take one, someone shouts, 'Goon up!' and the bushy-eyebrowed guard marches noisily into the hut, directly towards us. I grip the wooden edges of the bunk, like someone on a raft in a storm. He's come for me. It's over.

The guard takes the contents of our precious parcel and stabs the lid of each tin with a knife, but nobody seems surprised at this strange behaviour. When he's done, he looks around casually and then leaves. I breathe again and release my grip on the bed. Did I think I could hold on as they dragged me out?

Bill explains, 'It's so that we can't hoard the food, for escapes. It starts to go off as soon as the tin is pierced.' He turns to Ralph, 'Do we need rackets bags?'

'Not here. Not in this hut. We never leave it empty.'

Bill nods and turns to me again, and I can see it pleases him to be able to tell me things about this life, to be the expert. 'In some camps, some huts, men steal each others' food and clothes while they're out, so they have to carry it round all day in bags. Seems like we've landed in a good hut here. No tea-leaves – thieves.'

Max looks up from his book. 'All down to Ralph.'

Ralph waves a self-deprecating hand.

I bundle some of the tins back into the parcel, and Bill takes them out again to pack neatly. 'Let's hide some,' he says, 'just in case', and so we remove some and secrete them around our bunks. I hide the chocolate on the bunk above my head.

When we're done, Ralph says, 'Come on, then. I promised to take you for de-lousing and haircuts. And then, I'm afraid, you've got the honey-waggon this afternoon.'

I dread leaving the relative safety of the hut for the untold dangers of the de-lousing station and the mysterious honey-waggon, but have no choice other than to follow.

The three of us weave between the huts to the de-lousing station. Other prisoners lounge around outside the huts, talking. I wonder what there can be to talk about when you have been

160

together so much – for years maybe, like Bill and Harry were. Guards are patrolling the boundary fence. The one with the bushy eyebrows looks at me as we pass.

As they walk, Ralph and Bill are having the sort of normal conversation that any two strangers might share, as if my life was not hanging in the balance. I want to draw Bill's attention back to me, but instead I concentrate on walking like a boy, with my hands in my pockets.

'Where d'you come from?' asks Ralph.

Bill replies, 'London, Stoke Newington.'

'I think that's quite close to Max. He's from America originally – Brooklyn – but has lived in somewhere called Hoxton since he was fourteen.'

Bill is delighted. 'Hoxton's just down the road. We're practically neighbours! What about you? Somewhere up North?'

'Manchester. Ever been there?

'No. Is it nice?'

'Rains a lot. But home, you know.'

They are both silent for a moment at the thought of home, and I picture my mother milking the cow, feeding the chickens, having to cope somehow without my help. I send my apologies to her spinning into the sky.

Before the dreaded de-lousing, we stop at another hut. The guard with eczema is patrolling outside, scratching at his inner elbow. He looks at my hair and smirks. One corner of the hut has been set aside as a barber's shop, and men lean against the wall waiting their turn. The barber's another prisoner, who cuts everyone's hair the same: almost shaved at the back and the sides and short on top. I don't want my hair to be cut like this, but I have no choice; no choice – no choice about anything ever again.

In the waiting line there's animated discussion about a cricket game due to take place later this week. I concentrate hard, but it's very confusing and involves a lot of words that sound made-up: wicket, googly, yorker. Opinions are sharply divided about which men should be playing and which team is likely to win. They also talk about the two 'tests' this summer, the 'Stashes' – Stalag ashes. I think of school tests, and the life I would have had if I'd gone to university, if Hitler hadn't come.

As they talk, the men move forward in an orderly queue until their turn comes to sit in the barber's chair. Some of them don't really need a haircut, but sit in the chair and pass something to the barber, and he writes a note in a book with the stub of a pencil or ducks down under the chair and passes an item back, hidden in his hand. I try not to stare. Ralph and Bill don't say anything.

Bill goes first, and I'm sorry to see his lovely fair hair cut tight to his head. It's so short I can see his pink scalp through the blond hairs.

'There – that'll last you a bit and stop the bugs biting,' says the barber.

I want to run out of the hut, but it's my turn now, and I force myself to take my place in the chair. I can see myself in the broken mirror that the barber has propped up. My hair's grown, even in the eleven days we were on the run. It looks pretty. The barber places a dirty scrap of towel around my shoulders and picks up his scissors.

He lifts up one of my curls and calls out to the waiting queue, 'Shirley Temple, eat your heart out!'

All eyes swivel to look at me. Surely they'll see I'm a girl?

'Been on the Good Ship *Lollipop* a while,' jokes Bill. I fix a grin to my face. How can Bill laugh, when he remembers the day he

162

cut my hair, so gently and deferentially, and how he said he loved me with my short curls? '. . . And ends up here in Candyland!'

The barber scissors close to the back of my head. 'Don't you want to give us a song, Shirl?'

Ralph says quietly, 'He doesn't talk. Shell-shock.'

The men in the hut study me with increased interest, and I stare straight ahead at myself in the mirror. Myself, but not myself at all. Sick to my stomach.

'Poor blighter,' says the barber, slicing all the hair touching my left ear. 'Do we know where?'

'Not sure,' says Bill. 'Tobruk, maybe. That's where I was picked up. He can understand. Just doesn't speak.'

One of the men in the hut scrutinises our faces for a second, to see if he recognises us, but then glances away.

The discussion of cricket resumes as the hair over my other ear is chopped, and then the barber attacks the curls that were starting to fall attractively over my forehead. I am shorn, and the effect appals me. As if that wasn't enough, he takes out a razor and begins to shave the back of my neck and above my ears. I grip the sides of the chair and struggle to keep the horror off my face. I am so ugly! How will Bill love me now?

'There you go, son,' says the barber kindly, 'No Brylcreem, I'm afraid, so I cut it shorter on top, Yankee-style.'

He flicks loose hair from my neck with a shaving brush and whips off the towel. I feel cold and naked and utterly miserable.

Standing up, I run my hand over my spiky, prickly hair. Shorter than my brother ever had it. Horrible! Horrible! Turning to Bill, I can hardly meet his eyes. He seems a little surprised at how it has transformed me, but I don't see my own horror reflected in his eyes.

Ralph says, 'That's better' and they nod.

Bill clears his throat. 'Much better.'

Out in the air again, I take long, slow breaths, concentrating on not crying, and follow Bill and Ralph with my head bent. I feel the eczema guard observing me, but I can't meet his stare. After a moment Bill drops back, glances around and whispers, 'You're still the most beautiful girl in the world. Still my sweet'eart.'

I don't believe him, but his kindness brings me even closer to tears and I daren't make eye contact.

'I look like a skinned pig,' he laughs ruefully, but I don't smile. I'm trapped in a cloud of misery, which almost makes me forget my terror of the de-lousing station, until we arrive there.

There's only one guard on duty. He takes off his cap to scratch his bald, shiny head and barely glances at us. Perhaps my horrible new hair is making me more invisible. Perhaps it's that. He inspects our ID tags and writes a number in his book, raising his eyes expectantly to Ralph.

Out of the corner of my eye, I see Ralph give him a fist-full of cigarettes, and the guard opens the door to let us inside.

'I know you haven't got lice, and the new haircuts will help,' says Ralph, 'but maybe it wouldn't hurt to do your under-arms. Lice carry typhus, and they love underarms and groins.'

Bill adds, 'And they itch like the devil.'

Ralph points to a pail of white powder with a paintbrush sticking out of it, then goes back outside to the guard, leaving Bill and me alone. Through the door, I hear Ralph strike up a conversation in German.

Bill quickly kisses me, and we grip each other tightly for a long moment. I think I can feel his heart beating. This might be the last time.

He runs his hand over my shorn head.

'You're still beautiful,' he whispers again. 'I'll always love you.'

A huge lump in my throat prevents me from replying.

He strips off his battledress jacket and shirt and lifts his arm for me to paint the wispy blond hairs underneath, then turns to do the other side. His white body is covered in goose pimples.

'We should do the seams of our clothes too,' he says, removing his trousers and pulling them inside-out. 'The places the buggers love to hide. And down round your you-know-what. I'll do mine.'

He turns his back to me and rubs a handful of the powder down the front of his underwear, while I apply the powder to the seams of his battledress and trousers. When we've finished with his clothes, he waves to my buttons. 'I'll watch the door, if you can do yourself?'

I remove my battledress and unbutton my shirt, exposing Jan's long-sleeved vest, which covers my corset. Cautiously I sniff the brush, then apply a little powder to each underarm area, quickly rebuttoning my shirt. Like Bill, I dab a little powder down my shorts into my private hair.

Quickly I paint the powder along the internal seams of my battledress and trousers, yank the clothes back on and touch Bill's hand. He's kept his eyes on the door the whole time, legs parted, ready to go to war for me.

He turns towards me. 'You are my love for ever.'

And tears now fill my eyes.

'Hush now. Don't do that.' He wipes away my tears on the sleeve of his shirt.

I hold his gaze and nod, but dare not speak.

When he sees I've regained control of myself, he opens the door. 'That stuff reeks,' he says to Ralph. 'The fumes have really got to Cousins!'

I make a pantomime of rubbing my eyes.

The three of us walk slowly away, and I think: We've done it. We've got through the de-lousing.

I'm just starting a thank-you prayer when there's a shout from behind us, from the bald Nazi guard. I look quickly at Bill, in case it's the last chance I get to memorise his lovely face, and then I force myself to turn. The guard is holding up a piece of paper that Ralph has dropped. Relief floods through me again, and Ralph gives him another couple of cigarettes.

On the way back to the hut we call again at the latrine, and I glance in the mirror where the men shave. My eyes seem huge now, cheekbones angular, chin square. I would call it head-shaving, not hair-cutting. I hate it, hate it, hate it, want to hide my ugliness from Bill.

In the hut I empty my kit-bag onto my bed and rummage for the woolly hat my mother knitted. I refused to wear it when she gave it to me, saying it was too boyish and horrid, but now I pull it on, stuffing everything else back in my rucksack. I make up my mind to wear it always. I will not die looking ugly. A small voice in the back of my head whispers, 'I thought you were going to be Cousins? He wouldn't make all this fuss about a stupid haircut.' But I am not Cousins, not yet at least. I yank the knitted hat down to my eyebrows and over my ears.

'Feeling the cold?' asks Bill sympathetically.

Men are such idiots, I think.

At midday someone comes round with a dustbin of thin soup called 'skilly' and one small potato each, and afterwards Ralph's told the 'honey-waggon' has arrived for our latrine duty. Ralph flicks the hair off his forehead and looks anxiously at me. 'You might want a scarf, to tie round your nose and mouth.'

I recognise the purpose of the 'honey-waggon' as it pulls up close alongside the latrine block. I've seen the cesspit at home emptied and I know what to expect, though I've never been so close.

The waggon's like an oil tank mounted on a cart, pulled by an old nag of a horse. I pat the nose of the horse and miss my mare back on the farm, with a sharp stab of physical pain. There's a Russian prisoner in charge of the waggon, and I understand that this is our punishment – to do the work of the lowest. A hatch opens into the cesspit below and, as the Russian lifts it, the stench and fumes make me retch.

'Fuckin 'ell!' exclaims Bill, turning his head.

The Russian drops a rubber elephant's trunk dripping with filth into the hatch, and I quickly wrap the scarf around my nose and mouth, though it doesn't help much.

He demonstrates how to clamp the elephant's trunk and then flips a lever. We hear waste being sucked through the hose into the tank. It's disgusting. The trunking judders and flips, and I fear the clamps might fly off at any moment and cover us in excrement.

When the sucking noise changes, the Russian turns the motor off and pulls the stinking hose from the hole, then hands it to us to replace on the cart. I think we're finished now, but he indicates that we must go with him to the next latrine.

He leads the horse, and I walk on the other side of it, resting my hand now and then on its warm coat, wishing the familiar horsey smell wasn't overcome by the stink of human waste. At the next latrine we're in charge of the process, while the Russian stands back. I try not to touch the shit on the hose, but it's impossible, and I can feel its wet softness on my fingers. I hold my hands away from my clothes. When it's done, the Russian leads the horse to the entrance of the camp, where the waggon will be removed.

A guard I haven't seen before approaches and my heart bangs in my chest. He holds his nose as he tells us in broken English that we must meet the Russian here tomorrow at eight-thirty sharp.

'OK,' says Bill. 'Get it over with early. Which way back to Seventeen?'

The guard points the way back to our block of huts and, as we walk, I breathe into the scarf around my nose, but can still smell the excrement on myself. Perhaps I can smell my fear too. I feel the guard's eyes on my back and try to swagger like Cousins, not move like a girl. At our washroom we clean our hands and then remove our jackets, roll up our sleeves and thoroughly scrub our arms with carbolic soap. To touch the shit of other people! It feels as if I'll never be clean again.

I'd like to stay in the relative safety of Hut 17, but Ralph insists on taking us for a walk around the perimeter fence.

'You need the exercise,' he says firmly, 'or your muscles'll waste.' I feel in some way this is addressed to Max and not to me, and sure enough, Max pulls on his boots to come too.

Everywhere my eye lands on danger – a guard, a gun, barbed wire, prisoners who might hand me in for a piece of bread. I stride out, hands in my pockets balled into fists. I won't go without a fight. Cousins wouldn't. I am Cousins. Max and Ralph walk just ahead of us, sometimes talking, sometimes not, in the way that old friends do. I notice Ralph's slight limp again, and think Max must be slowing his pace to fit Ralph's.

Looking around me, I begin to understand the scale of this

place, where we can walk and walk and still be in the British compound.

In the evening the men divide into small groups within the hut. Ralph's at the table teaching German to one group. I listen for a while, longing to correct some of his grammar. Max is still on his bunk, scribbling furiously in a notebook. Bill and I look at a copy of the camp magazine called *The Clarion*.

That night I dream of home, and wake up with my face wet with tears, remembering the note I left my mother. I see my pencilled writing, neat and defiant. I picture her roughened hands and broken nails, with my careless letter clutched to her chest, or more likely screwed into a furious ball and thrown across the room, with Marek trying to quieten her anger. I weep silently into my kit-bag pillow, until I've cried myself out. Then I promise myself this must be the last time. Gee-gee Cousins would never cry. The sliver of light around the shutter turns from grey to white, and another day begins.

When we are finished with the stinking honey-waggon and are back in the hut, preparing for another long, empty day, Ralph asks, 'Would you like to visit the art and craft show this afternoon? It's our hut's turn.'

'An art and craft show?' says Bill, in apparent amazement.

Ralph laughs. 'You have to queue to get in. Some pretty astonishing things. There's some clever blokes here. Shall we go?'

The hours tick by, minute by interminable minute, until it's time for us to see the show, and then I pull my hat down over my ears to indicate my readiness, and anticipation mingles with my ever-present anxiety in a cocktail of jangled nerves and heightened perception.

Ralph and Max lead the way to a hut they call 'the school', and a long queue snakes up to the door. A guard with a red, bulbous noseand small beady bird-eyes patrols the line. I think he will be the one to unmask me.

As we wait, Bill and Max talk about places they both know in London. Haggerston, Shoreditch, Hackney. They lived only a few miles from each other. It seems strange to me that they should live so close and not know each other.

'What did you do in Civvy Street?' asks Max.

'Clerk at Paddington,' Bill says. 'Great Western. You?'

'Oh, this and that. The socialist bookshop one day, a printer's the next. Help out here and there with the Transport and General Workers' Union.'

I decide with a thrill that Max is a socialist, like my father.

Bill turns to Ralph. 'And you?'

'Oh, I was at university.' He sounds apologetic, as if it's some kind of disease.

Bill is a bit hesitant. 'What's your subject, like – if that's how you say it?'

'I went to do medicine, but couldn't stand the sight of blood, so after a year I switched to Classics. Not much use to anyone.' Ralph smiles wryly.

I've never seen Bill so lost for words, and I understand that neither of these men mixes in the kind of social world he's used to.

'How come . . . ?' Bill falters.

'How come I'm not an officer?' suggests Ralph. 'Easy, really. I couldn't see myself leading a charge out of the trenches, and all that. Being in charge of Hut Seventeen is more than enough.'

While we shuffle forward in the queue, I keep my head down to hide my face. Some of the other prisoners crouch on their haunches while they wait, some smoke, some talk incessantly and some are as silent as me. I wonder if they're afraid too.

Eventually it's our turn to go in, and the school hut turns out to be a cabinet of wonders. I relax a little as everyone stares intently at the exhibits and nobody looks at me. The craft section comes first, and includes a detailed model of a steam engine made from old food tins.

Bill smacks his lips appreciatively. 'I'd like to meet the bloke that made this,' he says, to nobody in particular.

There's a model of a farm, and I bend down to study it carefully. The house is quite separate from the barn and stables, which I think is a stupid idea. I want to tell them how much more sensible it is to have them arranged around a courtyard.

There's a model of industrial Glasgow and one of the harbour of Tel Aviv, and the greatest wonder of all – half a metre high, and carved, so the notice says, out of soap – is a model of the Mosque of Omar in Jerusalem. I marvel at their choices as well as their skill: Glasgow, Tel Aviv, Jerusalem. These men are citizens of the world, while my life's been so small and confined. But here we all are, together, all equally powerless.

We move on into a section for drawings and paintings. Many of these are comic cartoons, with jokes about camp life. Then we reach the back of a big crowd, where the prisoners have halted, creating a bottleneck. A British soldier keeps saying, 'Come on, you wankers, move on now. Other blokes deserve a cop of 'em.'

I crane my head to see past the shoulders of the men in front, and eventually we shuffle forward until I can see two large charcoal drawings of nude women, with long, flowing hair curling around their shoulders. The drawings show large breasts and luxuriant pubic hair, and I can't help blushing as I look at

171

them. Someone behind me groans and says, 'That'll keep your pecker up. If I had half an hour alone with her . . .' and someone else cuts in, 'Half an hour? Three minutes more like.' There's loud laughter.

I glance at my companions. Ralph is gazing mistily, but he might be looking slightly to one side of the pictures. Max's face is full of bitterness and anguish; these naked women are not bringing him joy. Bill's eyes are almost popping out, like in a cartoon. I am completely forgotten as he ogles the pictures, and I'm furiously jealous of these imaginary women with their cascading hair and balloon breasts. I want to shout to him, 'Me, look at me!' Then I realise that Gee-gee Cousins would be gawping at them too, so I shove hands deep into my pockets, digging my nails into my palms, trying to master my anger, forcing myself to make a close study of the dots that make the nipples, and the squiggles forming the pubic hair.

'Move on, son,' says the soldier-curator kindly. 'Let the others have a turn. You can toss yourself off later.'

Bill taps my arm, and we turn and push our way through the crowd around the nudes. I want to ask him if pictures like that make his 'pecker' stand up, and if he likes my small breasts as much as those large ones.

Out in the air again, I try to walk like a boy whose pecker has just been lifted, and wonder what that must feel like. How peculiar it would be to have a part of your body you can't control, that jumps up of its own accord and you can't tell to lie down. I wouldn't like that at all.

Max is silent on the way back to the hut, but Bill and Ralph discuss the things they've seen and laugh about the funny cartoons. Bill sighs over the nude drawings, and I want to smack him for thinking about them. Ralph sighs too, but I can't help feeling he's pretending as much as I am.

Close to our hut, Tucker falls in beside me and Bill, chatting about the drawings of the girls and rolling his cow-eyes at me. He's sauntering slowly, and by the time we reach the hut the others are ahead of us, just out of hearing.

'And another thing,' Tucker says casually, as though he was still talking about the pictures, 'I think it would be worth you giving me a little something from time to time, just to keep me mouth shut.'

Bill stops dead and looks around nervously. 'What d'you mean?'

'Well, it's hard to keep quiet when I'm so hungry, isn't it? And a word in the ear of a goon might get me an extra parcel.'

We have stopped walking, and I look from Tucker to Bill, expecting Bill to say something, do something, but all he can manage is 'You heard what Max said: they'd shoot her if they knew.'

Tucker smirks. 'That'd be a pity, of course. Her so pretty an' all. I don't mean her any harm. Just need a bit more nosh. And some fags. Got some debts to pay. You could leave me a tin of grub and some fags at the end of your bunk, just under your blanket. I'll come for them after lights out.'

Bill is looking at the ground. 'We haven't got any fags. We got a Canadian parcel.'

Tucker thinks. 'Well, make it two tins then.'

Fury rises in me, almost blinding me.

Bill growls, 'You bastard!' He has his fists clenched by his sides.

But Tucker hasn't finished. 'And of course if you tell Ralph Maddox or your other new mates, I'll be straight to the goons with your little bit of news.'

14

Bill and Izzy's first days at Lamsdorf begin to unfold in a mixture of terror, boredom and hunger. The search, the roll call and the latrine are the worst, and Bill's heart thumps in his chest every time Izzy is close to a Nazi, though he's full of admiration at the way she stares coldly at the guards. Almost every day the men from Hut 17 who know her secret are forced to stage some kind of diversion to draw the guards' eyes from her to them. During one routine search the lazy-eyed guard, banging his hands down her body, rests them for a second longer than necessary on her waist, but Bill, ever vigilant, pushes Max so that he trips forward in the queue into her, knocking the guard aside, and the moment passes. Bill is exhausted from feeling that he has to be alert to danger every second, that he can never take his eyes off her.

Each night they leave a small amount of food at the end of Bill's bed for Tucker, and it's always gone by morning. Bill and Izzy's rations are now cut beyond endurance, and their stomachs twist and turn with hunger. Tucker seems to take pleasure in reminding them how easy it would be for him to betray them, standing close to the tall guard in the washroom and indicating

him with a flick of his head, or hanging about near the guard
with eczema at the wire, opening his mouth as if to speak and
then deciding against it. Bill loathes him more than he's ever
hated anyone in his life. Every day he thinks he'll tackle him
direct, but can't decide how to do it in a way that won't send
him whining to the guards. Every day he makes up his mind to
tell Ralph, because he'd know what to do, but then he wonders:
How could Ralph stop Tucker going to the guards? There would
always be an opportunity for him to spill their secret. Bill finds
himself trying to dream up ways that he could kill Tucker without being discovered, and then is appalled at himself. Killing in
battle is one thing, but he doesn't know whether he could plunge
a knife into a body. The thoughts buzz round and round his
head, wasps trapped in a jar.

Each morning opens into a long, yawning day, filled with the
sweating closeness of men pressing in on every side, and he can
only imagine how Izzy, who is used to open spaces and solitude,
must find this oppressive. Even those who are protecting Izzy
spend too much time scouring her with their eyes, then quickly
looking away when Bill catches them. He can imagine how she
must suffer from the unbearableness of never being alone or
quiet, not for one single moment, not even in bed or on the toilet.
How she must long for the fields and the sky. He knows he does,
and he didn't grow up with nature all around him.

The days seem interminable, as if time runs on a different kind
of clock in the camp. When they were here before, Bill and Harry
would fill the hours by reading, or finding a football match to
take part in or a cricket match to watch, or Bill would go to play
the piano in the hut they used for a church. Now he and Izzy do
their latrine duty and take a daily walk around the perimeter with

Ralph, and sometimes with Max or Scotty. And after that, the long, long hours till bedtime. He takes Izzy to the camp library and chooses *Great Expectations*, which he begins to read to her, very quietly, tucked in his bunk, running his finger under the words so that she can see them, and Izzy writes down all those that are new to her. But you can only read for so many hours a day, and Bill misses the constant chats about anything and everything that he held with Harry. He marvels at Izzy's determination not to speak, but he longs for conversation to pass the time.

He wonders how Max can stand spending most of each day on his bunk, reading or scribbling rapidly in his notebook in tiny writing, or just lying with one leg always jiggling restlessly, staring at the slats above his head. Bill can't understand why Max doesn't go out and join a club or play a sport, or teach something in the camp school. Anyone choosing to stay trapped in the hut all day is a mystery to him. He thinks about the marriage service – for richer, for poorer, in sickness and in health. It didn't mention being stuck in a stifling hut all day.

He's ridiculously grateful when Ralph falls in beside him and Izzy on the way back from roll call and says, 'I saw you had a harmonica. Do you play anything else?'

'Just piano,' says Bill. 'Not well or anything.'

'What composers do you like?' asks Ralph.

'Oh, I never had lessons. Me mum and dad run a pub, and we always had a piano in the bar. I started messing about on it when I was a tiddler, and just sort of picked it up. Mum always said I should have lessons, learn to read music and all that. But Dad couldn't see the point. He said I could play well enough for the pub, and it wasn't as if I was going to be a concert pianist.'

'Pity,' said Ralph. 'You might have been.'

176

Izzy is nodding beside him, but Bill pulls a wry face. 'Too late now. But it's handy for a sing-song. I had a sax at home too, but need to be taught properly.'

'Maybe the band-leader could teach you. He's a good sort. I can ask, if you like?'

'Not planning to be here that long.'

Ralph smiles. 'Fair play.' And he opens the door to the hut.

Bill's heart sinks as they step back into the hut and he says, 'When I was here before, I used to go and play the piano in the church hut, when it wasn't being used.'

'Well, go again,' Ralph urges him. 'Go now! Me and Max will stay with Cousins. You need to get out.'

Izzy is nodding vigorously, and Bill is overwhelmed. He feels like running out of the door this very second. He shakes Ralph by the hand and wonders what he can do to repay him. 'Do you think the men would like me to play my harmonica one evening, for a bit of a sing-song?' He's done that many times before in the camps where he and Harry were imprisoned.

'We'll ask them,' says Ralph. 'I should think they'd welcome it. Singing raises the spirits.'

So that night Bill plays, for almost an hour, and most of the men join in, singing familiar songs. Max doesn't sing, but lies on his bunk with his eyes closed, and Izzy hunkers back on her bed, watching Bill.

As he drifts to sleep, Bill thinks how unfathomable it is that a species that can invent music and feel love can also kill and maim, and starve and blackmail one another.

With every day that passes, Bill thinks how right he was to put his faith in Ralph. He knows now that Ralph is one of the Nazis' 'men of confidence', in charge of their hut, relied on by the guards to keep control and able to speak German well enough to convey orders. But he also knows that Ralph's trusted by the men in the hut to treat everyone fairly and represent their needs to the commandant. That makes him a rare character. He's all right for a Northerner, thinks Bill. The North is all one undifferentiated place to Bill, who's never been further north than the top end of the Piccadilly Line.

Bill is more wary of sad-eyed Max. He's a curiosity with his occasional nasal Brooklyn twang, as though another Max is hiding inside this one, and perhaps another inside that, like Flora's stacking Russian dolls. Bill isn't sure he'll like the one in the centre, if he ever gets there. Max is obviously dead clever, but seems like a time-bomb, set to self-destruct, and Bill doesn't want to be close by when that happens.

Scotty is more straightforward, with no side to him. What you see is what you get. A diamond in the rough, Bill thinks.

He wonders if Izzy can hear the differences between their accents: his London one, Ralph's northern and the faint echoes of Yankee in Max. Perhaps all English sounds the same to her. Apart from Scotty, of course.

He thinks about the way that in peacetime you stick mainly to your own sort, gravitating to friends with a similar education and background, with parallel interests and views of the world. He'd never have made friends with a university student, an agitator, a riveter and a farm girl.

As the days pass, Bill is chuffed to discover that he's trusted in turn by Ralph. One evening when most of the men are out at the camp theatre, Ralph tells Bill he'd like them not to go. Bill would have liked to take Izzy to the theatre, but he feels proud to have been asked to stay behind. When the main group leaves the hut, only six prisoners are left. Bill is relieved that Tucker has gone out. A small degree of the constant tension drains from him when Tucker's out of sight. Bill toys with the idea of taking this opportunity to tell Ralph they're being black-mailed, but what could Ralph do?

A sentry is posted, and from a number of Klim dried-milk tins come the parts of a crystal radio, which Scotty expertly assembles. He has a folding knife, which he uses to strip the wires. When he's finished with the knife, he tucks it away, in a niche under a picture of his sister and her two children above his bed. Bill watches and thinks perhaps one day he'll use the knife on Tucker.

Bill's fascinated by the construction of the radio, and Scotty is delighted to show him the tube wound round with copper wire, and two more tubes covered in silver paper that fit inside each other. More wires run from one part to another, to a long string of copper. The whole thing is fixed to a block of wood no bigger than a book. Bill nods his appreciation to Scotty and whispers, 'I could make one of those' to Izzy.

Scotty climbs up to join the wire to another length of copper that is pinned above the rafters, down the full extent of the hut. This is the aerial, a fine thread of shimmering copper that will connect them to the world.

When the radio is set up, Scotty hands one earpiece to Ralph, and Ralph indicates that Bill should have the other. Bill knows this is a treat and a mark of Ralph's confidence in him. They listen as Scotty moves the silver tubes in and out to pick up a station. A voice comes loudly through the crackle. Bill says, 'It's German' and hands his earpiece to Izzy. Ralph begins to write what he hears in shorthand, and Izzy motions for a pencil and paper to make her own notes. Max finds paper and a pencil for her. Bill watches her intent expression and rapidly moving hand and is filled with pride.

As the broadcast unfolds, Ralph glances up at Izzy, and neither of them can hide their horror at what they're hearing. As the news item ends and they stop writing, the others look at them expectantly.

'May I?' asks Ralph, pulling Izzy's paper towards him, as if to confirm his own fears. The crease between his eyebrows deepens as he reads, and he adjusts his glasses, looking up at them. 'It might be Nazi propaganda,' he begins slowly, 'but they say the Polish Home Army has been completely routed and arrested. And – please God this isn't true – the entire civilian population of Warsaw has been rounded up and sent to transit camps.'

They all sit in silence for a moment to allow this idea to sink in. Bill wonders if it can be true. Every single man, woman and child from Warsaw in Nazi camps like Lamsdorf? Is that even possible?

Max bursts out, 'And where was Stalin? Where's the Red Army?'

Ralph shakes his head. 'Camped outside the city, the broadcast said.'

'Fuck,' says Bill.

Ralph hands the earpiece to Scotty to retune, and finally he finds what they've all been hoping for, a distant crackly voice from London. To Bill, it's like hearing the voice of God when you have almost ceased to believe in heaven. London is a real place, and it's still standing, and somehow the clipped words are here with them in Hut 17. They excitedly repeat what they're hearing. The English news is so different from the German. It talks about Stalin and Churchill meeting to discuss the future of the Balkan States. They all agree it's a sign that the war must nearly be over.

'Why didn't they mention Warsaw?' asks Bill.

Ralph shrugs. 'Maybe the Nazi one was propaganda.' But Bill can tell he doesn't believe that.

As the radio is dismantled and packed away, Ralph turns to Izzy. 'It's good that you can understand German,' he says, and looks at her notes. 'Your handwriting doesn't look very English. Would you like me to teach you shorthand?'

Izzy nods eagerly, and Bill is delighted that Ralph is offering her something to pass the time, something to use her brain. He wonders how many people in Warsaw have loved their wives as much as he loves Izzy and now may never see them again.

The other men return from the theatre, singing loudly and clowning around. Tucker leaps about, doing a silly dance, and Bill realises with a sick lurch that he's hardly thought of him for the last two hours.

Then someone steps on another man's foot and is pushed roughly and retaliates, and the singing is undercut by the shouts of two men. One throws a punch and the other clutches him in a wrestling hold.

Ralph and Bill jump between the fighting men, and others pull them apart.

'Stop it now,' shouts Ralph. 'You'll end up in the cooler!'

The bushy-eyebrowed guard throws open the door, drawn by the rumpus, and Izzy pulls herself back onto Bill's bunk. Silence is thrown over the room like a blanket.

181

Ralph's grip on one of the fighters slackens to a comradely embrace, and the only voice is Max, shouting from his bunk, for all the world as if he hasn't seen the guard, 'I tell you, it was LBW!'

Bill takes the hint and yells back instantly, 'That umpire wants his eyes testing.' And others join in, arguing volubly about cricket.

The guard watches suspiciously and then retreats.

'Quick thinking, Max and Bill,' Ralph nods. 'Now, you two, shake.'

The two men who were fighting shake hands reluctantly and go to their separate bunks, each complaining quietly to his own group of friends.

Bill turns to Izzy. 'Sorry. Fights break out all the time in camps. Everyone's nerves are shot.'

Izzy nods miserably, and he knows she feels it too. The boredom and tension, and so many people all around them, buffeting and jostling all the time, even makes them irritable with each other. He looks away from her, and Tucker catches his eye, eating their food in his bunk, raising his tin mug to Bill and Izzy. Bill thinks again of Scotty's knife.

It's no surprise to Bill that talk in the hut is mostly about food. It's been the same ever since he was picked up. Before he was captured he might have expected a group of men to talk about girls or sport, but instead it's a constant litany of fish and chips, steak-and-kidney pies and roast potatoes. In the absence of sex, food has become an obsession, similar to the early days of falling in love. All the prisoners are in love now with the memory of food, and hunger's there all the time, under the surface of everyone's minds. As soon as they finish one of their meagre meals they begin to plan the next, to worry about the parcels not arriving

182

on time, to wonder what will be in them. Bill's thoughts of food are magnified by the conviction that he should be providing for Izzy, keeping her fed.

One man obsessively writes menus of ever-more-exotic meals that he will eat after the war. These are pinned up on the foot of his bunk for everyone to see, like sharing posters of film stars or dirty postcards.

When the parcels don't arrive on Tuesday, Bill and Izzy are down to their last two tins – one of marmalade and one of Spam. Tucker stops by their bunk and points at the Spam. Izzy shakes her head furiously, but Bill holds her arm. 'We've got to,' he whispers. She's only considering her own stomach, when I've got her life to worry about, he thinks.

The smirk on Tucker's face as he takes the Spam is as bad as their hunger. They spread marmalade thinly on dry bread. Its bitter taste seems fitting.

The following morning Ralph comes into the hut with the worry lines etched deeply between his brows and holds up a hand for silence. 'Sorry, everyone. No parcels again today. Hopefully Friday. Try to make it last.'

Bill looks at Izzy in consternation. They have nothing for the next three days but the bread ration, some marmalade and the lunchtime skilly. He doesn't blame the Nazis for their hunger; he blames Tucker. He tries to tell himself it's only three days; he can go without much food for three days, to protect Izzy.

As Bill and Izzy are leaving the washroom the next morning, with Bill carrying the newly scrubbed, empty apple tub in his arms, Tucker suddenly appears from round the corner of the hut, falling into step with them.

'Morning, all,' he says cheerfully.

The tall guard is a few metres away, watchful as ever. Bill knows that's why Tucker has chosen this place to talk to them. His grip on the apple tub tightens with anger.

'Bit of a bugger about the parcels,' continues Tucker.

Again Bill doesn't reply, but speeds up to get away from him as soon as possible. Tucker lollops alongside, just out of Izzy's sight-line.

'So I was thinking,' says Tucker, 'you'd better give me your bread ration, till the parcels come.'

Bill stops dead and drops the apple tub. 'You fucking bastard,' he says, squaring up to Tucker.

Tucker retreats a step, smiling and batting his cow-eyelashes. Izzy grabs Bill's arm and pulls him back.

Tucker laughs. 'Or I could just tell the goon now?'

He turns towards the approaching guard, who calls, 'What's going on here?', hardly able to keep the eagerness out of his voice.

'Nothing,' replies Bill, and the tall guard stoops over them, a little breathless, staring close into each face.

Tucker turns to him and clears his throat. 'Just that—'

Bill interrupts. 'You can have it.'

'Just that Cousins here is a . . .'

'I said you can have it.'

'. . . Chelsea supporter. I can't stand Chelsea supporters.'

He smiles at the guard and turns to walk away, sure that Bill won't try anything here.

The guard peers closely at Bill and then at Izzy. Blood rushes into Bill's face as he bends to pick up the apple tub, heavy even when empty. He'd like to hurl it at Tucker, but he doesn't.

'It'll be all right,' he says to Izzy as they walk away. He hopes he sounds convincing. 'We'll give him half, not all, the bread. We'll go a bit short today and tomorrow, but there'll be another parcel on Friday, and if we get one with fags we can give him those instead.'

It's odd how he can tell that she's seething with him for not refusing. She doesn't need to speak – there's something about the way she holds herself away from him and doesn't look him in the eye. But what can he do?

That night they split their remaining bread ration and leave half at the end of Bill's bed for Tucker. They fall asleep with their stomachs empty.

15

I wake each morning hollowed out by hunger, with terror crouched heavily on my chest. I lie for a moment, letting the panic wash over me, then force it down, control my breathing, until my heart rate slows to something like normal and I can raise my head to face the day. Bill can see my fear, but he smiles. 'Chin up.' And his eyes are so full of love that I forgive him for letting Tucker blackmail us. I know he's trying his best to protect me. We have to prepare ourselves to confront whatever may come, side-by-side. I try to leave the frightened Izzy in her bunk and take Cousins out into the compound.

A very particular worry has begun to haunt me. My last period began a week before our marriage, and we were on the run for ten days. I am regular as a clock, at twenty-eight days. I suppose there's a small chance I could be pregnant, but Bill was so careful. At best I have a few days before a red stain spreading over my trousers gives me away. Then Tucker's threats will be like hot air.

To my surprise, this doesn't send me into a depression. It's quite the opposite. Life has never felt so precious. I watch Bill covetously, as if trying to feed on every movement of his head, his lovely hands. I see the leaves on the birch trees beyond the wire beginning to turn yellow, or a jagged streak of gold above a black cloud, or my head jerks up at the waterfall notes of a blackbird's song. Everything is brighter and sharper than I've ever seen it, as if I'm saying a long goodbye to life.

Common sense tells me that I have only a few days left to live, but another part of my brain holds onto a thin hope that maybe I can get through this, and perhaps there will be a life for Bill and me after the war. I make up my mind I must live 'as if', or I might as well hand myself over right now. So all the long, long day and evening, I concentrate hard on listening to the conversations around me, trying to improve my English. In the endless hours in the hut, I eavesdrop as the men play cards or talk about everyday things: lice, socks, parcels, food.

Often the speech I hear about me is too fast to follow and I can't say, 'Stop, please. What means this "bollocks"?' I have no way of knowing which words are acceptable in company and which only among soldiers. How would it sound if I went to take tea with English ladies and spoke like a prisoner in a barrack room?

Bill continues to read *Great Expectations* with me. It's a very long book and I'll never discover how it turns out, because I have so few days left. But I let him rattle on about his own great expectations of our life in England after the war.

'We'll get a little house, in the same road as my mum and dad and Flora, so they can help you get settled. Of course we might have to live in the pub to start with, but there's plenty of room, and an indoor toilet. How funny it'll be to have you in my bed in my old bedroom!'

Tucker passes the end of the bunk as Bill's talking. Behind Bill's head, he licks his lips in a slow, revolting way and my stomach rumbles with hunger.

On Thursday I devour my lunchtime skilly and potato, like our farm dogs when we feed them. Gone in seconds. My stomach grinds and clenches, and there's nothing to distract me from thoughts of food. I thought I'd known before what it felt like to be hungry or weighed down by boredom, but I had no idea. So much that I didn't know.

Now that Ralph has encouraged Bill to leave me with him and Max, Bill's always asking if he can 'pop off for a jiffy' to play the piano or have a game of football or watch the cricket. I'm pleased that he can escape the horrible hut, but if I'm honest with myself, I also resent him being busy and occupied and taking his mind off the hunger.

I wonder if this is how it will be, if we ever reach England. Will he go out to work, to football, to play his music, and will I be at home, cleaning and cooking, no more free than my mother? Perhaps if I get to England, I should continue to pretend to be Cousins during the day – and be allowed to do all the things boys can do.

While Bill is out, Ralph is true to his word and starts to teach me Pitman shorthand. When he presents me with the small notebook of squared paper and a short pencil, I feel as if I've been given gifts of huge value, and I keep them carefully. I'm desperate to have something to occupy my mind, and find I like the discipline of the learning and repetition, but also the cleverness of a system that can be used in any language.

During our lesson Max heaves himself from his bed and announces he's going to the camp library.

'D'you want me to come with you?' asks Ralph eagerly, lay-ing down his pencil, but Max shakes his head and leaves without even replying. I think he's rather rude. Ralph covers a look of disappointment and turns back to me and Pitman, though his mind clearly isn't on our lesson any more.

Looking about him, at the relative emptiness of the hut, Ralph starts to whisper to me about Max, in staccato, anxious phrases. 'You know you've saved him, don't you?'

I don't know what he's talking about.

'Max. Your coming has saved his life. That's why I can never do enough for you.'

I wait and listen, and Ralph continues, as though my silence is a magnet, drawing the words out of him. 'Before you came, about six days before, Max had a letter. The letter every man here dreads getting. Fears more than the Nazis, really. A letter from his fiancée, Rachel – selfish bitch – telling him she'd got married. And not just that, but she'd married his brother. Can you imagine that? Max's own brother, stealing his fiancée while he's a prisoner of war. It's the lowest of the low. And Max just took to his bed. I've seen it before: young men, young fit men, just turn their faces to the wall and wait for death. I thought I'd lost him.'

Ralph struggles to control his emotion, deepening the furrow between his brows. He looks up at me.

'You don't know – you can't imagine – how different he was before. He's one of those people you love and hate together, because they do everything well. It's not just that he knows so much, but he's funny, really funny, and always calm and posi-tive, rallying everyone when they want to give up. So many people owe their lives to Max. And sporty too – not like me.

Before the war they wanted him to try out for a professional footballer, but he told them he wanted to be a writer.' Ralph shakes his head in amazement. 'He writes such incredible stuff. Poems, stories . . . anything. I thought he was sort of invincible, like a god, the one who'd always be there and know what to do. And then, when the letter came, he just kind of collapsed in on himself. Wouldn't read or write, or eat or leave his bed.'

He pauses, remembering.

'And then you came and, d'you see, it gave him something to live for. He's even gone back to the library and he's writing again. So I owe you everything, because if anything . . .'

I nod and fleetingly touch the back of Ralph's hand. I know. And I'm pleased he's told me, because now Max's erratic behaviour seems completely explicable. What would I do, if Bill had married someone else? I wouldn't want to live, either. I decide I'll try to think of little things I could do for Max.

When he returns from the library, I pass him a note. It says: *What are you reading?*

He looks surprised, and the jiggling in his leg stops for a moment, but he turns and shows me the two books. 'Tolstoy,' he says, 'though I'm surprised they let us read the Russians, if they think they're subhuman. And H. G. Wells' *History of the World.*'

He hands me the history book, which is surprisingly short. I turn it over and over. It seems I could learn everything from a university in this one book. I almost want to steal it from him. I write, *Can I read after?* and the constant jiggling in his leg slows.

'Are you interested in politics and history?'

I am now. I nod and Max smiles. It may be the first time I've seen him smile, and it makes him look less skull-like. His teeth are very white and even.

'OK. I'll read a chapter and then tell you about it. And when I've finished the book, you can have it. Deal?'

I think what Cousins might do, and hold out my hand to shake his. So my political education – and my mission to save Max – begins.

Every day that it's not in use, Bill goes to play the piano, and sometimes I trail along behind him. On Friday it's raining, and many men are drawn in by the music. The tall guard follows and stays, out of the rain. Then Bill starts to play tunes they know and everyone joins in, song after song, through all the long, wet afternoon.

Bill plays the nightingale song, and the one about dancing cheek to cheek, and I know these are for me. The tall guard is watching me not joining in, and I try to mouth the words I can remember, swivelling in my chair so that he can't see my face. His eyes bore into the back of my head.

By evening the parcels have arrived, and we have an American one with cigarettes. Bill corners Tucker and does a hasty deal. This week it's to be the fags, not the food. But I don't trust Tucker to keep to any deal.

One of the ways our hut tries to forget its hunger and boredom for an hour in the evening is for Ralph to have a 'film night', when he tells us the story of a movie – every detail, like he's seeing and hearing it in his head. One of these is called *The Lady Vanishes*, and I think: That's me.

Another way to pass the time is to hold debates. One is on the question of socialism after the war. The two sides are drawn up, with eloquent speakers for each. Max is the main speaker for socialism, and he's ardent for a new order.

'Remember the Battle of Cable Street,' he says to all the men who've drawn up to listen. 'How we defeated Mosley's Blackshirts. If the war hadn't come, we could have had a Nazi Party in England. But the people of the East End rose up and prevented them marching.'

I glance at Bill as Max speaks, wondering if he was part of this glorious battle against the fascists, but he's looking down at his shoes, and I can't read the expression on his face.

Max is in full flood. 'When this is over, there'll be no more lords and ladies while the working men starve. Public schools must be abolished, and everyone will have equal education. No more governments full of Eton men. No more doctors for the rich while the poor die of preventable diseases. The Great War changed nothing for the working man. This war must change life for everyone, or what's it been for?'

Bill looks up now and nods his agreement. There's thunderous applause when Max finishes. The man speaking against socialism has a difficult task, and his speech is answered by boos and catcalls as he tries to describe the worst excesses of Russian socialism. The men are not in a mood to hear this.

'The Russians are our allies,' someone shouts, 'dying in droves' and begins to stamp his feet. Others join in the rhythmic stamping, and Ralph, who's chairing the debate, has to hold up his hand for silence. When the hut quiets again, the man speaking against socialism finishes lamely, 'Of course we all want a better world, with the wealth shared out more fairly, but we have to guard against socialist totalitarianism as much as fascism.'

He sits down to a thin smattering of polite clapping. Everyone agrees that Max has won the debate, and the hut breaks up into excited discussion of the different life they will enjoy after the war.

Max comes and sits with us. 'Education's the key,' he says. 'I never went back to school after we left Brooklyn when I was fourteen.'

'I left school at fourteen too,' says Bill. 'Passed for grammar school, but my parents couldn't afford the uniform.'

Ralph chimes in, 'I only went to grammar school because I got a scholarship.' I think he's eager to show he is 'one of them', despite his better education. He continues, 'Manchester University is full of the most witless types who came from public schools, drinking themselves legless and hardly bothering to attend lectures, when lads like you two would really make use of the opportunity.'

'That's what I want,' confides Max. 'I wanna see if I can get a place at Ruskin College, study politics, so I really know what I'm talking about.'

Bill looks at him with wonder, obviously encountering ideas he's never heard before or even considered as possibilities.

The three of them continue until lights out, charged with excitement about the different world they will inhabit after the war. I wonder if it will be the same for girls. I wonder if I'll live to find out.

A few days later, two weeks after our arrival at Lamsdorf, I'm standing on the touchline, watching Bill play football, with Ralph alongside me. Tucker is across the pitch. His eyes fall on me, and he keeps looking as he picks his nose and eats the contents. Cousins stares through him, beyond him. The men nearest to us wander away, and Ralph speaks in a low voice, well hidden under the shouts of the crowd.

'I've got something to ask you,' he says. 'It's a bit delicate, and I hope you don't mind me asking. I had three sisters, you see; I was brought up in a house of women. And even my one year as a medic taught me some things. I've been wondering when your "monthly visitor" might be coming, and what you might need.' I look at him in surprise, and he ploughs on. 'I was wondering when you had your last menstrual period. "The curse", my sisters called it, or their monthlies.'

Měsíčky! He knows about *měsíčky*! I feel a blush spreading from my throat up my face, and he peeks sideways, satisfied that we understand each other. I glance at the guard, to see if he's noticed my blush, but now he's staring the other way.

I feel a huge wave of relief and gratitude to Ralph and his sisters. I'd been wondering if Englishmen know that such things exist, and how on Earth I could tell Bill. The hidden compartment at the bottom of my rucksack contains some of what I will need: the oilcloth sanitary belt and a few rags. The oilcloth belt was my mother's own invention, to prevent leakage.

'If I get you some rags, do you have the other things you need?' asks Ralph, and I nod my deep gratitude, but can't meet his eyes. 'You'll have to let me know, I'm afraid, so we can shield you in the washroom.'

I nod again, feeling my face as red as if I was sunburned.

'We'll have a signal.' He's obviously thought this through. 'You come to me and lay your hand flat on your stomach.' He demonstrates. 'Got it?'

I lay my right hand on my tummy, where the pain will be, to show I have understood. He glances down at my hand.

'Good. I'll tell Bill what we've agreed. It'll be all right. It will.' He sounds as if he is trying to convince himself as much as me.

He turns his attention to the football, and we both watch as

Bill runs the ball down the far side of the pitch with his long, graceful stride. My deep blush slowly subsides.

It has to be all right. It has to be.

The day after Ralph spoke to me about the 'monthlies', Bill shyly hands me a neat pile of cut-up strips of rag. They are some of the *fuss-lag*, worn by men who haven't got socks – donations from the men who know our secret. I am horrified that my shame must be so public, but full of gratitude for their unselfish generosity. I wonder whose feet will be cold or blistered as a consequence. Not Tucker's, I'm sure. Bill's face is half-shamed, half-pleased, and my relief must be evident. This will be enough to see me through.

That night after dark, and under my blanket, I pull on the sanitary belt, lined with some of the rags. It's not a day too soon. In the morning I wake with the familiar cramp. As soon as I'm able, I signal to Ralph with the flat of my hand on my stomach, and he nods encouragement. The cramps are as bad as I've ever known and I have to stand still for two hours at the roll call, feeling the dragging sensation, the hot wetness, the grinding pain, and letting none of it show on my face. I try to think that I'm Cousins, with a stomach wound inflicted by the guards. He doesn't want to give them the satisfaction of knowing how much they've hurt him. I raise my head and stare beyond the wire, hands deep in my pockets, gripping my fists tight against the pain.

Bill sits in the hut with me most of the day, and it passes with excruciating slowness, one minute creeping after another. There's only so many hours a day that Bill can read to me. Sometimes he wanders off to play cards, and I lie on my bunk. I try to sleep to pass the time. We are both miserable and edgy.

The evening is the most terrifying of all, as I crouch at the furthest tap in the washroom, scrubbing blood from my used rags and watching it run down into the drain. Bill, Scotty, Max and Ralph casually arrange themselves around me. So much blood. It looks as if I've committed a murder.

The morning is easier, as I can wash my rags as I clean out the apple tub, but each evening my shame is there for anyone to see – a red accusation swirling away.

My friends position themselves carefully between the doorway and me, to prevent me from being caught at my humiliating task. I know I'll never be able to repay the kindness of the twenty men who hide me. Back in the hut, I hang the rags to dry from the slats on the underside of the still-empty top bunk.

On the evening of the fourth day of my monthlies I'm crouched as usual in my spot nearest the drain. The cold water has turned my hands almost as red as the blood running from the rags. I try to use my body to hide what I'm doing, but as the last stain washes away, I hear Bill's warning whistle and look up.

The tall guard is sauntering towards me, pushing Ralph and Max out of the way. He has the look on his face of one of our dogs when it scents a rat.

I look down and quickly wring out the rags. Scotty and one of the other men from our hut start a staged argument near the door, and the guard glances round at them, but they're not as interesting to him as me, and what I'm doing.

He comes and stands by me, and my legs begin to shake. His boots gleam. I squeeze the last water out of the rags and use one hand to push myself to a standing position. I'm trembling so much that I have to hold the pipe for support.

'What's going on here?' the guard asks.

Ralph replies casually in German, 'Some of the men pay him cigarettes to wash their foot-rags. Filthy job!'

The guard uses the end of his rifle to lift my left hand with the dripping rags.

'Why is he so ashamed?'

I'm amazed that Ralph can answer so casually. 'It's dirty work, I suppose, for a few fags. I wouldn't do it!'

The guard stares at me, and I stare back, as Cousins might, though my knees are like water. At last he sneers, 'All right, little washerwoman, you can wash my *fuss-lag* too!'

He considers me for another long moment before he turns away to Scotty, who's escalating his play-argument into a mock fight.

Ralph goes with him to break up the 'fight', and Bill comes round behind me.

'You want to give up smoking,' he says loudly. 'Then you wouldn't have to do this.' He takes the wet rags from me and begins to wring them out. 'What you need is a mangle.'

As he touches my hand he can feel the shaking that rattles my bones. I lean back against the wall as waves of sickness overcome me.

'Let's have a brew,' he says, and leads the way out of the washroom.

When we get back to the hut, he sits me on his bunk. My hands are like ice and he rubs them between his. I pull them away and sit on them. What if one of the men sees who isn't in on our secret?

'Come on, duck,' he says gently, though there's a tremor in his voice. 'I'll make you a nice cup of tea. Lots of sugar this time. That'll make you feel better. You'll see. Then we'll hang out these *fuss-lag* to dry.'

For once the sweet tea tastes good, and as I drink it, the shivering begins to diminish, although the thought of having to wash more rags tomorrow night fills me with dread. At least it will be stopping soon. One more day perhaps. I pray, 'Make the bleeding stop.'

This evening most of the men are out of the hut at an event. While Bill is busy with the blower, Tucker stops by our bunk, touching a can of pears that he wants us to leave for him that night. He glances over at Bill, who is out of earshot, and turns to me. 'What else've you got for me, then?' he whispers. 'Something hidden away? Bill won't notice.'

I start to shake my head vigorously, as if shaking could rid myself of the sound of his whiny voice saying, 'I'm too famished to keep this secret any longer. I bet the guards would have fun with you and reward me with a slap-up dinner.'

It infuriates me that so many men in this hut are risking every-thing each day to protect me, to hide me, while this pig is daring to threaten me. I gesture him away angrily, and Tucker picks up the tin of pears and slips it into his pocket.

'If you can't find me something better than this, I'll have a little word with the commandant at roll call tonight.'

This time the hard edge in his voice tells me it isn't another of his threats. He really means to do it. I watch Tucker saunter away and fury builds in me, like steam in a kettle. I won't allow him to destroy me. When he stops to talk to Ralph and Max, I slip out towards Scotty's bed and feel under the picture for his pocket-knife.

Pushing myself between Ralph and Max, I face Tucker. With a swift movement I pull out the knife and Tucker jumps back, assuming I'm going to attack him, but instead I hold it to my own throat. Grabbing his hand, I wrap it around mine, making him press the cold blade to my skin. My eyes bore into his.

'Do it, then,' I hiss. 'Big man. Kill me.'

Tucker looks terrified and tries to pull his hand away. He doesn't want to cut my throat, though he'd be happy to let someone else do it. Ralph and Max yank us apart. Bill hurls himself towards us over Ralph's bed, scattering parcel contents.

Ralph grabs hold of my hand with the knife, while Max and Bill grip Tucker, with his arms behind his back. Some people look up at the noise of a scuffle, but they see Ralph has it under control and lose interest.

'Cousins,' whispers Ralph urgently, 'what's going on?'

I nod to Bill. I've done my speaking, made my point.

Bill shakes Tucker's arm and, without loosening his grip, he whispers, 'This bastard's been blackmailing us ever since we arrived.' He punctuates his points by twisting Tucker's arm more and more. 'Taking food. Threatening to tell the goons about Cousins, if we don't let him. Threatening to tell them, if we came to you. I didn't know what to do.'

So swiftly that I think I must have imagined it, Max brings his knee up into Tucker's groin and he doubles over in pain. 'You fucking, wanking coward. You would've murdered her in cold blood.'

Ralph puts out a warning hand – 'Max!' – and Max suddenly lets go of Tucker. Bill releases him too, so that he falls on the floor between the bunks with both hands nursing his testicles.

Ralph bends over him. 'Do you know what would happen if I told the rest of the men what you've been doing, you filthy, miserable little rat?'

Tucker peeps up, his face scrunched with pain. 'Don't tell 'em. Don't tell 'em. I'll go to another hut. Skedaddle, like.'

'No, you won't. You'll stay here, and I'll put a watch on you.

There won't be a moment of the night or day where we haven't got our eyes on you. And you'd better keep as quiet as Cousins, or I'll let the rest of the hut tear you apart.'

Tucker is nodding like a clockwork toy. 'Don't tell Scotty, will you? Please. He'll . . .'

Ralph puts his face very close to Tucker's. 'He'll what? Kill you? Like you were prepared to do to Cousins? I'm very, very tempted.'

He and Max pull Tucker to his feet and frog-march him back to his own bunk. Ralph moves off to speak to some other men, and immediately two of them station themselves alongside Tucker's bunk. Tucker shrinks into the shadows of his bed.

I'm still boiling with anger. Bill reaches a hand to steady me. 'Are you OK? You're so brave.'

But what I did was pure fury, and I see now that it could have gone horribly wrong. More of the rash risk-taking I'd promised myself I would stop. I wave the folded knife at Bill and return it to its hiding place behind Scotty's picture. I've just turned away when Scotty comes back into the hut. Ralph nods to me, and I know that he'll explain what's happened and make sure Scotty finds a new hiding place for the knife.

Bill picks up the possessions that he sent flying as he leapt across the bed to save me. With everything gathered, he looks up at me and grins. 'It was nice to hear your voice,' he says. 'I'd almost forgotten how scary you sound.'

16

'We can't stay here,' Bill blurts out to Ralph and Max later that evening. 'I need to get Cousins to another hut.'

Ralph takes off his glasses and polishes them thoughtfully, hooking them back behind his ears. 'You're right,' he says. 'It's too dangerous here. But we might all be even better in a labour camp. There'd be fewer guards.'

Bill is nodding furiously, and I remember how lightly he was guarded at the Mankendorf sawmill and on our farm. It would be a huge relief to be somewhere like that.

Max joins in. 'Maybe we could find an *Arbeitskommandos* in Czechoslovakia,' he says quietly. 'There we might even have some chance of getting word out to the resistance.'

My heart leaps at the thought that my father or my brother might come at last to rescue me, and I grip Bill's hand. I don't know how hard it would be to hide my monthlies at a labour camp, but I do know that I don't want to be here when it happens again. And I want to be as far from Tucker as possible. Even under guard, I know he can't be trusted.

Ralph says, 'Just one thing. I couldn't bear to go down a mine.

Anything else, but not a mine. I wouldn't last five minutes in a confined space.'

I'm pleased they're all in agreement that we shouldn't go down a mine. My sight of the sky every day gives me hope. I know my mother and father could be looking up and seeing the same sun and clouds, and it makes me feel connected to them. I don't know if I could go on living in darkness.

Scotty sees our whispered conversation and comes over. He stands awkwardly, twisting his cap in his hands. 'If youse going for a work detail, I'd be glad to come with you, if ye'll have me.'

We all look at one another and nod. There would be something very reassuring about having someone on our side who has the reputation of knowing how to handle himself in a fight.

The next morning, instead of our usual walk around the perimeter fence, the five of us head for the hut that acts as a labour exchange, handling requests for workers in a huge radius around Lamsdorf. On the way, Max tells me there are 600 *Arbeitskommandos* labour camps connected with Lamsdorf, with British prisoners working for them. He says the Nazis aren't supposed to send us to munitions factories or anything else that directly helps the war effort, but it's well known that they do.

As we walk, I start to notice a curious, acrid smell in the air, and see men all around us lifting their noses to smell, and shaking their heads at one another.

'Wind's changed direction,' says Ralph.

I look at Bill. Does he know what this awful smell might be? He and Ralph and Scotty avoid my eyes, but Max falls in beside me as we walk.

'The smell?' he asks, and I nod. Max won't mince his words.

'The rumour is it comes from the camp where they take the Jews and the Gypsies. They say it's the smell of thousands of burning bodies. Women and children who aren't any use in the labour camps.'

I stand stock-still and look at Max. My own horror is mirrored in his face. Can this possibly be true? Could even the Nazis do this to other human beings? Fury surges up in me and I start walking again, fast, overtaking Ralph, Scotty and Bill. The three of them hurry to keep up with me and we pass other groups of men sauntering around the perimeter.

'What's the rush?' they call. 'Got a bus to catch?'

But I'm blind with rage at the world, the war, this cruelty beyond anything I could imagine. I want to run at the wire, to shake and shake it, screaming my anger, but all I can do is walk and walk, faster and faster, not knowing where I'm going, just desperate to escape from this terrible charnel house of a place. Ralph falls a little behind and Max drops back with him, but Bill and Scotty keep pace with me, circling and circling the huts, until eventually I start to slow down and allow Ralph and Max to catch up with us.

I hear Bill say to Max, 'You shouldn't have told him', and I turn on Bill with my eyes flashing.

Bill holds his hands up. 'Sorry, sorry. Yes, of course you have to know. It's just so awful, I wanted to spare you.'

'We have to stay alive and get out of here,' says Ralph. 'We have to live and tell the world what we know.' I'm sure he's talking to Max.

The 'labour exchange' is a hut set aside to match prisoners with suitable *Arbeitskommandos* work camps, and now I see for myself how the Third Reich exists on the slave labour of its captured enemies.

The hut is staffed by two 'trusted men', one British and one Australian. There are lists on the walls of the hundreds of factories, mines and quarries that are looking for workers.

'Ready to make yourselves useful to the Reich?' asks the Aussie.

Bill says, 'We hear Czechoslovakia is very nice at this time of year.'

The Aussie pulls a card index towards him.

'Not mines,' says Ralph. 'I'm claustrophobic. I'd scream the roof down.'

'Experience?' asks the Aussie.

'I've worked in a sawmill before,' says Bill, 'and done sledge-building and farmwork.' He indicates me. 'He's a dab hand with 'orses.'

'Not much agricultural work at this time of year,' says the Aussie. 'What about you two? What can you do?'

'Book-keeping, and I can speak German,' Ralph says.

The Aussie writes something down as Max says, 'I can organise a trade union.'

The Aussie's eyebrows raise. 'Hmm, better not advertise that.'

Scotty says, 'I've worked in a quarry, a shipyard, a milliner's and a biscuit factory. We'd prefer a biscuit factory, if youse got one.'

Everyone laughs, but I look at him with new interest.

The Aussie pulls a card from his index. 'Here's something. Not a biscuit factory. Saubsdorf quarry. E166. Jeseník district, Olomouc region. Wants five new men.'

He pronounces Jeseník with a j for 'jam', not a y for 'yes', so it takes me a moment to recognise where he means. Then my heart leaps. I'll be back in my own country! It will be so beautiful in the mountains. Surely that's where the resistance is hiding.

The Aussie scrutinises us carefully, and I see us with fresh eyes: Bill, thin but wiry; me, small for a man and skinny now, after a month without my mother's cooking and only half our parcel ration; Max, like a skeleton, full of nervous energy; Ralph, bespectacled and somehow feminine; Scotty, square and tough.

'It's hard graft. Are you sure you're up to it?'

'We'll just have a powwow,' says Ralph and we withdraw to a corner of the hut for a whispered conversation.

Scotty says, 'Heavy work in a quarry.'

Ralph indicates me, asking Bill, 'Can he manage it?'

Bill searches my eyes anxiously, reading my eagerness, before he says, 'Anywhere's better than here, and he's stronger than you'd think. We can cover for him maybe, or get him work in the office, once we're there.'

And so it's agreed. We'll go to Saubsdorf quarry. I'll be home in Czechoslovakia again and might even be able to send a message to my mother.

The Aussie completes the paperwork and hands us each a chit.

'You need to pack up your gear and transfer to the *Arbeits* compound till we can get you transport. Shouldn't be more than a day or two.'

On the way back to our hut I feel as if I'm flying. I'm going back to my homeland, where we can easily escape and find the partisans. My happiness must be apparent, because Bill and the others smile indulgently whenever they catch my eye.

We begin to pack our small possessions into our kit-bags, and the trusted men in our hut come over in ones and twos to wish us luck.

They all shake my hand vigorously, and some whisper things that make tears prickle the back of my eyes.

'I'd just about given up hope till you came.'

'If you can do it, we all can.'

'It gave me something to focus on, having you here. A purpose. I'll miss you.'

'I think we can make it, now I've met you.'

I can hardly believe Bill and I have been at Lamsdorf for less than a month. It feels like a lifetime. I wonder if I might miss the familiarity of Bert's thunderous snores, Chalky cracking his knuckles, even Harold cleaning his ears with his fingers. I look over at Tucker's bed, but he isn't there, and I feel a rush of panic.

Ralph notices my leap of fear and says, 'I promise he's under guard. They won't let him tell.'

We pull on our coats, shoulder our kit-bags, drape our blankets around us and carry the precious remains of the last Red Cross parcels in our hands as we wave goodbye.

We have to pass out through one layer of the perimeter fence to the *Arbeits* compound and show our chits to the guard.

The tall guard from the latrine is on duty here today, picking his nails with the fingers of the other hand. Bored. He brightens up as we approach and tells us to halt. I don't like the enthusiasm with which he searches our meagre belongings; he's enjoying it all too much. He makes a great play of opening each of our kit-bags and looking inside, of poking his fingers into some of our open tins, as if searching for something, licking his fingers and then shoving them into more of our food. And then, as I knew he would, he turns to me.

'So our little washerwoman is going away,' he says in German.

Bill and Scotty stir nervously, but Ralph holds out a warning hand as the guard circles slowly, looking down at me.

'There was always something that bothered me about you,'

he goes on. 'I never believed that story about you being *stumm*.' He pauses in his circling and then, without warning, brings the butt of his rifle crashing down onto the instep of my right foot. I can't help gasping at the pain and doubling over to grip my foot, but no words escape me. Ralph and Max are holding Bill firmly, and he mutters a stream of invective, but the guard ignores him.

I straighten up, and this time I'm not feeling Izzy's ungovernable temper, but Cousins' stony resistance in the face of bullying. The guard looks disappointed that he hasn't made me speak, but I am Cousins to my very core, staring straight into his face and silently mouthing, 'Fuck off!' at him, my right arm shooting up in the two-fingered gesture, holding it close to his nose.

The guard glowers at me and my fingers. This could land me in solitary, while Bill goes off to the work camp without me. But to my astonishment, the guard laughs. 'Go on, then – go and be mute down the mines,' he says and waves us through.

I limp towards the second set of perimeter wire, and we show our chits to a new guard, in charge of the *Arbeits* compound. The gate's locked behind us and we are led to our new hut. As we'll be here only for a couple of days, my friends have decided not to tell anybody my secret.

I have a moment of terror when I realise that the empty bunk beds are scattered throughout the hut, but there are two free spaces on adjoining bunks, and Bill and I take those. The straw mattresses are old and flattened. This time we are deep in the forest of bunk beds, with men all around us. I must be even more careful to keep absolute silence. Bill explains again to the prisoners immediately around us that I'm mute from shell-shock. 'He kind of tags along with me, since I found him.' Bill shrugs.

They look curiously at me for a moment and then return to whatever was occupying their attention before, and I breathe again.

At roll call the next morning a guard calls the names of those who will be leaving, and ours are not among them, so we have a whole day to fill without the distractions of the main camp. I pad my boot before lacing it, and I'm able to join the others walking around the compound wire a few times, like tigers in a zoo, carrying all our possessions in our kit-bags. We stop to watch a line of people being marched up from the railway station, towards the Russian camp, just beyond the woods. They pass close to the wire at this point and Ralph says, 'Oh God, look at them.'

The Russian soldiers are bearded and filthy, and their greatcoats hang off them in a way that makes it clear their bodies inside have shrunk to bags of bones. Some of them are barefoot, and their feet are lacerated and bleeding. One stumbles and his companion lifts him back onto his feet. The Nazi guards prod them with rifles and scream abuse at them, as if they are cattle being rounded up.

Max whispers, 'Hitler's classified them as *Untermenschen* — subhuman. Stalin didn't sign the Geneva Convention, so they can do what they like to the Russians.'

Bill swings his kit-bag off his shoulder and reaches inside for today's bread ration. Breaking it into three pieces, he throws the pieces over the barbed wire. The Russians catch the pieces and push them whole into their mouths. I open my pack too, intending to do the same, but the guards have spotted us.

'Stop that! Move away from the wire or I'll shoot. These animals don't deserve your good German bread.'

We start to move backwards as soon as the shouting starts, instinctively saving ourselves.

'Move away, or you'll have a month in the cooler.'

We retreat to a safe distance, but continue to watch the line of hopeless Russians shuffling past us. How can God let this happen? Is God even watching. Is he even there? I turn away from the others and cross myself to protect me from Cousins' blasphemous thoughts, and we trudge back to our hut in silence.

The next morning the tall guard comes to the wire with a hand-written message for Ralph from one of our friends in Hut 17. Ralph cleans his glasses, then reads aloud, 'Listen, everyone, it says: *Tucker found dead in his bed. The doc says rat poison in his food.*'

I clap my hand over my mouth, as relief washes through me.

'Good riddance,' says Bill, not meeting my eyes.

Did Bill do this? Is my gentle husband capable of killing a man to defend me?

Scotty slaps his thigh with delight. 'Rat poison!' He might have done it perhaps, but he looks too amused to be a murderer.

Not Ralph, I'm sure it wouldn't be Ralph. He says, 'All his tins had already been pierced, and everyone knows there's rat poison under the huts. It would have been the work of a minute. But who could have done it?'

Max exhales. 'Talk about the punishment fitting the crime.'

I think it might have been him.

Him, or Scotty, or Bill.

I wish it had been me.

We spend five interminable, second-ticking days in the *Arbeits* compound and I have to grip myself tight in frustration at the forced idleness. Only Cousins keeps me under control, telling me, 'Easy now, easy now.' And I've begun to itch – in my groin, under my arms and up into the back of my hair. It seems these mattresses are harbouring lice.

It's raining hard at roll call and I've almost given up hope of our names being called when I hear, 'Sergeant Ralph Maddox, Bombardier William King, Private Algernon Cousins, Private Maximilian Greenberg, Private Alistair Forsyth . . . report to the gate at ten a.m.'

We visit the latrine. I've been careful to have only sips of mint tea this morning, not knowing how long it will be until I can safely relieve myself again. We present ourselves at the massive gates with the Nazi eagle over them. Outside is the world. Poland. There are about another thirty prisoners gathered with us.

Our travel documents are studied, the gates are opened and we walk through, away from the hated watchtowers and sentries. Already the air smells different to me, rich with the must of autumn, as we march along the road towards the station. Here the trees are close enough to hear the wind in the leaves, and I'm looking about me all the time as we walk, at the different shades of green in the pines, at the birch leaves' gold and bronze. There's a scattering of bright-yellow leaves on the path and they swirl up in eddies as we pass.

Two guards line us up on the platform in front of the ticket office. There's something so utterly normal in seeing civilians buying tickets for a train and waiting on the platform alongside us, that I want to hug Bill with excitement. But my eagerness dwindles as we wait one hour and then another, and are finally allowed to sit down on the cold platform.

A goods train pulls in across the tracks from us, and the massive doors of the sealed waggons are pulled back to reveal hundreds of captured Russian troops crammed into the trucks. They stumble down from the train, supporting one another. They have many days' growth of beard and look half-dead with exhaustion and starvation. We look at each other in silent shock, and our mood is further depressed.

After we wait three hours, another train pulls into the station.

As Ralph predicted, we are loaded into a cattle truck, but there are only about thirty of us, so there's room to sit on the dirty straw. The big doors are slammed shut and I have a moment of panic that we may just be left to suffocate here, in the dark, but then my eyes adjust to the gloom and I realise that a trickle of light is seeping through air holes. With a lurch the train moves off and, despite the discomfort, joy rises in me again as we leave the camp behind. The train moves so slowly that it would be possible to walk faster, and after a while I doze, lulled by the movement. After a few hours the train stops, and we hope we've arrived somewhere.

'Must be in a siding,' Bill concludes, trying to look out through a small slit. 'I can't see anything,' he reports. 'Just trees.'

Finally we move again, and just as I think the journey will go on for ever, or maybe we've all died and this is the train through purgatory, we stop and the doors are hurled open. Clean air rushes in, and we throw up our arms to cover our eyes. As we jump down from the train, someone can't find a haversack of food, and it seems it's been stolen by another prisoner in the dark. I am disgusted that prisoners steal from their own countrymen.

A jowly, red-faced postern calls our names and we five separate ourselves from the other Lamsdorf prisoners. Our documents are checked, and the postern tells us to move to the other end of the platform. He gives Bill and Scotty a good poke in the back with his rifle butt and says, in German, 'Don't think you can try anything because I'm not regular army. You bastard English killed my brother.'

As we wait, Bill and I share a slice of bread and the last of the Spam. The meat is luke-warm, and I wonder if it's safe to eat, but we wolf it down all the same. The men discuss having a brew, but decide it would be too tricky, if our train suddenly arrived.

Another train pulls into the station, and this time we aren't loaded onto a cattle truck, but allowed into a third-class carriage. Bill is fizzing with excitement as we load our kit-bags and parcels into the luggage racks. He and Ralph have had long conversations about train journeys.

'Add this one to the list.' He beams at Ralph.

We sit on the wooden benches and watch the countryside fly past. It's wonderful to be able to see as far as the horizon, to see farms working just as usual, animals grazing in fields, late crops still waiting to be harvested. The guard in the corner doesn't bother us one bit. We are having a day out, a holiday! It feels like freedom, to be out and moving. Ordinary people pass our carriage in the corridor and look in, some with sympathy, others with curiosity, but one woman spits on the glass.

Our train passes from the flat lands of Poland into the Jeseník Mountains, climbing and climbing. Now there are no more birch trees, but only evergreen pines, with their broad branches spreading, ready to take the snows of winter.

Eventually our train arrives at Saubsdorf. We are in the Czech region of Silesia, where many of the people speak German, just as they did at home. Outside the station is a waiting cart drawn by two big horses.

I pat the nose of one of them as the postern hands us over to a middle-aged civilian wearing a well-cut green coat and a Bavarian hat. He is armed with a small pistol.

The civilian eyes us all as we climb into the back of the cart, and addresses us in German with a strong Czech accent. 'I am Herr Rauchbach, the owner of the Saubsdorf quarry.'

I hope his first loyalty might be to Czechoslovakia rather than the Third Reich.

Ralph translates for Bill, Max and Scotty, and replies to Herr Rauchbach in German, saying we are good workers who are eager to increase the productivity of his quarry.

As Ralph makes his little speech, Herr Rauchbach appraises us with his dark, deep-set eyes. He raises his eyebrows and nods, then clambers up beside the powerfully built younger man holding the reins of the horses. My stomach lurches as he speaks to him in my beloved Czech. 'This lot looks even worse than the last. Half-starved city types and a skinny boy.'

The skinny boy must be me!

The horse driver swivels in his seat to look back at us as Herr Rauchbach continues, 'Let's just take them to the main quarry and get some stronger men from there for Supíkovice.'

His companion looks me slowly up and down and smiles a thin, humourless smile. He says, 'Then it will be dark, and we'll have to start again in the morning.' He too speaks Czech with a Silesian accent, as though his first language is German. He's almost handsome, in a square-jawed, thick-necked way, but has none of Herr Rauchbach's intelligence in his face.

Herr Rauchbach clicks his tongue with impatience. 'Yes, yes, very well, Kurt. If they aren't any good, we'll take them to Saubsdorf in a few days. Do what you can with them. But don't push them too hard to start.'

Kurt touches the horses lightly with the whip and we are off, further up into the forests and mountains, far, far away from Lamsdorf.

PART THREE

SUPÍKOVICE QUARRY, OCCUPIED
CZECHOSLOVAKIA

October 1944 to January 1945

17

Bill and Izzy are thrown against each other like sacks of corn as the horses trot from the railway station to the quarry. Late-October dusk is descending fast as the cart rattles over potholes in the road. Herr Rauchbach and Kurt have their backs to the prisoners as they drive, although Kurt turns from time to time and waves his pistol. Bill has seen too many trigger-happy young men before, and this makes him nervous.

The floor of the cart is hard and filled with a white dust that coats everyone's clothes. They try to sit on their kit-bags, but are constantly thrown off them, and Bill can feel bruises blooming on his bony bottom and legs. He fears it will be the same for Izzy. As daylight slowly departs, the cold mountain air begins to penetrate their clothes. With difficulty, they haul their blankets out from beneath them and wrap themselves. Izzy huddles against Bill, though he can't imagine that any warmth comes from him.

When he glances down at her, he can see that despite the cold and discomfort she's gazing around her with undisguised delight at the beauty of the mountains in the deepening twilight. Peaks and crags and the spiky outlines of pine trees are silhouetted in black against an indigo sky. Izzy feels Bill's eyes on her and gives him a wide smile. He grins at her just as Kurt turns again, taking in their happiness and closeness. Kurt stares hard at Izzy in a way that makes Bill feel uneasy, and he feels her stiffen and drop her head. In a moment, Kurt has his back turned to them, driving the horses forward and talking in a low voice to Herr Rauchbach in Czech. Bill wonders if Izzy can make out what they are saying, over the clattering of the hooves and the whir of the wheels on the road.

It's completely dark by the time they arrive at the quarry. The horses are walking slowly, and great clouds of steam rise from their noses as they haul the cart up the steep hill towards the shadowy buildings. Kurt jumps down and runs round to let down the tailgate, motioning all of them to climb down, waving his gun in a dangerous way.

The five prisoners gather their belongings from the cart in the darkness and clutch them as they walk up to the buildings. Bill notices there isn't any wire fencing. To the right of them is a stone house, but they enter through the adjoining single-storey timber-framed extension. Bill hopes they won't be sleeping in it, as there would be little insulation to keep it warm in the winter. But it's not sleeping quarters. Inside is a messy office, with piles of papers and an unlit cast-iron stove.

Herr Rauchbach leads them through the office and unbolts the door into the stone house. Kurt brings up the rear. As they take off their hats in the hallway, Bill can see Kurt's hair is a dirty blond and prematurely receding, while the owner has a firm dark hairline. He doesn't think they are father and son.

Just off the dark hallway is a room with three bunk beds, but they are ushered past it, through to the rear of the house, where the warmth of a kitchen range and the strong smell of cabbage and cigarette smoke welcome them.

They drop their bags and blankets in a heap and shuffle forward. It looks a bit like Izzy's farmhouse kitchen, thinks Bill, with a deep sink, a range and a large table with about ten chairs, all occupied by British prisoners in khaki battledress. One of them stands up.

'Welcome t'otel,' he says, and holds out his hand. 'Johnson, Frank.'

Ralph steps forward and shakes his hand. 'Maddox. Ralph.' He ushers Izzy forward. 'And this is Cousins; doesn't speak, I'm afraid, but a good worker.' Frank looks her up and down doubtfully. The introductions to Bill, Max and Scotty are completed and the five newcomers gravitate towards the warmth of the range.

Herr Rauchbach says something in German, and Ralph translates. 'He's going now. We have to be ready for work as soon as it's light at seven a.m. Kurt will come to lock the doors.'

They listen to Herr Rauchbach and Kurt walk back down the hallway and, once they are out of the door, the bolt thunks back into place.

One of the other prisoners has moved to a big cauldron on the range.

'Is there any left?' Frank asks him.

'Should be enough,' he replies.

Bill and the others tuck in eagerly to bowls of steaming cabbage soup. He thinks it tastes wonderful, much better than the Lamsdorf skilly; it has lumps of potato and turnip in it and, once, a small square of rabbit meat. He turns to his kit-bag for the remains of their last parcel, to supplement the meal.

Frank eyes the parcel food enviously. 'The parcels are a bit slow getting through here,' he says, 'but Rauchbach feeds us better than a camp. Lots of spuds, and meat once a week.'

He has a strong Yorkshire accent, and he and Ralph make a joke about the Wars of the Roses and God's own county. Bill asks about the cricket. He notices Frank has a habit of repeating what someone else has said, as if making their thought his own. There's some talk about Lamsdorf and the camps where each of them has been imprisoned before coming here. Bill is trying to work out whether to trust these new men with their secret. He thinks he'll wait a little longer.

Ralph wipes his lips with the back of his hand. 'What's the boss like?'

Frank crosses to the door into the hallway and closes it.

'He's a good boss. Very fair. I don't think he's a fan of the Reich, but he plays the game. The work in the main quarry is hard – ten hours a day – and he has lots of orders to complete, with not enough time. That's why he's reopened this small offshoot to the main Saubsdorf quarry. But he's not a bad man. It's his sidekick, Kurt, you have to watch out for. Vicious streak. And you younger men shouldn't be alone with him, if you know what I mean.'

He nods significantly to Izzy, and she bends her head to show she's understood. Bill wonders uneasily if he's put her in even more danger, bringing her here. Ralph studies the floor.

'Rauchbach's daughter, Rosa, works in the office here,' Frank continues. 'That wooden building you came through. Lovely girl. Very sympathetic. She works as a translator. German, Czech and a bit of English. And we have a cook. And some Czech women take our washing and bring us black-market stuff, if we have cigs to spare. So could be worse.'

'At night?' asks Bill.

'At night? We've got three rooms. I'll show you in a minute. There's seventeen of us here now, including you five. Two bedrooms upstairs and one downstairs. Double bunks. We've all moved upstairs, knowing you were coming, so you can have the downstairs room. Not the best, I'm afraid – the one by the door as you come in, but next to the kitchen. Though don't get excited. The cupboards are bare.'

Bill thinks the upstairs rooms must be warmer.

Frank gestures to the empty shelves, where jars of jams and pickles should be laid up for the winter, and continues, 'Wooden bunks. The usual. And out there' – he indicates another door – 'is the latrine and washroom, in a hut. After we've used that at night, we have to leave our trousers and boots in there. Bit of a cold run back across the yard. I've got pyjamas, which I take in with me. And then Kurt locks us in. Bars at the windows, of course. Jam jars for the night-necessaries.' He shrugs.

As if summoned by the mention of his name, Kurt opens the door from the yard and steps into the kitchen. He points to the new arrivals and says something in German.

Ralph translates with an apologetic shrug. 'Last chance to use the "shitter", apparently.' He politely thanks Kurt in German, then turns to his friends. 'Let's get our pyjamas and recce the facilities.'

They follow Kurt down a few steps into the yard, where a long wooden shack is opened for them. At one end is the usual bench with holes in it, and closer to the door are three large sinks with taps above them. There aren't any showers. It seems this is where they must all wash off the dirt of the quarry. The washrooms aren't as clean as those at Lamsdorf and have no heating. Bill thinks the taps will freeze in winter.

Kurt isn't keen to stay in the smelly washroom, so at least they have the relative privacy of just the five of them. It's better than the forty-hole latrine at Lamsdorf. Bill is grateful to the others, who 'about-turn' as Izzy uses the latrine, loudly discussing the journey to cover her embarrassment, and who look away as she takes off her trousers and pulls on her brother's pyjamas.

When they are dressed, in an assortment of pyjama bottoms and long winter underwear, they add their boots and trousers to the large pile on the concrete floor. Bill thinks they'll be very cold to put back on in the morning. He wonders again if this has all been a terrible mistake and they should have stayed at Lamsdorf, especially now Tucker is dead. They run back to the kitchen in their stockinged feet. Kurt locks and bolts the back door from outside.

'Come on. I'll show you to your room,' says Frank. Bill, Izzy and Ralph follow him, leaving Max and Scotty in the kitchen, talking to the other prisoners.

Bill decides their bedroom must have been a front parlour when the building was used as a house, and it's cold compared with the kitchen. There's a wood burner in the fireplace, but it's not alight.

Three sets of double bunk beds have been placed against the walls, and there's a small table under the window, beneath a dim light bulb. Thin gingham curtains hang at the window and give an odd cheerfulness to the little room, despite the bars at the window. It's crowded for five people to sleep in, but it's a proper room, in a house, and there are only five of them to share, so compared to nearly a hundred in the hut at Lamsdorf, it feels like a kind of luxury.

Moments later Kurt is back, staring into the bedroom at them in their pyjama bottoms, picking out Izzy, who pretends to be busy shaking out a blanket.

Finally Kurt turns away, and they hear the interconnecting door close and the sound of a key being turned, before heavy bolts slide into place on the other side. Kurt is gone, but they are locked in like rats in a trap. Bill thinks if there was a fire, he'd never be able to save Izzy. It wouldn't only be Tucker who'd die like a rat. Ruefully he realises that until he met Izzy, he never worried about much except his next meal. Now worry is his constant companion.

'Safe and sound,' says Frank, popping his head round the door. 'Is there anything else you need?'

'Nothing, thanks,' says Ralph.

Frank starts to move away, then turns. 'It's pretty hard graft in the quarry,' he says. 'The lights here get turned off at ten, but you might want to turn in early.'

'Thanks,' says Ralph. 'I think we will. Do you have any news of the war? We've been days without a radio while we waited to come here.'

Frank hesitates for a moment, then tells them the Red Army is pushing forward, fighting alongside local partisans, and has liberated Belgrade, then East Prussia, then Romania. Izzy looks anxious and Bill wonders if her father and brother are now fighting alongside Soviet troops, or if they're still alive. He thinks maybe it's for the best that Izzy's dad didn't find them and carry them off to join the partisans. They could be in the thick of battle now.

'And Hitler has ordered a call-up of all men from sixteen to sixty for Home Guard duties,' continues Frank. 'Must mean they're getting pretty short of real soldiers. Maybe it really will be over before Christmas.'

'Humph,' says Ralph. 'Heard that one before. But thanks.' He looks around. Their kit-bags are still lying in the middle of the room. 'Which bed do you want, Cousins?'

'Don't let the bedbugs bite,' says Frank as he wanders back to the kitchen.

Izzy screws up her nose, examines each of the bunks and scratches the bites on her head.

Bill laughs. 'It's just an expression! But there might be bugs in any or all of them.'

Ralph says, 'Look, why don't you take the top bunk here, and Bill can go below.' He indicates the bunk against the wall adjoining the kitchen, and Bill knows he's given it to Izzy because it might be less cold.

Scotty and Max come in from the kitchen and eye up the other two sets of bunks.

'We could draw for it,' suggests Scotty. He digs in a pocket, pulls out two matchsticks and snaps the head off one of them, pulling them through his fingers so the same length sticks out. He holds out his hand to Max. 'Shortest gets the outside wall.'

Max hesitates for a moment and then chooses one. It's the longer match.

'Och well,' says Scotty, 'I suppose I'm hardier than you Sassenachs.' He throws his belongings up to the top bunk. 'Ye can put youse bags on the bottom here.' He climbs up after his bags, lies down in his clothes and lights a cigarette. The grey smoke curls around the bare light bulb.

Max unpacks his little library of books onto the windowsill behind the curtain and sits at the table, writing in his journal.

Seeing the others are all occupied, Izzy mouths the words 'I love you', and Bill mouths them back.

He lies awake in the dark for a long time, worrying about what he's brought Izzy into. Will the work be too hard for her? And is Kurt is going to be an even worse problem than Tucker?

18

I wake before anyone else, before the first light of dawn, and roll onto my side. To know I'm in Czechoslovakia again fills me with momentary joy as sharp as a lemon, and then with its equal sourness to know I'm so close to my family, but can't see them or speak to them. The wooden bunk bed is hard against my hipbone. I scratch under my arms and around my head. I can feel bumps around my neck. I was itchy in the *Arbeits* compound, and now I'm certain I have lice.

While it's still dark, the guard called Kurt opens the interconnecting door and shouts, '*Raus, raus*. Collect your trousers and boots', and all the lights in the house spark into life.

I climb down first and slip out to the washroom to find mine, thinking I won't have to encounter all the strange men wearing pyjama bottoms, but Kurt is there ahead of me and watches me bend to find my felt-lined boots and the smallest trousers. They are very cold to the touch. I remember the advice not to be alone with Kurt, and then others crowd into the washroom behind me and start to pull out their own chilly belongings. I slip past them to our own room to dress.

Everyone mills about in the kitchen for a breakfast of acorn coffee and watery oatmeal. Some take it back to their own rooms, while others sit at the communal table. Scotty seems pleased about the oatmeal, which he calls porridge. It looks to me like something we would feed our horses. Three or four at a time, we make our way to the washroom. Nobody has given instructions for this to happen, but the men seem to watch for others returning, to get the maximum privacy. Scotty and Ralph come with me, shielding me from the eyes of the other men. Not that anyone is looking at me. A column of silence surrounds each of them as they shave, or wash, or clean their teeth with splayed toothbrushes or their fingers. I feel invisible and as safe as Cousins.

Much too soon, a grey light permeates the barred windows and Kurt is back, harrying and hurrying us out to work. The cold slaps our faces and hands as we emerge from the house, but the view is beautiful. Close by in every direction is the deep green of dense forest; we are about one-third of the way up a mountainside, looking down through the trees on the little town with yesterday's railway station. Beyond the town the forest closes in again, and above it stretch the bare slopes of another mountain, with a cable car to the top; and beyond that, bluer and bluer, further ranges of mountain peaks. As I'm looking all around me, the sharp prod of a rifle in my side brings me back to reality. Kurt marches us down the track into the quarry itself, where he unlocks a shed and hands out tools. I get a shovel, a broom and a bucket. The others are given a pickaxe, a chisel and a sledgehammer each.

The small quarry is a bowl of noise: shouts counterpoint the chipping of pickaxes, as great slabs of white marble are released from the cliff by sweat and muscle. My friends are shown where

227

they must begin to hack away the precious stone. Frank gives instructions on how it's to be done. 'And make sure you do a good job, boys,' he says. 'These are needed for the war effort!'

Everyone laughs loudly and Kurt scowls. 'Work!' he yells in German. 'You aren't here to laugh. Get to work.'

Frank shows me my job, which he says is done by Czech women in the main quarry at Saubsdorf. I almost jump at the thought that he's discovered me, but Frank says, 'That doesn't mean it's women's work. It's still hard. It's just that you're small. Like a scrum half.'

Ralph overhears and calls out, 'He's a jockey!', which seems to impress Frank.

'A jockey!' he repeats.

My job is to sweep and shovel away the loose stone chippings and gather them in buckets. When my buckets are full, I have to carry them to the door of the tool-shed. Within half an hour my back and arms are beginning to ache, for all that I tell myself I'm young and strong, and so recently used to physical work on the farm. I make the mistake of filling the first bucket too full and can barely lift it. As I'm staggering to the tool-shed, I feel Kurt watching me.

Frank lays down his pickaxe and says, 'I was doing this yesterday. I filled the first bucket half-full, then took another half-bucket to top it up.'

I nod my thanks. I can see I'm the one who has the easy work. The men heft and wield their heavy pickaxes, time and time and time again, until sweat runs down their faces. Even in this autumn chill, some of them are stripped to their vests from the heat of exertion. Then they have to strain to lift and carry the huge slabs of marble to the waiting horse-drawn cart.

Blisters are starting to form on the palms of my hands, and the others have the same problem. Max and Ralph tear a spare foot-rag into strips, and we share them out between us, wrapping them around our hands. Kurt hurries over, shouting and waving his pistol to urge us to resume work, and Ralph explains in German that we'll work faster if we aren't in pain. Kurt spits into the dust of the quarry floor and I watch the little ball of spittle soak away. I'm careful not to make eye contact with him.

My hands are better for a little while, but then the blisters start to rise again and burst, wetting the dirty rag. And there are still hours and hours of this to go before we can lie down on our beds. Hunger starts to gnaw at my insides, and I try to take my mind off my pain by thinking about the food I'd most like to eat. I think of my mother's borscht, and of the delicious little parcels of meat and vegetables she would make, wrapped in cabbage leaves.

I try to calculate how many hours it will be until a dinner break, and then how many more until it gets dark. I thank God that the days are shortening fast, so that every day will have a little less working time than the one before.

I look over at Bill, his face caked with dust, apart from the smears where he's wiped away the sweat with the back of his arm. He is wearing his shirt, but the underarms and back are dark with moisture. I worry that this will be too hard for him when we have so little to eat, that he will become ill.

'Concentrate on shovelling and sweeping,' Cousins tells me sternly. The watery sun lifts from the trees and makes its slow progress across the sky.

I jump into the air as a loud bell rings. The old hands tell us to retreat towards the offices, while dynamite is detonated. Once we are all clear of the quarry, there is a loud explosion, which makes my ears ring. On the way back, Bill and I call at the quarry latrine. I sit at the end of the plank, and he pisses into the hole next to me. I think how in normal life a husband and wife would never see each other urinating, never smile secretly at each other while they are doing it. Bill asks me how my hands are, and I nod as bravely as I can, knowing the rags have now fused into the burst skin of the blisters, but I can't complain when I'm sure his are the same, or worse. I wonder how they'll ever heal when we have to do this every day.

At midday we are allowed back to the house, and a fresh pot of soup stands on the range, being stirred by a large-boned Czech woman who clearly has enough to eat. There's fresh bread too, proper bread, not like that sawdust muck at Lamsdorf. Herr Rauchbach gives out a loaf to each of the 'combines' of men.

'How long does this have to last?' asks Bill, and Frank tells us the ration here is half a loaf a day for each man. Half a loaf of good bread seems so much better than one-third of a rotten one, even if we are having to use so much energy. I'm thrilled to discover the soup is sour, like my mother's. The Englishmen complain and pull amusing faces, but I love it. The soup's full of vegetables, and there's enough to have a second portion. I long to pass just one word with the Czech woman who's cooked it, to talk to her about the ingredients, to speak my own language. She smiles at my obvious relish of her soup and offers me more. She has slightly hooded eyes and strong cheekbones. I refill my mess tin three times. When she reaches out towards me with the ladle, I notice that her hands are large and her wrists are twice the width of mine. I think she would make a better man than me. Ralph asks her name, and she says she's called Berta. Her German is poor.

The longing to speak Czech to her is so strong that I have to clamp my teeth together.

Scotty wanders over to the range and sniffs the pot appreciatively. 'It's got some herbs in it,' he says to Ralph. 'Can you ask her what they are?'

Berta says *majoránka* and *libeček*, but she doesn't know the German names. She tells Ralph that she'll ask Rosa, and she beams at Scotty.

'Didn't know you were a cook,' says Ralph.

'Aye, in the canteen at the biscuit factory. No' that we used any herbs there. Plain food for plain working men and lasses.' Scotty sighs. 'We'd think nothing o' geein' leftovers to the pigs that I'd merrily kill for now.'

After a twenty-minute break Kurt hurries us back to the quarry and, on the way, Frank tells us that Rosa and Berta and the Czech women who do our washing will bring us black-market eggs and rabbit in exchange for soap and cigarettes. He says they've even smuggled in radio parts, and a crystal radio is assembled every few days to make sure we have news of the war. I wonder if the Czech women could be trusted to take a message to my mother.

The afternoon is never-ending noise and dust, pain in my hands and aches in my back and arms. I try not to show how hard I'm finding this. I remind myself this is all my choice, that Cousins can work this hard and harder.

By four o'clock the sun is setting, but we work on into the dusk, until Herr Rauchbach comes down to tell Kurt it's time for us to stop.

'What are you thinking of?' he asks Kurt in Czech. 'They can't see what they are doing. The marble will be ruined. And this is a very special order.'

231

Kurt obviously doesn't like being told off in front of us, even though he assumes nobody can speak Czech, and he protests, 'But, Herr Rauchbach, we are already running behind, and these new men are too slow.'

He takes our tools from us as we file past, locking them away again for the night.

Herr Rauchbach grimaces. 'You don't need to remind me. But they can only work while they can see. It's too dangerous, and the slabs will be uneven and spoiled.'

Kurt slams the door of the tool-shed.

Ahead of us on the track, at the entrance to our quarters, the men stand in line and wait for Kurt to finish locking away the tools. He hurries past us all and stations himself at the door, where he pats down each man – searching, I suppose, for anything that could be used as a weapon, or to aid escape. The old Lamsdorf terror surges through me as I get closer and closer. Then it's my turn. I lift my arms to the side as the others have done, and Kurt leers into my face as his hands pat my waist and hips. 'Breathe easy,' Cousins tells me. 'Breathe easy.' Kurt bends to grope around my ankles and I think I could kick him over and run. Then the moment's past and I stumble into the light of the house, my heart banging like the hammers and chisels I've been hearing all day.

I can barely find the strength to haul myself up to my bunk, where I lie, waiting for my heartrate to return to normal, waiting for the pain in my back and limbs to subside, waiting for enough energy to go to wash and eat. Ralph and Max are lying down too, but Scotty and Bill sit on the lower bunks, unwinding the bloody rags from their hands and showing each other their blisters. I can hear my mother's voice: 'Surgical spirit hardens the skin against blisters.' And I hear Bill, almost as if he is repeating her, 'Surgical spirit hardens skin', and Scotty replying, 'Aye, mebbe, but where'll we get some o' that?'

I drift to sleep, and Bill has to wake me to wash and eat and use the toilet before lock-down. I wash my face, but ignore the dust in my hair. It will only be back tomorrow.

Max is writing in his journal. 'It's November the first,' he says. 'We missed Hallowe'en.'

'Every day is Hallowe'en here,' says Scotty grimly.

'All Saints' Day today,' says Bill, and Max asks what that means.

'All the saints are remembered today, and tomorrow it's All Souls' Day, when we pray for the departed.'

Everyone is quiet, remembering their own loved ones who've died. I wonder if I should be saying special prayers for my father or Jan. I have no way of knowing if they're dead or alive, although I think I would somehow know if they'd been killed. Some fabric of the universe would have shuddered, and I would have known.

Exhaustion overcomes me and I sleep as deeply as a baby.

At lunch the next day Berta notices my blisters, and in the evening a bottle of surgical spirit and a clean rag have appeared in our bedroom.

In the quarry, over the next few days, and always under Kurt's gaze, my friends take turns to work alongside me, and as we work they talk more to me, and I begin to fill in the jigsaw puzzle of each life. Although it's hard for them to work and talk, it's as if my silence draws the words out of them.

Ralph tells me more about starting university as a medical

student. 'The sight of blood made me physically sick,' he laughs wryly. 'I was such a disappointment to my family; they were all working so hard to help me become a doctor.' He hefts his pickaxe a few times as I sweep around him, and then resumes, in bursts between his blows. 'When I switched to Classics, I was in heaven. To have a whole library full of books. And, for the first time, friends who really understood me, who I could walk all day with, just talking, with no one to say which way or when to stop.'

Some days he passes the time by telling me stories from the ancient Greeks, from the *Odyssey* and the *Iliad*. I think it comforts him to remember that this world of books and stories hasn't entirely deserted him. He doesn't simplify his vocabulary or patronise me, but sometimes when a word is particularly obscure, he'll explain it as he goes. I think he would make a marvellous schoolteacher, if that's what he decides to do. He tells me about his sisters and his mother, and the guilt he feels that there wasn't enough money for all of them to go to the grammar school.

His eldest sister, Jean, is a Red Cross nurse stationed in Malta. I would have liked to do that – to be off on a great adventure, nursing the wounded men. The middle one, Grace, was apprenticed to a bookbinder, but has gone to work as a Land Girl, the very job I've struggled to escape. The youngest, Hilda, has been working in a department store since she was fourteen, selling men's ties.

'Imagine that,' Ralph says, 'a world where men walk into a shop and spend hours choosing a tie. It's easier for me to imagine Ithaca!'

He describes his sisters so vividly that I almost feel I'd recognise them on the street. I hope I'll meet them one day and be able to tell them how wonderful their brother is. Ralph seems to tell me everything about himself, until I realise he has never mentioned a girlfriend.

In the evenings, if we aren't too exhausted, he continues to teach me shorthand, and I correct his German grammar. In our room, with the door shut, I sometimes feel brave enough to whisper a word or two, but mostly silence has fallen down over my shoulders like a nun's habit, and I can no longer remember what I used to chatter about all day. I've become the quiet man, Cousins, and conversation now happens in my head.

As the weather becomes colder, and the initial aches in our backs and arms have become second nature, Ralph's limp is worse, and his face often contorts in pain. Eventually he admits that his foot is becoming more and more unbearable. He developed frostbite soon after he was captured. He shows us his foot, and the toes are so red and swollen that they must be pressing against his boot every moment.

Bill insists that Ralph tells Herr Rauchbach, who immediately takes him down to see the local doctor. The doctor says the foot must be bathed in warm water two or three times a day and then some cream must be applied. Herr Rauchbach says he will allow Ralph and me to be a little late to work in the quarry each day, and that if it gets worse, he will find him work to do in the office, where his excellent German will be useful.

Each morning, as the other men leave for the quarry, Ralph sits at the kitchen table, and I bring him a bowl of warm water to bathe his foot. Afterwards I dry it for him and apply the cream. 'You'd be a good nurse,' he says, 'like my Jeanie. Or maybe a doctor. A better doctor than me.'

And I think: Yes, maybe after the war, instead of being a translator, I could become a nurse or a doctor. I long to ask how

235

much it would cost, and if it could be done on a railway clerk's wages. And if they would take a woman. Perhaps I'd need to continue to be Cousins during the day, returning to being Izzy just at night with Bill.

After a few days in the quarry, Herr Rauchbach takes Bill and me with him to set the dynamite, and tells us why the marble has to be so perfect. 'It's used for the graves of Nazi officers killed in battle, and brought home to be buried with full honours.' There is irony in his voice as he adds, 'The glorious dead.'

Suddenly the work doesn't seem so arduous, if every slab we sweat and struggle to hew from the rockface is going to cover a dead Nazi.

Day by day, Bill and the others are more and more aware of the way Kurt follows me around with his eyes. I hear them talking about it when they think I'm asleep, and it fills me with foreboding. How ironic it would be to be attacked by one of my own countrymen, when I'd fooled all those Nazi soldiers in Lamsdorf. I don't tell Bill how Kurt clutches my bottom when he's searching us, and there's no way I can avoid the searches, although most nights my friends manage to create some kind of diversion to move Kurt quickly from me to the next prisoner.

Whenever I go to the latrine in the quarry, Kurt finds some urgent work he has to do close by. Only once does he actually follow me inside, but Scotty is close behind him, letting out a loud fart, which makes Kurt turn and leave rapidly. I laugh into the grimy sleeve of my jacket. It's the most I've laughed in weeks, and so hard to keep it silent.

Some days I work alongside Scotty. I find that his accent lacerates the words, as he talks to me of life in tenement slums and the jobs he did before the war, but I connect with enough words to make sense of what he's saying.

'I was on the ships at fourteen – apprentice riveter – but it's no a life. They lay you off and take you on, and the metal is sae cold in your hands, and riveting makes you stone-deaf in the end. All the old fellas lip-read you know. Nobody taught them how to do it; they just picked it up because their hearing was gone.'

He tells me that he left the shipyard after a year and then did a range of jobs: in the quarry he'd mentioned, as a hod-carrier on a building site, a month in a milliner's shop, and then in the canteen of the biscuit factory where his sister's husband was foreman.

'He nae wanted me, but did it to stop my sister nagging. He was a bastard to us workers almost as much as he was to her.' He straightens his back for a moment and looks long into my eyes. When he turns back to his work, Scotty begins, between hefts of the pickaxe, to slowly tell me something else. I'm sweeping next to him and I concentrate hard on his words, knowing he is trying to tell me something important.

With a shock the meaning springs clear.

'I've ne'er told anyone this. And mebbe I shouldna tell you now, but it's eating at me, bad as the hunger. I did for him, you see. Killed him mysen. I'm nae proud of it, but he beat her once too many times. And beat the bairns too. Even the wee one. Can you credit it? Och, that was a sight to turn your stomach: the wee mite with bruises on her pretty face. Next time he might have murdered her.'

I wonder how Scotty killed him – a knife, a rope, a push beneath a train? Maybe poison? And does this mean he killed Tucker?

But Scotty continues, 'I ran right for the recruiting sergeant. I thought they'll nae come looking for me in the army, and so I was right. And he had plenty enemies. I was more afeared o' jail than o' the rope. Ha! And now in jail these last three years. I reckon I've done my time here, but the bailie wouldna see it like that.'

We work for a while, the only sounds the arrhythmic percussion of the quarry.

'Mebbe I'll go to Australia when we get out. Mebbe they wouldna catch me up there, d'you think? I'd like to see ma sister again and her bairns, but mebbe in time she could come to Australia to join me. If I get a good life there. No sense going home to the tenement or the hangman.'

I look around to see if we are near anyone, and then I whisper, 'I hope you see her again.' Scotty jumps, as if a dog has spoken.

As we finish for the day and he places himself between me and Kurt, to hand back our tools, he says, 'I know ye wouldna tell a soul.' And I think one day I would like to tell Bill, feeling sure he would understand, but I nod my promise to Scotty and he's satisfied.

Less often, Max takes a turn near me. He tells me about his work in the trade-union movement, and things I don't know, such as F. D. Roosevelt having polio as a child, but overcoming that to have three terms as President of the United States. I think one day Max might be a famous politician, perhaps even prime minister. He talks and talks, and when he talks, he shines with a kind of fierce passion, an icy fire. It's hard to believe that before I came, Max had lain on his bed for days, getting up for roll call and then returning to his bunk, barely eating, willing himself to die.

I wish he'd talk to me about that, but he never does. Perhaps he'd said to his brother, 'Take care of Rachel for me', and his brother had taken care of her in every way. But Max never mentions her; he only talks about strikes and better deals for the working man and woman, and ridiculous dreams of free health-care and pensions for the old, and money for women with children. Impossible ideas. He offers to lend me his books, and I nod gratefully. Mostly in the evenings he writes in his journal, sometimes copying passages from a volume he's reading. Once I glimpse something laid out like a poem. I wonder what he can find here to write poetry about.

On other evenings there are speaking contests, or debates, or hands of bridge or darts, or one of Ralph's 'film nights'. Bill and I had to leave *Great Expectations* in Lamsdorf, unfinished, but now Max has loaned me a novel called *The Ragged Trousered Philanthropists*, and although it's difficult, I read that to myself. My shorthand continues to improve, and I scribble almost as fast as Ralph when the radio is assembled to listen to news from outside our tiny goldfish bowl of a world. They don't dare set up the radio too often, in case it's discovered.

In mid-November we hear that General Patton's troops and tanks have crossed the Moselle River. Our hopes rise for a quick end to the war. Roosevelt has won a fourth term as US president, and Max explains to us the difference between Democrats and Republicans. I think I am a Democrat.

But as November stretches on, everyone becomes glum and frustrated again. The Allies don't seem to be making any advances in Italy because of heavy rain, and there's less news of the Soviet advance. I worry for my brother and father. I wonder how close the Red Army is to my farm, and whether my mother has already had to face the Russians.

239

The rain affects us too, and the quarry becomes an even more dangerous place as the marble becomes slippery. Bill is working next to me; we are soaked to the bone and trembling with cold, when he brings down his pickaxe and it glances off the glassy rock and almost embeds itself in his foot.

That evening Herr Rauchbach orders us to stop work until the rain ceases, and we are filled with relief at the prospect of some rest. We peel off our wet clothes and are able to give them to Berta to take to the washerwomen in the village. We've spent the last few evenings burning the lice from the seams of our dry clothes, and Berta has given us paraffin to wash our hair with, which is supposed to kill the lice, so I'm hopeful that the itching might lessen for a few days. My body must be covered in weals.

That evening Frank tells us about a time back in 1941 when summer rains stopped the work and they were allowed to swim in an abandoned quarry.

'One of the blokes banged his head playing the fool and almost drowned. All the good swimmers were diving for him, but it was like swimming in milk and they couldn't see anything. They were just about to give him up for dead when one of them touched him and was able to dive down and haul him out.' Frank pauses. 'They say he's the man who Rosa was sweet on. And that's why he got moved.'

Everyone falls silent.

'Do you think it's possible,' asks Bill, 'a prisoner and a local girl?' I keep my eyes on the grain of the wood in the table, and my heart beats fast.

'A prisoner and a local girl,' muses Frank. 'There's another story from here, of a local girl and a French prisoner. It's said he got her pregnant.'

240

One of the other men in the room pipes up, 'Trust a Frenchman! Can't keep their cocks in their trousers!'

Bill glances at me at the word 'cock' and I realise it's not a word he'd use in front of me. 'Should've used a French letter,' he jokes, and everyone laughs. I have no idea what this means, but don't have time to puzzle over it, because Frank picks up the story.

'It didn't end well. The guards dragged the Frenchman out and put him in front of a firing squad. And she was taken away, supposedly to prison, but when the Czech women tell the story, they look at each other and cross themselves, so I think they must have shot her too.'

There's a brief silence, and I feel I'm struggling to breathe.

'Well, I don't see how they'd ever get the opportunity,' says Bill.

The man from upstairs replies, 'I don't know how he could even get it up. I haven't had a hard-on for months. It's this starvation.'

'I suppose if the girl was pretty enough,' says Ralph, and I smile to myself at his transparent attempt to be one of the boys.

We all have our secrets, I think.

19

The rainy days and longer evenings mean we are spending so much time in one another's company that everyone is starting to get on my nerves – and maybe I'm getting on theirs.

Scotty has started to carve a chess set, and the sound of the whittling knife makes me clench my jaw in irritation. I'm always relieved when he goes off to one of the other bedrooms for his endless card games.

Frank's habit of repeating what people have said begins to get under my skin, and even Bill annoys me sometimes. He takes down my blankets in the morning and folds them for me, which I could do myself but don't think is necessary, and when I stand up from sitting on the edge of his bed, he pulls the blanket straight again, like an old woman.

Max's jiggling legs and Ralph's fiddling with his glasses both drive me mad.

We haven't had any parcels for weeks, but Scotty spends time in the kitchen, devising concoctions that can be made from the ingredients brought in by Berta, the cook. She has noticed that the others don't like sour soup, but I do, so she sometimes brings a little sour milk for me to add to my mess tin. Then she stares questioningly at me, but Cousins simply nods his thanks.

Bill astonishes us all by announcing that he wants to do some knitting. Berta brings needles and scraps of wool, and Bill settles down to begin to knit a scarf. He and Flora learned together when they were children and had a fierce rivalry to see who could make something fastest, or who could learn to do a new stitch.

'I even learned to knit socks, on four needles, just to get ahead of her. Turning the heel was tricky, but I was better at it than Flora. She got in such a mess and flew into such a rage!' He laughs at the memory, but I'm sick with jealousy of this girl who has been so close to Bill for so long.

I wonder briefly if many Englishmen can knit, but the surprise and interest of our friends assures me it isn't common. Scotty says that fishermen can knit, and that makes it more manly. Not that Bill cares. His needles flash furiously all evening, click, click, clicking as they talk. And the clickety-clack of them irritates me too.

On Sunday afternoons, if it isn't raining, we are all allowed to go into the village to play football, and that's a welcome relief from the close quarters in which we live. The pitch is stiff with frost in the mornings. Kurt watches us keenly, but Herr Rauchbach says he will take responsibility if any of us abscond. Nobody tries to escape, whether because of Kurt's gun or because everyone knows there is Nazi-occupied territory for hundreds of kilometres in every direction, as well as hazardous mountains all around us, or because the war must surely end soon. For Frank, I think it's because of Rosa. There's a rumour that he sneaks out to meet her at night, and I think of the time Bill did the same to meet me.

Ralph sometimes stands on the touchline, because his foot is too painful to run about. I find it too cold to stand still, even though I'm now wearing my brother's winter underwear. So I whisper to Bill that I'll play football too, and I'm quick on the pitch and helpful to the team. Jan would be proud of me.

Max is a surprisingly good footballer for a bookish man and scores a lot of goals, but Bill sometimes scores too, and then he immediately looks to me for approbation. I slap him hard on the back. I don't know how we have the energy to run about after the gruelling work of the week, but somehow it seems to refresh rather than exhaust us, and the others are full of talk of who ran where and kicked the ball to whom, for hours afterwards.

It's so cold now that Herr Rauchbach has brought us an extra blanket each and given us wood for the stove in our bedroom, which we light each evening when we come home from the quarry. It doesn't exactly make the room warm, but it does take the chill off it during the evening. Some men have taken to dressing in the kitchen, which is the warmest place. One night Herr Rauchbach comes in as we are running back from the washroom in our pyjamas and bare feet.

'The trousers and boots must be cold to put on in the morning?' he asks Ralph, who answers, 'Freezing. They can stand up by themselves.'

The next night Kurt orders the men to carry two big baskets into the hallway and we put our boots in one and trousers in the other. Then they are hauled into the office overnight. It's a slight improvement.

Herr Rauchbach has also ordered that a tin bath is pulled into the kitchen on Sundays, and each bedroom has one Sunday when they can use it, though the water is tepid and chilly after the second or third man has been in it. I'm filled with joy at the idea of cleaning my whole body, properly, and my friends unanimously agree that I should go first.

Bill and I boil the big pans on the range and pour water into the bath, while the other men are still sitting round in the kitchen. It takes an awful lot of water to cover even the base of the bath, and Bill says, 'We could boil more, but the water in the bath is going cold while we wait for it.'

'Yes, the water will go cold,' says Frank, sticking his finger in the water. 'We only had about this much for the first man last week,' he says. 'You can keep the pans on the boil while the first and second man bathe, and then the third can have it hotter and deeper. Even if it is a bit grimy!'

'OK, we'll do that. Cousins is first.' Bill clears his throat. 'A bit of privacy for a chap?' he requests.

Everyone looks astonished and then begins to laugh and catcall.

'What's the matter, Cousins – think we haven't seen a cock before?'

'Wanting a quiet wank?' One of the upstairs men makes a hand-signal I've never seen before.

'I wouldn't like to get in his water!'

'When I was his age, I wanked three times a day.'

'And had wet dreams every night!'

I look at the floor and don't know how to arrange my face. Part of my brain logs the new words, and though I'm not sure what it all means, I understand this is a kind of man's world that I ought to seem familiar with, so I raise my eyes slyly, look from one to another, then shrug and wink. There's loud laughter, and as they gather up their possessions and leave the kitchen, I hear animated discussion of the last time any of them managed to 'get it up' and how they blame the starvation rations. Even my short acquaintance with these peckers tells me that their owners have absolutely no control over when they are up or not. I can't help wondering about Jan and my father. Do they use words like those in Czech? Did they too do those things to themselves?

When the others have all departed, Scotty leaves by the washroom door, and I know he'll stand out in the cold, guarding it, until we give him the 'all clear' signal.

Bill stations himself outside the other door, in the hallway, and I quickly remove my outer clothes. It's too dangerous to strip completely, so I get into the bath still wearing my brother's woollen underwear and the bust-flattening corset, which I've loosened. As I sit down, I dip my head down under the water and rub it with the bar of red soap. The water is already grey and scummy. It's hard to get the soap out of my hair, and I feel sorry for the men who'll come after me.

I wash myself under the long-sleeved vest, and up under the corset. It's a shock to feel how much my breasts have shrunk as I've lost weight. I'm almost glad Bill never gets to see them now. Some of my lice bites are swollen and hard. I wash myself inside the long johns, and even though this isn't a proper bath, it's a joy to feel water on my skin, and to picture the wretched lice drowning. I rub my underarms and my groin fiercely with the soap. The soap stings where I've scratched myself. But I mustn't take long; it's Bill's turn next. This is the most dangerous moment. Standing up with water streaming from my baggy underwear into the water, I quickly pull off the vest and corset and drop them in the water, rubbing my top half dry, goose pimples covering my body, nipples tight and hard, even in the

246

relative warmth of the kitchen, taking only moments to pull clean underwear over my damp torso. Then I drop the long johns into the water and do the same with my bottom half. I haven't dried myself thoroughly enough, and that makes it awkward to pull on the fresh underwear, but I feel wonderfully clean. I hope I'll never again take the joy of washing for granted. I yank on my battledress, loose enough to hide the lack of breast-binding. Wringing out my underwear as best I can, I throw it into the big butler sink.

I knock on the door to the hallway and Bill comes in and closes the door behind him. He kisses me on my nose. 'You smell of carbolic!'

I risk a whisper. 'Even my lice are clean!'

And he laughs. 'Let's get poor Scotty in from the cold.' As Scotty comes through, Bill continues, 'You rinse out your underwear then, and I'll hop in your water.' He looks at the grey water with a soap scum and quarry dust and bits floating in it. 'Not too dirty,' he lies cheerfully, and I smile.

He adds another kettle full of water to the bath, and I carry my sodden long johns to the washroom while Bill takes his turn. I can hear him singing through the closed door. Scotty comes with me, and when I've rinsed everything as well as I can under the freezing water, he wrings it out for me. Then he rolls the corset and shoves it up his sleeve. 'We'll leave everything but this in the kitchen for the washerwoman to take away tomorrow,' he says.

Bill is already dressing as we pass back through the kitchen, and he helps Scotty pour more hot water into the dirty bath for his turn.

*   *   *

Ralph has exchanged cigarettes for extra logs, and we put one on to keep the stove in our bedroom lit overnight, to dry my breast-binding. Before dawn I creep down from my bunk to get it and wrap it back around myself. Moving across the room with my body unbound is such a strange sensation. I wish I didn't have to flatten myself like this, and hope it won't cause permanent damage, but at the same time it feels familiar now, and safe – perhaps in the way that a baby stops crying when it's tightly swaddled. I pull on my woolly hat, so that my hair won't be full of dust again in an hour.

The itching has lessened overnight, and I hope that after a few more baths and paraffin treatments the lice might be gone for ever. I tell Bill my hair needs to be shorter, and one day Berta has scissors in the kitchen, and we all take turns for a cut.

Although I'm grateful for the days when my friends work alongside me, I'm always, out of the corner of my eye, aware of where Bill is in the quarry, and most pleased to work alongside him. He talks about the news we've heard, and although I like it when he talks about serious things to me, or treats me like his mate Cousins, I like it even better when the others are far enough out of earshot for him to talk about our future. It doesn't seem to occur to Bill that his parents might hate this dark-haired stranger with the funny accent. His mother might not let me into her kitchen, I think. But in the evenings I can sit in the pub and listen to Bill play and sing on the piano, and I'll learn all the songs and join in, and people will say I have a pretty voice, and no wonder he married me.

Bill says when we've been home a little while, we might go to live in one of the railway cottages, and now he knows about growing food, he could have an allotment nearby. His eyes shine.

'I'll grow all our vegetables. I'll never let you and our children go hungry.'

Again I start to watch the moon and count the days, dreading the onset of my monthlies. On 17th November I wake with the familiar cramps beginning, low in my stomach. Blushing, I walk over to Ralph and place my hand on my tummy, in our signal. He understands immediately and smiles reassurance. 'Don't worry. We'll watch out for you.'

In the washroom I rinse my rags in the sink that's furthest from the door; the others block sight of me with their bodies. If Kurt comes near, they devise a diversion to draw him away. The five days of my 'monthly' crawl slowly past.

My need to speak and to be heard grows, and sometimes I could wail at full lung-power. Then Cousins steps in and calms me, whispering as he might do to a shying horse, 'Be still. Easy now. Easy now. It'll be all right', until the rage ebbs out of me.

I certainly don't need the excitement of Kurt's unwanted attentions. One night, after the baskets of trousers and boots have been locked in the office, he returns and stands in the doorway of our bedroom, pretending to inspect the room, but really watching me as I climb up to my bunk. I lie down, breathing fast, turning my face to the wall, and Ralph asks him in German what he wants.

Kurt shrugs and says in Czech, 'You know exactly what I want. Are you jealous, or do you just want to keep him for yourself? Have you all fucked him? Does he service you all? Then why not me?'

His words rush through my head like a hurricane, and I'm trembling with the effort of not shouting back. And although I had worked out that Ralph was not quite like the other men, how does Kurt know?

I squeeze my hands into tight fists, struggling to contain my fury.

'Well, don't worry,' sneers Kurt. 'I'll get that tight little arse too. You just wait.'

He slams our door behind him and we hear the outer door bang shut and the bolts thrown into place.

Immediately Bill is standing on his bunk, leaning over me. I still have my eyes squeezed tight shut, my heart pounding with anger.

'What did he say?' asks Bill, touching my arm. 'Iz, are you OK? What did he say? Whisper it. Or do you want to write it down?'

But how could I write such filth? I open my eyes and shake my head, and Bill turns to the others.

'Don't know,' he says, 'but we all know it wasn't nice.'

Ralph looks pale. 'We must never let Cousins out of our sight.'

Later that night I'm woken by the sound of Kurt singing an old Czech drinking song on the lane leading to the house. As he approaches he becomes quiet, but I can hear him stumbling, cursing as he falls over something. I sit up, and see in the dim moonlight through the curtains that Scotty on the top bunk by the window is also awake. Bill moves on our lower bunk and I know he's listening too.

We hear Kurt crashing through the office.

'He's coming this way,' says Bill.

Scotty swings down from his bunk. 'Aye, and he's ganna get a wee surprise. Cousins, you get yersel' over here.'

I quickly climb down, and Bill gives my hand a squeeze as we hear the bolts pulled back on the door to the offices. I run silently across the room and climb into Scotty's bunk, lying on my side to peep between the slats.

Scotty is up in my bunk before Kurt opens the door to our room and stands silhouetted in the doorway. Bill gives a convincing snore, and Kurt moves forward, trying to creep, but weaving unsteadily.

He sneaks round to the foot-end of the bunks and stands up on the edge of the lower bed, bringing his head level with where I should be sleeping. As he reaches forward under the blanket, I hear a dull crack and see him thrown backwards, banging his head on the wall behind. He crumples to the floor, making a low mewling sound. None of us move. Slowly Kurt picks himself up, holding one hand to his face, and staggers back to the door, pulling it closed behind him. We all lie still until we hear the key and the bolts again, and then his footsteps stumbling away from the building.

Then Scotty sits up, and Bill and I do too. Max and Ralph both seem to have slept through everything.

'Whatever did you do?' asks Bill.

'I was having a wee nightmare of a ghosty or a ghouly comin' to get me. I must have kicked out in my sleep,' says Scotty.

Bill laughs out loud. 'Good man. I don't think he'll be back soon.'

Scotty climbs down from my bunk and begins to pad back across the floor. 'No, mebbe not, but let's set him a wee mantrap just in case.'

He leans one of the chair-backs under the doorknob and moves the jam jars for night-weeing into the path of the door.

'That should do it,' he says, and we cross on the way back to our own beds. I put out my hand to say thank you, and we shake hands in an oddly formal way. And then Bill is there beside me and although he never makes a display of affection in front of the other men, he puts his arm round me and leads me to his bunk. He sits beside me, holding me very tightly, mistaking my pent-up fury for fear.

'I'll never let him hurt you,' he whispers. 'We'll never let anyone hurt you. None of us. You do believe me, don't you?'

I nod and lay my head on his shoulder and concentrate on the memory of Kurt falling backwards from Scotty's kick. I try to let that wash my mind of his dirty, repulsive words, but I know now that he's not only a predator I must fear, but also my enemy, who will want revenge.

20

The days shorten rapidly through December and it's bitterly cold in the quarry, as if the bowl of it traps the frozen air and refuses to let it go. I'm used to Czech winters, but most of the prisoners aren't. Bill begins to rub his left wrist and tells me it aches where he broke it falling off the shed roof as a boy. Ralph's feet become daily more painful. He doesn't complain about them, but we can see by the way he limps and occasionally winces when he thinks nobody's watching.

We wear as many clothes as possible, but that means it's hard to move our arms to work efficiently, which makes Kurt cantankerous. Herr Rauchbach has ordered more logs for the range and our stoves, but we suspect Kurt is siphoning off some and selling them, because there's never enough to keep the stove alight all night.

Despite the extra logs, the patterns of frost are thick on the windows when we wake. The latrine is frozen now, which helps with the smell, but when we pee into it, our urine puddles on yesterday's layer of ice. As Bill predicted, the taps in our washroom have already frozen twice. Kurt brought a cut-up blanket – better quality than the blankets most of us are using – and we wrapped it around the pipes. Straw would have worked just as well.

We wash in the most perfunctory way in the freezing water, rubbing our hands together quickly. Now everyone wipes a cloth over their faces like girls, rather than immersing and splashing like men. I dread the thought of having to rinse out my rags when my monthlies come again. Scotty has stopped shaving, and a huge red beard is starting to sprout, but Bill and Ralph, and sometimes Max, stand loyally beside me each morning. As I pretend to shave, they do so in reality, cursing the blunt razor blades and cold water. They think it draws less attention to my smooth chin if they are clean-shaven too. Max lets his beard grow for a few days, but then says it itches and shaves it off again.

Red Cross parcels aren't as frequent here as at Lamsdorf, so we are overjoyed one Sunday in early December when an army truck rattles up and there's a delivery. We don't know if it's a mistake, but there are enough parcels for one each, and there's swift bartering in our house between those who have American parcels with coffee and those who have British ones with tea. I have something called Cadbury's Fruit and Nut chocolate, which I think may be the most delicious thing I've ever tasted. There's also an Australian bulk package of raisins, which Scotty proposes that we use to make some 'hooch' for Christmas, and there's great debate about the best possible recipe. I wish they could taste my mother's plum brandy, and could kick myself for not paying attention when she was making it.

Many of the men have letters and personal parcels too. Max has one letter, which he retreats to the window with. I hope it's good news for him. Bill has two letters from home, sent months apart, and one parcel.

'A letter from Mum.' He beams. 'And one from Flora.'

Scotty and I are the only people in the house who have nothing.

'I kenned it was wiser not to let anyone know where I am,' he sighs. 'Ne'er mind, Cousins. Come and play rummy while they read their mail and open their presents. Card games are good for blocking out other thoughts.'

But I can't help watching Bill's face while he reads his letters. Everything he feels shows in his expression. I'm sick with jealousy that he's reading the letter from Flora with such evident relish. I lose hand after hand of rummy, and Scotty says mildly, 'Ye needs to put your whole mind to it.'

Then Bill calls me to open the personal parcel with him. It was sent from home last May, first to Italy and then all the way up to Lamsdorf and finally to Saubsdorf.

He wrenches it open with the eagerness of a child, and I watch his joy at the simple things inside: a photograph of his mum and dad taken in a studio, looking self-conscious and unhappy. I study this hard, but can see no sign of Bill in their faces, though his mother is blonde, like him, or maybe grey-haired. It's hard to tell in a black-and-white photograph. They both look overly well fed. His father has a moustache, but much smaller than my dad's. I long to have a picture of my father and mother. Already I'm finding their faces difficult to picture. I don't wonder Bill's parents look sad when this photo is intended for their only child, whom they haven't seen for five long years – a prisoner in a strange land, so many, many miles away. If we ever have a child, I'm not sure if I would be able to bear that.

The parcel contains: some underwear better suited for summer in Italy, though any new vests are welcome; some socks, which are sorely needed; some Carters Elastoplast and an iodine pencil; and, best of all to Bill, a new harmonica, made of brass, with more holes than his, and a note from Flora saying she got it from an American airman who was a jazz fan, but hadn't mastered the art of playing it. I hope Flora's fallen in love with the GI and will go back to the United States with him, but Bill turns the harmonica over and over saying, 'Well, I never!' before finally putting it to his lips. Everyone looks up as he blows. It certainly makes a richer sound than his old one, more like chords than single notes, and he determines that we'll have a sing-song as soon as he's worked out what it can do.

When everything in his personal parcel has been admired and exclaimed over, we turn again to the Red Cross food parcels. Herr Rauchbach has ignored the orders to pierce the tins, so we know this food will keep as long as we need it to, or as long as we can bear not to eat it.

'What'll we have tonight?' asks Bill. 'We could use some of the dried egg and the cheese to make an omelette. Would you like that?'

He's so eager that he reminds me of a puppy, though I long to simply cram the biscuits into my mouth, one after another, until my cheeks are so full that I can't move my jaw.

Max's parcel has books and a belt and a shaving brush. Ralph's has playing cards, leather bootlaces and a knitted balaclava for someone with a very small head.

'You'd better have this, Cousins,' he says doubtfully, but I think it's only big enough for a toddler.

He unfolds a droopy hand-knitted sweater and holds it up against himself. 'Was I ever really this big?' he asks.

'We've all lost a lot of weight,' says Max.

'I was almost chubby when I joined up,' admits Bill.

I'm astonished. I can't imagine him overweight, and wonder with a rush of anxiety if I will still love him if he becomes overweight like his mother, when we get back to England. I try to imagine his finely sculpted face padded out with layers of fat, but it's impossible.

'We should weigh ourselves tomorrow,' suggests Max. 'Where we weigh the marble.'

Bill is eyeing up Ralph's sweater. 'I could probably make two out of that, if I unpicked it,' he says. 'Or a jumper with a matching scarf and mittens.' He has been knitting furiously, using patterns and wool brought by the amused Berta. If Berta wonders how he understands the Czech patterns, she never asks.

Ralph laughs and wraps his sweater back up in the brown paper. 'I'm sure you could,' he says, 'but hands off. It's mine. Knitted by my sister.'

The next day Ralph asks permission from Herr Rauchbach and we weigh ourselves, where they weigh the quarried rocks. Bill is fifty-seven kilos, and I've dropped from fifty-four to forty-four. This is with my boots and outdoor clothes on, so I guess my real weight might be even less than this, maybe only forty-two. There's a long debate between Ralph and Max about the conversion from kilos to stones and pounds. Apparently there are fourteen pounds in a stone and sixteen ounces in a pound. I wonder how I'll ever be able to bake a cake or buy groceries. It's just as well I'm good at numbers.

Eventually the calculations are done and Bill exclaims, 'So fifty-seven kilos is nine stone. I was thirteen stone when I joined up. I haven't been nine stone since I was fourteen. And Cousins

must be – hang on a minute – under seven stone. Six-stone-
something. Blimey, that's not much.'

Herr Rauchbach has been watching: at first with interest and
then with some consternation.

Ralph sees his opportunity and saunters over. 'Herr Rauchbach.
As you see, the prisoners are losing weight. The work here is
so heavy. I worry that they will become too weak to be produc-
tive.' He points to me. 'Cousins here is only forty-four kilos. A
strong puff of wind could blow him over.'

'Yes, yes, I can see that. Don't worry. There will be extra
potato rations from now, and dumplings; and God knows it's
not easy, but I'll try to get sausage, and Kurt can shoot some
rabbit.'

'Thank you, Herr Rauchbach. Whatever you can obtain will
be much appreciated.'

The quarry owner hurries back to the house, and sure enough
that dinnertime, Berta has cooked up a stew with additional
potatoes, and we each have a portion of sausage, no bigger than
the end joint of my thumb, but at least it's meat. We all still feel
hungry, but the rest of the house is delighted and everyone
shakes Ralph's hand to thank him. We all agree to have one
ladleful for lunch and save the rest for the evening. I go to bed
feeling less hungry for the first time in two months.

Ever since the letters and parcels came I've been thinking
how much I want to write to my mother, trying to work out
what I could say that wouldn't give away our whereabouts.
Finally I decide Bill must write to Flora and ask her to send
a thank-you note to the farm where people were so kind to
him. We pore over it together as he gives Flora the exact words
to use:

My cousin Bill has asked me to write to say thank you for your kindness and generosity to him. He is well and happy, and taking great care of the gift you gave him.

Of course the Oily Captain will know what it means, but Bill's letter has to go all the way to England and won't mention our location, and then Flora's letter will come from England to Vražné, and by then surely we won't be here any more. I ache for the day I can write to my mother myself.

One personal parcel somehow became separated from the rest and arrives a few days later. It's for Max, and he goes white when he sees the handwriting. Most people rip open the parcels from home as soon as they arrive, but Max thrusts his under his bunk. Nobody makes any comment.

When we are all in the kitchen, he slips away to the bedroom, and when he returns, some time later, the dark circles under his eyes seem to have deepened. We all pretend not to notice the fact that he doesn't speak all evening and retires early. When I go to bed, Max is curled away from us facing the wall, but I know by his breathing that he's only pretending to be asleep. During the night I hear him blow his nose as quietly as he can.

The next day in the quarry Max beckons me over to where he's working, indicating the chippings around his feet. I begin to sweep them up into my bucket. 'It was from Rachel – my parcel,' Max says in a rush.

My heart is full of sorrow for him, but he isn't looking to me for sympathy. He is bursting with the need to speak, and my silence seems to draw more words out of him.

'She sent it over a year ago. Full of things she knew I liked. She must've still loved me then, mustn't she?'

I know he's talking to himself as much as to me, before he explodes with these pent-up thoughts.

He glances up at me. 'But you don't know, do you? My fiancée wrote to me. About ten days before you came.'

The words wring slowly out of him, with each fall of the pickaxe. He doesn't lift his head again.

'I had a letter. First one for ten months. From Rachel. Saying she had. Married. Someone else. My brother. Married my brother. D'you see?'

He pauses, sweat and tears running down his face, and looks directly at me.

'How could they do that to me? My own brother and my fiancée?' he asks.

Max shakes his head, and freezing droplets spin from his face as he resumes work with a hammer and chisel.

'How could they?' he asks.

'I'm so sorry,' I whisper, and I touch his arm, fleetingly. I hope that conveys the words I want to say: that I don't understand how she could do that to him, but one day perhaps he'll meet someone else and they will be happier than he could ever have been with Rachel.

Max's voice is raised, as if he is convincing himself, and it attracts Kurt's attention. 'The only way I can get over it will be to have a different focus in my life. To put all my energy into the defeat of fascism. It's all I've got left. I'll never have a wife and kids. Not now.'

He lifts his pickaxe and a few more blows fall.

While I'm nodding to show that I understand, Kurt arrives,

as if he has a kind of antenna for emotion. He stares hard at Max and points to my half-full bucket of chippings. I lift it to take up to the tool-shed and, as I walk away, I hear Kurt say to Max in Czech, 'What's the matter? Won't he let you shaft him? Or is it a lovers' tiff? Has he thrown you over for a new one? Don't you worry. When I catch him I'm going to bugger him unconscious.'

I stagger away with my bucket of chippings, terror like a cold hand around my heart, taking care not to slip on the wet stone. As I put the bucket down, I imagine these chippings are for Kurt's grave. I see myself pouring them over his dead body.

When my monthlies come again in mid-December, there's less pain than last time, and the bleeding only lasts for three days. I feel my body is returning to the size and shape it was when I was fourteen, before the curse ever began. I wonder if my breasts will shrink to being little bumps behind the nipples and then finally flatten away like a boy's, and if I will become hairless again, like a young girl.

On the morning of 17th December, Kurt greets us with huge excitement. The Germans have launched a big offensive in the Ardennes.

'The war will turn now,' he says in his bad German. 'You will never go home.'

I think I hate and fear him more than I've ever hated anyone in my life – even more than Tucker.

We all suffer from huge red chilblains on our fingers and toes, which itch furiously as soon as they regain any warmth. I tell Ralph to ask Rosa for onion juice or potato juice, and Berta hands it to me saying, 'I hope it helps' in Czech. Her face is full of fake innocence. I bite back the automatic '*Děkuji*' and try to look as blank as Cousins would. The kitchen empties and Berta stares hard at me, quietly insisting, in our own language, 'You're a Czech boy, aren't you? Resistance? That's why you don't speak?'

I look into her eyes, and the desire to tell someone is too much for me. I whisper back in Czech, loving the sound the syllables make in my mouth, 'Yes, from Vražné. Please don't tell.'

She shakes her head and snorts at such an idea. 'When they go, I can hide you. We'll dress you in women's clothes. Get you back home.'

I want to laugh at the irony of being hidden in women's clothes, but it's deadly serious. She must know that she would be shot by the Nazis for helping a prisoner to escape. And she has children. Despite my longing to see my mother and my brother, I shake my head. 'No, no,' I say, 'too dangerous. For you. For all of us.'

I can't tell her that wherever Bill goes, that's where I must go, to the end of my days.

Bill steps into the kitchen from the hall, and Berta turns away, muttering vaguely to herself in Czech, 'Well, just think about it. You can change your mind. Right at the last minute.'

'What did she say?' Bill asks, but I shake my head, appalled that I've given my secret away. I can't tell Bill what I've done, because I'm so furious with myself. I've been a terrible fool to admit I'm Czech, and maybe at this very second Berta is telling a Nazi guard where I can be found. I shake my head, sick to my stomach, wishing I'd said nothing. That night I have trouble getting to sleep, as I wait for the sound of marching boots.

But the boots don't come, and the days unwind. We begin to make plans for Christmas. It's essential to have something concrete to look forward to, when the promised end of the war moves away like a mirage. We pool our cigarettes and give them to Berta, to bring us a rabbit for Christmas Day. Ralph writes a beautiful menu card, and extra Red Cross parcels arrive just in time. Again we're given a whole one each. I yearn for Christmas at home and wonder how my mother and Marek are coping alone on the farm, and I wish there was something I could give Bill as a gift on Christmas Eve. But there's nothing. All I can give him is my love. I hope that'll be enough.

Bill tells me about Christmas at the pub in Stoke Newington, and how the regulars crowd in for a sing-song in the morning and how, at closing time in the afternoon, he and his parents go down the road to his aunt and uncle's house and stay there till late in the evening, because the pub doesn't open on Christmas night. He doesn't mention going to church on Christmas morning, but I can't imagine Christmas without singing carols and hearing the old story with its hope for all the good that might follow hardship and poverty – and the promise it holds that one day all of us prisoners who are so hungry and tired might eat until we can't manage another morsel, and rest in soft beds with clean sheets.

Bill lists all the things his family will eat on Christmas Day. I wonder what a figgy pudding tastes of and how it differs from the plum pudding, the Yorkshire pudding and the Christmas pudding. I think that perhaps when we have our own home I might introduce my Czech Christmas too – the delicious, gold-coloured, sweet *vánočka* bread on Christmas Eve, and in the evening all his family will gather round our table and we'll eat pea soup and fried carp with potato salad and black *kuba* made from mushrooms and garlic. I think how much he'll love this meal once he's tasted it. We'll have the Christmas biscuits I'll have been cooking and putting away, starting at the beginning of Advent: the sweet and aromatic vanilla crescents, or 'wasp nests' made from walnuts, or Linz cookies with marmalade, or our delicious Christmas gingerbread.

On Christmas Eve, Berta takes pity on us all and brings us a tin of Czech biscuits, a whole carp and a jar of black *kuba*. One of the other men opens the jar and sniffs it, recoiling from the garlic and passing it on. 'What's this fucking muck?' The others smell it and laugh, calling it 'shit' and 'diarrhoea', and I'm pleased Berta doesn't speak English, though she must understand the faces they're pulling. I'm furious at their bad manners on behalf of my countrywoman. So when the jar is handed to me, I dip in my finger and savour the delicious flavour of home. The other men say, 'Ugh!' and 'How can you!' but Berta's watching me, and I smile my appreciation.

She nods, imperceptibly. She hasn't told on me, and now I know she won't. The other men don't want the *kuba*, so I keep the whole jar for myself.

Berta can't be spared from her own house to cook the carp, but tries to instruct Scotty, giving detailed instructions in Czech and miming the frying of the fish and chopping of the potatoes for the salad. She sees me listening and cocks her head to me, inviting me to translate. I look away. When the mime descends into a hilarious stalemate, she brings in Rosa, who gives the instructions to Scotty.

'Fish for a Christmas dinner?' the men exclaim in astonishment. 'And potato salad?' Some of the men say they don't like fish – or not without something called batter – and Scotty asks if any extra eggs could be spared.

'I could try to make the potatoes into chips,' says Scotty, 'though I don't know how they'll fry without lard.'

'Fish and chips!' The men declare themselves highly delighted with this travesty of a Christmas meal. I'm disgusted at their lack of willingness to experiment and very glad Berta won't be here to see what they make of her carp. She hurries away to her own family, no doubt imagining that the British prisoners will have a proper Christmas feast.

When we return to our room, Scotty begins to throw everything off his bed and the bunk below.

'I cannae understand it. I know it was here. Some bugger's stolen it!'

'What's the matter?' asks Bill, and we all crowd around, prepared to help look.

'My chess set. I finished it yesterday. Every piece finished. And now it's gone. Some bastard's made off with it.'

Ralph calls an immediate meeting with the unofficial leaders of each of the bedrooms, but an hour later the chess set has not reappeared, and Scotty is yelling profanities and cursing the man who has been low enough to take two months' work.

His shouts bring Kurt into the house. 'Ah, yes,' he says, 'I have taken that. It is the property of the Reich.'

Ralph doesn't need to translate. Scotty lets out a howl of fury and launches himself at Kurt, whose hand drops to the pistol in his belt.

Bill and Ralph grab Scotty and pull him away from Kurt.

'You fuckin' bastard son of a whore,' shouts Scotty, flailing to release himself from his friends' grip. I drop down and wrap my arms around his knees.

Kurt waves his pistol at all of us, but hastily retreats to the door to the offices and locks it loudly from the other side.

Scotty struggles free from us and we stand back as he throws his tin mug and plate across the room and kicks the bunk bed, continuing to scream his rage.

'I'll get that fuckin' bastard if it's the last thing I do.'

It takes us almost half an hour to calm him, and I gather up the things he's thrown about the room. Bill folds the clothes and returns them quietly to his bunk, before surreptitiously checking his own kit-bag full of knitted items, in case those have been stolen too. His silence tells me everything is still there.

Eventually Scotty takes himself back to the kitchen to prepare the 'fish-and-chip supper'. Every time he remembers his chess set, his anger erupts afresh, but the act of skinning and filleting the carp gives him something new to focus on. I take a scale from the carp and put it in my pocket, and another for each of our friends. I don't tell them. This is my present to them – enough money for the following year. I always believed completely in this superstition till now, and although my conviction falters under the weight of irrefutable evidence about our situation, old habits are hard to break.

We all crowd into the kitchen in our pyjama bottoms, battle-dress tops and stockinged feet for the Christmas Eve meal of fish and chips. Each of us receives a small portion of fish, horribly coated in a soggy yellow batter, which adheres in some places and not others. We also have four or five fingers of potatoes, which have been fried. I think the stove hasn't been hot enough – it's hard to control a wood-burning range unless you have years of practice – and they have absorbed more fat than Scotty probably intended. Alongside these two yellow offerings is a small teaspoonful each of bright-green squashed peas. I think it's a shame to make delicious peas into a mash, but it seems to be the finishing touch all the men wanted, as one after another they exclaim, 'Fish and chips and mushy peas!' and clap Scotty on the back, until I think he almost believes he has made something delicious. The lovely fresh carp is subjected to a heavy dose of salt, and then vinegar, left over from pickling, is poured over it. I can't see the point of pickling something and then eating it immediately, and I find that the batter and vinegar together have completely stolen the fresh flavour of my Christmas carp. I have to work hard at being Cousins and pretending to smack my lips. Nobody else wants to try the black *kuba*, so I pick the carp out of the batter and eat it with that.

After supper everyone stays in the kitchen and Bill plays his harmonica for longer than I would have thought possible, as they sing music-hall tunes, Hollywood musical numbers, folk songs, rugby-club and barrack-room ballads, which I know to be rude because of the anxious glances my friends throw at me. Luckily, the increasingly tuneless quality of the singing renders the words almost impossible to make out.

Eventually everyone tires, and Bill says, 'It's almost midnight. Shall we finish with a carol?'

Everyone waits, and he plays the first notes of '*Stille Nacht, heilige Nacht*' and the hair rises up on the back of my neck. I think how strange it is that both sides in this terrible war will be singing the same carol about peace on this same night. All the men except Max begin to sing, and it's more tuneful and harmonious than all the previous songs. In this quieter choir, one voice rises above the rest, clear and true, and I see that it's Scotty's. His voice reminds me so much of my father's that tears well into my eyes and begin to fall down my cheeks, and I don't bother to hide them or wipe them away, because one by one the other men stop singing as they too are overcome by emotion. In the end it's only Bill's new harmonica and Scotty's true tenor:

Sleep in heavenly peace
Sleep in heavenly peace.

And as the notes fade away, we all sit still — they have joined me in silence and we are all united in identical longing. Then faces are wiped on the backs of sleeves and someone starts to applaud Scotty. Everyone joins in, and people are exclaiming, 'You dark horse!' and 'Didn't know you could sing like that!'

I think they should be thanking Bill too, and sure enough Ralph says, 'Three cheers for the singing chef and for the musical accompaniment! Hip-hip . . .'

'Hooray!' choruses everyone.

They begin to clap one another on the back and wish a 'silent night' all round. My back is stung with many hearty blows, and I make sure Cousins reciprocates.

I want to tell Bill how proud I am of him. His practising with the new harmonica has all been worth it. I feel sure that after the war he will be able to get some training and become a real musician in a famous orchestra.

We all climb into our beds and Bill whispers, 'Sleep well, and happy Christmas.'

I allow myself two squares of chocolate as I lie thinking about my mother and Marek. I can almost feel my mother lying awake in her bed, wondering where I am and if I'm all right. I try to send her a dream of me, happy and well, so she'll know I'm still alive.

* * *

On Christmas morning there's no wake-up call, so we sleep until the watery sun is as bright as it ever will be.

All my bunk room wishes each other a merry Christmas, and I mouth the words too, not sure if anyone will be passing our door. Bill delightedly dives into his kit-bag and presents us each with something he's knitted. Max has a hat with flaps that come down over his ears, and the boys agree he makes a perfect Sherlock Holmes – they have to explain to me who he is. Ralph has thick socks that he says will be a tonic for his poor feet; Scotty has a pair of mittens; and I have a scarf so long I can wrap it around my neck twice, and a matching hat with a fluff on top like a rabbit's tail, which Bill calls a bobble. I'm very curious about how he made this bobble, but most importantly, the hat and scarf are very warm.

I'm deeply moved as Scotty, Max and Ralph each bring me a Christmas gift. Ralph gives me a new notebook and pencil, Scotty brings me chocolate, and Max gives me half a pack of precious coffee. I cast about wildly in my mind, mentally listing the contents of my kit-bag, but know I have nothing to give them in return apart from the carp scales I tucked away for them. I feel too embarrassed to offer those.

My expression must clearly convey my consternation because Ralph says gently, 'You have no idea what you've given to us, do you? You've given us all hope that, even in this hell, there can still be love and courage.'

'Aye,' agrees Scotty, 'you gee us something to work for, to fight for.'

Max nods. 'It's even more than that, for me. I think I owe you my life. Half a coffee ration isn't much in return for that.'

'Enough of all this,' says Bill. 'Cousins will have his head turned! And we've got a feast to make.'

We have agreed to take shifts in the kitchen of two hours for each bedroom, pooling all our saved Red Cross rations to make a feast, and trying overly hard to be cheerful. When the five of us have our turn in the kitchen, we open the 'hooch' that Scotty has lovingly fermented. It tastes terrible, but everyone slugs it back and immediately I feel quite light-headed. Within a few minutes the dizziness becomes an overwhelming desire for Bill. I can hardly look at him, longing to signal to him somehow to sneak back into our room. I imagine he might grip my shoulders and press my back against the door to stop anyone coming in, and he might start kissing me and I would be panting, and he would put his hand over my mouth to stop me crying out with joy as he pushed himself inside me and thrust until we are both trembling and satisfied. I keep my head down, so the others can't read my shameful thoughts, and when the hooch bottle comes round again I shake my head.

'What's the matter, Cousins?' laughs Max. 'Can't take your drink?'

I mime a wobbliness to my head, and their laughter eggs me on to stagger about the room until they are laughing so hard they're wiping tears from their eyes.

'Better than Charlie Chaplin!' gasps Bill.

There's a knock at the door, and Berta comes into the kitchen, looking at our feast laid out on the table. We have tinned fish and beef, most of a loaf each, a big plate of saved-up biscuits and a strange scone-like pudding made from flour, sugar, margarine and jam. We didn't expect to see Berta today. She should be with her family and must have come straight from church. She's carrying a plate, covered with a bowl, which she places on our feast table. 'I saved a little of our Christmas Eve dinner for you,' she says in Czech, as if to nobody in particular.

Ralph lifts the bowl on a small portion of carp prepared properly, and potato salad and more black *kuba*. Everyone thanks her politely and she wishes us '*Veselé Vánoce*' and hurries away. I begin to wonder if it would be safer for my friends if I just slipped away with Berta, when the time comes for us to leave. I don't think the Nazis would bother searching for me. Not with the whole Red Army bearing down on them. I think perhaps that leaving Bill is the final act of bravery this war demands of me. My ultimate act of resistance. I shake my head. I'll think about this when Christmas is over.

As soon as the door closes, we fall on the feast, like the starving men we are. I pull Berta's delicious dinner to me and don't offer it to anybody else. This is all mine. We eat fast, trying to make up for so many months of hunger.

Conversation is all about Christmases past – anecdotes about uncles who fell asleep after lunch and had tricks played on them; Christmas when it snowed and Christmas when it didn't. I'm amazed that there could be Christmas without snow.

Ralph says, 'So what was everyone's best Christmas ever, and best Christmas present? Scotty, you first.'

He thinks for a minute and then says, 'I was seven, and me mam and dad were still speaking to each other, an' I had a pair of roller skates, which was just what I'd asked for, so I truly believed that Father Christmas had brought them to me. My dad drove me into Edinburgh to the roller-skating rink. It was the only time I ever went there, but it seemed such a magical place, where people could do things which I kenned were impossible – even turnin' roond and skating backwards.'

'I never tried roller skates, but I went to Central Park to ice-skate once or twice when I was a kid,' says Max. He takes over. 'My family couldn't celebrate Christmas, of course, but didn't celebrate Hanukkah, either. Atheists. I always felt as if I was missing out – half my friends had Christian holidays and half had Jewish holidays, and I didn't have either. All we had was the Internationale! But I do remember one Christmas, because we looked in a Brooklyn toy-store window. There was a big whispered debate, and in the end they took me in and bought me a model aeroplane. It came all the way to London with me, even though we had to leave the States in a hurry after some strike my dad organised, and it's still in my room at home. At least I think it is.' There's a moment's silence, and I guess we are all thinking of the last time we saw our homes, wondering if they are still standing.

Then Ralph takes up the thread. 'We had lovely Christmases as children. My sisters all used to dress up, and we'd play charades, and there would be delicious food, but I think my best one was going home the year after I'd changed from medicine to Classics. It was a joy to know that I'd be going back to a world I finally fitted into.'

'Best present?' prompts Bill.

Ralph thinks hard. 'Maybe a train I had when I was a boy. I loved that train. What about you, Bill?'

I think he'll say something about the pub and Flora, and a whole world I've never been part of, and I'm prepared to be jealous, but he looks steadily and seriously at me and says, 'This is my best-ever Christmas, and my best-ever present is sitting next to me.'

I see Ralph's eyes are bright with tears as he raises his tin mug. 'A toast.' We raise our mugs as Ralph makes a toast: 'To those who've found happiness, that they keep it for ever; and to those who are still looking for it, that we find it in equal measure.'

We bang our mugs and say, 'To happiness.'

Bill adds, 'And to friends.'

We drink again and Scotty adds, 'And to the end of this effing war.'

Bill stands up and raises his cup and solemnly echoes, 'The end of the war.'

21

With January comes more snow than Bill has ever seen, and the work in the quarry slows as the marble is buried under drifts. Some days it's a light enough snowfall for the prisoners to sweep away, but the marble has become slippery and work soon has to be abandoned. It's colder than Bill could possibly have imagined. Herr Rauchbach tells Ralph it's minus-twenty centigrade at night, and Ralph says that's minus-four Fahrenheit. Bill thinks that's a long, long way below freezing point. For days together, the men are unable to leave their quarters, and everyone gets on one another's nerves.

One never-ending day Ralph, Bill, Max and Izzy are sitting in their room. Bill has started knitting a new scarf, with a complicated pattern. Ralph asks him the name of the pattern, saying it's like a cricket sweater, and Bill says, 'Cable stitch.'

'Like Cable Street,' says Max. He turns to Izzy. 'The most marvellous battle against Mosley's fascists,' he says, 'in 1936. We nearly had a Hitler ourselves, you know.'

Bill puts his head down and concentrates hard on the knitting.

Max is enthusiastic. 'They were all marching, the Blackshirts, and tried to get into the East End. They were anti-Semites like the Nazis, you see, and us Jews all lived in the East End. But we rose up – they say there were twenty thousand of us: Jews, communists, anarchists! We built a barricade, at the Christian Street end – you know it, Bill . . . ?' His eyes glitter.

Bill pretends to be focused on his knitting, knowing what's coming, but with no idea how to avoid it. He'd like to jump up and hurry from the room, but that might look worse.

'The police were trying to let the bastards through, and we were fighting the police with chair legs, broom handles, anything we could find. The women in the houses were emptying piss-pots down on the police, and kids were chucking marbles under the hooves of the police horses. Mosley backed down and they left, and we carried on fighting with the police, because they were on the side of the fascists against us. And I was arrested and nearly had my arm twisted off, but it was worth it.'

Ralph asks how long he was in prison, but Max doesn't answer. He's looking oddly at Bill.

'Were you there, Bill?'

Bill lifts his head from his knitting and gazes long and slow at Max. His heart is thumping, and he knows there's going to be trouble. 'I was there,' he says in a neutral voice.

Max scratches his head. 'You weren't . . . you weren't one of the Blackshirts?'

'No – no, I wasn't.'

'But not fighting them, either?'

'No. Not fighting. Just interested.'

'Interested in fascism?'

Izzy gasps and clamps her hand over her mouth.

'Interested in Mosley?' Max's voice is low and dangerous.

Bill carefully lays down his knitting and looks from Izzy to Max. 'Look, you've gotta understand. Mosley was a great speaker. We used to listen to him out of my friend's window. When he spoke you could feel yourself being swept up, and thinking: He must be right; he seems to be able to explain everything.'

'Yeah, like Hitler and Franco and Mussolini and Stalin could explain everything.'

Max and Bill are both sitting very upright, as if squaring up to each other for a fight. Izzy's face is a picture of horror at what she's hearing.

'Well,' says Bill, picking his words carefully and watching Izzy's expression, 'they wouldn't have had followers, if they hadn't said things that people agreed with.' Bill holds up his hand to stop Max cutting across him. 'It was all wrong, what he said – I know that now – but it seemed so convincing at the time.'

Max's voice is beginning to rise. 'And when did you discover that? At Tobruk? When your pals got their legs blown off? When you got your first beating from a Nazi guard? Or not till the wind turned at Lamsdorf and we could smell the smoke from the death-camps? Eh? When?'

Max is on his feet and bristling for a fight, but Bill stays sitting, tense and ready to duck a blow, not wanting to enrage Max any further. The effort to keep his voice calm makes it squeaky. 'I said I was wrong, didn't I?'

Ralph comes nearer, ready to intervene. 'Come on, Max, he said he was wrong!'

But Max is yelling and pacing. 'Yes, it's all right to say it now. Now that millions of people have had to die. It's all right if it doesn't affect you, isn't it? He's sitting pretty, isn't he, with his fucking knitting and his fucking bint . . . ?'

He flicks his hand towards Izzy, and she draws back in shock as if the word has hit her in the face.

Bill leaps to his feet, and his knitting clatters to the floor. He stands between her and Max, with his fists up.

Ralph steps between them and grabs Max by the arms. 'Stop it. Stop it now. Go outside and cool off.'

Max strains at his grasp. 'I'll take him outside and show the fascist bastard not to mess with the little Jew-boy.'

Ralph starts to push him back towards the bedroom door, which opens as others are brought out by the shouting.

'Get him out of here,' yells Ralph over Max's furious, 'Come outside, come on, you fucking coward.'

As the other men drag Max out of the room, Bill can still hear him in the kitchen, swearing and kicking the furniture. Bill hopes he isn't telling everyone that he's a fascist or, worse still, telling them about Izzy.

Ralph reads Bill's thoughts. 'I'll go and make sure he doesn't say anything about Cousins.'

And then Bill is left alone with Izzy, and the disgust is clear on her face.

She spits out the whispered words, 'Is true? Are you Nazi?'

Bill is anguished. 'No, no! Listen, you have to understand. We were hungry. There was a Depression. There wasn't enough work. Everyone was blaming the Jews. Well, some of my mates perhaps, but not me. I've never told you this: my life was saved when I was born by a Jewish woman from the upstairs flat. I was delivered with the cord around my neck and I was blue, but this woman knew what to do, and she literally breathed life into me. So I ain't never been prejudiced. How could I be?' He pauses, trying to find the right words to make Izzy understand – and not to hate him. He blunders on. 'But when everyone keeps saying something, you think it might be true . . . It was Jewish bankers and moneylenders they went on about. And foreigners coming over and taking our jobs, when so many English families was going hungry. I was fifteen, that's all. And Mosley was a speaker like you've never heard. He could draw pictures in the air with his words, and you felt yourself pulled to him like a magnet. He made it all seem so clear, and he had answers. He was like, I don't know, some sort of prophet.'

Bill takes a stride towards Izzy with his hands out, but she steps back, searching his face, as if asking what kind of man she has married. Bill's hands fall to his sides.

'Do you really think that of me?' he says, sick with desperation. 'Do you really believe I'm no better than these Nazi scum?'

How can Izzy think so little of him?

She whispers, 'I not know you.' And he can't bear the cold distance opening up between them.

'I was fifteen,' he repeats. 'Out with my mates, for a laugh and a few beers. We didn't know that a few clever words could lead to all this.' He sweeps with his arm and his gesture includes the Russian soldiers; the death-camps; his friends, mutilated and killed in battle; four long years of imprisonment and starvation. 'All this,' he repeats. 'All this.'

His eyes search her face again and, not finding the love he expects to see, he sits down heavily.

'I not know you,' she repeats bleakly.

He wishes she was angry with him, anything but this chill of no love.

'Didn't you ever do anything stupid when you were fifteen?'

he asks bitterly, then drops his head in his hands. If he has lost Izzy, then he has lost everything. He might as well be dead.

There's no sound or movement in the room for what feels to Bill like hours, and then Izzy is on her knees in front of him, lifting his head from his hands, kissing and kissing his face, whispering, 'Sorry, sorry, sorry.'

'Shh!' He lifts a hand to her cropped hair. 'Shh! It's all right. As long as you still love me, it's all right.'

In answer she kisses him on the lips, fiercely, as if her life depends on it.

Then they pull apart, and he lifts her from her knees to sit next to him on the bed and is saying, 'Because if you don't love me, it's all for nothing, and I might as well . . .', when there's a light rap on the door, and it opens.

Ralph puts his head round the door. 'Am I intruding?'

'No, come in. Shut the door,' says Bill, dreading the thought that Ralph now finds him abhorrent too. He wipes his face with the back of his arm, and Izzy slides a little away from him on the bed. 'It's all right,' says Bill. 'I mean, we're all right. I've explained. I was just a kid. I was all wrong, a stupid idiot.' He searches Ralph's expression and finds nothing but compassion in his eyes.

Bill's anxiety lifts as Ralph says, 'I know. I understand. Lots of people were taken in. Just as they were in Germany, in Spain, in Italy, everywhere.'

Bill says sadly, 'But Max'll never see it like that.'

Ralph sighs. 'No, he probably won't. Not yet anyway. He wants to move to another room. He's just said that it's a political disagreement. Frank's offered to swap. You need to give Max time, that's all. It's being cooped up like this.'

Max comes in and starts to clear his books from the little

window ledge. He hesitates and hands *The Ragged Trousered Philanthropists* to Izzy.

Bill stands up and holds out his hand. 'Look, Max. I'm sorry,' he says awkwardly, 'Please don't go.'

But Max doesn't reply and doesn't take the proffered hand. He won't even look at Bill, but turns to Izzy. 'I'll still do everything I can to keep you safe, but I just can't be in here for now.'

Izzy nods in sorrow as Scotty bursts in, to see Max removing his belongings from his bunk. 'Och, come on, man!' he says. 'We all have our rows. It's to be expected, shut up in a place like this. Cabin fever. But . . .'

Max is near the door now. 'No, this is best. It's not as if I won't see you all again tonight and tomorrow, and all the rest of our shit lives in this dump. Let me through.'

Scotty stands aside and Max leaves.

'I'm so sorry,' says Bill to Izzy and Scotty. And he is. Sorry to be the reason for losing one of the men who've taken such care of his beloved Izzy. Sorry for things he did in his youth, which he can't go back and change. Sorry that Izzy is obviously so upset to lose Max. He feels a hundred years old.

'Och, there's something been eatin' him for months,' says Scotty.

Ralph returns to the room with Frank, who's agreed to swap beds with Max.

'Evenin' all,' says Frank. 'I gather there's been a rumpus. I was ready for a change. Can't stand Blake's snoring. Hope none of you snore. Where am I?'

Ralph points out Max's bunk, and they all look at one another. Bill decides that one more man must be let in on the secret.

'There's something we need to tell you,' he says quietly, shutting the door.

280

Frank's reaction is more oddly mixed than that in the original bunkhouse in Lamsdorf.

'God all-fucking Almighty! That is . . . Sorry. Can he speak English?'

Izzy nods, slightly amused, and Frank stares hard at her.

'Of course. Of course she's a—'

Bill holds up a warning hand, nodding towards the door, and Frank swallows the word as he continues.

'Of course she – he – understands. Sorry about the language.' He seems excited and buoyed up, pacing up and down and looking closely into Izzy's face, as if she's a waxwork at an exhibition. 'God almighty. It's true. So he's not mute?'

Izzy grins widely, and Frank holds out his hand to her, pumping hers up and down, saying, 'I never thought a wom—Sorry, I don't know how you keep so quiet, if you don't mind me saying.' Then he leaves off and begins to shake Bill's hand. It looks as if he wants to kiss them both. 'You did it,' he exalts. 'You bloody did it.'

'Nobody must know,' cautions Ralph.

'Nobody. No, of course not.' Frank makes the sign of a cross on his chest. 'Cross my heart and hope to bloody die. Well, well, you only bloody did it. Right under their noses! One in the eye for the Nazis. I won't breathe a word. I swear. I bloody swear!'

He laughs aloud, and Bill knows he's thinking of Rosa and of all the things that might be possible, if he's just patient.

'Nobody. Not even Rosa,' says Bill.

Frank looks around the room and sees that everyone knows about his feelings for Rosa.

'Not even Rosa,' he repeats solemnly. 'But if it can happen for you . . .'

They all nod, and it's like the men at Lamsdorf said: what's happened for Bill and Izzy gives hope to others. Hope spreading like a virus.

The wind changes. It's coming from the east, and it tastes of ice and snow. In the house Izzy starts to seem withdrawn, as though she's turned in on her own worrying thoughts. Bill asks her if it's Kurt, or if she's ill, or if she's homesick, and she simply shakes her head. So he's relieved when they're in the bedroom with Ralph, and he asks Izzy, 'Shouldn't you have had your period by now?'

Bill's ashamed that he has no idea when this is due. Perhaps married men are supposed to know stuff like this. Izzy nods miserably, and she looks really scared. For one moment Bill wonders if she's pregnant, despite the fact that they haven't had sex since they were arrested.

'It's just because you've lost so much weight,' Ralph reassures her. 'You must be below six-and-a-half stone now. Don't worry – you'll be able to have babies in the future. It's not a permanent thing.'

When tears of gratitude well up in Izzy's eyes, Bill knows that Ralph has guessed correctly.

'Thank God,' she mutters inaudibly.

Bill doesn't know if she's thanking God because she doesn't have to cope with the bleeding again, or because one day she will be a woman again. Both, he suspects.

At night now they can hear the Soviet guns, like a constant drumroll. Herr Rauchbach tells everyone, through Ralph, that they're only twenty-five kilometres away and he's had notice that the prisoners will be moved back to Lamsdorf as soon as a truck can come for them.

'Fifteen miles,' says Ralph. 'Less than a day's march.'

'You've been good workers,' Herr Rauchbach tells them, 'and I wish I could have done more for you.'

Kurt scowls, his eyebrows meeting in a line above the nose that Scotty broke by kicking when he sneaked into their room.

Bill talks to Ralph about how much Herr Rauchbach must fear the Russians, who would shoot him as a Nazi collaborator, and wonders how he'll hide Rosa from them. He remembers Izzy's mother making plans to disguise her as a boy, and his own eagerness to get her out of the path of the Red Army. There's a rumour circulating in the house that Herr Rauchbach has bought Rosa a ticket to Prague, but she's refusing to go, because of a prisoner. Bill hopes it's Frank, but fears it must be the man who was here before.

The prisoners begin to make preparations for their journey, although some of the men are whispering about trying to escape instead.

Bill asks Izzy, 'Should we try to escape, d'you think? Tell Berta who you are and see if she can get us away?' He's used now to answering himself. 'But then you might fall into the hands of the Soviets. Better maybe to try and reach the Americans. That'd be safer for you. Shall we go back to Lamsdorf and see what's planned? Maybe the guards'll hand us to the Yanks. They won't want to come up against the Russians, either. Not after the way the Nazis have treated the Russian prisoners.'

Izzy nods, though Bill's not sure what she's agreeing with.

He continues thinking aloud. 'If Berta could help us escape, we might make it to the partisans, but it would be so dangerous, and either of us could get shot as escapees. Or we might meet the Russians first. No, our best chance of getting out of this alive and together is to remain prisoners, even if it means going back to Lamsdorf.'

Everyone is trading with the local women for anything useful. Bill and Izzy make a list.

'Your boots are still good,' he says to her, inspecting them closely, 'but mine are in rags. What d'you think? Hobnailed, if possible.'

She writes down *thick socks* and *wool underneaths* and *paraffin wax or other wax, even candles.* Bill is puzzled by the last item, but doesn't question it.

His new boots and additional underwear cost all their pooled cigarettes and all but half a bar of soap, but he knows they'll be worth it. They now have three sets of long johns and long-sleeved vests each, and now they're so skinny, they'll all fit under their army uniforms.

Izzy and Bill are the last prisoners in the kitchen one dinnertime, when Berta beckons Izzy over to the stove and pulls the tin of wax from her apron pocket. She hands Izzy the tin, but holds onto it, saying something quietly to her in Czech. Bill freezes. She knows. He's sure Berta knows. Izzy looks from him to Berta and almost speaks, then clamps her lips together and hurries back to their room. Bill is close behind her.

'She knows, doesn't she?' he whispers urgently. 'And she's offered to get you away?' But Izzy keeps walking.

Bill's head spins with confusion. Has Izzy been holding out on him, and is she planning to escape with Berta? Would she be safer without him? Would she be happier? And how would he find the strength to carry on if he woke one morning and she was gone?

In their room, Izzy spreads Bill's, Scotty's and Ralph's coats on the floor, rubbing wax into the shoulders, back and torso. Frank looks bemused until Scotty explains that it will make them waterproof. Bill watches her with a mixture of pride and quiet misery at the prospect of losing her.

'Fishermen do it,' says Scotty.

Frank hurries to fetch Izzy his coat and asks if she'll waterproof his as well. There isn't much wax, but she does. Bill still has the waxed hood and cape her mother made.

Ralph says, 'I wish Max . . .' and Izzy nods. He goes and returns with Max's coat, although this means she can't do anyone's coat thoroughly. When the tin's empty, Izzy gives each of the men a candle and shows them how to rub it on their hats and the outsides of their gloves and boots.

Then they carry everything into the kitchen and lay the coats over the range until the wax begins to melt and they can rub it deeper into the fabric. Some of the upstairs men complain that they're hogging all the heat, so Bill takes the last of their supply of firewood and lights the stove in their room. They all work now on their own coats, Bill helping Izzy, rubbing the warmed wax deep into the fabric. Later they pack their kit-bags, so they'll be ready to leave at a moment's notice. Bill can hear the guns. They sound so close.

Despite his kind words, Herr Rauchbach is keen to get one more order fulfilled before his workers are taken away, and the prisoners are still in the quarry from dawn to dusk. Max usually tries to work in a different part of the quarry from Bill now, but Kurt orders him to join Izzy, Ralph, Scotty and Bill at a new section until the light is almost gone, while he goes off to gather in the tools and search the other prisoners on the way back to the house.

'I don't think Kurt's coming back,' says Ralph. 'We should just stop.'

'I can't see what the hell I'm doing,' complains Bill. 'This is too dangerous.'

Max shoulders his pickaxe. 'I'm going back. It's stupid.'

The five of them trudge up the lane from the quarry, aching, cold, too hungry to think, when suddenly, by the tool-hut, Kurt blocks their way with a gun trained on them. His fingers trace his flattened nose, eyes glittering revenge. He cocks his gun. They all freeze, and there's no sound but one another's breathing. Kurt advances slowly towards Izzy and levels the gun at her chest. Bill is anchored to the spot. He wants to rugby-tackle Kurt to the ground, but knows he wouldn't be able to move quickly enough to stop him firing the gun and killing Izzy. He holds himself tight and forces himself to wait for an opportunity.

Kurt says something to Izzy in Czech – indicating a pile of marble slabs. The others look from him to Izzy, and her face is a mask of terror. Bill can't bear it. Not knowing she's already understood every Czech word, Kurt repeats what he's said to Ralph in German. Even in the half-light, Bill can see Ralph's face blanch, but he still doesn't know what's being said. Ralph doesn't translate.

Kurt turns to Izzy with the gun still aimed at her breastbone and says, in English, 'Coat. Off. Trousers down.' He points to the pile of slabs and demonstrates bending over; then he grins widely and does a grotesque mime of what he plans to do to her.

Her eyes blank with horror and despair, Izzy begins to fumble at her coat buttons with shaking, gloved fingers. She can't look at Bill and the others.

Keep calm, Bill thinks; if I can keep calm, I might have a

chance to knock the gun from his hand before his filthy cock touches her.

'*Raus, raus,*' Kurt urges Izzy, his voice hoarse with excitement and anticipation. Izzy pulls her gloves off with her teeth so that she can unfasten her coat. She drops her gloves and coat onto the slushy snow, and Kurt indicates for her to undo her trousers and turn round. He switches the gun to his left hand, but keeps it aimed at her body as he unbuttons his flies and his prick leaps out, stiff and ready.

Izzy looks away from it and begins to unfasten her trousers, trembling all over. Acid rises to Bill's mouth, and he holds himself like a runner, awaiting his opportunity, knowing that if he intervenes too soon she'll be shot, and if he leaves it too late she'll be raped. She pushes her trousers to her knees, leaving her long underwear pulled up, and glances quickly at Bill, warning him not to endanger himself. Then she turns from them and bends over the pile of marble slabs.

Kurt moves close behind her, holding the gun to her head with his left hand as his right hand pulls down her underwear. For a moment Kurt's left hand with the gun waves wildly in the air, as he concentrates on using his right to guide himself into position.

Knowing this might be his only chance, Bill leaps forward, but someone else is ahead of him by half a second, a dark shape from his left, knocking Kurt to the ground. A gunshot rings out and, as Bill lands on top of Kurt and the other man, he sees Izzy fall from the pile of slabs into the snow, lying on her stomach. Bill's thumping the body he's fallen on with both fists, while turning his head to see if Izzy has been hit. She doesn't move. If she's dead, he might as well be dead himself.

Then she screams out, an anguished, 'Bill!'

'I'm here,' he calls, scrabbling across the bodies and through the snow towards her.

Ralph yanks the gun from Kurt's hand and sends it spinning into the slush. Izzy is struggling to roll over, hampered by the trousers and underwear around her thighs. Bill still fears she's been shot, and all thought of Kurt is gone from his head as he rushes to help her, yelling, 'Did he get you? Are you hurt?'

Simultaneously she cries out, 'Did he shoot you?'

He hoists her to her feet, as she yanks up her underwear and trousers.

'Are you all right?' he asks again.

And Izzy stutters, 'Yes, all right. You, are you all right?'

'Yes, yes.'

They look each other over quickly to check they are telling the truth, then turn to see Scotty lying face-down on Kurt. Max and Ralph heave his body to one side, and he is heavy and inert, lying prone in the snow. Bill grabs the pistol and kneels on Kurt's chest, crashing him in the face with the butt of the pistol, shouting, 'You fucking bastard!' But Kurt is completely still. A thin band of moonlight is enough for them to see a red slash has been opened across his throat, and blood is pouring out onto the path.

Ralph and Max roll Scotty's body over, and they can all see he's taken the bullet that was meant for Izzy. There's a huge hole in his stomach, pumping dark blood into the snow. Bill knows it would have been him lying there, if Scotty hadn't moved a second sooner. In Scotty's hand is the knife he used to carve his chess set, wet with Kurt's blood.

Bill aims the gun at Kurt's lifeless face, but Ralph wrenches it from his grip. 'Stop now – it's done. It's over.'

Izzy is shivering violently from shock and cold. Bill picks up her coat and gloves and wraps the coat around Izzy's shoulders. 'Here, put these back on.' Black puddles spread around Scotty and Kurt, as Bill helps her push her arms back through the sleeves of her coat. 'Hush now,' he says. 'It's over.'

Lights flashed on in the house at the sound of the gunshot, and now Herr Rauchbach and some of the office workers are hurrying down the path towards them with strong torches.

'There's been a terrible accident,' calls Ralph, repeating it in German.

Herr Rauchbach lifts his torch above his head to cast light on the bloody scene. Kurt and Scotty are sprawled in the snow, both obviously dead, with a stream of black gore from each of them now running down the path towards the quarry. Ralph begins to retch and turns aside to vomit into the snow.

'What happened?' demands Herr Rauchbach.

Clouds of steam rise from their breath as they wait for Ralph to wipe his mouth with the back of his hand and straighten up to speak. He doesn't look again at the bodies.

'An argument,' stutters Ralph. 'A terrible argument between them. Scotty must have had a knife. And, look, Bill's found Kurt's gun.'

Bill frowns at Ralph; he was planning to keep the gun. But he hands it to Herr Rauchbach, who drops it in a pocket.

Thin flakes of snow begin to fall.

'We can't leave them here,' says Max. 'They'll be covered in snow by morning.'

'How about the tool-shed?' asks Ralph. 'Not very respectful, I know, but away from the wolves, until they can be buried properly.'

Herr Rauchbach nods assent, and between the four of them they carry Scotty and then Kurt. As they lift Kurt, Herr Rauchbach takes in Kurt's open fly and flailing member. He steps forward and tucks it away. Kurt's and Scotty's arms and legs slip from their grip and they make slow progress, but eventually lay them side-by-side on the shed floor.

Herr Rauchbach says something in German and Ralph translates. 'A violent man meets a violent death.'

Herr Rauchbach padlocks the tool-shed and they trudge slowly back to the house, shocked into silence.

For once nobody is hungry, and Bill lies for most of the night thinking of what almost happened to Izzy, feeling that he's failed her utterly. He isn't the one who saved her, and if he had, it would be him who was dead, not Scotty. He reaches the painful decision that she might be safer escaping with Berta. These thoughts chase one another round and round his head till he falls into an exhausted sleep just before dawn.

In the morning Kurt's family comes to claim his body, and two Nazi guards arrive from Saubsdorf. They instruct the prisoners to lift Kurt onto the cart. His body is as stiff as frozen washing now and easier to carry. Izzy doesn't glance at his face, but Bill looks hard and remembers what Kurt wanted to do to Izzy – what he would have done to others throughout his life, if he'd had the chance – and thinks: I hope he burns in hell.

Herr Rauchbach covers him with a blanket. Kurt's mother is crying noisily, but everybody else is silent. Herr Rauchbach says something in German and the Nazi guards salute. He repeats it in Czech, and Kurt's father spits in the snow.

Once the cart has pulled away, the guards instruct Ralph and Max to dig a grave for Scotty in the woods. They clear snow from a patch, but the ground is thick with tree roots and, even with pickaxes, they can't get down more than a few inches into the frozen earth. Berta and Herr Rauchbach and Rosa and the other prisoners stand around watching as they lift Scotty's body into the shallow grave. He is barely below the surface of the earth. Ralph lays a handkerchief over his face.

Bill hunts around for two suitable sticks to make a cross. As soon as he understands what Bill's doing, one of the guards cuts off side-branches with his bayonet. Berta goes to the kitchen for a length of string to tie the cross together. Then everyone stands around the makeshift grave with their heads bared, even though the snow has started falling again.

Ralph stutters, 'He was a good man, and we'll never forget him.'

Bill's never seen Ralph lost for words before, so Bill takes over. He says the Lord's Prayer, and Herr Rauchbach repeats it in Czech. Izzy crosses herself, and Bill sees Berta exchange a long, long look with her. Izzy's going to stay here when we leave, thinks Bill. And the thought is like lead in his stomach.

Bill and Max shovel soil over Scotty's poor body, but he's barely covered by it. The wolves will dig him out before morning.

'There are buckets of chippings from the quarry,' Ralph says. 'We could heap those over him.'

The guards give their approval, and Izzy, Bill, Ralph and Max begin to ferry the buckets of marble chips from the tool-shed. Although their fingers have now lost all feeling, they carefully build a cairn with all the white marble chippings. They carry a heavy marble slab between them and lay it on the top. Bill thinks Scotty's grave is as good as a Nazi general's. He remembers Scotty

291

cooking the Christmas meal and knows his death has saved both Izzy and himself. A debt like that can never be repaid. Should he repay it by insisting that Izzy escapes with Berta, or by refusing ever to be parted from her? They stand quietly until the snow is thick on their hair and shoulders.

'Come on,' says Bill eventually, 'we need to pack our things.'

As they gather their small belongings together, Bill wonders who else might die because of him and Izzy. Or has she already decided she puts them in too much danger?

Later in the afternoon a truck arrives to take them back to Lamsdorf. As Bill returns from the latrine, he sees Berta by the range, whispering urgently to Izzy in Czech. There's fear as well as hope in Berta's face, and Bill knows what a risk she would be taking. For a moment he imagines Izzy hiding in her house, dressing in her daughter's clothes with a scarf around her short hair, being smuggled by one neighbour and then another, until she's knocking at the door of her farm. Her mother opening the door. And then? What then? What about the Russians? Has Scotty saved her from Kurt only to face worse?

Izzy raises her head to him, and Bill thinks he can't bear this to be the last time he ever sees her. She looks deep into his eyes and slowly places her right hand over her heart. Then she's moving towards their room, stammering something to Berta as she leaves the kitchen with Bill.

Berta follows with a basket of bread and drops a packet of raisins and a small bottle of plum brandy into Izzy's pocket, whispering one last thing in Czech and crossing herself. Bill is in a hurricane of emotion – relief and joy that Izzy isn't leaving him, whirling with anxiety and fear about what they might have to face next. He thinks he can face anything with her beside him. He thinks she is the bravest person he's ever met. Herr Rauchbach, Berta and Rosa stand on the track to watch them leave. Frank, in the back of the lorry with them, is slumped in despair, because Rosa's eyes are sad but dry. He isn't the man she loves, and he knows it. Bill hopes she'll get away before the Russians come.

The truck is canvas-covered, and although that keeps the sleet off them, it does nothing to keep out the cold. They are wearing all their clothes and wrap themselves in blankets, but are almost frozen by the time they arrive at Lamsdorf. On the road Bill thinks of Scotty and the life he might have had. He swears to himself that he and Izzy will make it home, and one day they'll tell their children about Scotty – about the man who died so they could live.

22

It's late afternoon when we arrive back at Lamsdorf, and there's chaos in the Stalag. Although the guards are still at the gate, there's none of the usual form-filling and bureaucracy. Nobody to look me up and down and tick off Algernon Cousins in their book. We can hear the sound of artillery fire, loud and close.

'It won't be long now,' one man says, with relish.

We're directed to a hut that looks as if a whirlwind has gone through it, with clothing and even tins of food strewn all over the bunks and the floor. There are books, which Max begins to pick up. We're told that a thousand men were given an hour's notice the previous night and marched from the camp, out into the snow. The plan is to send the rest of us out in groups of one or two thousand.

Ralph remembers being told there could be 13,000 British prisoners at any one time in Lamsdorf, and 12,000 more out at work camps. 'Twenty-five thousand Brits,' he says, 'and God knows how many of all the other nationalities. That's a big evacuation. Though I suppose they had practice with Warsaw.'

The prisoners who remain are making hurried preparations,

in case they are one of the groups that will leave tonight. We watch as packing cases are torn apart to make sledges. Shirts are buttoned up to make rough backpacks that bulge with tins. Frank meets some of his old friends and plans to march with them. So our old foursome is together again, though Bill and Max don't look at each other or speak. We drop our kit onto one of the abandoned bunks.

'We haven't got much time,' says Bill. I've never seen him take charge before, but suddenly there's a need for his practicality, rather than Ralph's and Max's book learning. 'We'll need a sledge to take as much food as we can pull. I can do that. We used to make them in the factory at Mankendorf.' He begins to yank the slats from one of the abandoned top bunks. 'I'll take these to the carpenter's shop. Ralph, can you take Cousins and get food? Max, are you with us?'

Max looks at all the strangers bustling around us.

Ralph says, 'Please?' and I lay my hand on his sleeve. Max looks from me to Ralph and nods.

'Warm clothes and blankets,' Bill continues. 'Find anything you can that might stop us from freezing, if they really go through with this madness. We should hide our bags up here while we're all away.'

We shove our kit-bags and blankets up into the rafters, while Bill continues to pull timber from the bunks, and then Ralph and I run to the hut where Red Cross parcels are distributed. Normally they're handed out through the window, but now the door is wide open and prisoners are taking as much as they can carry. The lazy-eyed guard is at the door, but he just watches. A fight breaks out as two men try to grab the same parcel. The guard steps in and fires a warning shot. Other people are ripping open the parcels and selecting food. One man is stuffing his pockets with cigarettes. I carry three parcels and Ralph carries five, piled up in front of us. They are heavy and awkward.

Back in the hut, Max is saying goodbye to his little library of books. He's managed to find us an extra blanket each, an assortment of other clothing from the stores and a pile of coats.

'They were issuing Dutch and Belgian greatcoats,' he says. 'Must have had them there all the time, the bastards. I brought us one each. They aren't waxed like ours, but might do as extra blankets.' He addresses Ralph. 'They say that men who aren't able to walk are to be left behind and taken by train. Do you think . . . ?'

Ralph shakes his head. 'I know my feet are bad, but I'll keep up as long as I can. I'd rather take my chances with you.'

I wonder how far he can possibly walk on his damaged feet, and think perhaps we could pull him on the sledge.

Max says, 'The guards have been making the prisoners here run laps to get them fitter. They must be planning a long walk.'

'We're fit,' says Ralph. 'Think how we've been working in that quarry. And we've been better fed than the prisoners here. We'll be all right.' He doesn't even sound convinced himself.

Bill comes back, triumphant, with a well-made sledge. I'm so proud of him and clap my hands spontaneously. Even Max looks reluctantly admiring.

'One bloke offered me a hundred fags for it,' Bill says. 'And someone else tried to steal it from me. I had to smack him one.'

'So much for universal brotherhood,' mutters Max.

'We shouldn't try to carry too much,' cuts in Bill. 'We aren't strong enough, and the weather's terrible. It's going to be hard enough just to walk. Let's get everything we can on here, then have a brew.'

As we pile the parcels onto the sledge, Max asks Ralph, 'Did you hear anything about where they might be taking us?'

Bill says, 'One guard says it's direct orders from the Führer. They don't want to leave us behind to join up with the Russians.'

'Blimey,' says Ralph, 'I don't want to fight for the Russians.'

'You didn't hear the other rumour then?' asks Max. We all look up and he hesitates. 'I'm not sure if I should say.'

'We'll hear it sooner or later,' Ralph points out.

'OK, well, they're saying Hitler plans to use us as a human shield for his last stand. All the Allied prisoners from here and the work camps and the other prison camps. Sixty thousand Russian prisoners, they say. That might make three hundred thousand prisoners in all. That would be quite a shield.'

We work in silence, tying our kit-bags to the sledge with some rope Bill found. It makes sense, of course, but I'm flooded with despair and fear. Have I really come this far with Bill, for us to be used as a human shield?

Max continues, 'They also say Hitler issued an order that we should march without trousers, to stop us trying to escape, but the camp commandant's defied that.'

'Thank God for small mercies,' says Bill.

Once the sledge is full, we cover it with our blankets and the spare greatcoats Max found, tying it all tightly. Bill uses the last of the rope to form a long cord for us to pull it by.

Each of us will carry a kit-bag containing the blowers, a day's rations, some fags and soap as currency, some toilet paper and any personal items. We've left out some food to eat tonight: the last of Berta's bread from the quarry, some margarine and some tinned sardines. I put Berta's plum brandy and the raisins in my kit-bag.

297

'I never liked sardines,' says Ralph, 'but we'll need the protein.'

Bill raises his tin mug of tea. 'To Scotty,' he says. 'And to us.' We all drink.

Ralph adds, 'I hope Rosa gets away and finds the bloke she loves.'

'Did you notice?' says Max. 'They were Jewish. The Rauchbachs.'

We all look astonished. 'On the back door of the house,' he says. 'They'd sanded it down and painted over where it'd been, but it was the shape of a mezuzah.'

'A what?' asks Bill.

'Mezuzah. A finger-sized scroll with verses from the Torah. Religious Jews have them on every doorpost in the house. I think it's a prayer for protection. Fat lot of good it's done.'

We're all remembering the little concessions Herr Rauchbach made to us, how he tried to ease our lives as much as he dared.

I wonder if God is dead or just cruel, like in the Old Testament, and then I fear He'll no longer look after me and Bill, so I quickly say the Lord's Prayer to myself, even though doubt runs like a river deep under ice.

At 10 p.m., when the lights would normally go out, a siren begins to sound. The door of the hut is flung open and a guard tells us we're leaving in fifteen minutes. We put on all our clothes, layer upon layer. I wind my Christmas scarf around my neck and pull on my bobble hat. I notice Max isn't wearing the hat with ear-flaps that Bill knitted him. He's a fool. Bill helps me put my mum's waxed cape and hood over my coat; he insists it must be mine. We have to help one another awkwardly pull our kit-bags onto our over-padded backs, and over all that we cloak ourselves in a blanket each. We're pouring with sweat from the effort as we carry the sledge into the night.

Outside it's chaos, with men running this way and that in heavy falling snow. There's a big bonfire smelling of cigarettes, and someone tells us that a successful gambler with a stash of 7,000 fags has set fire to all that he can't carry, rather than let the Nazis have them. There are metres of toilet paper thrown up over the huts like streamers, again to destroy anything that can't be carried. The ground is littered with ripped clothes, squashed cigarettes and trails of powdered milk.

On the unlit parade ground, a strong wind blows the snow directly into our faces. We pull our hats down and our scarves up. The wind also carries the sounds of heavy Russian artillery closer than we've ever heard it before. But to my astonishment, all around us men are laughing and joking, as if we're heading out on a midnight holiday. A hearty and filthy conversation starts up around me about the number of them who had wet dreams last night, knowing that today might be the day they finally leave Lamsdorf and start to head home.

Most of the guards are coming with us, with just a few left to gather the wounded onto ambulance trains. We are to leave in batches of 1,000 or so, over the next few hours. The tall guard and the bald guard are in our section. By 11 p.m., when we pull our sledge out of the gates into the black night beyond, the snow has turned to a blizzard. It whirls about our heads and blinds us. There's joyful singing for the first few metres, but it quickly peters out as the snow blows into our mouths, our noses, our eyes. We fall to silence, put our heads down and begin to trudge forward, already looking like a long line of snowmen.

PART FOUR

THE LONG MARCH WEST
January to March 1945

23

I can't lift my head, or the swirling snow will blow into my eyes. Our long line shuffles into the blizzard. Despite the bobble hat pulled low over my eyebrows and ears, and a scarf pulled up over my nose, my face is so cold that it feels like nails being driven into my cheeks. My eyes water and the tears turn to ice on my eyelashes. My exhaled breath freezes to an icy fringe on the edge of my scarf. I'm wearing two pairs of gloves, one inside the other, but my fingers are alternately numbing and burning. I clench and straighten them repeatedly to keep the blood flowing.

We are all walking bent forward from the waist, to keep the snow out of our faces. I fix my eyes on my trudging feet, as much as I can see them in the dark, for fear of falling over and twisting my ankle. We shuffle in the wake of the men in front of us. All around us the air is thick with the thunder and smell of artillery bombardment. Flashes of gunfire shimmer through the falling snow. The Red Army is that close.

The tall guard and the bald guard walk alongside us. They are better shod and clothed than most of us, but are carrying heavy rifles and packs. The bald guard seems to be struggling already. They shout to us to go faster, but their shouts are half-hearted because they can't move any quicker themselves, and they haven't had any sleep, either. Only their terror of the retribution of the Russians drives them on.

At about 2 a.m. the wind starts to drop, and the snow slowly turns from a whirling cloud to a light feathering, and finally eases to a few stray flakes fluttering down on us. The snow underfoot has been trodden by thousands of men ahead of us and is compacted to ice. We slip and slide. Bill holds firmly onto my arm, and Max grips onto Ralph. Ralph limps, but pins his lips together tightly and says nothing.

Images of Kurt and what he tried to do to me replay in my head, and I can't staunch them. I remember leaning forward in the cold snow on the pile of marble slabs as I waited for the world to end; my terror when I thought Bill had been shot; Scotty with the hole in his stomach, the blood in the snow. I try to block them out, to think of nothing, to think of putting one foot in front of the other.

We take turns pulling the sledge. It's well made and easier to pull over the icy ground than it was through the newly fallen snow. Already we see the wreckage of sledges made from packing cases that haven't held together and are now abandoned by the side of the road. Tins of food are scattered around some of them, and although other prisoners bend to pick them up, they can't carry any more and soon have to let them fall again.

'We can't manage any more tins,' says Bill, and the sound of his voice makes me jump. Nobody has spoken for a long time. 'But we could maybe burn the wood.' He and Max scoop up some pieces of the light timber as they pass and shove them onto the sodden blanket covering our sledge. They work together without making eye contact.

Some of the other PoWs laugh at us with our heavy sledge, because the Lamsdorf guards have told them we won't be going far, so they haven't brought much food.

A man near us slips and falls. There's a surprisingly loud crack as his arm breaks. We look round for a doctor, but of course there isn't one. The tall guard knows Ralph had some medical training, and he lets us pull out of line while Ralph tries to set the break. Ralph's face is white with nausea. It's almost impossible to set the break properly through so many layers of clothes, but if the man took his coat off, he would freeze to death. Ralph uses a length of our packing-case firewood to make a splint and ties it with the man's scarf. Nobody has anything to give him for the pain.

'That's the best I can do,' Ralph says. 'I'm sorry.'

The tall guard says he'll try to find a medic when we make camp. The man mutters his thanks as we all re-join the endless, shuffling line.

At 3 a.m. we are allowed a half-hour rest.

'The Russians are close,' explains the guard. We don't need to be told. The sound of their guns is all around us. Ralph says it's just as well we aren't being allowed to stop for longer, because falling asleep could be fatal in these temperatures. We sit down in the snow. The skirt parts of our coats, which I couldn't wax, are already soaked through, and so are our scarves and the blankets we've wrapped round us. As we sit still, our trousers and coats freeze to the ground. The waxed shoulders and hats seem to keep out some of the wet, although we're so cold that it's difficult to tell. I have icicles on my eyelashes, and the scarves we've breathed into are stiff with ice.

On every side of us we can see tiny flames of blowers, as men use the snow to make themselves a hot drink. Bill and Ralph set to work with theirs and, when the water has boiled, they drop a pinch of tea and sugar into it.

The sodden blankets we wrapped round us are heavy with ice, so we tie them on top of the sledge, and that makes it easier to walk when the call comes down the line for us to get up and move on.

Ralph winces as he puts his left foot to the ground, and although we all look worriedly at him, he dismisses us with a flick of his hand. Bill rubs his wrist from time to time. I alternate between sliding my feet, as if I'm skating on the compacted ice, and walking in the slushy snow to the edges, which soaks through the eyelets of my boots. I'm so tired that I don't know how I'm continuing to walk, but too afraid of being left behind to stop.

As the sky lightens for dawn, the line comes to a slow stop. We stand for a long time, banging our hands on our sides, stamping our feet, clouds of steam around our heads. We've perhaps said five words to one another in as many hours. The raggedy queue shuffles forward for a few hundred metres and comes to a halt again, and a rumour is passed back to us.

'They're billeting us in farms. We'll be inside soon and able to sleep.'

I think it'll take a lot of farms to fit us all, but at last I can lift my head and take in the lightening world around. Snow-covered fields rise towards woods. A deer walks out from the trees. It looks down on us for a long time, before the bald guard spots it and raises his rifle. The crack of the shot echoes all around us, but the deer's unhurt and leaps back into the woods.

The gunfire sends ravens shooting into the air, cawing their outrage, black against the snow-heavy sky.

On the trees nearest to us are great clumps of mistletoe, just like at home. Further up the hill, in the dark wood, the snow on the uppermost branches of the trees is the purest white, lighter than the sky. Tall firs have their branches weighed down to the ground. The birches glitter.

It's completely light before we're in the yard of a farm. We are among the first being counted into a large barn. I point up to the hayloft.

'Up there,' says Bill for me. 'Might be less cold, and hay to bed down in.'

It's very awkward to pull the sledge up the ladder behind us, and the men below shout loud complaints to us.

'Fucking idiots! Leave it down here.'

'You're holding us all up. Get a move on.'

But we are determined not to be parted from either our belongings or the sledge itself, so we heave and haul until it's up in the loft. We manage to get it into a corner and start to pull hay into our area to sleep on, wringing out our wet blankets and hanging them in the rafters above our heads. More and more men keep coming up the steps of the hayloft, until there isn't enough space left for us to lie down.

'Move that fucking thing,' growls a heavily bearded man, pointing to the sledge. We stand it on its end, so it takes up less room. Then we lie down next to it, claiming the minimum space we'd need to sleep.

All around us, pressed close, men are trying to gather their possessions into little nests of frozen, wet clothing. Many men light up fags or set their blowers going to make a brew, and I'm horrified. My mother would sack a man who smoked in the hay barn. It could all catch light and go up in minutes, and we'd never be able to get out.

Bill sees my agitation. 'Any of us could roll on a fire and put it out,' he points out. 'We're all soaked through. Now then, a brew before we sleep?'

I remember the raisins and the plum brandy Berta gave me and we share them out. The brandy warms our insides, if not our extremities. Ralph unlaces his boots, and I dry his feet with straw while he rubs some of the cream into them. They look swollen and raw.

The barn is locked from outside, and men carefully extinguish their cigarettes. There are no toilet facilities, so people pee next to the places where they've made their beds. Angry cries come up from beneath us. I haven't drunk much in the last nine hours, so I think I'll try to hang on until they let us out again. Cigarette smoke hangs in the damp air, mingling with the smell of urine, and steam rises from our wet clothes and our breath. Some men are gorging on the food from their parcels, but for once I'm too tired to feel hungry.

'We ought to ration the food,' says Ralph, watching them. 'God knows if we're going to get anything from the guards.'

We all nod miserable assent.

Part sitting and part lying, Bill and I lean against each other in our wet clothes.

I sleep fitfully, for only a few hours, and when we're woken by the sounds of the barn being unlocked, I'm stiff. My clothes are still thoroughly wet and very, very cold. I didn't think it was possible to be so chilled and damp and still live. The ice is unmelted on the skirts of my coat.

Some men have eaten too much of their Red Cross rations while we slept and the reek of sickness and diarrhoea is added to the strong ammonia scent of urine. I cover my nose and mouth with my frosty, wet scarf.

We stand and stretch, and the ache in my legs and back from yesterday's long march makes me feel like an old woman.

As we shake our arms and legs, trying to get some warmth back into our limbs, Max shouts, 'Thieving bastards! Who is it? Come on, who is it? Low, bloody scum. I hope you choke on it.'

While we slept someone has untied a corner of our sledge and taken a whole food parcel. And above our heads in the rafters, Bill points out that one of our blankets is missing.

'Not me, mate,' protest all the men around us.

I try to read their faces to see who's lying, but all I see is desperation.

Some clean air enters from the open barn door, and I can't wait to get out. Two men have been bitten by rats while they slept, but there's no antiseptic for their wounds.

In the snowy farmyard there's been a Nazi army-truck delivery, and the tall guard gives us a dense black loaf to share among six. The four of us team up with two other prisoners, and Max carefully measures the loaf before cutting it with his identity tag. He lets the two men we don't know choose their portions first. Ralph has some margarine in his kit-bag. It's too frozen to spread on the bread, so we hack off slivers to suck. I rub some margarine on my cracked lips and chapped face, and the others do the same. Ralph gives us each a thin slice of Spam, which only makes me hungrier. For a second I see myself grabbing the whole square and running off to ram it into my mouth. I see other men eyeing it hungrily. What will happen when we've eked out our rations, but others have nothing left?

Bill heats snow for tea.

'Always find the cleanest, whitest snow and make sure it boils properly. You don't want dysentery,' cautions Ralph.

The tall guard tells us we covered twenty-nine kilometres since leaving Lamsdorf, and Max protests, 'But the Geneva Convention says prisoners can't be made to march more than twenty kilometres a day.'

The guard shrugs expressively. What can he do about it?

'How far is twenty-nine kilometres?' Bill asks Max.

'Eighteen miles, I think. Leicester Square to somewhere like St Albans.'

'Blimey, it felt like Leicester Square to Manchester.'

This is the first time they've spoken to each other since the Cable Street row.

Then we're on the road again, putting weight gingerly on our sore feet, stretching the aching muscles in our thighs, calves and backs. For the first time I think: We aren't fit enough to survive this. And I look with panic at my companions – three young men, bent and limping like pensioners.

It's midday; we only stopped for five hours. The long, dark line of thousands of men stretches on ahead between rows of trees, a black band through the snow-covered open fields, showing the way we have to travel. Every half-hour or so there's a house surrounded by a small patch of garden. A river runs close to the road, but its silence tells me it's completely frozen.

Some men set up singing down the line, but most walk grimly on. The singing is defiant, but the men around me – even

310

Bill – don't sing and don't speak, as though we are folding our energy reserves into the heart of our frozen, damp bodies. It's as if my silence has passed like an infection to everyone else. I know how exhausted Bill must be, if he isn't humming or whistling, and my fear for him is like a stone I've swallowed. What if I've come all this way only to lose him now? Our sledge bumps along behind us. We walk and walk and walk. Every so often I think: When I reach that tree, or when we pass that gate; and then I allow myself to nibble my small hunk of bread. It's soon gone.

In another three hours, dusk is beginning to fall, and the line slows to a stop and moves to the side of the road. Civilian families pulling handcarts piled high with their belongings pass us. Mostly they are women, children and old people, with their faces set hard. The men who should be helping them are somewhere else, freezing in snowy trenches, shuffling like us in lines of prisoners, or dead.

A village or small town slowly emerges from its snow-camouflage, buildings solidifying out of a mist.

Carefully holding my coat, I take the opportunity to pee in the slush beside the road, which is already yellow with urine. Groups of prisoners are counted off and directed to different buildings around the village, barns and halls. We are to sleep in the church. I cross myself when I enter, and someone behind me scoffs, 'Pray hard, kid, and maybe a fuckin' angel'll flap you out of this.'

I tut. He shouldn't say 'fucking' in the church.

We choose pews in a side-chapel, away from the night-soil buckets provided by a thoughtful verger. Again there are complaints about the space our sledge is taking up, and it seems even harder to lift and manhandle tonight. We are already getting weaker. It's cold in the stone building, but at least we don't have to sleep on the floor. I put my kit-bag at one end of the pew for a pillow and I long to wash my hands and face. Ralph shares a tin of processed cheese between the four of us. I suck my portion for as long as I can. Then he opens a can of strawberry jam. We don't have anything to spread it on, but hand it round, each taking a couple of fingers' worth, before passing it on.

'It's calories,' he says, 'though not nearly enough.'

The smell of it is so thick and sweet that I inhale deeply before I eat, as though the smell alone will sustain me.

We don't take off any clothes, but pull the damp blankets over us. The pew is hard and uncomfortable, but it feels good to stretch out properly. The sledge stands at the end of our pews. I wonder if men will dare to steal in a church. Some are already smoking here, which I think is wrong, but Ralph says smoking helps to keep the hunger at bay. Perhaps I should take it up.

The lice have begun to itch again, in my underarms, groin and hair. I take my hat off to scratch my head, and Bill and I try to flick the little devils out of the knitting before I put it back on. I'm sorry they've infiltrated the hat Bill made me.

When the church goes quiet, I pray for us all, for strength to endure, and my mind drifts to Scotty, to all he achieved in his life – how he saved his sister and her children, how he saved me. I give thanks for him.

Despite the hardness of the pew, the hunger which gnashes at my insides, the itching of the lice and the coldness of my damp clothes, I fall into a dreamless sleep. Perhaps that's how my prayer is answered.

In the morning we are given another loaf of hard, black bread among six. Ralph and Max discuss the logistics: how they are managing to bake and distribute such large quantities to hundreds of thousands of evacuated men, and how long it can continue.

Bill opens a tin of condensed milk and pours some onto his bread. I drink my three spoonfuls of the sweet, sticky cream, but keep my bread in my pocket to eke out throughout the day. As the afternoon passes, the white of the fields meets the white of the sky with no horizon line. Buzzards circle overhead, and I think we are walking carrion.

Over the next few nights we sleep in different places – a village hall, a factory, a cowshed. One night Bill and I bed down with the pigs in their sty. It's the warmest we've been for days.

In every village the local people come out to watch us pass. Prisoners barter cigarettes, soap and chocolate for bread or sausage. My companions decide we should keep our cigarettes and soap until our food parcels run out. They are more valuable currency than gold coins sewn into the hems of our clothes. The food from our parcels is rapidly diminishing. Even carefully rationed, it doesn't go far among four.

When the snow starts to fall again, we walk with our heads down to stop the snow blowing into our eyes. Even with my neck bent, I can't keep my eyes open properly. The guns sound more distant now, and all I can hear is the wind and the trudge of footsteps, and beyond us the great uncaring silence of nature.

One house we pass has logs piled up outside it and smoke rising from a chimney. It's almost unbelievable that on the other side of that wall are warmth, company, family, food. I wonder if the people look out at this line of straggling, starving wretches, or if they just keep the curtains closed and face the fire.

At Strehlen there's a church with an onion dome, like in Vražné, where we were married so many hundreds of years ago. But no priest comes to help us.

On the sixth night the tall guard tells us we won't be locked in; we must bed down where we can. We cram into a draughty tool-shed, but it's so crowded we have to sleep sitting up. Bill removes his boots to look at his blisters. His feet are raw and bleeding and he decides to leave his boots off for the night. 'The air might do my feet good,' he says doubtfully.

But after a few minutes he sees the pinkness of his feet turning white and pulls his bloodstained socks back on. From his pack he takes a second pair, which he knitted himself and which are rather misshapen, but still warm. As he yanks them over the first pair, I see another man eyeing the socks as if they're gold nuggets.

'Give you a hundred cigs for those, mate,' he says, but Bill refuses, tucking the blanket around his feet to prevent the socks from being stolen as he sleeps. I sneak a look at the man's feet and see that he is only wearing *fuss-lag* and wooden clogs. Bill sees that too and ties his boots to his wrists by their laces.

It's so cold in the shed that by the morning the wet leather of Bill's boots has frozen like iron and he can hardly force his feet back into them. It's snowed again in the night, and I clutch Bill's arm as I realise some prisoners were forced to sleep outside. Most of the mounds of snowy clothing don't move.

24

The endless line of men winds through open country where the wind has bent trees to strange shapes. We can see the snaking line of prisoners kilometres ahead of us – black shapes shuffling against the snow. Sometimes up ahead we see the dark silhouettes of buildings or church spires, and hope flickers for a few minutes. Perhaps we'll be allowed to rest here. Perhaps there'll be bread.

In some villages the women come out to line the road with buckets and pans of soup or acorn coffee, which they set up on chairs beside the road and hand to the first lucky prisoners who pass by. Sometimes it's just hot water, but we're grateful for anything warm. Our guards mostly ignore the women and let us pause for a second or two to drink whatever's on offer, though occasionally there's the stain of coffee or soup in the snow, and we know that a guard further ahead has overturned whatever the woman had made. Once there are small pieces of vegetable in the stained snow from spilled soup, and men scoop them into their tin cups to warm later or pick out the frozen vegetable cubes to suck as they walk.

One elderly civilian man is handing out newspapers, urging them on men who don't understand what he's saying.

'We can't read bloody Polack,' someone says, pushing them away.

The man tries in German. 'For insulation, to line your clothes.' And Ralph takes some, translating loudly for those around us and thanking the man. Behind us the pile of newspapers is quickly depleted. At our next stop we wrap the papers around our bodies, shoving them down the trousers and up under our battledress. To my surprise, I can feel a small difference.

In one nameless ordinary village a woman swaddled in shawls ladles thin gruel out of a pot, and we stop to fill our tin mugs. When I look closer she's not old at all, but about the same age as my mother, with prematurely grey hair. She never takes her eyes off me. My friends thank her in English and German, and she replies in Polish. We shake our heads to show we don't understand. She slowly translates into German. 'Perhaps . . . some other mother . . . will do this for . . . my son,' she says. Ralph repeats her words in English. I put my head down, because tears have filled my eyes.

That night – our seventh on the road – we are led again onto a farm, but this time we are too far back in the line to be able to find spaces in the outbuildings. We drag our sledge from one shed and barn to another, but every centimetre is taken by exhausted men, crammed and scrunched, without space to lie down.

'Move over,' says Bill, but there's nowhere for them to move to and, as we leave the last building, I begin to panic. As night falls, the temperature's dropping fast again, and we'll be the unmoving bundles of rags in the snow tomorrow morning unless we can find shelter. Ralph seeks out the bald guard and pleads with him in

German. 'Please take us to one of the other billets – the next village perhaps. There's nowhere left for us. We'll all die. Please.'

The guard looks exhausted. I can see ice beginning to form in his one-day stubble. He looks us over and hesitates for a second.

'We can pay you,' says Ralph. 'We've got some tins left.'

The guard still hesitates. 'One hundred cigarettes,' he says at last.

Ralph replies, 'We've only got a few cigarettes. Coffee maybe? Please. We've come all this way together.'

The guard weighs up effort and reward; then he shrugs and says, 'These are my orders. Tell the other prisoners to move up and make room.'

'For the love of God!' Ralph begs. 'Even just for two of us? For the boy?' But the guard turns and shuffles away. Ralph swings back to us, desperation in his eyes. 'I'm so sorry. He wants a hundred fags.'

Max says, 'It's good to know my life is worth twenty-five fags.'

The guard disappears into the snow. It's no good going after him.

'We could maybe build a shelter against a wall of a shed,' offers Bill doubtfully. 'We could use the sledge somehow . . .'

Thin snow begins to fall again, and I make a decision. Checking we're out of sight of the guards, I stride out towards the farmhouse, the others following behind.

'What're you doing?' Bill asks, but I don't answer.

I knock firmly on the back door. It opens a couple of centimetres, and the light from a kitchen candle falls out into the snow. In the slit of the door I can see an old man, skeleton-thin, with luxuriant white hair.

I speak very little Polish, but we all understand as he hisses, 'Go away!' I've put my boot in the door, so he can't shut it. He's muttering something else, about the Nazis. Probably that they'd shoot him if he helps us, or that they are coming back, having been billeted on him.

'*Varshahvay*,' I interrupt gruffly, in my best imitation of a Polish accent. '*Varshahvay*.'

He releases the pressure on the door a tiny fraction so that my foot isn't so tightly jammed, and he peers out at us in the sliver of light from his kitchen.

I point to us and say, '*Cztery* – us four. *Varshahvay*', and we can see him hesitate.

He tries to look behind us into the darkness, to see if we are being watched. Then he lets go of the door handle and slips through, joining us out in the yard. The snow is falling thicker as he scans the four of us and flicks his head to look all around him like a wary bird.

'*Varshahvay*?' he asks, and we all nod.

He reaches back into the kitchen for a shovel and his coat, then scuttles away down the side of the house and beckons us to follow. Measuring distances with his hands from a window, he stops and begins to clear the snow, heaped waist-deep against the outside wall. After a few minutes he's tiring, although the snow is light, and Bill takes the spade from him, digging down to ground level. All the time the farmer's looking around him, terrified. Then the spade makes contact with the hollow sound of a wooden trapdoor and we scrabble the snow aside, until the door to the cellar can be opened. We grab our kit-bags from the sledge and he hustles the four of us down, as quickly as possible. We half-tumble over one another down the little ladder onto a hard stone floor. Ralph tries to bring the sledge with our last parcels, but the farmer pushes him away with the shovel, down into the cellar. The trapdoor bangs shut above our heads and we are in total darkness. We can hear the farmer shovelling snow onto the trapdoor, and for a second I think he's burying us and this will be our coffin. Then Bill's fumbling for a match in his kit-bag.

'My bloody hands are too cold,' he whispers, trying to strike it over and over again.

'Maybe the box is damp,' suggests Max. 'Try the floor.'

We hear the swish of a match on the stone floor, and there's a flare of light as it catches. Bill stands and lifts the match above his head and we see we're in a small cellar, with empty shelves where food was once stored. There's just enough room for us to lie down, and we have our blankets wrapped around us, but no provisions, and our sledge is outside.

'I've got a few candle stubs,' says Max, and we hear him opening his kit-bag and rifling through it. A match is struck again and, after a candle's lit, our shadows leap up the walls. Max lines up three more candle stubs, but we can all see they won't last till morning.

We sit down on the hard floor and we all open our kit-bags to see what food might remain. Bill has a wizened turnip, I have a tin of pilchards and Ralph has prunes. Max says he doesn't have anything.

There's a hasty discussion.

'Once he's gone, we could go back out and look for the sledge,' suggests Bill.

Ralph isn't sure. 'But we might get caught coming out.'

'Better stay here,' agrees Max.

'I'm famished,' argues Bill.

I say quietly, 'We die from cold out there', and the others all stop and consider me for a second, before their voices tumble over mine.

Ralph says, 'You've saved our lives. We can manage on this food for one night.'

Max is curious. 'Whatever did you say to him, to persuade him?'

'Just one word, like "Open Sesame",' says Bill.

Ralph nods. 'And he helped us, though you could tell he was terrified.'

I say it again in Polish, and Ralph repeats '*Var-shah-vay*', tasting the shape of the word to fathom its meaning, but he can't guess.

'*Warschau*,' I say to Ralph in German, and he shakes his head in admiration, then translates for the others. 'Warsaw. Of course. Genius! Warsaw. The one word in the world to persuade him to save our lives.'

'But why?' asks Bill. 'Why would that work?'

'When the Nazis broke the Siege of Warsaw, every single one of the civilian citizens was rounded up and sent to prison camps,' Ralph reminds him. 'Every man, woman and child. Who knows what they've suffered? No self-respecting Pole could deny sanctuary to people who fought the Third Reich and helped his countrymen in Warsaw. That one word reminded him who were his enemies and who his allies. And he'd think that if we escaped, maybe others did too.'

Max nods in respect, while Bill allows himself to gaze on me in wonder. 'However did you think of that?'

I shrug and say aloud, 'Just thought.' And I feel a small glow of pride as we divide up the raw turnip and chew it. The first candle stub gutters and we decide that when it goes out, we'll huddle together and try to sleep.

The darkness is more complete than I've ever seen. The cold from the floor penetrates up through our clothes, and the stone is unforgiving against our bony frames. But we fit ourselves close together. I'm in Bill's arms for once, because here nobody can see. I have his arm to rest my head on. Ralph sleeps with his back to Bill, and Max is on my other side. Despite our hunger and discomfort, we are so exhausted that one by one we fall asleep.

We don't know how many hours later it is that we're woken by scraping above our heads as the farmer clears the trapdoor. Max helps push it open from inside and, although it's still night outside, it's a blessed relief to see the light from the stars. In the east is a thin greying, indicating that we've lived to see another dawn. The farmer pulls us out roughly, wanting us away from the house as soon as possible. As he starts to shovel snow back onto the cellar door, he indicates a rough drift to one side, and underneath is our sledge, with the remains of the final parcels. We heave the sledge out and start to help him with the shovelling, but he's looking round anxiously and is very eager for us to leave. He thrusts the branch of a fir tree at Ralph and indicates how we must cover our tracks, then yanks from his pocket a paper bag, which he gives to me, looking deep into my eyes. '*Dla Warszawy.*' It sounds like *Varshahvay*. For Warsaw.

I grip his hand for a second. '*Dziękuję ci* – thank you.' And the others all echo their thanks, but he's pushing us away, terrified of being found with us. We pull the sledge over the fresh snow, back towards the farm buildings that were too full to take us, passing the snow-covered bodies of men who were not so lucky. Ralph crunches backwards, obliterating our tracks, and tosses the fir branch under a tree.

Ahead of us, the tall guard is banging on the door of a shed, calling, '*Raus, raus.*' We slip round behind, to look as if we're just emerging from another building, yawning and stretching into the dawn light. He barely glances at us.

'What did he give you?' asks Ralph, and I open the top of the paper bag. We peer inside. Oats. Like we'd feed the horses. 'Porridge for breakfast!' beams Bill, as if it's all he could ever imagine wanting in the world. I know we're all thinking of Scotty, and wishing he was here to share it. As we're making the watery porridge, the tall guard comes around looking for Ralph.

'*Arzt* – doctor.' He beckons urgently. '*Komm mit mir.*'

Ralph struggles to his feet. 'Cousins, can you come too?' And we follow the tall guard down towards the farmhouse where we spent the night.

The white-haired farmer recognises us and freezes, ready to deny everything, but I signal to him to say nothing. The tall guard stumps upstairs to a bedroom and we follow to where the bald guard is lying on the bed in his long underwear, gasping for breath, his face ashen and sweat pouring down it.

He's clutching his chest. Even I could make Ralph's diagnosis: 'Heart attack.'

For fifteen minutes Ralph and the tall guard and I take turns pressing on the bald guard's chest, trying to bring him back to life, but eventually the tall guard makes a decision. '*Nein.* It's no good. He's gone. Stop now.'

I lift my head and stop the pounding. The room is absolutely still and silent. Ralph leans in, to close his eyes and mouth, and I cross myself, while at the same instant the tall guard does the same. He nods to me and pulls the sheet over his comrade's face.

Ralph and I turn to leave, but the tall guard taps us on the shoulder and puts out a hand to shake. '*Danke schön.*' We both solemnly shake his hand, and he seems to be trying to think of a way to thank us. He points to himself. 'Hans,' he says.

Ralph replies, 'Ralph, and this is Cousins.' He shakes our hands again, and we escape back down the stairs into the freezing air.

A little further on, late in the morning, we enter a village where some children come out and walk alongside us, nudging one another. They are laughing and want to ride on our sleigh. Of course we let them climb aboard, two at a time. We are so weak that it takes three of us to pull the extra load, but it's worth it to hear their squeals and giggles. All around us men are smiling at them, squaring their shoulders, lifting their heads, visibly cheered by the laughter and gaining new determination to stay alive, to return to their own children. Tonight there are fewer men to house in our section, and we all squeeze together into the designated barn.

In another village a dark-haired Polish girl smiles at Max, and a passing Hitler Youth boy happens to see. He swings out his rifle barrel and knocks her down. She flies sideways into the snow and curls into a ball, waiting for more blows. Max moves to help her, but the Hitler Youth trains his gun on us.

'He'll shoot, for sure,' says Bill.

Max wants to argue, but he knows Bill's right. We reluctantly shuffle forward.

'Fucking scum,' mutters Max.

Until she's out of sight, one after another of us looks back to see if she's managed to clamber to her feet. When we turn the corner she's still curled up in the snow, with the Hitler Youth standing over her. I think about her for hours.

There's a column of Russian prisoners somewhere out ahead

of us. We know this because every day we pass nine or ten of them lying dead beside the road. They are no more than skeletons in coats, and many of them are barefoot. Their feet are lacerated, red and shiny, or black from frostbite. Some may have had boots on when they fell, but they've been taken by others who need them more. One has cut the ends off a pair of boots that are far too small for him, and his blackened toes leer out at us. Some of them have been shot, and blood has spread out into the snow around them, like a warning.

After eight days of marching we reach a larger, more prosperous village, and we stand for two hours in light, swirling snow, waiting to be billeted. The four of us are directed to join a group going to a sawmill just outside the village.

'Home from home,' remarks Bill, looking around. 'Just like the sawmill at Mankendorf.'

He hurries us across the icy yard to the building adjacent to the offices, where there might be a stove. The tall guard, Hans, tells us tomorrow is Sunday and we'll be there for the whole day, with a chance to rest. He sounds relieved himself.

Bill and Ralph prop our sledge in a corner, and Bill begins to gather up wood shavings and sawdust.

'We can make a bed – that'll lift us off the floor,' he says.

We take turns to stay with our sledge in the corner we've staked out, or to help gather armloads of shavings and sawdust, which we spread in an area big enough for the four of us to lie down.

Ralph unstraps the last two parcels from the sledge and puts them under the head end of our sawdust bed, as lumpy pillows.

I lie between Bill and Ralph, looking at a wood shaving, at the beauty of its curling shape, and I inhale the warm smell of it.

In the morning we are given a loaf to share among six, and it tastes as if it isn't only the bed that's been made of sawdust. This time some men we hardly know cut the bread, and they don't give us first choice of the pieces. Max complains that one of their pieces is bigger, and one of the other men squares up to him.

'And if it is, what are you going to do about it?' he sneers.

Bill pulls Max away, and Max doesn't shrug him off.

Later in the day the guards drive up on a truck and unload a bucket of soup. It's gone cold on the journey from the cookhouse, but it has some real pieces of potato in it. We spend the day sleeping and resting, and the tall guard lets us out into the yard. We gather snow to make drinks and to try and wash ourselves. It's too cold to remove many clothes, but I dip a rag in the snow and hurriedly scrub my face and reach in under my clothes. Ralph and Bill heat a little water and rub a sliver of soap through their beards and scrape them off, so that my beardlessness won't look so strange. Max's beard is growing black and curly. He says it's full of lice, but gives him some warmth.

Ralph carefully removes his boots and socks. His toes are like a patchwork: pink, swollen and shiny, or white like frost itself. I inhale in horror as I see that the little toe on his left foot is starting to turn black.

'You should get those looked at,' says Max.

'By who?' snaps Ralph. 'I'm probably the nearest thing to a doctor for fifty miles, God help us. It's frostbite, not cancer.'

We heat a little water and I try to warm the deadened skin, and rub in the last of the cream. I wonder how he can stand the pain.

Several hours of the day are spent trying to kill some of the lice. We light a cigarette and run it up the seams of our coats and battledress, to sizzle them.

Bill takes the opportunity to make some improvements to his sledge. Someone offers him 1,000 Reichsmarks for it. I'm amazed that anyone can have amassed so much money, but Ralph tells me that he's the man who used to run the secret 'casino' at Lamsdorf.

And then we're back on the road, stopping overnight and setting off again each morning. For hour after hour the scenery is identical. Sometimes a small flock of sparrows circles over us and wheels away. Sometimes there are power lines, and the telegraph poles show up blackly in the snow. Sometimes the road is raised above the fields. Sometimes there are no trees lining the road, and fences have been erected to stop snowdrifts blocking the carriageway.

Then fir forests become closer and closer to the road on our left, until they are so near that I wonder if we could simply slip away into the woods. Far ahead of us I hear a gunshot, and wonder if someone else tried it.

From time to time we see a man who's just sat down by the side of the road and given up, from cold and exhaustion. The padre is going up and down the line, exhorting these men to get to their feet, to continue. I hear him use language I wouldn't have expected from a priest.

After three more days we have another rest day, and there's soup again, of indeterminate flavour. Bill, Ralph and Max constantly count and recount the items left in our food parcels. Our little stock is running out. A guard tells us we're headed for Görlitz PoW camp and that there might be fresh Red Cross parcels there. The guard says Görlitz might be four days' walk away. He asks, embarrassed, if we've got any cigarettes, and we say only if he can get us extra food. He disappears.

Ralph says, 'Let's divide what's left into four days then. Or five maybe.' And the others agree. It's even less than we were having before, and when I put my hands on my hips, it feels as if my body isn't where I expect it to be. The time for my monthlies comes, but there's no blood.

I hide one square of chocolate at the bottom of my kit-bag. It comforts me just to know it's there. I eat my last prune and suck the stone for hours. When I finally drop it into the snow, I hope it will grow in the spring.

For days we've been walking across almost flat land, but now it's becoming hilly. The snow is thicker, deep to the edge of the forest, and we heave the sledge up a long, steep hill. As we come over the top, shaking and breathless from the effort, we see rolling snow-covered hills to both sides and purple mountains up ahead.

We shuffle slowly past a castle on a hill. The snow has stopped falling at last, and clods of settled snow begin to drop from the deciduous trees, though it stays and freezes on the fir branches. The cattle we glimpse here are hairy, as though they are wearing long fur coats.

I name the things we pass, in Czech, to keep my words alive: the red brick chimney of a factory, birch woods, a tattered advertising poster for glass-blowing, a pigeon loft. And still we are climbing. On the road now there are even more civilian refugees, who stand aside to let us pass, or walk doggedly on as we thread past them in single file. At a railway station we watch German soldiers disembark from cattle trucks. They're filthy and almost as ragged as us, with long, unkempt beards. They are wounded, sick, terrified, young. One of our guards says they've come from the eastern front, fighting the Russians.

Every day Ralph's feet get worse. Skin that was swollen and pink has bleached white, the toes that were white begin to turn green and then black. He hobbles more and more painfully, until a day comes when he admits he can no longer walk. There's a waggon for the injured, and the tall guard lets us drop back to lift him onto it. The waggon's pulled by prisoners with friends on board, who are given an extra bread ration – though not enough to make up for the calories they're using up on pulling a heavy wooden vehicle, laden with the sick and injured, over the icy slush. Bill and Max take their turns, but Bill refuses to let me. 'I need you to stay strong enough to walk.'

We heap all our blankets onto Ralph, but lying still on the waggon, he shivers uncontrollably. At night we lift him down and bring him to sleep with us, trying to warm him with our own bodies. I try to use a little water and some rags to warm the frozen skin of his feet, though the cream is long gone. He grips his lips together in a thin line, so as not to let any groan escape. When the pain diminishes a little he says, 'You lot'd be better off without me. You should just look after yourselves.'

I poke him hard in the ribs, and even through all his clothes, I can feel he's no more than bone.

As he shivers on the waggon, I pull the sledge alongside. I pray in time with each footstep, 'Don't let him die. Don't let him die.'

On the mountain to the right of us is a ski-slope with motionless cable cars. Clouds cover the tops of the mountains. We pass a tall observatory tower on a hill, and then a town with factories. The houses are half-timbered, like in a fairy tale. One is thatched.

It's the hardest thing I've ever done in my life just to take one step after another, and pulling the sledge up the steepest hills is pure pain. Then after the crown of the hill the sledge wants to run down the other side, and I have to hold it back.

We pass a grand house with stables, perhaps a riding school, and a flock of geese. At a railway station the tracks head off in different directions, and I wonder if it would really have been worse than this to be carried in cattle trucks.

There's a red-brick church with a Gothic steeple, and we begin an agonising climb to a high plateau, where the wind snatches away every breath as though the world begrudges us even that. An old windmill spins implacably. I can almost smell the corn it must be grinding.

On 5th February, word comes down the line that we're almost there – just one more hill and we can rest. But even one more hill feels like an impossibility. Max heaves the sledge. Bill's with the men pulling the waggon of the injured. More men have fallen in to help with that, both pulling and pushing to get their comrades to safety. I don't know how they are finding the strength to risk their own lives for one another.

We somehow sweat and struggle to the top of the hill, and before us is peaceful, snowy country with clumps of trees, and a huge prisoner-of-war camp. The line slows to a crawl. It's only two weeks since we left Lamsdorf, but it feels as though I've been forcing my exhausted body to keep moving for months or maybe even years.

Eventually ahead of us loom the tall gates with the eagle and swastika emblazoned on them. The wire fences and watchtowers spread out over the top of a huge flat hill. We stagger into Görlitz, Stalag VIIIA.

25

Görlitz is so crowded with thousands of men from all the Eastern European camps that nobody counts us or takes our details. We're told there may be room for us in Hut 37, but when we find the hut, all the bunks are taken and there's barely space for us to find a patch of floor. Ralph struggles down to sit on the floor, and Bill props our sledge beside him. I sit down too, huddled close to Ralph to make room for the others.

'You stay here,' says Bill. 'I'll go and see if I can find anywhere better.'

'I'd better come with you,' says Max, 'so that one of us can stay to guard the place we find, and the other can come back for these two.'

I feel stricken as I watch Bill walk away. I try to hear Cousins' voice in my head, 'Steady on,' he says kindly.

Ralph's watching me. 'It's OK,' he whispers, tapping my arm. 'He'll be back soon.' Sometimes I think Ralph understands me better than Bill.

Max comes back alone, and my heart leaps into my mouth.

'We've found somewhere,' he says. 'It's not much better, but there's one bunk, and we can take turns. We decided Bill looked better able to defend it than me!'

I exhale in relief. This means they're on speaking terms at last.

He leads us to the other hut. It's hard to pull the sledge through the icy mud of the parade ground. The empty bunk is a top one, which means insects will fall from the ceiling, but there'll be a little more warmth. The warmth now matters to me more than the insects.

'Can you get up there?' Bill asks Ralph, but he shakes his head.

'I'm off to see if I can find a quack,' he says, and we all know he must have come to the end of his endurance even to consider such a thing, because it will mean parting from us.

Max nods. 'Bill, why don't you hold the bunk and our stuff, and we'll pull Ralph to the sickbay on the sledge?'

Bill agrees readily, and I can see he's longing to stretch out and sleep, even on a lumpy, lice-infested straw mattress. We pass up our blankets and kit-bags. Max's rucksack is surprisingly heavy, and I wonder if he's stockpiling food and hiding it from us. Then I'm ashamed of the thought. I want to stay with Bill, but I know Max can't manage Ralph on his own.

Max and I drag Ralph on the sledge to the sickbay hut, which is full, but has a stove lit and is at least less cold. Patients sit on packing cases and the floor, as well as on beds. A British soldier takes Ralph's name and asks what the problem is.

'Frostbite,' Ralph grimaces.

'Oh, another! Well, over there and wait.' He looks at Max with the sledge. 'You can't bring that fucking great thing in here.'

'We'll, I'm not leaving it outside, to get nicked by the first tealeaf who passes.' Max makes a decision. 'I'm taking it back to the hut,' he says. 'Then I'll come back. You stay with Ralph.'

I sit close to Ralph on the floor and see that most of the sick and injured have a buddy close by. I think how human beings cleave together in pairs – husbands and wives or close friends – and how truly lost we are when we're alone. I think of all the years that Bill had Harry with him, and how he left him behind to run away with me. Ralph's hand rests on the floor. Out of sight, I cover his hand with mine.

Max returns just as a harassed medical officer arrives to look at Ralph's feet. I help him remove the boots and peel off the socks. All Ralph's toes are black now and they seep with pus. The doctor says, 'Well, you aren't walking a step further. You'll be taken on by train – if the Russians don't get here first.'

'Are they so close?' asks Max.

'Apparently.'

But Ralph has other concerns. 'Will I lose my feet?' he bursts out.

The doctor considers. 'We haven't got anyone to do it, but if your mate can come in and bathe them in warm water every couple of hours, we might be able to save them.'

I nod eagerly. The thought of Ralph with his toes or feet amputated is a horror. I remember how much he loved walking with his friends, and I think I'll do everything in my power to give him that again, after all he's done for me. I point to an imaginary watch, and the doctor looks questioningly at me.

Ralph explains, 'He doesn't speak. Mute. Some sort of shell-shock.'

The doctor looks interested. 'Do you want to stay here too and go on by train?'

I shake my head with such force that the doctor laughs. 'OK, OK. Well, for as long as you're here, come at two-hourly intervals. You can start now, if you like. There should be some water on the stove. Just warm, mind, not hot.' He turns to Ralph. 'It'll hurt like hell,' he says. 'I'm sorry I haven't got anything to give you for it.'

'I know,' says Ralph, and we know he does. 'But if it means I don't lose my feet . . .'

Max says, 'I'm going to see if I can lay my hands on any grub. I'll come back.'

We stay in Görlitz for ten days. After three nights another bunk comes free in our hut and Max moves to that. Bill and I share the one up near the ceiling, 'topping and tailing' as two men might do. We are fully clothed of course, but under the blankets we can at least hold hands.

The normal rules are much relaxed, but we are still confined to barracks at night. There's a change in the way the guards look at us all, as though they know that the tide of war has turned and one day soon they might be held to account for their actions. Although broadcasts in English from the Nazi propagandist Lord Haw-Haw are still played regularly through the camp's loudspeakers, telling us of Germany's successful battles against the Allies, we no longer believe anything we hear, and men openly shout insults in return.

Max and I take turns bathing Ralph's feet every two hours during daylight hours, and he tries to do it himself once it's dark and we're confined to barracks. I'm careful not to have the water too hot, but he grips the seat of his chair in pain, as if I've immersed them in boiling fat, as the skin begins to warm through. I know he dreads each treatment session, but I'll go on doing it as long as he can stand it, and as long as we're here.

After a couple of days he looks down and says, 'Do you think there's less pus?' I agree, but he has to look away. 'Ugh! Revolting!' I wipe away the offending discharge.

We learn from the other patients that we were 'lucky' to be in the second wave of evacuees from Lamsdorf. The first was led by Hauptmann Schultz, who forced the men to march further and faster than us every day, sometimes with no shelter for the night and with even less to eat. Nobody could guess the number of prisoners who'd died on the route. Some of the men in the sickbay were forced to abandon friends who'd come through five years of battle and imprisonment with them. The man in the bed next to Ralph says, 'Remember Schultz's name, lad . . . Tell the authorities when you get home.'

Bill spends most of his days scrounging around for food. We get the usual daily ration of bread and soup, but the Red Cross convoys can no longer break through the lines of battle with parcels, and we're hungry all the time. Although we're able to rest, there isn't enough food to regain the weight we lost on the march, and all of us look like scarecrows. We cut the string that secured our parcels to the sledge into shorter lengths and use them to hold up our trousers. Bill, Max, Ralph and I have finished the last parcel we carried from Lamsdorf, though Ralph gets 'invalid rations' in the sickbay. He tries to share these with Max and me, and sometimes I don't refuse, just to please him. We don't dare leave any food on our bunks, but carry the meagre bread ration with us all day in our kit-bags. Every day I see a fight break out over food. Bill has located the tall guard, Hans, and he manages to exchange our last cigarettes for a sausage. We allow ourselves a couple of centimetres of it each a day.

Our principal occupation is trying to rid our clothes of lice, and we are able to wash our long underwear for the first time in a month, though I can't imagine how I can wash my corset, which must be harbouring whole legions of lice.

The sounds of the war are close to us all the time: the rumble of heavy artillery and the constant drone of planes overhead. On two nights running, the number of huge bombers flying over makes the windows rattle all over the camp, and the sky to the west is lit with red light. The guards tell us it's Dresden burning. They are bitter and angry that one of their most beautiful cities is being destroyed by fire-bombs, when the war must be so close to ending. I imagine women running with babies in their arms, children with nowhere to hide from the bombs, the awful screams of people being burned to death or perishing by suffocation under the weight of a falling building.

After Dresden, the mood in the camp darkens. Even Hans and the other guards from Lamsdorf are cold with us, but there's also a new attitude among the prisoners.

I see a guard strike a prisoner with the back of his hand. The prisoner slowly takes a cigarette paper and a stub of pencil from his pocket. 'What's your name and serial number?' he asks the guard.

We are frozen with horror. Surely this will result in days in the cooler or a more determined beating. But the guard just looks at him for a long time and then turns and walks away.

On 18th February we're informed that we'll be leaving in the morning, on foot again. This means we'll be forced to leave Ralph behind. The sick are told they'll be taken on by truck or train. Most of them hope they'll simply be abandoned, to be liberated by the Russians.

The men have been moved around in the sickbay, and there's

a stranger in Ralph's bed. For a horrible moment I think he's died in the night, but other men who've seen me there before tell me where to find him. As I leave, they call out, 'Good luck, lad' and 'Say hello to Piccadilly for me.'

I scan the faces of the patients until I find Ralph. After I've washed and dried his feet for the last time, I take my notebook and write in shorthand, with my hand shaking and my eyes prickling, *I never forget everything you have done for me.*

He says aloud, 'And you for me. Come and find me when you get back to Blighty.' He writes his parents' address. 'Or if I don't make it back' – I shake my head fervently, but he wants to know that he's said it – 'go and see my mum and dad. Tell them . . .'

I nod. Of course I know what he wants to tell them, and he doesn't have to finish.

He looks over my shoulder and scratches his head as he continues. 'And please, would you look after Max for me? He means . . .' I wait, nodding solemnly. He swallows and tries again. 'Max isn't as resilient as he looks. He could give up. And you're the strongest of all of us. Promise me.'

He wipes his face roughly with the back of his sleeve. I lay my hand on his and nod again.

I write in his notebook, seven little shorthand squiggles: *I promise. I won't let him give up.* Of course I'll look after Max. He and Bill are all the family I've got left.

One of the medics stops and looks closely at me. 'Out on the march, I want you to keep telling yourself that the human body is the toughest device ever invented. You can make it, if you believe you will. Don't forget that, will you?'

I nod, full of dread at what we may be facing.

Ralph and I both have tears in our eyes as I stand by his bed

336

and formally shake him by the hand. I leave with my head bowed and a strong feeling I'll never see him again – that only one of us, or perhaps neither, will make it to England.

As I cross the compound back to our hut, although Cousins holds back the tears, I feel hollowed out, a husk of the person I was.

Just after dawn on 19th February we're called out onto the parade ground. We're wearing all the clothes we possibly can and have our kit-bags and blankets lashed to the sledge again. This time there are only three kit-bags and no food parcels, but we still need our blankets, and it's easier to pull a sledge than carry anything in our weakened state. We're all counted, in the old, familiar way, but this time the derision and mockery from the prisoners' ranks are loud, and mostly ignored by the guards. The old taunts that have been called for so long are now louder: '*Unser Tag wird kommen*' – Our day will come; '*Den hattet ihr schon*' – You've had it. We're told that this time we'll be sent out in groups of 200–300 at a time, following slightly different routes to make it easier to find billets for the night.

Our old Lamsdorf guards are standing back, and new men from the town of Görlitz are assigned to accompany us. I look along their faces; they are furious at the unpunished taunting, and the old fear floods through me. Maybe one of these new guards will spot the secret I've kept hidden for so long.

The order comes to 'About-turn', and the great gates of the prison camp are swung back for us to leave, as once again we march out onto the open road.

26

Bill senses the mood of the march darkening further as they leave Görlitz, still pulling their sledge behind them. It's even more than a grim fight for survival; it's like being at war all over again. Their shorter column of 300 or so prisoners may be easier to bed down for the night, but Bill fears that Izzy might be harder to hide. Their guards are posterns and *volkssturm* rather than regular army; either adolescent thugs, indoctrinated by the Hitler Youth from the time they could walk, or old soldiers in their sixties who lived through the First World War and the terrible conditions of the Armistice. The young are the worst, because they're arrogant, aggressive and self-important, completely certain, despite all the evidence to the contrary, that the Nazis are still winning the war. They are distrustful, trigger-happy, mean. They haven't been through what the Lamsdorf guards suffered with the prisoners on the first leg of the march. They haven't known any individual prisoners long enough to see them as human beings. The new guards loathe the Allies for the slaughter of civilians at Dresden.

Bill's constantly worried that Izzy will be discovered as a woman by these new guards, who seem eager to show their superiority in every way. He knows they wouldn't hesitate to have their sport with her in front of him, before killing both of them. He watches Izzy doggedly putting one foot in front of the other through the snow and can't believe everything she's faced, just to be with him.

Now they are in the old pre-war Germany, and Bill feels there's a difference in the guards. They are in their homeland and he knows they'll fight to defend it, just as Izzy was prepared to do for Czechoslovakia. They seem to take the ice on their eyebrows and noses and lapels as badges of honour. They call to the prisoners constantly to move faster up the long, murderous hills, as if they weren't going as fast as their bodies could move. Despite their days resting at Görlitz, Bill knows they are in a very poor condition, hundreds of starving men, edging forward through the snow.

But just as something has hardened in the guards, so it has lightened in the prisoners around him, who are marching west towards their own people. This time they are kitted out against the cold better than on the first march. They have had more time to prepare, and everyone knew they weren't going on a short hike. Two friends have raided the sports cupboard in the camp: one is wearing wicket-keeper gloves and his mate has cut open a leather football to make a hat. One man shows Bill his gloves and says they're made of dog-skin, the warmest thing he's ever felt.

'Look, look there,' says Bill to Izzy, pointing as they trudge. 'Posterns digging in with machine guns. They know the Allies are coming very soon.'

Jeering and insults are thrown at the posterns and singing starts, up and down the line. Bill joins in, roaring out the words of 'It's a Long Way to Tipperary', 'Keep the Home Fires Burning' and 'Take Me Back to Dear Old Blighty'.

Rumours keep starting that there will be Red Cross parcels in the next village or the one after that.

Hauling their sledge up these long, gradual hills, Bill, Izzy and Max can take in their shorter column, two or three abreast, stretching ahead along the snowy, potholed country tracks they're travelling. Although they're now in Germany, Bill notices that the number of civilian refugees seems even greater than before. Nobody wants to be left for the Red Army, he thinks. If the Russian soldiers showed no mercy to Czech women, then his blood freezes at the thought of the revenge they'll mete out to German women. And now he's pleased that Izzy didn't stay with Berta. Perhaps Izzy's mother and Marek are on the road by now too.

They trudge through endless pine forests, with snow fallen from the branches of the trees, but still lying deep beneath them where the sun doesn't reach. The farms are bigger than in Poland, with bigger barns. The villages have red roofs that ought to look cheerful.

At the first night's rest stop, the posterns treat the prisoners like animals, kicking out of the way men who have collapsed with exhaustion.

Bill says, 'Who'd have thought we'd miss the guards from Lamsdorf?'

A man near him says, 'There were some bastards there too, but that one with eczema asked me why I went round all day with an empty pipe in my mouth, and I told him it was because I hadn't got any tobacco. And every day after that he brought me a pinch of tobacco for my pipe.'

There's a moment's silence, then Max says, 'Well, none of them showed me a moment's kindness. And we should get the names of all these bastards, so they can be made to pay.'

The guards push and shove them into a huge barn, bigger than Bill's ever seen and alive with rats. Some prisoners try to catch them for food. Bill thinks again of Tucker and wonders if it was Izzy who laced his food with rat poison. Could she have done it? Would she?

The mood is different in the villages too. Bill remembers the Polish women who came out with hot drinks for them, but now many of the Germans throw stones at them and spit on them. 'This is for Dresden,' they shout. 'Murdering swine.'

News comes down the line that the posterns are having to guard the RAF prisoners from the locals as they pass.

On their second day Bill hears the line ahead go deadly quiet, as they begin to come alongside men and women who've been made to stand back from the track for them to pass. There must be 2,000 of them, wearing thin pyjamas and bloodied wooden clogs. Their heads are shaved and uncovered. They have no coats, no underwear, no hats, no *fuss-lag*. They shiver uncontrollably, some holding the others up. They stare ahead or down, but aren't focusing on the prisoners, not expecting anything from them. They line both sides of the road, like a terrible warning that however cold and hungry the British PoWs may be, even worse is possible. Max tries to press a crust of bread into the hand of a young person who might be a man or a woman, and one of their guards crashes a rifle butt down on his hand. The morsel of bread falls into the snow. Bill thinks they can only offer them respectful silence – prayers perhaps, from those who still believe.

For a long time after they've passed, Bill can still see the blankness in their eyes.

Max whispers, 'Jews. I think they were Jews. If my grandfather hadn't gone to America, I could be there with them.'

Izzy links her arm into his, and they tramp on.

The new guards are harsh with anyone who drops out of line to answer a call of nature, so they try to wait until the rest stops. With so little food, they only have to defecate every five or six days, and because the new posterns rarely let them stop for water, their urine has turned dark yellow. Izzy is very careful now only to crouch down when the posterns' backs are turned, with Bill and Max to shield her.

As well as the gnawing hunger, Bill is thirsty all the time, with a terrible craving for water that he's never experienced before. He cracks ice off a puddle and hands out chunks of it to the others. They break it into their tin mugs, waiting for it to melt. One man says it's his birthday, and the guard gives him half a cup of water. Bill sees many men scooping up handfuls of the yellow snow from beside the road, and he remembers Ralph telling them only to eat clean snow, only to drink boiled water, not to use the same hand to eat as to clean themselves. Bill wishes Ralph and Scotty were still with them. It's so hard only having Max to help him watch over Izzy. He is exhausted with having to be vigilant every minute.

The food ration is intermittent. At some overnight stops there's bread or even soup or potatoes, but sometimes there's nothing. When there's a pause to rest, the guards let them into the fields to forage for turnips, mangolds and potatoes, which they dig out of the frozen ground with their bare hands and eat raw, with the earth still on.

They are still covering more than twenty kilometres each day on the treacherously icy roads. They pass Bad Muskau and the River Spree, with factories farting their smoke into the sky. There's a huge chemical works, and then a field of hop poles. Bill remembers going down to Kent once on a working holiday with Flora's family to harvest hops, everyone laughing in the summer air. He is hardly able to believe a day will come when these will be hanging with green vines, and people will laugh in these fields.

They walk on, still pulling their sledge, until the track again enters the dark and gloom of a thick pine forest. Bill wonders if they have wolves in Germany, but thinks he'd better not ask, for fear of worrying Izzy. He thinks the prisoners are all such sick weaklings now that wolves could pick them off like baby deer.

For three whole days they eat nothing at all. They've still got a cake of soap, but the villages they pass through have either been bombed or are shut up tightly against them. Bill begins to grab at something in the air before him as he shuffles onwards. Izzy catches his hand, and he looks at her, puzzled, not knowing who she is for a second. Then he focuses. 'Sorry,' he says. 'It was right there in front of me. A big slab of bread and drippin'. Right there where I could grab it.'

At the next village they drop back in line until the postern is ahead of them, and they look out for someone ready to barter. A woman in a headscarf and shawl is standing close to the column, watching them pass. Bill catches her eye and shows her their last cake of soap. She nods and reaches into her apron pocket, quickly snatching the soap and pressing a bread roll into Bill's hand. Bill pulls the roll into three portions and shares it with Izzy and Max. It isn't fresh, but they press it quickly into their dry mouths, chewing and chewing.

They overtake more civilian refugees. A young woman with two children hanging on her skirts stands next to a cart piled high with her possessions. The cart has one wheel missing. Her clothes were once well cut, good quality, but are now dusty and ragged. She holds out one hand for food, but doesn't look at them. As they come level with her, Max unstraps his watch and presses it into her hand. Bill just catches the astonished look on her face as they shuffle past, and shares her disbelief.

'You shouldn't have done that,' says Bill. 'That was your last birthday present from your folks.'

'I know.'

Bill is urgent. 'You could've swapped it for food for yourself. That's what your mum 'n' dad'd want.'

'It might be enough to keep all three of them alive. They're the next generation,' says Max reasonably. 'And I've got a feeling I'm not going to need it.'

They walk on in silence, and Bill says quietly, 'You're a good man', although he can't help thinking Max could have used his watch to feed his friends, not a family of strangers.

In every barn Izzy scratches the floor, searching for a trapdoor covered in earth leading to a basement where potatoes, beetroots, carrots and corn might be stored. Bill watches her indulgently; though he doesn't believe she'll find it, it's important to have hope. But one evening she comes to them, eyes shining with triumph, and pulls Bill and Max over to see. As soon as Bill opens the trapdoor, he can smell the dry, clean smell of stored vegetables.

Max hisses, 'Shut it quick. Goon up!'

They wait for the postern to close the big barn doors for the night and then Bill takes charge, calling out, 'Quiet, everyone. Cousins has found some food here.'

Men nearby move aside as Bill hauls up the trapdoor. Max and Izzy hold it open while Bill drops down, lights a match and calls back up, 'Yes. Spuds. Turnips. Something else.'

They help him back up, and all the eyes are watching him, somewhere between hope and desperation.

Bill says, 'Quiet now. Don't let the goons know. Form an orderly queue. I'll get down there and hand it up. Let's say one spud each for now. Then we'll get it all up and share it out properly. There's enough for everyone, but if you push in, you don't get anything.'

He drops back down and begins to hand the vegetables up to Izzy and Max to distribute. The other prisoners line up for Izzy and Max to give them their share, each taking their potato and either eating it raw or cutting it up into tiny chunks to cook on their blowers. When each of them has one potato, Bill continues to hand up the rest of the winter store. Max counts the men in the barn and they divide it so that everyone has something to take away with them, to eat tomorrow.

They pass through bomb-wrecked towns and villages, some with houses still burning. Occasionally the side of a house has fallen away, leaving a room like a theatre set, with a fireplace, wallpaper and curtains flapping at a window, as if the actors will step back into it at any moment and the action of their lives will continue exactly as before. All along the road Bill sees makeshift graves hacked from ice. Many are child-sized.

Out in the countryside again, up in a snowy field close to the shadow of the trees, a dark shape catches Bill's eye. Something

345

standing with its ears pricked up, ready to run or fight. He points it out to Izzy and Max.

'I think it's a hare,' Max says.

'I ain't never seen one,' says Bill, and Izzy looks astonished.

The hare seems important to Bill in some way he can't fathom, like a message to him in a language he doesn't know. If only he could understand it, then this whole sorry mess would make some sense.

Max is doing some calculations. 'I think it's the first of March,' he says. 'A mad March hare! Fancy that.'

One afternoon the greyness of the interminable days suddenly lifts and the sun breaks through. They can feel some warmth on their backs, and begin to find it more difficult to pull the sledge. It slowly dawns on Bill that the temperature has risen a few degrees, enough so that the snow on the road is melting under his tramping feet. First the snow gets thinner, then patchy, until it's completely gone and their sledge is bumping over the pitted road or cobbles or grass. Within an hour he and Max have decided this is impossible. They have to take turns pulling every five minutes or so, and it's too hard to let Izzy do it. All along the roadside other makeshift sledges have been left behind.

'If we could keep going till tonight, we could at least burn the wood for some warmth,' puffs Bill. They keep on, switching and switching about for another mile or two, until there's a short rest period, then he agrees with Max that they have no choice but to abandon the sledge. He's proud of its construction, and sorry to leave it behind. They unload their kit-bags and blankets.

'We must keep the blowers,' says Bill.

'There's no room in my bag,' says Max, and Bill thinks: That's odd.

Izzy takes one blower and Bill takes the other. Bill wraps his two blankets crosswise around him and ties them with string. Izzy wears hers like two cloaks over her kit-bag. Izzy and Bill don't have any food to weigh them down, and apart from a couple of turnips covered in earth, their kit-bags only contain their mess tins and cups; blowers; pyjamas; small, dirty towels; Izzy's stained rags; Bill's photographs; and Izzy's last square of chocolate. He keeps his remaining harmonica in his battledress pocket. He thought they were all wearing all their clothes, and yet Max's bag looks heavy when he swings it up onto his back. Bill has a rush of suspicion that Max has got some tins of food that he's keeping for himself. He'll have to keep an eye on him, he thinks.

The next section of road has been bombed, and they pick their way through rubble.

'We couldn't have pulled the sledge across this,' says Bill, at last convinced that he's done the right thing in leaving it.

They cross a river, still frozen, pass mills, warehouses and red-brick factories. There's a huge tavern right by the roadside, and it seems to taunt them. Bill thinks that inside there must be beer and food, while outside other human beings are starving. He salivates at the thought of beer.

He's so exhausted that he can hardly form thoughts, hardly recognise sensations, so he fails to recognise the feeling of being warm, as if it's for the first time in his life. The blankets are unbearably heavy.

Someone behind them begins to sing 'The Sun Has Got His Hat On' and Bill joins in. The singing seems to lift everyone, quicken their shambling pace, as if the sun has given them a message of change: that this can't go on for ever. Bill begins another song, 'Oh, I Do Like to Be Beside the Seaside', and everyone sings it tauntingly into the faces of the posterns.

They pass along Freital high street with its *Kino*, still showing a new film each week, as if the lives of the prisoners and refugees were more shadowy and unimportant than the flickering images on the screen. They cross a railway line and look up to the mountain behind the town, with thick snow still on its slopes. The sun sets in a ball of orange fire and the sky is clear.

'It'll be cold tonight,' says Bill as if it wasn't cold every night. But he's right. Without the cloud cover, the temperature plummets again. Bill and Max insist that Izzy lies between them, where she might be a little warmer, and they throw their blankets over the three of them.

The next day the winding road runs alongside the railway through a steep valley where trees climb the slopes on both sides. Every half-hour or so a train passes and curious passengers look out at them, at mile after mile of trudging scarecrows, while they hurry to their business appointments or new postings, or to visit families. A church is perched on top of a rock, and Bill wonders if anyone attends it. Harder to get to than the kingdom of heaven, he thinks, if that exists.

In the afternoon of the next day, when their billet for the night is in sight, Max begins to stumble like a man who's drunk. Bill wonders if he's eaten something that had gone bad or if he's getting sick. They support him on both sides, knowing that if he drops out of the line, he might be shot or they'd have to leave him to freeze to death. Bill swings Max's kit-bag onto his own back, ignoring his protests, and bursts out, 'Good God, man, what've you got in here? No wonder you can't walk. This must weigh twenty pounds.'

Max, almost incoherent, is supported between them. 'It's my books. I couldn't leave my books.'

They carry him between them into the riding school where they are to spend the night. In the yard, where they wait to be directed to their sleeping quarters, Max crumples down onto the concrete, and Bill drops his kit-bag beside him, letting it fall from waist height. There's no clank of tins.

They are directed to the stables, painted and carved and decorated like a palace, and retreat into a horse stall, where fresh straw has been piled for them and the owner has left pails of clean water. There they all collapse onto the straw, resting to get their strength back. Bill struggles to a sitting position first and pulls open Max's kit-bag. Max watches, but doesn't stop him.

'It *is* bloody books!' Bill pulls out one volume after another – the whole library Max has carried with him from Lamsdorf to the quarry and back. Nothing but books, notebooks and the hat with ear-flaps that Bill knitted him.

Bill lines up the books in front of him, and Max watches without saying anything. What a fucking idiot, thinks Bill. There's no food at all in his bag. Not even a carrot.

'What happened to your ration from the barn cellar?' asks Bill.

'I had to leave it. I couldn't fit in any more.'

'No, I can see that!' Bill is running his hand back and forth through his hair, making it stand on end. Izzy lays her hand on his arm, but he shakes it off.

Max cowers in front of him.

Bill hardly ever loses his temper, but now he rages like Izzy.

'What did you want to do – kill yourself for a few books?' He opens one and tears out the first few pages. Max shudders and his hands flutter forward, as Bill shoves the crumpled pages under his nose. 'Go on then, eat them! Eat the pigging books, you bloody swot.'

Max doesn't retaliate, but seems to shrivel into himself.

'What have you got to say, eh? Eh?'

Izzy pulls at Bill's sleeve again, and this time he notices her.

'What've I got to do – look after both of you? Is that my job? Is that what I signed up for?'

Izzy clamps her hand over her mouth with the effort of not retaliating, and jumps to her feet, to kick furiously at the post separating the stalls.

'Hey, give it a rest in there,' comes a shout from the next stall.

'I don't want you two to fall out over me,' says Max. 'It'd be better if I just took myself off . . .'

Izzy stands over him with her arms folded, to make sure Bill understands she doesn't want Max to leave, and the rage goes out of Bill, as rapidly as it flared. He never stays angry for long.

'OK,' he says. 'Sorry, sorry. It's just . . .'

Bill can see Izzy is still fuming with him for shouting at Max. She looks like she did when she bit him – like the old, fiery Izzy – and a flood of irrational love rushes through him. He tries to think of something to soothe her.

'Maybe,' he suggests, 'maybe we could light a fire with the books, just outside the stable, and boil up the vegetables we've got left and make a nice soup?'

He can't understand why Izzy smacks him hard on the arm.

Max protests, 'You don't understand. I haven't carried them all this way to burn them.'

Bill is petulant, already tasting the stew he'd be able to make, thinking they are both equal fools. 'Well, why did you, then?'

Max pulls at the collar of his greatcoat. 'For all the ideas of goodness that have disappeared. I thought as long as I had the books, there was a chance those ideas might stay alive in the world. But it's too late. It's all gone.'

Bill knows he's thinking of the stick-limbed people in the striped pyjamas, as well as their own men left to die by the side of the road. Izzy has her hand over her mouth again, and Bill thinks that all the words she's been damming up might come gushing out of her.

He shakes his head, then looks around him. Below the window behind the stall is a shelf with tackle and brushes. He clears the shelf, dusting it with the cuff of his coat sleeve, picks up the books and carefully, one at a time, places them spine-out on the shelf.

'Here you are,' he says. 'Someone will find them here. Some stable boy.' He looks at Izzy. 'Or girl. And they'll understand.'

Max's voice is hoarse and indistinct. 'But it's too late, d'you see? It's all too late. There's no point to anything. If we live, and all those others die, what's the point?'

Izzy goes to him and wraps her arms around him, but Max's body is stiff and unresponsive. Bill watches, embarrassed, then goes out into the yard. Max and Izzy seem to understand each other better than he does, he thinks with a stab of jealousy.

But when he comes back, Max and Izzy are sitting apart, heads down with fatigue. All the fire in her has been doused by exhaustion, and the sight of it twists Bill's heart.

'There's some soup,' he says. 'Bring your mess tins.'

The riding-school owner has provided buckets of steaming pea soup and an inch of sausage each. It tastes better than anything

351

Bill's eaten for weeks, even though it's not like proper bangers. He smacks his lips over the soup and says, 'Sorry' to Max.

'No, I'm sorry,' Max replies. 'It's just . . .'

'You don't have to explain.'

Bill unpacks the vegetables from his own and Izzy's kit-bags and divides them into three on the straw.

Max says, 'No, I can't. Those are yours.'

'Oh, we need you to help us carry them,' Bill grins. 'They were getting too heavy.'

There's a commotion outside, and Bill sees the riding-school owner bringing buckets of hot water for the prisoners to wash and shave in. One of the posterns is arguing with him, sneering at the filthy prisoners. The owner says something in German and then repeats it slowly in English. 'My son is a prisoner of the British,' he says. 'I hope they would let him shave and wash. Would you be less than them?' The postern reluctantly stands aside.

They take their mess tins to get a share of the warm water and use thin, grey rags to wipe the water over their face and necks. Max and Bill both shave, and Izzy pretends to do the same. Some men are trying to wash under their clothes. One has opened his shirt and is scraping lice from his chest hair into a matchbox. He laughs and nods at the postern who didn't want them to have the water. 'I'm catching these little beauties to throw at that one tomorrow – a little present from me. I got some right down the back of one of their necks today!'

Bill laughs aloud and thinks he'll try to catch some of his own.

27

The following afternoon it begins to rain steadily, soaking our blankets and making them heavier and heavier, until I stagger sometimes under the weight. Max opens his kit-bag and pulls on the hat Bill knitted, the one with ear-flaps. I know Bill notices, though neither of them mentions it. We carry our mess tins in front of us to catch rainwater to drink.

'At least we won't die of thirst,' mutters Bill.

Now the whole column is shuffling and limping rather than walking, heads down, looking at nothing but our own feet – left, right, one in front of the other.

I try not to look ahead, not to focus on any landmark in the distance, a brick chimney or farmhouse. Once you've seen something like that, your eye strays back to it and you walk for hours, or maybe days, but it never seems to get any closer. I've learned that it's better to let your eyes rest on the small things by the road: a rabbit hole, a dripping drainpipe, a sparrow's skeleton with its head missing. Those things can be passed and left behind. Small progress.

We see one of the posterns kick over a stool on which an old lady has set up a bucket of steaming acorn coffee. He tells her she's a disgrace to her nation, and she answers back, 'But I won't have to answer to God for my actions.'

In another village a woman holds herself and rocks, constantly calling out, '*Kinder, Kinder, warum kämpfen wir?* – Children, children, why are we fighting?' I can't find an answer. I know my brother doesn't hate her son.

The boots have rotted on some men's feet and they are walking with sacks wrapped around them. Even so, from time to time a defiant shout comes down the line, 'Are we downhearted?' And Bill and Max lift their heads to roar '*No!*' with the others.

'My boots are letting in water,' says Max, and I pay attention to the strange sensation around the toes of my left foot. My boots are wearing through too, and the felt is soaking up water from the puddles. Much of the road is awash, and some puddles are deep enough to let water through the lace-holes.

A Russian fighter plane appears from nowhere, flying so low that it seems to skim the top of the hedges. We all dive to the ground, nose-down in the mud.

When we get up, the front of our clothes are sodden too. For the first time I think: I can't do this. I'm just going to have to stop. But I know Bill wouldn't let me just sit down and die; he would insist on staying with me, and then he would be shot too. So I keep on, one foot in front of the other, bent double like an old woman under the weight of my wet coat and blankets.

And then, just when I think I can't go a step further, the posterns point out our next resting place. Tall chimneys rise from a brick building and fear shudders along the column of men. 'Chimneys,' they whisper to one another. 'Death-camp.' Max's and Bill's eyes mirror the panic I'm feeling.

But then word comes down the line that it's nothing more sinister than a brick factory, and we breathe again.

As soon as we enter it, a wonderful warmth dries our wet faces, and our clothes begin to steam. It's warm everywhere from the kilns; even the brick floors are warm. And it's big enough for all of us to have space. Someone has scattered dry straw on the floor and, as we find a corner to bed down in, I wish blessings on them and their family.

We pull off our coats, and through my exhaustion I note that the waxing on Bill's and Max's coats has still worked – their shoulders and backs aren't soaking like the front of their clothes. Our coats and blankets can be dried simply by hanging them from nails on the wall. Most men immediately strip to their underwear, which is grey and ragged, and their wet clothes festoon the factory.

A cry goes up. 'Warm water! There's warm water to wash in.'

Bill goes to investigate and comes back full of excitement. 'There are sinks. We could wash ourselves. Maybe even our underwear.'

Max says, 'I'll look after our stuff. You go and see.'

Men are forming an orderly queue, as if in barracks or at a holiday campsite. There they might have had a towel over one arm; here they are holding their filthy underclothes. Many are stripped to the waist, and some are dressed in a second set of long underclothes, or pyjama bottoms, or shorts. A few are naked and look like skeletons with skin loosely hanging from them. In the steamy room ahead there's laughter. I can't see how I would hide my sex here, and I'm bitterly disappointed at the thought of not being able to wash.

We return to Max.

'We could wash the clothes first,' Bill suggests to him. 'And you and I could wash ourselves while Cousins stays with the bags. Then tonight, when everyone's asleep, I could take him back to wash. What do you think?'

I nod and nod. I'm willing to risk almost anything to be clean.

Sitting behind Bill and Max, I wriggle out of my trousers and three sets of long underwear and pull on Jan's grubby pyjama bottoms, tying the cord tighter than it's ever needed to be before. I keep on my battledress top, but contrive to remove the long-sleeved vests beneath it, leaving just my chest corset, which is crawling with lice. I'd like to get rid of it completely. In the secret part of my kit-bag I still have the small vest belonging to Marek, clean and smelling of home. I think that would now be enough to hide my shrunken breasts.

I make a sign to Bill by laying my hand on my chest, and indicating the lacing down the side. He understands immediately and reaches up the side of my battledress to unlace me. I reach in through the neck and use my tag to saw through the straps, then I can pull out the whole contraption. Sure enough, when I pull out the corset, it's alive with lice. I quickly roll it and stuff it under my dirty washing. The inside of the battledress top is scratchy against my bare nipples.

We queue to wash our clothes. There's no soap, but we rub the fabric hard in the warm water. I dip my head under a tap and hope some of the lice will drown. Around me are men washing their bodies, trying to rid themselves of infestations. Their private parts flap against their scrawny thighs.

We return to our corner and hang our washing to drip onto the warm floor.

Bill and Max go to wash, while I light one of Max's remaining

356

cigarettes to burn lice from the seams of my trousers. While they're away, one of the posterns swaggers over, eyes alert with excitement.

'What've you got in those bags you're guarding?' he asks, and I realise he must have been watching us, waiting for the boys to leave me alone.

I shake my head as if I don't understand. My heart's beating loudly in my ears as he bends to Max's kit-bag, tipping a shrivelled turnip and his notebooks out onto the floor. He flicks through the notebooks, but obviously doesn't speak English and drops them carelessly, kicking one out of the way.

Some prisoners I don't know can see what's happening and start to come towards me.

'Hey, leave that stuff alone,' one says, and I scramble to my feet, arms crossed over my front, as much to hold myself together under this assault as to protect my unbound breasts. But the postern continues, now emptying my bag onto the floor. I have a blower, plus a potato, a box of matches, my brother's summer undershorts and pyjama top, my filthy towel, the stained foot-rags and one last square of chocolate. He dives on the chocolate and shoves it in his mouth. Then he shakes the bag again, feeling something moving in it. He turns it inside out and, at the bottom, finds the hidden section.

'I knew you were hiding something!' he says triumphantly. A small crowd is gathering, but he waves his gun threateningly at them, and they stay back, wary but curious.

From the hidden compartment he yanks Marek's small vest, which he throws to the floor, and the sanitary belt and another small heap of stained rags.

My vision goes black and red. I begin to quake. Bill will come back, and I'll simply be gone, dragged away to the fate of so many women before me.

'What's this?' he asks, waving my sanitary belt about.

My head is spinning as if I'm going to faint, but the part of me that is Cousins steps forward and takes it from his hand, shoving the potato into the waxed gusset and yanking the elastic back like a slingshot, aiming at his head.

'A catapult!' shouts one of the prisoners. 'It's a bloody catapult. Go on, let him have it.'

'David and Goliath,' shouts someone else, and for a fraction of a second I'm tempted.

The postern looks at the device, and I nod furiously and relax the elastic. There's a murmur of disappointment from the crowd. I hold the 'catapult' out to him, keeping the potato. He stuffs it into his pocket, with the elastic trailing out, and turns to Bill's bag, tipping out a carrot, the other blower, his photographs and one of his harmonicas.

'Ha!' he cries and swoops down on it. '*Mundharmonika*.'

He brings it to his lips and begins to suck and blow, making a cacophony like a donkey braying – a world away from the heartbreaking melodies Bill can draw from the instrument.

This is the moment Bill and Max return, pushing through the crowd to get to me. Bill hurls himself at the postern, who knocks him away with the butt of his pistol. There's a sickening crack as it connects with Bill's face and he falls back, blood pouring from his nose.

'You've broken his nose!' shouts Max, and there's a surge forward all around us. For a second I think the crowd will close in and tear the postern to pieces, but he shoots into the air above their heads and the circle expands again.

358

The postern shoves Bill's harmonica into his pocket with my 'catapult' and shoulders his way through the prisoners.

I'm down on my knees beside Bill, as bright blood drips from his nose. Terror for myself now transmutes into fear for him and cold fury against the postern.

'Give us some air here,' says Max and the circles steps back again. 'Are there any medics?' Nobody moves, and I take Bill's newly washed shorts and ball them against his nose to staunch the bleeding. He flinches as his nose is touched, and his eyes are watering, but he keeps his lips clenched together. He takes the shorts from me, and I can see he's pressing harder than I would have dared.

'Tip your head back,' says someone, and he does.

The shorts become redder and redder and I begin to despair, thinking: He's never going to stop bleeding, he's going to die here, in front of me, and there's nothing I can do.

An age passes and some men drift away, then Bill pulls the bloody pants from his nose.

'I think it's stopping,' he says. 'But it don't 'alf 'urt.'

'Must be broken,' says Max anxiously. 'Pity Ralph isn't here. Though he wouldn't have liked the blood.'

Bill looks up at me, woebegone. 'I'll look like a boxer.' He grimaces. 'Sorry.'

But all I can see is my beautiful boy, my beautiful Bill, with his face bloodstained by that beast. My hand flutters in a signal that's supposed to tell him I don't care about the shape of his nose. I don't care about anything, as long as I have him with me.

Black bruising starts to spread like an eye-mask across Bill's face.

'Thought I'd get through this caper unwounded,' he says ruefully.

'Could have been worse,' says Max, nodding at me, and Bill agrees.

'Could have been a lot worse.'

We look at our few remaining possessions scattered around us, and I collect Bill's photographs. Max carefully puts his note-books back in his bag, then stops.

'Where's the other harmonica?' he asks, and Bill taps the breast-pocket of his battledress.

'Safe and sound,' he winks through his closing eye.

Later I go back to the washroom with Bill, to wash his bloodied pants and, hopefully, my filthy body and my corset. The queue has gone as men settle down to pull straw together for mattresses and eat what very little they have. I rinse the blood from his shorts and he splashes it from his face. When we turn round, we are alone in the washroom.

'Quick,' says Bill. 'Wash yourself. I'll watch the door.'

I don't need prompting to thrust his wet shorts up inside my battle dress, under my arms, around my scrawny body and down the front of my pyjamas as far as I can reach. Then I roll up my trousers and wipe my legs. I'm damp all over under the clothes, and even though I know it won't have got rid of the lice, I feel clean for the first time in weeks. I unroll the corset and quickly scrub it.

We return to Max just as the lights are put out all over the factory, without any warning. In the dark we fumble for the raw vegetables – our only meal of the day. I prop my corset around the base of a column, close to the wall, to dry.

'Maybe there'll be bread in the morning,' says Bill.

In the dark I pull on Marek's vest and Jan's pyjama top. The vest is now only a little tight; I am the size of an eight-year-old boy. I stretch out on the straw, in my clean clothes, feeling the glorious warmth easing its way up from the brick floor.

In the morning Bill is almost unrecognisable with his two half-closed black eyes and his swollen nose. I want to kiss each eye and the poor, shattered nose. But I don't. I check that all the washing is dry, and then I pull my brother's long underwear and a tatty shirt back on and sit on the warm floor, flicking lice from the seams of my battledress and grinding them underfoot. Later in the morning there's bread – a loaf among four – and soup and a potato each. Almost a feast. All day we doze, and I listen to Max and Bill talk, and I miss Scotty and Ralph, and my mother and father, and Marek and Jan, until a dark hole aches in my entire chest.

From time to time Bill gingerly fingers his nose or checks the breast-pocket of his battledress for the other harmonica.

When the lights go out, I re-lace the corset under my clothes. At least it's another layer of clothing.

28

When they set out the next day, Bill's eyes are half-closed and his broken nose throbs with each step he takes, although at least his clothes feel clean and his coat and blanket are dry. He hopes that Izzy feels stronger for the rest and the meagre food, and marvels at her resilience. Who'd have thought a girl could survive this? Perhaps they'll make it, he thinks.

It isn't just him – he can see that everyone is more hopeful, lifting their heads to take in the view as they reach the top of another hill, rather than simply shuffling forward. He realises that even a little food and warmth and rest can bring hope. But it's as if the Nazis are playing a cruel trick on them, because after the brick factory there are no further food rations for three days, and now they are truly starving. To make matters even worse, many men have developed dysentery. Sometimes they are allowed to crouch down at the side of the road to empty their bowels, but often the posterns refuse to let them stop, and the watery, bloody bowel motions run down their legs as they struggle onwards. At rest stops, Bill sees sets of filthy, blood-stained underwear left by the side of the road.

They come across a boy sitting on a gate, watching the ragged column walk past. He pulls a big carrot out of his pocket and opens his mouth to bite into it. Bill stops and tries to beg it from him. The boy is unmoved, looking the three of them up and down to gauge what he could ask for in return. He obviously isn't impressed by anything he sees. Bill's hand slowly goes to the breast-pocket of his battledress and brings out his precious remaining harmonica.

The boy's eyes light up, and he stretches out his hand for the harmonica. Bill indicates, 'Carrot first', and they hand them over simultaneously, each holding on to their own offering until they're sure the swap has been made.

The boy runs off, leaping into the air with joy, and Bill offers Izzy the first bite of the carrot. She nibbles at it and hands it back. Bill takes a bite and hands it to Max, who refuses for a moment.

'All for one,' says Bill, and Max digs his teeth into the hard flesh. As they trudge on, they each take a small bite. When the carrot is finished, they feel just as hungry, and Bill, who for a few minutes felt proud of his sacrifice, now wants to weep for the loss of the harmonica that Flora sent him.

In the next village a civilian man is standing in a shadowy doorway. He makes eye contact with Izzy and beckons her towards him. She pulls on Bill's sleeve, and the three of them drop out of line for a moment. The man thrusts a bag of hot potatoes into her hand and disappears into the shadows before they can even thank him. They hide the potatoes under their blankets and eat them slowly without being seen. Bill thinks surely the men around them will smell their delicious scent, but perhaps they think it's a hallucination, like the bread and dripping he thought he saw. When the last scrap of the chewy skin is swallowed, and the warm food is moving down into his stomach, Bill thinks: If this man had come along sooner, I'd still have my harmonica.

And then the thinking slowly ceases again, and his body puts one foot out in front of the other, one foot in front of the other . . .

They haven't been walking long the next morning when five RAF planes fly low over the column of shuffling prisoners. Everyone cheers and waves, and Bill throws up his arms. Joy surges in his chest. Perhaps this is the end! He thinks: They've found us and come to save us. But the planes circle back and, as they come in closer, there's a deafening sound and the flash of gunfire as they begin to strafe the line.

'Get down, get down!' shouts everyone, and Bill, Max and Izzy throw themselves to the ground and crawl into the ditch.

Max grunts. 'They think we're Nazi soldiers.'

An RAF man stands up from the ditch, waving his distinctive blue airman's greatcoat. For a second Bill holds his breath and thinks the fighter pilots have understood and recognised a comrade, but then they open fire again and the RAF man's body jumps and twitches, spraying blood. Bill throws himself over Izzy, so that any bullets will get him first. Her life is more important than his own.

The RAF planes circle back three times, and the bullets bounce on the track all around them. The noise is like a deafening hailstorm, a great machine of death, and it pounds in Bill's temples, taking him back to the last terrible battle at Tobruk. He can smell the stink of the hot interior of the tank, hear Harry's voice making jokes through it all, subduing their terror. He hopes Harry is safe.

They continue to lie in the ditch with their hearts beating loudly for minutes after the planes fly off. Bill, Max and Izzy struggle to their feet, but many prisoners have been badly wounded or killed outright. There are men screaming like animals; men calling out for their mothers; hands and feet and a head blown off, which disgorge bright blood into rivulets on the road; a torso hangs from the branches of a tree. Izzy's face is rigid with horror, and Bill thinks: Yes, this is what a battle looks like. This is why we keep it from you women and children. If he could cover her eyes and ears and protect her from it, he would. It's another hell he's led her into.

But Izzy looks around decisively and moves to help an injured soldier. Max turns over the body nearest him and finds he's already dead. Without knowing he's going to, Bill begins to take control, directing those who can move to help those who are injured – calm and in control. He's proud to see Izzy pulling the rags from her kit-bag and using the strips as tourniquets for one man's arm and another's leg. There's so much blood that he doubts the men will survive, but he doesn't tell her that. The smell of blood all around them is metallic and hot. Some survivors sit with their heads in their hands; their bodies are the shape of despair. Some men weep bitterly that their friends have come so far, through so many years of war, and survived battles, imprisonment and starvation only to be mown down now by so-called friendly fire.

Izzy watches one man wiping blood from his open wounds with muddy water from the ditch, while another drinks the same water without boiling it. She marches straight up to one of the older posterns with their three mess tins and speaks in German, waving her arm towards the wounded and over to the field beside them. Bill freezes with fear for a moment, at the risk she's taking, and then sees the postern indicate to her that she can go to look for clean water.

Bill turns back to his job of organising the wounded to gather together in a 'muster station', and he watches Izzy out of the corner of one eye as she strides down the hill towards a line of trees. The postern is watching her too, hand on rifle in case this is an attempt to escape. The trees must line a frozen brook, and Bill can see her breaking the icy surface with the heel of her boot, to dip in the tins. The postern relaxes as she carefully carries back the filled mess tins. She takes a sip from one to demonstrate to him that it's clean water, and he sends a younger guard to fill bigger water containers.

Izzy returns to the stream time and time again, with as much water as she can carry – giving it to men to drink and cleaning their wounds.

Bill is busy separating those who can still walk from those who can't go any further. A man with his foot blown off leans on Max and hops to the mustering place. On Bill's orders, the bodies of the dead are lifted and carried to the ditch at the side of the road. The posterns stand in groups smoking, watching as the prisoners clear the road of their comrades and bind up the wounded as best they can.

Eventually someone comes from a local village with a horse-drawn waggon, and those too injured to walk any further are loaded onto it. As Bill helps one of them to the cart, Izzy notices a dark stain on the back of his coat, near the shoulder.

She turns him round. There's a small tear in the centre of the stain.

'You are bleeding,' she whispers accusingly. She presses the place gently and he winces.

'I didn't notice.'

'Take off coat.'

Bill pulls off his coat, straining to look over his shoulder, and now that she's pointed out the wound, the pain begins. When he removes the coat, Izzy sees his battledress and the jumper below are bloodier still. Bill can't tell if he is badly wounded or whether the bleeding has stopped, but the pain is spreading and throbbing insistently. He runs his hand up through his hair, looking at the semi-conscious men laid out on the waggon. Izzy presses a wad of rags to his bloody jumper, and he wrenches himself away from the pain. He's got more important things to think about than a little flesh-wound.

'Someone ought to go with the wounded,' he says, 'to speak up for them, make sure they're treated well.' He yanks himself away from Izzy and tries to put his battledress back on, but his left arm won't work any more, and he can't push it through the sleeve. Izzy drapes the bloodstained battledress and coat over his shoulder.

Bill looks around for someone who could go with the wounded, and a wave of nausea overtakes him as the pain grows stronger. All about him the survivors are busy helping to carry the dead into the ditch or lying, exhausted, or sitting with their heads bowed. There's nobody he can send.

'You,' whispers Izzy. 'You are best man. You go.'

'But . . .' The waggon lurches forward. Bill looks from it to Izzy, torn by indecision. He can't leave her. But he could come straight back, once he's seen that the men are being looked after. He could easily catch up. 'Will you be . . . ?'

'Go. Make doctor look at your shoulder. And your nose.'

He looks again at the bodies on the waggon, men hardly

moving, unable to demand the care they deserve, and he decides, 'I'll catch up and find you as soon as I can.'

Izzy gives him a half-push, her eyes dark with worry.

Bill runs a few steps to catch the moving waggon, and with difficulty, now unable to use his left arm, he climbs up and turns to Izzy, trying to hide from her the pain of his wound, forcing his face into a smile as the waggon pulls away.

29

I feel sick to my stomach as I watch the waggon begin to trundle off, and I run to climb aboard myself, but the postern won't let me. 'Wounded only,' he says, pushing me with the butt end of his rifle.

'I'll catch up and find you as soon as I can,' calls Bill weakly, and I can only stand and watch him, his broken nose and black eyes still visible against the white of his face, carried away from me, half-slumped on the waggon floor, trying to smile. What have I done? How can I let him go? I need him to see a doctor as soon as possible. But how could he leave me? Perhaps it's only because he knows how badly he's wounded and doesn't want me to watch him die.

As the waggon turns a bend in the road, Bill raises his hand in salute, just as he did when he first came to the farm, and I suddenly know, with the chill of absolute certainty, that I'll never see him again. I pray, with fierce intensity, 'Bring him back, please. I'll do anything – give up anything – if you let him come back to me.' But I don't know if God is listening. I think of the life-blood pulsing from Bill's wound, wishing they'd let me go with him. It all happened too quickly. We didn't say goodbye.

As the waggon disappears, I try and hear Cousins stemming my panic, telling me it will be all right. 'Steady now,' he says. 'There's work to do.'

I join Max and help to lay body parts and whole dead men into the ditch, and I carefully collect up their identity tags, so their families will know, so the world will know. We have no tools to dig the frozen soil to cover them. Again I go to the older postern and demand, in German, 'The dead must be buried.'

He wafts me away like a bluebottle. 'Yes,' he says. We'll get the townspeople to do that. It will all be done properly.' Then he looks hard at me. 'Your accent?' he asks. The younger guard, with an almost-shaved head and many angry pimples, lifts his head and looks at me too, and I realise it might all be over. Somehow I'm too tired to care, because without Bill nothing matters any more, but as the young guard picks up his rifle, my brain leaps to a plausible answer.

I cough my voice down low and try to iron out my Czech vowels, to speak my mother's perfect High German. 'My teacher was from' – I search my memory for the German name for Jeseník – 'from Freiwaldau. I think it's in Silesia.'

He still looks suspicious and the young guard steps forward, but then the postern shrugs. 'Ah, yes, a Silesian accent,' he says. 'Country bumpkin.' And he turns aside from me.

The young guard looks at me for a moment longer and I meet his eyes, defiantly, as Cousins would, before he also turns away.

I stumble back to where Max is sitting and briefly lean my head on his arm. Bill, Bill, where is Bill? Every cell in my body wants him. Every few minutes I find myself looking in the direction he disappeared, willing him to come back. I make a bargain with God. 'If one of us has to die, let it be me, not him. Kill me, and let him live.'

The strafing has killed a horse as well as so many men, and that night we have soup with meat, brought around in buckets. But there is no joy in the meal. It's almost as if we are eating the flesh of our dead comrades.

Perhaps it's the richness of the meal, or from drinking dirty water before I brought clean water from the stream, but by the next morning Max has developed dysentery. Bill isn't back, and I want to wait where we last saw him, but the posterns force us to walk on without him. Sometimes they let Max crouch by the road, and I stand beside him, feet planted apart like Cousins, guarding my friend; but sometimes they make him keep walking and the thin faeces trickle down his legs. He keeps turning to me. 'Sorry. I'm so sorry,' he groans before the pain doubles him up again. By the afternoon he's so weak that he sits down by the side of the road and refuses to get up. If I left him, I know he would die in hours, from dehydration, or the cold at night, or a gun-happy Hitler Youth would use him as rifle practice.

I lean in, close to his ear. 'I am not go on without you. You have to get up. You cannot leave me alone.' But Max doesn't budge. I lean in and order him furiously, 'You must live. Tell people what we see. Make sure this never happen again. You have work to do.'

After a long minute, he lifts his eyes to mine and nods imperceptibly. I drag him to his feet and pull one of his arms over my shoulder. We shuffle on together, one foot in front of the other. When the others aren't looking, the older postern offers Max some charcoal to chew, to ease the pain.

* * *

371

Coming out of Tharandt, we drag ourselves slowly up a long climb to the summit of a hill and a flat plateau. I think over and over again that the two of us won't make it to the top of the hill, and this is where it will all end. But somehow we do, and at the top we're allowed to sit for fifteen minutes to look down on small, picturesque villages dotted about the frozen country-side. And then we're on the move again, heading into a massive forest that stretches to the horizon. I remember my promise to Ralph that I'll look after Max. I will keep going as long as he's alive. It may not be long.

Every couple of kilometres we shuffle past huge piles of logs waiting to be picked up by forestry trucks. There's a lake, still frozen round the edges, with ducks standing on the ice or swimming in the centre. We pass a house with a millpond.

Overnight we stop in a school building. We are sleeping in the main school hall, which has a large blackboard on which someone has written Hamlet's 'To Be or Not to Be' soliloquy, which I remember learning at school.

A soldier I don't know asks, 'Do you think someone knew we were coming?'

I don't think so, because I can see the difficult words underlined, and I imagine the teacher who was trying to explain this speech to a class of bored children who'd never experienced despair. Max sits in front of the board, staring at the words for a very long time. He's sitting there when the lights go out, but he doesn't say anything. I think he is choosing not to be, and I have failed in my promise to Ralph.

I wake in the morning to the loss of Bill. It kicks me in the stomach, so that I curl myself around the pain. And as if the universe is laughing at me, I've also developed a severe head-cold.

My nose runs, my eyes water and my head aches and feels full of fog. I have hot sweats and cold shivers. I have no choice but to walk, using a rag to wipe my nose, wringing it out to reuse.

After the forest, we begin to descend again on a road the guards call the Silberstrasse. We pass big riding stables and a fast-flowing unfrozen river. Why couldn't this river have been near us when the RAF attacked? Maybe then everyone would have had clean water, and Max wouldn't have dysentery.

Every time we shuffle down a hill it's in the knowledge that in a few hours we'll have to drag our bodies up another. Sometimes Max can stagger on his own; sometimes he walks with his arm linked to mine. Travelling up the hills, the two of us support each other, and I feel a strange sensation of water trickling down my face and my spine as we reach the top. I think it's the fever from my cold.

I look at Max, and his hair is wet with sweat as well. A man behind us says, 'I'm sweating cobs', and I realise the day is getting warmer, as if we have leapt from winter to summer in a couple of hours.

Along the route we start to see discarded greatcoats and blankets. First one or two, then more and more. I know it can still get cold again after a false spring, and I'm determined to keep my coat and one blanket, but I discard the second blanket, the scratchiest one. I'll try to change out of my long winter underwear, if there's somewhere private enough at our stopping place tonight. I can feel it becoming damp and heavy with perspiration.

Max insists on dropping his coat and one blanket. 'I can't carry the weight of them any longer, I'm too weak,' he whispers.

I certainly don't have the strength to carry them for him, so he leaves them by the side of the road.

We pass under double railway bridges, a big railyard and a water tower, with a chimney tiled all the way up with roof tiles. In the open country there are groves of trees, ploughed fields, crops starting to come up in the uncaring cycle of the seasons, the gradual greening of the land. We eat a handful of grass and some rye shoots. I find a *kostival* plant and pull off its hairy leaves, stuffing them into my rucksack. Someone asks, 'Can you eat those?' and I shake my head. I could explain that the leaves are just for wounds and could even be poisonous if eaten, but he doesn't pick any.

More and more, on and on, come the same agonising long, slow hills, up onto a plateau and down into the next valley. My nose stops running, but now it's blocked, so I have to breathe through my mouth. I'm always thirsty, and I begin to cough, a chesty persistence that shakes my frame. I daren't raise my eyes to look ahead, knowing there will be another hill we'll have to climb.

I don't know what enables everyone else to keep going, but I think now I'm powered only by a steady flame of rage, fed at every step: rage at myself for not going with Bill or preventing him from leaving; rage at human beings who can treat one another worse than animals; rage against the ordinary people who failed to stand up against fascism until it was too late. I understand those who simply sit down and say they can't go any further. I'd do the same, if not for my promise to take care of Max.

The felt has now worn off the inside of my brother's boots and they are too big. At a stopping point I inspect my blisters, which I know are becoming infected, and I wrap the *kostival* leaf around them to draw out the badness. I find some newspaper and wrap that around my feet. Somehow the pain each time I put my foot to the ground tells me that I'm still alive.

We pass clumps of snowdrops and a lone crocus under a tree. I register these without the usual leap of my heart. It means spring will come again, but what sort of spring will it be? At night now, if we are in a low-lying village, comes the familiar whine of mosquitoes, joining the lice to suck the last of our blood. I sleep fitfully, coughing, itching, hungry, thirsty, grieving for Bill. Some strong instinct tells me he's dead. The wound was worse than we thought and he bled to death, or it has gone septic. He's dead, I think. Dead. And I don't want to be alive without him.

We trudge on, heads down. Some days I'm almost carrying Max and simply supporting him on others. I learn to walk in a lolloping way that puts least pressure on the sore points of my feet. I cough with my head turned away from Max, fearful of infecting him if it's TB.

We pass some retreating SS men sitting beside the road, carefully cutting the insignia off their uniforms. For the first time the posterns look really worried. They talk amongst themselves in low voices, but they follow their orders, forcing us on.

One day a farm vehicle comes the other way and, as it passes, the back of it is emptied of milk and chickens. I drink some milk, and it tastes fatty and rich. Somewhere I can smell a chicken cooking, and my mouth waters at the thought of the crispy skin and soft flesh, but we don't get any. Mostly we live on turnips from the fields, fish heads from dustbins, grass. There's a fight between two men over some swede peelings.

At the top of yet another hill we lie on the ground. I cough my lungs clear, spitting green phlegm into the grass.

'Look there, some big town,' says Max, pointing.

My eyes focus on the rising smoke from many industrial chimneys, making clouds that hang over the factories.

'That's Chemnitz,' says the older postern. 'It means we're nearly there. Nearly at Hartmannsdorf.'

My heart is like lead in my chest at the thought I'll get there without Bill. There's no meaning to anything without him.

The men pass the word back and forward in the column: 'Nearly there!' 'Nearly there.' And singing starts up. Not the patriotic songs of before, but show tunes, popular songs, 'Happy Days Are Here Again . . .'

Our feet continue to walk and finally, in the middle of the afternoon, we see the huts of a great PoW camp spread out across the top of the hill: Stalag IVF. I never thought I would be so glad to see a Nazi prison and so ready to wish myself inside it. A man behind us says my thought aloud, and someone else laughs. 'I was just thinking the same.' Perhaps every man in the column is sharing the same thought at the same moment. Max says nothing, but his head hangs from his neck as if it's too heavy to support. I cough and cough, spitting gobbets of green slime.

Then we wait, patiently, like cows waiting to be brought in from the fields, and after a while, when nothing seems to be happening, we sit down on our packs. It starts to rain, that light rain which soaks insidiously through every fibre, wetting to the skin.

Every ten minutes or so the line moves forward and we all struggle to our feet, or crawl forward on all fours, and move another few metres.

As we get nearer I realise we are being counted in, and the old fear licks up in me, clean as a flame, and the fog that has been swirling round my head is blown away. The guards are collecting us into groups of ten and sending us through the gate. What if I get separated from Max?

Someone runs back to us. 'There's a hot meal and a bath when you get inside. The goons have promised it,' he shouts.

A meal and a bath are the two things everyone longs for most in the world. Everyone except me. Max lifts his head, sees the panic in my face and fleetingly touches my hand.

'I expect both are a mirage,' he says.

30

We shuffle through the prison-camp gate in our group of ten, and Max leans on my shoulders. He seems very heavy for such a skinny man, or maybe I've just become very weak. Someone asks the date, and the Nazi guard tells us it's 10th March 1945.

It's been four days since I last saw Bill. Has he died of his wound, or is he still trying to catch up with me? For the hundredth time today I taste my instinct and it has the flavour of death.

'Shower,' the guard says, pointing to yet another queue.

I indicate Max, leaning on me with his head bowed.

'Sickbay,' I croak in a voice that doesn't sound like mine. My cold and cough have deepened it to gravel.

The guard glances at Max's flopping body, soiled trousers and boots, and the stench of him tells its own story. 'That way.'

We leave the line for the showers and join another, where many men are holding up their sick friends or standing beside their prone bodies and helping them forward. All around us are crowds of starving tramps, moving this way and that. Some are fresh from the showers and have clean faces and hair above their filthy rags of clothing. I find myself watching the feet as they move past us: some bare and muddy or wrapped in bloodied sacking; some in clogs and *fuss-lag*; others in boots on which the uppers have come apart from the soles and threaten to trip their owners with every step; a few – very few – in worn boots and socks. The legs go past us and past us, in hundreds or thousands. None of them are Bill's.

Our queue shifts slowly alongside rows of coffins. We don't know if they're full from those who've died in the hospital wing, or empty, taunting the sick and dying.

It must be an hour before we reach the medic at the front of the queue. He's brusque.

'Problem?'

'Dysentery,' says Max.

'That all?' He looks at Max's hollow face. 'Dehydration.' He's already lost interest, and repeats a prescription he's obviously given many times. 'Clean water. Bland diet. Rest.'

'Not sickbay?' I ask, forced to speak.

The medic sighs. 'Look, eighty per cent of you have got dysentery. All of you have got malnutrition and dehydration. I've got TB and typhus to deal with. Find him a bed in a hut. Get him plenty of clean water to drink. Let him sleep. Next!'

I quickly sit down on the ground and unlace my boots.

Max lifts his head. 'Will I live?' he asks.

The medic looks him in the eye. 'If you want to,' he replies.

I peel off the *kostival* leaves and hold my feet towards the medic.

Max sucks in his breath. 'Why didn't you tell me?'

I shrug. What would have been the point?

'I thought you were all supposed to have showers?' the medic says crossly, and I realise that I must smell bad. I feel humiliated and would draw my feet away, but the medic prods my infected blisters. One is behind my right heel, and the other runs over the top of my left foot, where the sock has worn through and the tongue of my boot has lapped daily at my foot. They weep pus, and the skin around them is red and angry. 'He'll dress them,' the medic says and points to another man, who also has a queue waiting.

A coughing fit overtakes me, and the medic watches as I cough into my rag. He takes it from me and inspects the muck I've coughed up.

'Bronchitis,' he says with new kindness. 'No medicine, I'm afraid, but you're young. Just rest and you'll get better.'

I nod. Rest – rest is all my body craves. Rest and the sight of Bill.

The medic puts a hand on my sleeve. 'Come back if you cough up blood.'

I join the queue for the foot treatment, which turns out to be a clean rag, a small bottle of iodine, some salt in a twist of newspaper and instructions to clean the wounds each day with salt water and then apply the iodine.

'If you see red streaks up your thighs or in your groin, come back quick – that's septicaemia.'

I wish there was honey for my cough.

We shuffle away and Max grunts, 'Just let me sit down for a minute.'

I pull him over to the wall of the sickbay hut and bend to whisper, 'You wait here. I come back.'

He sinks into the mud and I join the milling crowds, pushing my way into one hut after another, seeking spare beds, looking for Bill. Sometimes I see a blond head, or someone with his build, and hope leaps in me for a second, until I realise it's yet another stranger.

All the huts are full, and I'm beginning to despair of finding somewhere for Max and me to rest when finally, way across the compound, I find a hut with two empty top bunks close to each other. I shrug off my blanket and ease my shoulders out of my kit-bag. All it contains now is my mess tin and cup, my brother's pyjamas and summer underwear and my small, grubby towel. I throw my blanket onto one bunk and my kit-bag onto the other, but bring my mess tin and cup with me, in the hope of finding some food or drink to put in them. I pray I won't find other men sleeping on our bunks when I get back with Max, or discover my blanket and kit-bag stolen. They are the last things I have from home. And it strikes me now that I have nothing to prove who I am or even where home is. Nothing to show I am married to an Englishman. Was married. Might now be the widow of an Englishman. Only Max could speak for me now.

As I work my way back to where I left Max, through the meandering rivers of men, I'm carefully memorising my route and constantly scanning the crowds for Bill's face. The pain in my feet is so bad that I consider going barefoot in the mud.

When I find him, Max has fallen asleep, slumped sideways against the wall of the sickbay, and for a second I think he's dead. I have to shake him hard to wake him. Taking his arm, I half-support, half-drag him through this mass of shuffling strangers. If we fall, they will just continue to walk forward over us, I think; no one will care if we are dead or alive.

I locate the hut again and we step inside, to the familiar noise and stink of men. Most of the bunks we pass are occupied, with prisoners lying motionless. I lead Max towards the bunks I've found, in the murky interior of the hut. Deep in the gloom of the back row of bunks are the two empty places along the top level. Nobody has taken them.

Max looks up at the bunk rearing above his head. He shakes his head, gripping the post of the bed for support. And then, for the first time, he starts to cry. The tears roll down his face and splash on the bunk below.

The man on the bottom bunk is lying on his back, staring up at the slats above his head. He seems to be barely breathing.

I touch his sleeve. 'Can you help, please?' I ask in my hoarse voice. 'I need to get him up to the top.'

The man turns slowly onto his side and looks at Max. 'Shouldn't he be in hospital?'

'We should all be in hospital,' says someone else.

The man heaves himself to a sitting position. 'He can have my bed, if you get those shitty clothes off him first.'

It seems to take the last ounce of the stranger's strength to ease himself to the edge of the bed and stand, and then to climb to the top level. I pass up his blanket and kit-bag.

'Thanks,' Max groans.

And I echo him. 'Thank you.'

'Phew,' says the man in the next bunk, holding his nose. 'Can't you leave his cacky clothes outside?'

I remove Max's boots and help him pull down his trousers and long johns. His scrawny bottom and thighs are caked with dried blood and excrement. I rub his body with a cleaner part of the trouser leg, but have nothing to wash him with.

Max rolls away onto the bed, and I cover him with my damp blanket, shoving the towel from his kit-bag under his bottom, then weave between the bunks and men with my stinking bundle of clothing. I throw Max's trousers under the hut. This feels like a daring act of rebellion.

When I return, Max is hunched on the bed in a half-sitting position. 'I can't lie down. It makes the cramps unbearable.'

I'm so tired that the only thing I want in the world is to rest and close my eyes, but I bend down, rearrange the towel under him and whisper, 'I am going to find water.'

I take my own towel, my brother's pyjama bottoms and our mess tins and cups. At the latrine block I fill my cup and swig it in three gulps. It tastes metallic. I drink two more mugfuls, which makes me feel sick, then I visit the 'forty-holer', sitting with my coat bunched in front of me, too exhausted even to be afraid. Under my coat, in the dimness of the latrine, I strip off my trousers, peel off my long woollen underwear and hope the lice will go with them, and pull on Jan's old pyjamas to wear under my army trousers. I drop the crawling underwear down the hole of the latrine. And then I go to wash.

The water's so cold it makes me gasp, but there's carbolic soap, and I push up my sleeves to scrub my arms as well as my hands, and then my face and head. Stripping off my boots, I wash one of my battered feet after the other, and dissolve a little of the salt in water. When my feet are dry, I dab my blisters with salt water and then iodine, which makes them sting so much that I have to bite my lip not to cry out. It's purgatory to shove my feet back into my boots. I dip my head under the tap to wash my hair, and the shock of the cold sets off a coughing fit that racks my body, so I have to sit down to recover. An older man touches my shoulder. 'You all right, son?' And I nod, waving him away.

Finally I fill the tins and cups to take back to Max. He's barely able to lift his head, but sip by sip I get water into him.

Someone comes round with a bucket of potato mush. I'm amazed at the way the starving prisoners queue politely for it, until I remember that the guards are still there in their watchtowers, with their rifles trained down on us. I'm given half a cup of potato each for me and Max, steaming hot, and retreat to the end of Max's bunk with it, scooping tiny mouse-portions into my mouth. I've seen what happens when starving people gorge themselves, and I don't want to vomit it straight back up. In between my own small mouthfuls, I try to persuade Max to eat, and he manages to swill a little around his mouth before his eyes close.

Then, at last, I allow myself to climb to my bunk with its dirty straw palliasse, lie down and close my eyes. I wonder if I should have said goodbye to Max, in case he's dead in the morning. But I don't have the strength in my limbs to climb down again. Sleep drags at me and I sink unresistingly into its bog, though in my dreams I'm still walking, as if I will never stop, and coughing, coughing, coughing.

In the morning I'm still in a deep sleep when the familiar '*Raus, raus*' is shouted into the hut. For a few moments I don't know where I am, and the man lying at arm's length from me in the next bunk is a complete stranger, with a hand down his trousers, scratching the lice in his groin. I panic and whip my head over to my other side. The man who moved up and let Max have his bed grimaces at me. 'I could eat a horse.'

It's just the sort of thing Bill would say. But Bill is gone. Gone. Gone. And I have no one. No husband. No family. No papers. Nobody but Max.

A voice comes up from below. 'You'll be lucky, mate!'

It isn't Max's voice. I lean over the edge to try and see him, and he's still half-sitting, just as I left him last night, with his knees up and his head lolling on them. A cold hand grips my stomach, and I think he might be dead. My only friend in this dangerous, murderous world.

A coughing fit takes me and, when it subsides, I force myself to swing down and poke his shoulder. There's no response, but he doesn't fall sideways. I grasp his shoulder more firmly and shake him properly. I almost jump back when Max stirs and raises his head, recognition in his brown eyes.

Thank you, thank you, I think, though I don't know who or what I'm thanking. Carefully I feed him some more sips of water and another small amount of cold potato. Then I help him out of the hut, barefoot and naked from the waist down, with his blanket wrapped around him.

'There is soap in the latrine,' I quietly tell Max and help him stumble there, often stopping and waiting until a spasm passes. He's too weak to stand and wash himself, but he leans on the basin, while I scrub away at the dried blood and diarrhoea on his legs and bottom, with a bar of soap and a corner of his towel. Once he's clean, I treat my own feet again, then take Max back to bed while I hobble to the cookhouse to collect some mint tea for both of us.

For the first days in the camp, perhaps for a whole week, we lie all day on our bunks, sleeping, waking, sleeping, rousing ourselves only to struggle out to the latrine or to take the half-cup of soup or potatoes on offer. Ten days have passed since I saw Bill and, with each day, the small hope of seeing him again diminishes further. I hardly know why I'm bothering to eat, but my body craves food. The loss of Bill fills my chest like a heavy metallic lump inside my ribcage.

Max's dysentery slowly ceases, until he's able to lie down and even to eat the miserly rations. My cough begins to subside, and I treat my feet diligently, watching the new pink skin starting to form. I wonder if pink skin ever forms again on a broken heart or if it's always scarred. As soon as I'm able to walk again, I prowl the camp, scanning the faces of the men playing football, standing around in groups talking, queuing at the cookhouse, cleaning their teeth in the wash-house, waiting on the parade ground. After a few days I start to recognise the same people, but none of them are Bill. They could vanish in a puff of smoke, for all I care. How terrifying it is that our own happiness hangs on the well-being of so few others.

The other prisoners are showered and de-loused, and clean clothes are issued. I hide from the showers and de-lousing, slipping back between the crowds, but I do manage to get issued with clean underwear and a Belgian uniform. Max brings me back some of the de-lousing powder in a twist of paper, and I rub it over my head, under my arms and down into my pubic hair, though it doesn't seem to do much good.

As the days open over one another, I start to spend the hours when I'm not obsessively hunting for Bill sitting in the sun outside the hut. I watch the crowds endlessly shuffling to and fro, but Bill is not among them. What shall I do without him? I think. What shall I do?

Some days it rains and the sky hangs low over the camp. Then I can hardly drag myself from my bunk. I make my rounds in search of Bill until I'm too wet and miserable to walk any further, but few men are out and about in the rain, so I give up, hang my wet things on the end of the bunk and return to bed. I try to sleep as much as possible.

Days roll into one week and then the next, in the careless rhythm of the camp, its hours of yawning boredom, the heavy weight of sorrow over Bill. Max watches me descending into emptiness and persuades me to come with him to the camp library. He chooses me a book called *Jane Eyre*, and I begin to read, discovering that I can take myself to other places and even distract myself a little from thinking about Bill, though each time I lay the book down, I know I have lost my Mr Rochester and the world is empty. I have sunk back into silence. There is no one I want to speak to and nothing I wish to say.

Max moves in the opposite direction. He joins a debating society and begins to campaign for the election of the Labour Party when the war is over. It seems he's decided to live and, despite myself, my body too works on bringing me back from the brink of starvation: my feet heal slowly; my cough gradually vanishes. Beyond the wire I hear birds singing, and I think what joy it would be to be alive if Bill was here with me, even in this filthy place. Max tells me of miraculous places called Bluebell Wood and Kew Gardens, but I know I'll never see them now. As soon as we are liberated I'll have to return to the farm – to the life I detested, to the rule of the Russians. I picture my future self staying at home for ever, nursing my mother in her old age, all my life empty from the loss of Bill.

One day a Swiss lorry enters the camp with Red Cross parcels, and for the first time in weeks we have protein and sugar. Some men eat too much too fast, and the hut stinks of vomit and diarrhoea. Max and I know better, and we eat gingerly, pecking at the food like sparrows.

We begin to hear artillery fire in the distance, and it comes closer day by day, hour by hour. Suddenly there's food, as if the Nazis know they mustn't be found with spare food and starving prisoners when we are liberated. Sacks of beans, peas and carrots are quietly 'made available'. Parcels are mysteriously located and handed out. One of them contains fudge, and I bite off tiny portions and let them dissolve in my mouth, wanting the sensation to go on for ever.

Late one afternoon Max hurries back to the hut from his political group and finds me in my usual spot, sitting in the sun with a book.

'D'you know what day it is?' he blurts out.

I've no idea.

'March the twenty-sixth,' he says. 'Isn't that your birthday?'

I nod slowly. I am twenty-one, but my mum and dad aren't here to wish me '*Všechno nejlepší k narozeninám*' and now I will never hear Bill say, 'Happy Birthday, Izzy.' I remember he said he'd take me dancing. I haven't seen him for twenty days. The start of a lifetime of nothingness without him.

Max says, 'I haven't got anything to give you.'

I shrug. What does it matter? What does anything matter?

He crouches down beside me. 'Look,' he says, 'I've been thinking. If Bill doesn't show up, we could pretend you're married to me, and I could get you back to England and we could look for him there.'

I think: Bill's dead, and nothing matters any more. The heaviness sits hard on me today, and it seems too much effort to speak, but I struggle to listen to Max, who is still talking.

'And later, if we can't find him, and if you wanted, we might really get married. We've both lost the person we love, and I'll never marry anyone else – and God knows you've seen me at the very worst. I've got nothing to hide from you.'

388

I look up at him with incredulity. To be married to Max?

He misunderstands my look and babbles on, 'Oh, not for sex. We wouldn't have to do that. But you've saved my life twice now, and I want to do everything I can for you. Maybe we could both go to Ruskin College. I think we'd rub along all right.'

The idea swims around my brain like a black cloud. To be married to anyone other than Bill is unthinkable. And yet it would save me having to go back to the farm and the Russians. I think: I'd be better marrying Ralph, if he's still alive. He'll never have a wife.

I pat his hand and whisper, 'Maybe. Thank you.'

But as I watch Max walk away and my mind settles, I know that the impulsive, self-centred girl who expected her daddy to rescue her and her husband to protect her has died somewhere on the road. If I am never to see Bill again, I'll have to find the strength to make it on my own in the world to come. I won't be dependent on anyone else, but I'll forge my own path, just as Cousins would. I think of England, where I know no one. Will I really be brave enough to go there?

Later, Max comes to me with a birthday present of a tin of coffee and two more squares of the exquisite fudge, swapped for all his newly acquired cigarettes.

Everything is changing in the camp. I overhear guards trying to reassure each other '*Befehle sind befehle* – orders are orders', and I know this means they're really scared. We notice that more and more of the guards have taken the insignia off their uniforms, and one tells a prisoner that he's never been a Nazi, and that Hitler is a *Schweinehund*.

To our astonishment, the postern who broke Bill's nose at the

389

brick factory seeks me out and holds out a hand in which my 'catapult' and Bill's harmonica are clutched. 'I am returning confiscated belongings,' he says without looking us in the face.

There's jeering from all the men around us. 'Bloody thief,' they catcall.

I slip the harmonica into the breast-pocket of my battledress, near my heart. The postern elbows his way through the jostling prisoners and back out of the hut.

Every day now the whole sky seems full of aircraft, with flares of every colour going up. The noise is incessant. We watch a plane falling from the sky, on fire from wingtip to wingtip, with sheets of flames billowing from it. All day we hear dull booming and see vivid flashes. One afternoon the whole camp is engulfed in an enormous smoke cloud. On the horizon we can see the red glow of towns burning.

That night we lie awake in the darkness and listen to the sound of a violin being played for an hour. The music seems to voice all the unspeakable sorrow in me: for Warsaw; for the starving people we passed; for my home and my family; for Scotty and Ralph; but most of all for Bill, and for love that is lost to me for ever.

One bright afternoon in late March I'm sitting in my usual spot, deep in a book about a village called Middlemarch, when a sound makes me lift my head. It's a whistle – someone whistling. A long way off. I lay down my book, not even noting the page number, and tell myself, 'Lots of men whistle . . .' But the tune begins afresh, moving away from me, and I recognise the song about the nightingale in the square that Bill always played for me. My heart leaps and I jump to my feet, weaving between the huts and around the groups of men to follow the sound. It stops and I panic. Maybe it's him, but we'll miss each other for ever in this great maze of humanity. Then it starts again, and the words come back to me: 'Angels dining at the Ritz.' It's closer now, and I begin to run, rounding the edge of the cookhouse and running slap-bang into the whistler.

'Oi!' he yells and pushes me away.

I stumble back, half-losing my footing, and catch a momentary glimpse of a dark-haired, lanky stranger.

'Watch it!' he snarls.

I back away, muttering, 'Sorry, sorry.'

I round the edge of the nearest hut, with his voice following me: 'You wanna mind where you're going!'

I crouch down against the wall, curling into myself, in a tight ball of pain. It's not Bill. It will never be Bill. All my life I'll hear snatches of song, or catch sight of a blond head in a crowd, and think it's him. And it never will be. I pull my knees into my chest, hugging the pain, holding my breath, willing myself out of a world that no longer has Bill in it.

Footsteps stop close to me, and someone says, 'All right, mate?'

I lift my head and grimace.

A man with sergeant's stripes nods encouragingly. 'Nearly over now.'

I nod, and he moves away. But it's not over for me. It will never be over for me.

On Good Friday, 30th March, the guards set lookouts to scan the horizon for tanks. In one direction they report sightings of Nazi Tigers, in the other American Shermans. Our prison camp is smack in the middle, under the flimsy protection of the Red Cross flag. There's a vibration of nervous tension, as if all the men around me have drunk too much coffee. The sound of gunfire is incessant and seems to come from all directions, all around us, as though we are in the centre of a typhoon that may wipe us out as it spins away. I pray that I'll be hit by a stray bullet. I don't want to live without Bill.

I watch prisoners exchanging addresses on the parade ground as if it's the end of term at school. A plane flies low over the camp. All around me men shout, 'Hit the deck' and throw themselves to the ground, covering their heads with their arms. I stay on my feet, shading my eyes to watch the plane going over, letting it target me if it will. But it doesn't open fire. A few days earlier the prisoners were given paint and allowed to climb onto the roofs of the huts to paint 'PoW' in giant white letters. Perhaps the crew of the plane has read the message on the roofs.

And then, as the men are getting to their feet and brushing down their coats, there's utter silence. The firing has stopped. We all look round nervously, as though this is the prelude to some gigantic explosion. But nothing happens.

'Maybe this is it,' whispers Max.

Others join in. 'Perhaps it's all over?'

A tremendous roar goes up from the gates, as if the final goal has been scored at a football match, and someone shouts, 'It's the bloody Yanks!'

Max grabs my hand, and I'm pulled along by him, towards the gate to see what's happening. I can't get a view, for all the heads in the way, but Max raises me up to see a US jeep, with six GIs sitting in it laughing, as it's lifted from the ground by starving prisoners and carried into the camp.

Everyone around us goes crazy, crying, laughing, hugging one another. They whoop and yell for joy. 'It's over. It's bloody well over.' Many men have tears pouring down their faces; others embrace each other rapturously as a stream of trucks enters the compound. Max hugs me and presses his lice-ridden head to mine, but I am a stone.

All around me men are saying, 'It's over! It's over! It's over!' as though only saying it will make it real.

Outside the fence, columns of armoured cars decorated with American stars speed past, their occupants standing to throw packs of cigarettes and chocolate to us. There's a scramble near the wire to gather up the bounty, but Max says, 'There'll be more where that comes from. Let's not get trampled in the rush.'

The side is dropped from one of the trucks that has driven into the compound and two American women with perfect hair, wearing red lipstick, begin to serve coffee and doughnuts. The smell of sugar and real coffee coming from the truck feels like another mirage. The camp loudspeaker crackles into life and we pause for a moment to hear an announcement, for someone to tell us all this is true, that we are free. But no announcement comes. Instead we hear the scratch of a needle on a record and the opening of a dance tune booms over the camp.

'It's "In the Mood",' laughs Max, and the music, plus the over-powering smell of doughnuts and real coffee, is more convincing than any words could have been. Stick-men in rags start to dance with one another. The whole camp has transformed into a fair-ground, a circus. Another food truck dishes out meat sandwiches, made with the whitest bread I've ever seen in my life.

Near the cookhouse the Americans have gathered the Nazi guards into a huge cage. They look terrified. One of the US soldiers guarding them says to me, 'Go on. Point out who was cruel to you. I'll kill him now. No one'll know.'

I raise my eyes and scan the faces for the man who broke Bill's nose. But when I find him, I think: What's the point? And I shake my head.

And then, beyond him, behind the cage of guards, across the parade ground near the latrines, something catches my eye. I shift and grab Max's arm to stop him.

'What is it?' he asks, following my gaze.

I duck left to try and catch another glimpse, but the caged guards are blocking my view. A shape. For just a second, I thought I saw . . . half-hidden. I strain to get a clear view past them. They move and block my line of sight. The sound of whistling reaches me. It's the nightingale song. But I've been disappointed before, and now, rather than lifting, my stomach plummets. It will be that stranger again, whistling our tune, taunting me.

We reach the end of the cage and we would now have a view across the parade ground to the latrines if my vision wasn't clouded with tears. I stumble, and Max, catching my arm, stops dead, lifting his hand to shade his eyes, gazing where I was looking before. The whistled notes rise, and I blink my eyes clear. It's a figure I'd know anywhere. He turns and looks straight at me.

It is.

It's Bill.

Epilogue

Bill takes my hand. 'Come on,' he says. 'Let's go and find someone in charge.'

I pull Max by the sleeve. He has to be with us, to be there at
the end.

The three of us press on through the crowds of singing,
dancing, laughing men.

'Like Trafalgar Square on New Year's Eve,' says Bill.

We come to the offices where the camp commandant used to
work, and at last I believe that this is real. I have found Bill and
we are going to England.

Bill says very firmly, 'We need to see the person in charge' and
there's something about the urgency and conviction in his voice
that the American soldier hears. For a few minutes we stand and
watch the fairground the camp has become, and I think of the terrible distance we have walked and of all those who fell on the way.
I bless Scotty's generous soul. Without his sacrifice, I wouldn't be
standing here. I see the faces of all those I love, not knowing if they
are alive or dead, in pain or suffering, somewhere on this war-
ravaged continent: my father and mother, Jan, Marek, Ralph. I grip
Bill's and Max's hands on either side of me. They are all I have
left, all that I know, all that I have to take into the future with me.

Those of us who've survived will have a huge job to do, to

rebuild the cities and towns that have been reduced to rubble, to rebuild lives torn by grief and separation, to build a new and fairer world, where the poor will be housed and fed, where this will truly be a war to end the senseless waste of war for ever. And looking out at the celebrations in front of us, I feel strength flowing through me. If we've survived all that we've experienced, we can do anything.

A GI ushers us inside. I've never been in the commandant's office, but behind his big oak desk now sits a tall and rangy American colonel. Bill and Max automatically salute him. I wave my hand ineffectually, feeling oddly calm and detached.

'Yes, soldier?' he asks. 'Something urgent?'

Bill steps forward and pulls me beside him.

'Yes, sir,' says Bill. 'This prisoner isn't a soldier. She's my wife. She's Czech.'

'Good God.' The colonel rises to his feet, staring into my eyes. I remember Ralph's astonished face, six months and 800 kilometres ago. The colonel starts to come around his desk to examine me more closely. Fear has fallen away from me, and I look back at him, gazing clear-eyed into this new world I've been spared to inhabit. Bill's hand is squeezing mine like he'll never let it go, but this moment is mine, earned from all the terror and hardship.

I hold up my other hand for silence and clear my throat, pulling myself up tall. 'Good afternoon,' I say in the English accent I've been practising in my mind for so long. I turn my head to Max and then to my darling Bill. They are both smiling encouragement, and I find I'm grinning all over my face.

I step forward, and the words rise up and circle my head like uncaged larks.

'My name is Mrs Izabela King. I'm very pleased to meet you.'

Author's Note

This astonishing story was first told to me in 2007 by Sidney Reed, who lived in the same sheltered accommodation as my mother. We were in the lift when he said, 'I bet I could tell you a story about the war that would make your hair stand on end.' I could hardly believe what he was telling me, so a few days later I arranged to go back and talk to him some more about it. We sat for a couple of hours, and I took pages of notes. I couldn't doubt the authenticity of what he was telling me – the details of how the Czech girl's presence was announced to the hut, how she coped with her period, the way the men worked together to protect her felt absolutely true. I knew I had to write this story, and it had to be in the voice of the Czech woman trapped in a perilous world of men. Despite my experience as a historical documentary researcher and producer for the BBC, I was daunted by the difficulty of writing it as a novel. I toyed with the idea of writing a radio play, but I was a recognised poet, and in the end I wrote a long narrative poem that was published online in 2008. I thought I was done with it, but the story kept nagging at me. I wanted to know more, and I wanted to share it with a wider audience than poetry readers.

I returned to Sidney Reed for another afternoon, but by this time his memory was less sharp and the details seemed muddled. He told me he'd been in Straflager E166, but his son said he'd been imprisoned at Lamsdorf, Stalag 344. I began to doubt the story. But thanks to Philip Baker's Lamsdorf website, I discovered that the English work camps were given E numbers and that there was indeed an E166, and it was at Saubsdorf quarry, which Sidney had described so clearly to me. Now my hair really did stand on end and my research began in earnest.

I visited the Imperial War Museum, the National Archive and the British Library. I read published books and private diaries and joined the Lamsdorf Association. I realised that a prisoner in a labour sub-camp of Lamsdorf would have been subjected to the terrible Long March from Eastern Europe into Germany. According to a report by the US Department of Veterans' Affairs, almost 3,500 US and Commonwealth PoWs died as a result of the marches. I wasn't at all sure I could write something so harrowing.

My husband went with me to the Czech Republic and drove the route from Vražné, through Poland and Germany to Hartmannsdorf as I took hundreds of photographs, and we searched out locations for the novel, including a possible farmhouse for Izzy and a church in which she might have married Bill. As we drove, we tried to identify barns and buildings in which thousands of men could have been billeted overnight. We visited the site of Lamsdorf prisoner-of-war camp on an appropriately snow-covered day in March 2016.

Then I began to write. The pages of notes I had from Sidney Reed could only give me a sketchy outline. For the rest, I had to depend on written accounts and my own imagination. Sidney couldn't remember the name of the Czech girl or her husband, and although he was sure he'd heard they'd made it back to England, possibly via Liverpool, he had no idea where they might have been living. So the characters of Izabela and Bill are invented, as are their friends Ralph, Max and Scotty. The character of Scotty grew from a memory of Sidney's of a member of the notorious Glasgow razor-gang at Saubsdorf, while Kurt was based on a sexually predatory guard recalled by Sidney.

This is a novel, not a documentary, but every researchable element is based on historical truth. My dad was a PoW in Italy and Austria, and some details came from the experiences of him and his friends. It was a stroke of luck that Saubsdorf happened to be the work camp at which the prisoner Horace Greasley fell in love with the quarry owner's daughter, Rosa Rauchbach, and that he wrote a book about his escapades.

Details of prison-camp life have been drawn from a range of sources. Every step of the terrible Long March comes from eye-witness accounts, drawing particularly on those so meticulously chronicled in *The Last Escape*. There were three principal march routes across Europe from the different PoW camps. I chose to send Izabela and Bill on the shortest. Many prisoners walked further, for longer, and suffered worse deprivation and cruelty, and many died before they could reach safety. Some incidents that I have included actually happened after the timespan of this novel. For example, on 19th April 1945, at a village called Gresse, thirty Allied PoWs died and thirty were seriously injured (possibly fatally), when strafed by a flight of RAF Typhoons.

Although this is a work of fiction, it is also the true story of what happens when fascism is allowed to flourish.

Facts and Figures

In terms of getting the facts right, I am particularly indebted to Sebastian Mikulec for checking the accuracy of the chapters set in the Lamsdorf camp and for answering endless detailed questions with unfailing patience; and to Martin Vitko, who gave me painstaking feedback on the Czech chapters and explained the complexity of the country's history. The names of many places in this story have changed since 1945. The village now called Vražné was actually called Gross Petersdorf (Dolní Vražné) in 1944; Lamsdorf is now Łambinowice; and what was Saubsdorf during the war is present-day Supíkovice. I hope I will also be forgiven for using the names Poland and Czechoslovakia when referring to regions called by different names during the war. Historians will know that in 1918, after the fall of the Austro-Hungarian Empire, the Czechoslovak Republic was created. The new country included Moravia, Bohemia and Silesia – German-speaking regions that were known collectively as the Sudetenland. Hitler's annexation of the Sudetenland in 1938 was widely welcomed by the German-speaking inhabitants. The village now known as Vražné was home to 90 per cent German-speaking people, although the wider region was nearer 50 per cent German- and 50 per cent Czech-speaking. After the war most of the German-speaking people were forced to leave.

Prisoner numbers are also difficult to verify. As Lamsdorf was a processing centre for the *Arbeitskommandos* work camps, the numbers of prisoners it housed fluctuated daily. However, there were 13,000 beds for British soldiers, plus about 12,000 British soldiers out at the *Arbeitskommandos* at any one time. Seven hundred sick British PoWs were taken from the camp on 15th January 1945, just before the mass evacuation on foot began on 22nd January. This continued over several days, in groups of 1,000–2,000, until 21,867 British PoWs from the camp and the *Arbeitskommandos* had set off on what became known as the Long March or the Death March.

We do know that Lamsdorf was the largest camp for British PoWs – every third captured soldier wearing a British Empire uniform was eventually moved there. The German authorities called it *Britenlager* – the British camp. However, these 'British' servicemen included 271 Indians, 1,543 Canadians, 1,829 Australians, 2,217 New Zealanders and 1,210 Palestinians, all of whom were Jewish. We also know that the International Committee of the Red Cross classified Lamsdorf as the worst prison camp for British prisoners, and inmates referred to it as 'hell camp' because of overcrowding, malnourishment and hard work.

In some labour camps, men were paid in what the prisoners called *Lagergeld*, a paper currency which could be exchanged in special shops.

It is impossible to know how many men died on the Long March because it's hard even to be certain about the number of Allied prisoners held by the Nazis. In 1944 the number of British prisoners was thought to be 199,592, but at the end of the war the number of PoWs logged as having returned home was only 168,746. What happened to those other 30,846 men? It may be that the first figure was wrong, but many of them must have died on the Long March. There are reports of one working party from which 1,800 men set out on the Long March and only 1,300 completed it, with 30 per cent dying en route.

Finally, Sidney Reed didn't know exactly where the Czech girl came from, or her name. I hope that someone reading this novel might be able to identify the real 'Izabela' and 'Bill', so that I can pay tribute to their courage and love.

Selected Bibliography

Peter Doyle, *Prisoner of War in Germany* (Shire Library, 2009)

Horace Greasley, *Do The Birds Still Sing in Hell?* (John Blake, 2013)

H.J. Gudgion, *A Gunner's Scrapbook memories of 1939–1945* (privately printed)

H.J. Gudgion, *Pass the Parcel* (privately printed)

Robert Kee, *A Crowd Is Not Company* (Cardinal, 1990)

John Nichol and Tony Rennell, *The Last Escape: The Untold Story of Allied Prisoners of War in Europe 1944–45* (Penguin Books, 2003)

Anna Wickiewicz, *Captivity in British Uniforms: Stalag VIII B (344) Lamsdorf* (Central Museum, Opole, 2018)

Philip Baker's Lamsdorf website: https://www.lamsdorf.com

Acknowledgements

My first thanks are to Sidney Reed for telling me this story – and to the serendipity that brought us together, in a lift.

I can't thank my husband, Tim Butt, enough for driving the route of the Long March through snow and ice with me, and for giving me all the encouragement, time and space I needed to write.

Thanks to my initial readers, especially Katie Butt whose response convinced me to keep going, and to Tim Butt, Johanna Charnley, Pippa Winton, Stephanie Cabot and Ellen Goodson Coughtrey, who gave such useful feedback. Also to Amy Butt and Millie Hoskins for reading later versions.

I would never have found the time to write the book if I hadn't given up my full-time job, so I have to thank the Royal Literary Fund for giving me the fellowship which enabled me to do that and focus on my writing.

I am indebted to a group of historians, museum curators and writers:

To Sebastian Mikulec, curator at Centralne Muzeum Jeńców Wojennych, Łambinowice, who showed us around the Lamsdorf site in the snow, then read the Lamsdorf chapters for accuracy and answered so many emailed questions.

ACKNOWLEDGEMENTS

To Philip Baker for the marvellous Lamsdorf website, Facebook group and meeting day.

To Mgr Martin Vitko (previously of the Regional Museum in Nový Jičín – Muzeum Novojičínska; now in the State District Archives Nový Jičín) for explaining many Czech things and reading the Vražné chapters. And to Dr Anna Hrčková from Muzeum Novojičínska (Regional Museum in Nový Jičín), and Mgr Jiří Střecha, director of the Czech Postal Museum (Česká pošta, s.p., Poštovní Muzeum).

And most of all to the writers Robert Kee, Horace Greasley, Peter Doyle, John Nichol, Tony Rennell, Anna Wickiewicz and the many private diarists whose books I have plundered for the episodes that make up my story. Most especial, heartfelt thanks go to my dad's prison camp and life-long friend, Harold Gudgion, whose war-time diaries were transcribed by his son, John, and which have proved such a valuable resource.

Finally, this book would not exist if my incredibly clever agent, Millie Hoskins, hadn't believed in it, and told me to cut out 30,000 words. Then I was so lucky that the book was picked up by the extraordinary editor Selina Walker, who has spent many, many hours coaxing it into shape. Thank you, Millie, Selina, Pippa and the whole amazing team at Century. And to my new American friends, Kate Seaver and the fantastic Berkley team.